WALKER BETWEEN THE WORLDS

A Novel By

Diane DesRochers

1995
Llewellyn Publications
St. Paul, Minnesota 55164-0383, U.S.A.

Cover art by Erin McKee
Cover design by Tom Grewe
Interior illustrations by Anne Marie Garrison
Interior design, editing by Laura Gudbaur

Cataloging-in-Publication Data
DesRochers, Diane, 1937-
    Walker between the worlds: a novel / by Diane
        DesRochers.
    p.   cm. --
    ISBN 1-56718-224-0
    I. Title.
PS3554.E8437W35 1995
813' .54--dc20   95-3286
                                                      CIP

Llewellyn Publications
A Division of Llewellyn Worldwide, Ltd.
P.O. Box 64383, St. Paul, MN 55164-0383

The Most Difficult Challenge

"They were all that remained of an ancient and mighty nation that had once held sway over an entire world: a nation that was now convulsing in its final death throes. It was too late to rescue his stolen priestess or the millions of worshippers that had once led in the service of the great mother and her horned consort.

"Still, he had to make the attempt."

Alan Kolkey is a man of many talents who has been chosen by the Goddess to battle Kali: a massively destructive comet on a straight course to Earth! Using his high intelligence, ESP and PK powers, Alan comes to the aid of Earth and Her people, all the while being reluctantly drawn into a world hero role. Seeking solace in his science/space station one afternoon, Alan meets the woman of his dreams in a climactic out-of-body experience that changes his life forever. As Alan becomes obsessed with his new love, insanity begins to encroach upon the inner recesses of his mind: he cannot have her because his PK powers could kill her in one moment of ecstasy!

The primordial bond between Alan and his love interest is rooted in past life experiences and karmic lessons whose time for reconciliation is up. As Alan struggles in his achingly lonely life, he faces the losses that come from change, and meets—for the first time in his life—the mundane challenges of sex, love, trust and friendship.

"A clever blending of modern technology and traditional myths from around the world, the reader is brought face-to-face with the mystery of the Earth Mother and Her need to survive. As Alan Kolkey learns to control his own fits of ESP, the reader learns to acknowledge those same depths within themselves."

—Tzipora Katz
author, *Celebrating Life: Rites of Passage for All Ages*

One man's magic is another man's technology.
　　　　　　　　　　　　　　　—Robert Heinlein

WALKER
BETWEEN THE
WORLDS

Forthcoming books by Diane DesRochers:

Shadow Walker

This book is lovingly dedicated to:

Marcelle White: my big sister. She bought me my first thesaurus and has never stopped believing in me.

John and Ann Pyra: for introducing me to the Macintosh computer and the wonderful world of word processing. They saved my life in more ways than they will ever know.

Jacqueline Lichtenberg: for critiquing, story conferencing, boundless patience and sage advice.

Brian Marsden: of the Smithsonian Astrophysical Observatory, for technical advice.

Stewart Grossman: for technical advice, for his martial arts expertise, and especially for choreographing all fight and combat scenes.

I Have Loved You Before

by Frances Vandine

I have loved you before,
In another time and place,
In another dimension,
On the other side of space.
If the world ends tomorrow
And again we grow apart,
Our love remains immortal.
You know this in your heart.
So let the fire of Hell be kindled,
Let Heaven open up her gates,
We only have fear to fear.
We are eternally soulmates!

TABLE OF CONTENTS

OVERTURE

FOR EONS She had been slowly waking into awareness of Self. She was Mother, soul of the third planet out from Her consort, Sol. A Man-child had just been reborn and now it was time. She was as dependent on all Her children, as they on Her, for they were the very cells of Her body. Her need for this particular child, however, was paramount. He had sworn an Ancient Oath of love and fealty. This time both She and Her children needed him. She had permitted lifetimes enough already for him to heal a dozen times over. Now it was time for him to acknowledge his vows, armed with the tools and weapons of his station. This time She would permit no place to hide. This time he would remember, recognize, acknowledge Her once more, and swear again the Sacred Oath. This time he would stand and prove himself equal to the task, or be cast to the demons of his own creation.

She projected a tenuous extension of Herself far beyond the track of Her farthest sister. She sought the distant Oort cloud. Here proto-comets sleep until rare collisions with each other or the infinitesimal but cumulative gravitational effect from neighboring suns rouses and diverts one of them onto a sunward course. She sought one, sufficiently roused, whose path was unstable enough for Her tenuous contact to influence.

At last, one that suited Her needs! Half a light year distant, a dark star had recently passed. Its gravitational effect was only now becoming evident. Ice mantled, with a rocky 25-mile-diameter basaltic core, the proto-comet was sluggish in waking from its 4.5-billion-year inertial sleep. Finally, acknowledging Her call, it slowed, dipped sunward, then grudgingly slid into a new trajectory that would send it crashing into Her bosom within thirty-eight of the Mother's circuits about Her consort, Her central luminary.

•••

An orbiting telescope was making a routine, programmed scan. It was the first to take note of the new visitor entering the heavily populated neighborhood of asteroids. Computers ran long mathematical analyses of the data being relayed and offered prognosis, first to the scientific community and then to governing bodies across the planet.

The temporary numerical designation assigned to it by the International Astronomical Union was Minor Planet 2000CC$_3$ (MP2000CC$_3$). The newcomer in the neighborhood was on collision trajectory with Earth. Projected impact was 335 days, three hours and thirty-eight minutes from time and date of entry.

Despite efforts to maintain security, knowledge of the impending cataclysm leaked to the media. One of the first of the investigative reporters to hit print with the story was a self-proclaimed student of Eastern Religions. Bending rules of journalism, he metaphorically called the new comet Kali, the black Goddess linked with death and destruction in the Hindu pantheon. The name caught the public imagination and soon even astronomers were referring to $MP2000CC_3$ as Kali.

Public concern forced member nations to grant temporary emergency powers to the United Nations. Grudging international cooperation and enforcement of a global state of Martial Law were the only workable options for pooling resources and efforts to divert the ball of ice that was speeding toward Earth. The comet was now beginning to grow a tail of ice, dust and ions. Failing that they had to be ready to help the world community dig in and salvage as much as possible.

•••

On a tendril of thought, the Mother rode along as a cavalry of nuclear warheads, mounted atop huge space-going steeds, was launched. Her daughter, Luna, had circled five times before they impacted with their target. Her Promised One, now grown to manhood, would not so easily escape his vows. Kali was for he alone to tame, or die in the attempt. Kali would test his mettle and decide whether or not he was worthy. Thousands of telescopes watched the immense serial explosions, which should have shattered the comet into harmless scattered debris or, at the very least, significantly altered the angle of approach. Their collective effect had succeeded only in melting and chipping away small chunks of Kali's icy mantle.

Twice again Luna circled. The Mother watched with maternal pride as one lone, manned ship streaked skyward. Television screens across Her surface were linked to the giant orbiting telescope. Vicariously traveling along, many of Her children were taking small comfort in periodically monitoring the progress of the solitary vessel, on its way to tilt at interplanetary windmills.

The target was closer now, and the ship traveled at a much higher velocity than the previous swarm of drones. The tiny manned vessel arrived within seven diurnal rotations of launch and began sending back live video monitoring of work in progress. Billions of Her children watched in rapt attention as a nuclear armed missile was launched and detonated close to the comet's surface. Within a three mile radius and to a depth of nearly a mile, the surrounding icy mantle was instantly vaporized. The ship slowly aimed a nose-mounted cannon at this newly created region of bare rock. A laser-tight beam of light-that-was-NOT-light shot out and began cutting what looked like a battery of gigantic rocket tubes. Landing amidst the mile-deep holes, suited workers swarmed across the surface readying nuclear charges at the bottom of each tube. The task took almost as long as the journey; but when they were simultaneously detonated, the live broadcast of the pyrotechnic display was seen by almost everyone on Earth who owned or was able to find access to a television screen.

With an almost audible groan, Kali grudgingly altered the angle of Her approach, but not quite as much as would have been needed for a safe fly-by. Not as much as had been calculated, even with the extra built-in margin for error.

Religious leaders proclaimed a miracle. Scientific and secular communities called it a billion-to-one combination of known and unknown variables. No way should it have happened. No way could it ever happen again. But it did.

Two more circuits of Luna. Like some ancient mythological Goddess, with tresses of light streaming behind Her and filling up the night, Kali arrived. Speeding in on a close, grazing orbit, she was quickly snared in the gravitational net of the Mother.

Her adopted daughter soon settled into a tight orbit that, even during the day, dominated the sky. Faithful to Her name, Kali immediately began wreaking havoc, with the ocean's tides first. Her repertoire rapidly grew, however, as She became a catalyst, everywhere touching off massive tectonic and volcanic activity.

PART I:
KALI

CHAPTER I

A LAN KOLKEY activated the cumbersome grav-shield that took up almost all of the two lowest deck levels, then held his ship motionless over Tabriz. Illumined by the first light of morning, fissures, like dry canyon riverbeds, wound in and out through the devastation. The ancient Iranian city sat like a shattered eggshell, hardest hit within the earthquake-ravaged Kurdish province surrounding Lake Urmia. Overnight, entire sections had been transformed into tiny mesas rising several feet above the ruined streets. Scattered lakes were sprouting from broken water mains and the Aji River's efforts at cutting a new channel for itself. Forty miles to the west, urbanized areas bordering the inland salt lake were awash from miniature tidal waves caused by the earthquake's after-shocks that were still hitting. Everywhere fires burned out of control. Everywhere bodies of dead and dying lay, as yet unattended. Everywhere hundreds who were still able to walk desperately dug for buried survivors, many with only their hands for tools, while others shuffled about like directionless zombies.

Troops had already begun arriving from billets near the Iraqi border. They were setting up tents for an emergency hospital and a command center just southeast of the city. Several hundred feet east of the encampment Alan Kolkey spotted a relatively flat unoccupied clearing large enough to accommodate the *Peregrine* and her cargo.

He closed his eyes in concentration, establishing PK link-up with the tiny, psychokinetically controlled electronic voice box that allowed for much faster, more direct communication with his on-board computers, then brought his ship in for a feather-soft vertical descent landing. He opened the large cargo hatch on the aft starboard side, extended the loading ramp, and closed down all but his internal security systems as he withdrew his psi link.

Waves of fear, pain, despair, and silent hysteria: the telepathic awareness all about him of lives blinking out! Wishing desperately for some way to block it all out, the way his ship's grav-shield could block the effects of gravity, he walked briskly down the loading ramp. He was flanked by the twelve team leaders of the vanguard rescue paramedics sent by M'Butu Moshey. The emergency restructuring of the United Nations that had elevated Moshey from Secretary General to UN President was the nearest Earth had ever come to global federation. Inside the *Peregrine's* hold, Kolkey's 600-man search and rescue command was busily preparing to unload the ship's cargo of heavy earth-moving equipment, all-terrain vehicles and emergency supplies.

Dark and brooding like his eagle back home, who was far, far more than pet or mascot, Kolkey stepped onto Iranian soil. Arriving uninvited as they had, he wondered how they would be received. Proud and militantly nationalistic, this tiny war-and-refugee ravaged nation still held itself aloof from most of the other nations of Earth that had banded together into a temporary confederation of exigency.

He gazed with grim fascination at the bitter irony as he surveyed the carnage around him. It was almost a year since he had been torn from his comfortable womb of solitude to do battle with this damned comet. Its official designation was MP2000CC$_3$, but it had become more popularly known as "Kali." The idiotic appellation had been coined by the same media nitwits, no doubt, who were lately having a field day portraying him as everyone's favorite messiah: saint, savior, and knight-in-shining-space-ship, all rolled up into one neat ball-and-chain.

Alan Kolkey was major stockholder and guiding genius behind Applied Space Technologies, Inc. When the UN's own efforts had failed to deflect the comet from its collision trajectory, President Moshey, not-always-affectionately referred to as "The African," had appealed to the huge aero-space, high tech research corporation. Reluctantly, Alan Kolkey had allowed himself to be talked into helping, and had succeeded, though tragically, not exactly as planned.

Somewhere a crucial variable had not been taken into account, a variable that still eluded him despite countless checks and cross checks. Because of this one tiny, fatal miscalculation, the angle of deflection had not been sufficient, though only by the smallest fraction of a degree. According to his exhaustively researched calculations, the comet should have gone streaking harmlessly sunward in a clean miss. Instead, like a huntress after her kill, Kali had charged in from behind. Had her trajectory not been anything other than exactly what it was, she would have continued soaring harmlessly on past. However, in a billion-to-one shot, the new orbit she had been kicked into had positioned her just so between planet, moon, and sun. Their combined gravities had been sufficient to brake her headlong flight. Captured within a gravitational cage, Kali was now locked within a very tight orbit around earth: so close now that her own otherwise insignificant gravity had become the proverbial straw. The delicate equilibrium between sun, moon and planet had been lost. Wherever tectonic stresses had built up along fault lines, volcanoes woke from their slumbers and new ones were born. Tidal waves scoured coastlines and earthquakes rumbled, turning the land in some places to constantly quivering jello.

Dammit! How could he have missed such a critical variable? Why did his miscalculation still so stubbornly persist in eluding him? It was as though Kali had taken on a perverse life and will of her own. Because of his inexcusable bungling, everyday people were dying by the thousands, and all he could do was organize rescue and mop-up operations such as this one. Even so, he could only be at the scene of one disaster at a time; for every victim saved, hundreds perished. He had been condemned, as much by Kali as by his own hyperactive conscience, to become the glorified errand boy of the African and his precious UN.

The entire population of the fast-materializing tent city had begun gathering to greet the advance party. They were shouting repeatedly in chorus, a phrase that probably translated into something like "Yankee go home!" Alan focused on the ranking officer, now stepping forward with a crisp military salute. Though salted with silver at the temples, Colonel Seyyed Ali Rajai had hair almost as black and curly as his own. Despite his dusty and torn uniform, the Iranian possessed an imposing dignity that more than made up for his lack in physical stature. Alan was careful not to stand so close that his heavily muscled frame and six-foot-three-inch height could be perceived as threatening. The Iranian officer was an educated man whose well-disciplined mind was the most informed and relatively comfortable for him to step inside of.

He regretted the necessary psionic invasion of the colonel's privacy, not to mention the emotional as well as quite literal physical pain he was causing himself; but he needed an immediate crash course on the local language. Alan took great care not to intrude into conscious levels of his temporary host's brain function. Careful also not to damage or cause discomfort, he merged himself almost completely, for a moment becoming Colonel Rajai. His own mind became a sponge as it blanketed the older man's cortical language centers, absorbing vocabulary at first, then grammar and syntax. By the time Bajinsky, Alan's second-in-command, and Colonel Rajai's translator had completed formal introductions in both English and Persian, Alan had withdrawn all but one slender connection with his unwary host's language memory.

Returning the young officer's salute, he managed an awkward, halting, but technically correct greeting in Persian. His effort was rewarded with an enthusiastic cheer from military and civilians alike among the still-growing crowd.

"Truly, Sheikh, you are a most welcome messenger from Allah," Colonel Rajai announced with the dignified reserve of one who has suddenly inherited responsibility for the survival of an entire city.

"President Moshey sends his greetings," Alan replied, carefully choosing his words, but breathing easier. The African's diplomacy had, doubtless, preceded them, greasing the way for this uninvited rescue mission. Seeing the degree of damage, it was highly doubtful that help of any sort would have been turned away. It was the fourth, and worst, earthquake of catastrophic proportions to hit in recent years, and the second with an epicenter here in Tabriz, killing untold thousands and bringing this once-proud Islamic nation to its knees. "I have been asked to assure you that transport choppers with reinforcements and supplies will follow later on today. We are only a vanguard, but my men are all seasoned paramedics, trained in rescue and disaster relief." His lips and tongue had difficulty shaping themselves around the unfamiliar words. It would require days of steady practice before he could even hope to begin feeling comfortable with this new language.

Colonel Rajai's polite reserve warmed by several discernible degrees. "While your men unload, shall we withdraw to my tent? I have maps of the city that we will both need to study before dispatching any more diggers. I ordered out every man I could spare the moment we arrived. Their searching is random and desperately wants for organization if we are to find all the survivors while yet they live."

"What is the situation in the other outlying communities?" Alan asked as they walked toward the colonel's tent.

"Nowhere nearly so frightful as here. Tabriz was the epicenter," Colonel Rajai replied with forced military detachment as he held back the flap of his tent for his guest to enter. "Tabriz is the area of highest population density; and tragically it was here where the shifting was most violent. Almost eight on the Richter scale, I was told. Other Battalions have already arrived in Rezaieh, Khoi, Maragheh, and Mianeh. They have reported to Tehran that they have adequate manpower to handle the situation in their sectors. Their greatest need is basic medical supplies, equipment, and, of course, shelter and food. Tabriz is where you and the men you brought are most urgently needed."

As maps were spread out, Colonel Rajai explained what he knew of the city from earlier visits. An aide arrived from the mess tent with coffee and morning cakes. The coffee was potent and bitter, the cakes dry, crumbly and nearly tasteless—typical army fare, but it was nourishing at least. If nothing else, it would stop the growling in his stomach. He had not stopped to eat since news of this latest disaster broke, and Lord only knew when he would find time for another meal, such as it was.

"I think we've covered just about everything," Alan announced, trying to conceal his impatience as he stepped back from the map table. They had already wasted more than an hour studying maps he needed only moments to assimilate. "My men are waiting. So, if you will excuse me," he added moving toward the tent opening.

"Surely such leadership skills as yours would be of greater value here in camp." Rajai protested. "I am certain your command can function quite efficiently on its own."

"I have no doubt you will be amply supplied with trained administrative personnel from Tehran and the UN before the day is half gone," Alan replied with an impatient smile. "I carry sensitive instruments hooked to my tool belt that can accurately pinpoint the locations of buried survivors. The sooner we get to them, without wasting time on fruitless digs, as you have already pointed out, the better will be our chances of finding them still alive." He decided the story would provide satisfactory cover for the use of his esper "gifts" in locating the victims. In truth they had proven far more curse than gift, ever since their full emergence, years ago, during puberty. Their existence was still a jealously guarded secret shared only with the aged couple who had adopted and raised him after the death of his parents. He had been only twelve at the time, his esper senses just beginning to surface at full strength. Not even the African knew his young protégé was a psychokinetic telepath, nor would he ever.

As he left the tent, Alan's men snapped to attention. They stood in squads of fifty behind each team leader, each wearing a backpack emblazoned with the insignia of UN paramedics and armed with digging tools. Behind them, engines idling and ready to roll, waited the rescue armada they had brought with them: trucks, jeeps, ambulances, bulldozers, backhoes, and two choppers.

Anticipating heavy digging, Alan had already changed out of the self-contained environment "space" suit he customarily wore while piloting his ship. It was "woven" from the same scarlet, semi-translucent material that formed the almost impervious hull of the *Peregrine*. "Plasti-metal," it had whimsically been dubbed by his research and development people. Technically, it was a highly sophisticated derivative of metal-ceramic composite materials and long-chain polymers. Rolled fabric-thin, it was extremely flexible, virtually puncture-proof, and very easily cleaned. It was also somewhat bulky and cumbersome; so he always kept several changes of work clothes tucked under the control console on the *Peregrine's* bridge. Today he was ready, uniformed in his usual black turtleneck shirt and black denims tucked neatly into black leather climbing boots. He would need all the comfort and mobility he could get. He was also wearing a heavy belt that carried special tools, a stun weapon, communications equipment and his imaginary life-signs detector.

"A thousand apologies, Sheikh. I fear your men will have to travel on foot, for the time being at least, until we can start clearing the streets and make them passable once more." Rajai wore an apologetic expression as he stepped forward, gesturing in the direction of the large motorcade. "By your leave: I have assigned an aide of mine who speaks English to serve as dispatcher for the helicopters you brought. They are most urgently needed for transporting the injured back into camp."

Before Alan had time to frame a reply, a citizen came running up leading a white mare, bridled and saddled.

"Please, Haji, take my Reza. She is very strong. You will need a powerful jumper to get about the city. Perhaps then, Allah will forgive and allow me to find my wife and children yet alive. I live not far from Tabriz. I should have been home with them. I have sinned grievously and am punished." The man was in tears as he handed over the reins then disappeared back into the crowd of soldiers and refugees.

Alan could still feel the man's pain long after he had vanished from sight. Respecting the privacy of the Iranian's thoughts, he wondered what the "grievous sin" had been. The man's fate recalled again the violent deaths of his parents. Lord! Would he never be free of that nightmare?

The gift was welcome nonetheless. Large and heavily muscled, the mare indeed appeared to possess the necessary strength as well as the endurance he would be demanding of her today. She would make it possible to move much more swiftly between the rescue teams as he directed their efforts. With silent gratitude to his vanished benefactor, Alan mounted. Ordering four of his paramedics to stay with the choppers, he turned his mount in the direction of Tabriz. Waving a hand over his head, he signaled a forward advance that started his little army moving. Its ranks were already greatly expanded by Iranian soldiers and able-bodied citizens who needed only the stimulus of a visible leader to motivate them. Still in shock from the magnitude of their loss, the citizens of Tabriz seemed like helpless children as Alan looked briefly over his shoulder. Then he recalled his own weeks of almost catatonic withdrawal after the childhood loss of his parents. With clinched teeth and fists, he closed his eyes and mind to the past. He was grateful that soon he would be too busy in the present, too saturated with the pain and grief of others to be dwelling on his own.

As the column left camp, the train of heavy equipment rumbled off to join Rajai's men. They had already begun the immense task of making the roads and streets of Tabriz passable once more. Alan led the way through the outskirts of the provincial capital, working his way toward its center where they would then systematically begin spiraling outward in their search for survivors trapped in the ruins. As they trudged through pools of water and thick mud surrounding broken water mains, the uniforms of the paramedics changed from smart blue to lifeless dun. The digging tools strapped to their backs clanked loudly as they picked their way between burning and still-smoldering ruins. This was all that was left of the ancient, once-thriving city.

They trudged past toppled buildings, detouring around giant chasms where walls of earth had parted company along fault lines. They climbed over mountains of debris, some so steep Alan was forced to dismount to conserve the mare's strength. She was a grim reminder of more pleasant times. Until the devastation spawned by Kali that now consumed his every waking moment, he would still go on occasional, brief camping trips into the foothills and mountains of the nearby Sierras. As a boy, though, when the old professor who had adopted him had still been able, they would often rent horses from a neighboring rancher and disappear into the mountains for days, sometimes weeks, at a time.

Everywhere, working independently or alongside the military, civilians were pulling bodies and belongings from the wreckage. They labored silently, eyes and minds vacant. Alan felt himself at one with them, grateful for the intense work that provided temporary shelter from his own emptiness.

They passed a group of collapsed apartment buildings. Scattered about, splintered fragments of trees mingled with buckled slabs of concrete and shattered turf. Here was the twisted tangle of what looked to have been swings and monkey bars; and there, half buried under tons of fallen masonry, was a child's tricycle. Its tiny owner's mangled legs were caught in a hopeless jumble of pedals and broken spokes. The earthquake had hit during the night. Had the child died trying to rescue his treasured possession?

The last of Alan's carefully constructed shelter crumbled into dust. Children had always been special to him. In their company, he was always completely at ease, with nothing to hide. Death having struck here was affecting him more than all he had witnessed thus far today. Forcing himself to look away, he urged the mare into a faster gait.

Ahead of them a fire raged, ringed by military equipment and soldiers trying to contain it with chemicals. Iranian Army choppers were dropping water bombs on other fires. A wave of Alan's hand sent a paramedic squad scurrying to help a group of soldiers laden with injured survivors who had just emerged from a partially-intact portion of an apartment complex. Further ahead, diggers were attacking the remains of what appeared to have been an office building. It was doubtful the structure would have been occupied when the earthquake struck.

He brought the mare to a halt and closed his eyes while he scanned the building. Nothing. Increasing the range of his scan as he swept the entire area, he intercepted a weak but distinct sensation of panic, of being trapped— minds crying out for help.

"Hatch, get your men working on that pile of rubble over there! It used to be a hotel and people are trapped in the basement level," Alan shouted to one of his team leaders. His outstretched arm pointed across the street from where civilian workers were digging under the direction of a young officer. In his left hand, Alan brandished a small electronic radiation detector from his instrument belt, pretending to scan the area with it. The ruse, to cover his use of telepathy, would survive all but the closest expert scrutiny. Satisfied that his men were working where they had the greatest chance of breaking through to the survivors, he gave a gentle kick and nudged the mare back across the street. The lieutenant in charge was a monument to stubbornness. No amount of argument was going to convince him that all they would unearth from the office building would be the lifeless remains of two hapless janitors.

A call from his men brought Alan back to the wreckage of the hotel. An opening had been cleared to the lower levels; but further progress was now blocked by a fallen girder. Dismounting, he worked his way under it, took a deep breath and heaved upward. The girder gave slightly then caught again, as though it were fighting back. Three men from the paramedic team were now able to find purchase for handholds and leverage. They braced themselves then added their strength to his. Grinding his teeth against the strain, Alan planted his feet more firmly and directed a scalding stream of invective toward that damned comet. Then, from some reservoir deep within him, together with his men he called forth the needed strength. Groaning in surrender, the steel beam grudgingly let go and began inching upward. For a moment it paused, suspended above their heads. Then, with one last heave, they sent it toppling off to one side. The girder crashed to earth, smashing into splinters the ornate gilt sign that once had so proudly proclaimed the name of this establishment. Two smaller cross beams were more easily moved and the way was clear.

Before they could climb down into the darkness below, a triumphant cheer went up from the members of his command, echoing accolades followed, this time in Persian as well. Several Kurdish voices joined the brief chorus, proudly and defiantly shouting in their own provincial dialect. The diggers from across the street had joined the press. Some were shouting while others stared in silent awe, whispering among themselves.

Alan scowled in annoyance. Precious moments had to be wasted shouting everyone back to work. More valuable minutes would also have to be sacrificed clearing out the last of the rubble, widening the opening. At last, Alan and several paramedics were able to secure a rope ladder and lower themselves into the hole. Thirty people emerged from the darkness. They were grime-covered, bruised, some bleeding, and all squinting painfully in the unaccustomed light.

Once more there was a round of applause, louder than before. First aid was administered, stretchers called up. The small party of those still able to walk began threading its way down toward the rapidly growing tent city, guided by civilian volunteers. The more seriously injured were carried to a relatively open area. Several paramedics had to be sacrificed temporarily to wait with them until the chopper ambulance that had been called for arrived.

Across the debris-strewn street, two bodies had been uncovered: exactly as predicted. Awed but still proud, the Iranian lieutenant came to place himself under Alan's direction. Others began arriving as word spread. Yet, as the morning dragged on, despite the rapidly swelling numbers of volunteers, need continued to far outstrip available supplies of manpower. With only an occasional pang of conscience, Alan found himself obliged to conscript civilian refugees who were wandering around, still dazed. Giving them a brisk shaking to rouse them somewhat, he shoved tools and commands at them. The work, more often than not, gave renewed purpose, helping to revive them.

Someone down at the tent city was thinking of them. By mid-morning runners began arriving with water, then later with coffee, military issue, but still welcome, sandwiches, and urns of hot soup. There was no feed for the mare, but Alan watered her out of a soldier's helmet and fed her several loaves of stale dry bread fetched by a thoughtful runner. There were also bits of dried and overripe fruit donated by dozens of soldiers.

It was nearly dark. Outside reinforcements had begun arriving by late afternoon, yet still there were not enough hands to free all those still imprisoned in the earthquake's aftermath. Alan was as exhausted as his workers, but dared not stop. Manpower was too precious to waste on random digs. He had to be there to point out the tombs that concealed living tenants. Pain, fear, even the flickering lamps of those unconscious or near death were beacons, directing and driving him.

He was riding ahead, searching through one of the poorer districts when he was suddenly overwhelmed by the silent scream of a child in agony.

"Mamma! Why won't you answer?" A child's voice rang in his head. That little house over there, the one with the tree toppled across what was left of a roof. Jumping down from the mare, he ran toward it. Yes! In there! The entire dwelling had been reduced to little more than rubble, and yet a child still survived within—a child he had to reach.

Anger became a stimulant, reviving him from rapidly overwhelming fatigue. Kali would not claim this sacrifice. The passion of determination set his heart pounding, cleared the cobwebs from his brain. The tree had to, would be, moved out of the way.

He grabbed a limb, pulled. It moved, but only slightly. It was caught somewhere. Again he felt the child's panic wash over him, setting his heart to pounding. Alone this time, too apprehensive to wait for help to catch up, he wedged himself under the main trunk and heaved. Crying out with the agony of muscles that threatened to rip away from the bones where they were anchored, he commanded yet more of them. They responded. With creaking protest, the dying tree inched up, and then fell aside, out of the way.

Reeling from pain and nausea, Alan paused only long enough to regain his balance. He drank in great swallows of air to feed his starving lungs and brushed a sleeved arm across his brow to wipe away rivulets of muddy, salty perspiration that were burning his eyes. As soon as he could clear his vision, he dove into the pile of debris that barred entrance to what remained of the tiny house.

"OK, Charlie, hit it!" He only half heard the voice behind him. "This is Dan Alexander again, at the scene of the Iranian disaster. We've just located Alan Kolkey, the man who stopped Kali. As just about everyone in the world must know by now, he is the reclusive owner and guiding genius behind the meteoric growth of Space Tech Industries. Its most famous and thus far greatest technological achievement: the spaceship, *Peregrine*. I'm going to try to get closer.

"Uh…Mr. Kolkey…Sir? Could we have a moment of your…"

"Not now!" Alan snarled over his shoulder as he continued his assault on the rubble.

"But Sir… The world is waiting to hear some word of assurance." The burly newscaster in rolled-up shirt-sleeves held tenaciously to his microphone while he scrambled over mounds of rubble. He was forced to perform several acrobatic maneuvers, in order to stay close to his subject while the camera crew circled in for close-ups from different angles. A careless step brought debris down into the opening where Alan was working, aided now by several civilian volunteers who had just joined their efforts with his.

"Dammit! Either you grab a shovel and give a hand, or get the hell out of here!" He grabbed a large, deceptively heavy-looking chunk of plaster and hurled it, accidentally-on-purpose, in the general direction of the gathering knot of media personnel, scattering them.

At last, an opening into the ruined dwelling. There was crawl space for only one to enter. Alan had decided it would be him. No one else. He blinked several times, trying to adjust to the almost non-existent light and to clear his eyes of the dust raised by the frantic digging.

Sheltered under a massive, crudely built wooden table, propped up in lean-to fashion by its two remaining legs, he saw a woman's body. Her head had been reduced to bloody pulp by that same table, her legs pinned under at the other end. Crouching down, he reached past to dislodge the small body still tenaciously clinging to her.

A warning sound of splintering timber. Alan looked up, just in time tucking his head under his arms as a broken section of support beam came crashing down on top of him.

For a moment the world blinked out. Opening his eyes again was a slower more painful process. There was dust from earth, plaster and masonry clinging to his lashes. Freeing a hand to brush it away was slow tedium. Fortunately nothing was broken: just weighted down under a large chunk of broken timber and a pile of debris. He was bruised and his head ached savagely, but otherwise, everything checked out.

"Mr. Kolkey! Can you hear us?" The muffled sound of Hatch's voice.

"Here! How long have I been out?" he shouted back. A wave of nausea threatened to empty the contents of his stomach.

"Couldn't have been more'n a minute or so, sir. We've got diggers assembled. We'll have you out in no time."

Alan was not about to wait helplessly while others slowly dug their way to him. He was in pitch darkness, but he had managed to free both arms now. If he could just reach, get hold of that length of timber pinning his shoulders down. Got it! There was room off to his right. Arching his back as he pulled and prodded with both hands, he finally succeeded in dislodging it.

His head was not hurting so much now. He was able to focus his mind sufficiently again to concentrate on the task ahead. A whimpering cry reminded him why he was here. Thank God! The child was still alive. Doubling his efforts, he freed himself sufficiently at last to sit up and then reach across the woman's body next to him. Fumbling blindly, his groping hand finally connected with a tiny warm body. It flinched fearfully at his first touch, but finally allowed him to drag it over its mother's icy stiff body and into his lap.

Alan gathered the trembling child close in his arms, gently rocking back and forth until its terror gradually subsided. Despite a lifetime spent rigidly schooling his emotions into submission, a telltale tear escaped, tracking a muddy trail down one cheek.

A crack of light appeared in front of him, accompanied by the sound of tumbling debris and clanging tools, the sound of voices shouting profanities in two languages: they were sweet music to his ears. Slowly, the patch of light began growing until it was large enough to offer safe exit. Anxious shouting gave way to cheers of celebration.

O'Keef, one of Alan's team leaders who was also a valued chief design engineer back at Space Tech, came running to relieve him of his tiny burden as he emerged, stumbling drunkenly into the cool evening air. He waved the man away. This child was too special to entrust to others.

As he mounted the mare, the boy snuggled deeper into his arms. He looked down to find himself in miniature: eyes as blue as his own, hair as black, curling softly over ears and neck. He clucked the animal into a fast walking gait and turned her head toward the encampment.

Far swifter than the pace of his exhausted mount, memory carried him back through the years, returning him once more to his own childhood, his own loss. This child was no more than six. He had been twelve when his own parents had as violently been torn from him. He had never been able to cry for them and yet their loss still colored the fabric of every day.

The child in his arms wriggled, whimpered, then finally fell into exhausted sleep. The earth had spoken out in angry protest and had taken the family of this small boy, just as the sky, lashing out in its fury, had opened up and swallowed his own. He was thirty-eight now: a grown man. Supposedly. To the world he was Alan Kolkey, owner of Space Tech Industries, designer and sole pilot of the *Peregrine*. Conqueror of Kali. A hero to some; to others even a messiah of sorts. Right! People everywhere insisted on seeing in him the realization of their prayers. Yet, when thunder talked and lightning walked the land, he still cowered, forced over and over to relive the horror of that long ago night. Alan held the child's body closer, craving comfort as much, perhaps more, than the orphan in his arms.

He was only vaguely aware of hands reaching up to help him dismount. Someone was promising that the mare would be well cared for as she was led away. He was certain there had only been two attendants, but it felt as though a crowd had turned out to herd him into one of the hospital tents. The astringent smell of antiseptic hanging heavily in the stifling air could not wash out the sound of weeping or the agonized cries of the injured and dying. Neither could exhaustion completely drown out the wave after wave of loss and pain that crashed like breakers against the shores of his aching, unshielded mind. Arriving at the back of the tent, a matronly woman who reminded him of his adoptive mother managed to coax the child out of his arms. A doctor and several nurses backed him down onto an empty cot with assurances that, yes, they would wake him in an hour if he would just agree to rest for a while.

Fighting a gradually losing battle against sleep, Alan watched silently while a doctor examined the small boy who had been placed on the bunk next to his. He reached out to mentally probe the child's physical and emotional condition for himself, but his mind would no longer focus. All he managed to glean was a name, Hassan, and a disjointed collage of scenes and emotions as searing as the flames that still licked the bosom of Tabriz.

"Nothing broken. No palpable internal bleeding. Reflexes adequate. Didn't the Sheikh mumble something about the child's mother, and possibly his father, being dead? He'll bear close watching." The doctor was speaking Persian, but with a noticeably strong Kurdish accent.

Reassured that Hassan was in reasonably responsible hands, Alan closed his eyes, surrendering to his exhaustion.

•••

He felt a momentary after-shock, not enough to rouse him, but somehow precipitating an incredibly vivid dream in which he found himself struggling up a steep, boulder-strewn mountain path. Again, the earth heaved violently beneath his sandaled feet, making him lurch drunkenly.

Looking down he found himself garbed in a white tunic and a long scarlet wool cloak that partially concealed the sacred ceremonial sword, sheathed now in its jeweled scabbard at his side. Around his neck hung a large gold and silver medallion: a winged pentagram. The silhouetted head of an onyx horse with a tiny silver star gracing its forehead adorned the center. His black hair, damp from the sweat of his exertions was a mass of long, tight ringlets. It seemed the only feature of his dream self that he could recognize. In a paradox of confusion, this was, and yet at the same time, was not him.

He was searching for something. Someone. A horrifying dread of having betrayed an ancient and sacred trust was overwhelming him. A grievous wrong had been committed that for too long had gone unavenged, a holy office too long untended. As the earth gave yet another violent heave, he found himself clinging to a rocky overhang on a solitary mountainside that overlooked a ring of islands. They were all that remained of an ancient and mighty nation that had once held sway over an entire world—a nation that was now convulsing in its final death throes. It was too late to rescue his stolen priestess or the millions of worshippers they had once led in service to the Goddess: the Great Mother and her Horned Consort. Still, he had to make the attempt. He had to die in the discharge of his duty, grievously belated though it was. He could only pray that the death of the infidel who had brought this doom down upon them all, his blood bathing this consecrated blade, might yet wash away the stigma of his cowardice.

Looking up, he saw his destination: a mighty granite fortress. Ramparts unguarded, its outer walls in ruins, it could now be easily breached. The leaden sky crackled with lightning, boomed with thunder so loud it drowned out the shrieking protest of myriad ships overhead. They were ferrying refugees to safety on larger continental land masses. Scores of giant starships, dwarfing all the others, were carrying the hardiest, most venturesome colonists out, searching for asylum on other worlds circling other suns.

He was inside the main citadel now, searching ruined halls and upper level chambers. Guards and retainers raced blindly past, ignoring him. Chaos was his ally. At last, success! But as he had feared, too late to save his priestess. She lay in a pool of her own blood, her hands still clutching the dagger that pierced her exquisite breast. She, who had been the Living Vessel of the Great Mother, was as beautiful in death as ever she had been in life. Kneeling beside her, cradling her head with its magnificent halo of golden hair, now bathed in crimson, was the faithless defiler. He had killed the Holy Chalice, as surely as though he had, himself, plunged in the knife.

Unsheathing the ritual sword, he raised it to strike. The murderer looked up. So much pain reflected in the emerald eyes of this silver-haired warlord! Grief-stricken remorse, as well, to rival his own. Something stayed his hand. The rapist, this defiler of women, would die. Oh yes! But not by this most holy sword which had never before tasted blood. Justice—vengeance—was no longer his to dispense. He had forfeited the right by his own cowardly inaction. It belonged now to the Horned One Himself and would momentarily be meted out to both of them, for deeds done and, most especially, for deeds too long left undone.

The floor buckled in one last, violent convulsion. Blocks of stone and masonry began raining down on them. Something blunt and heavy struck his head and brought him to his knees.

•••

Alan woke with a start. Someone was hovering over him, holding him down. He looked up into a swarthy, mustached face, darkened further by a concerned frown. "What…?" he mumbled, fighting his way through cobwebs of sleep that still blurred his vision.

"I was fearful for you, Haji. You were crying out, thrashing about so violently. I wonder that you didn't topple us both to the ground. Are you all right now?" The dark face spoke softly in the soothing, cultured tones of his native tongue.

"Apparently I must do battle with earthquakes even in my sleep." Alan sat up slowly, kneading the last of the sleep from his eyes as he planted his feet on the ground. "My

God, that dream was vivid!" If that's all it was, he added silently. He was amazed how clearly and indelibly each detail had registered into conscious memory. The scenes, the emotions they had evoked were as starkly real as the recurring childhood nightmares that still compelled him, over and over again, to relive the death of his parents. This latest nightmare would probably join in haunting him for weeks to come. Was it only a dream, he could not help wondering. Or could it have been the long-buried memories of some ancient incarnation dredged up into dream consciousness by the trauma of the day's events? The ancient doctrine of reincarnation: was it more than mere superstition? Was it indeed fact? Did something survive after the death of the flesh? No, he scoffed silently. Reincarnation was nothing more than the pseudo-religious romanticizing of men and women too cowardly to accept their own mortality: man reassuring himself that death was not total dissolution. No, the dream, despite its vivid detail and emotional impact, was nothing more than his unconscious mind replaying in symbolism his ongoing battle against being swept onto the playing field of global politics as a major player. It was a role he neither sought nor welcomed. Of course it was only a dream! And yet he found himself grieving for the fallen priestess almost as keenly as he still grieved for his mother and father.

Forcing himself back to the here-and-now of earthquake-ravaged Tabriz, Alan looked up, this time recognizing the black wavy hair, the long graying sideburns melting into a short, impeccably manicured beard and pencil thin mustache. The man hovering over him was Iran's defense minister, Jafar Shoja. Time, war, and natural disasters had gradually mellowed the Iranian government's revolutionary zeal of twenty odd years ago, dulling its edge with logistical considerations. The new political climate, one of expediency, had provided fertile ground for a gradual return of diplomatic relations with the Western world. Although an Islamic Conservative, Shoja's first concern was for the welfare of his nation and its people. He had been largely instrumental in Iran's return from Fundamentalist extremism and her rapidly improving relations with other countries.

Alan had always found Shoja's aura, for lack of a more scientifically correct terminology, far more comfortable than those of most diplomats and politicians. Right now, however, it positively glowed with a pride, respect and admiration that fell just short of outright worship. The diplomat's thoughts and feelings were projecting too strongly to ignore. This wealthy and powerful young man, he was thinking, proclaimed hero and savior by every nation in the world, had come to the aid of his countrymen in this terrible catastrophe. Somewhere too, along the way, Haji Kolkey had considered it important enough to have made the effort to learn their language, which he spoke with amazing fluency. There was something hauntingly familiar about the "flavor" of the Iranian minister's aura right now, recalling the gentle, never-forgotten touch of his mother's mental imprint. She also had come from this corner of the world. It put him at ease in the older man's presence.

"Coffee?" Shoja offered, pouring the steaming liquid into a battered metal cup from a thermos that had been sitting on a nearby packing crate. The heady aroma was almost intoxicating, reminding Alan how hungry he was.

As he took the cup, he looked down at his watch. "How long... My God! I've been out of it for nearly twelve hours. I told those damn medics to wake me in one hour." He jumped up, gulping coffee and raking a hand through his hair to get it out of his face.

"You had been working out there since first light yesterday, Haji Kolkey, and it was very late when you came back in. They told me you were so exhausted you had to be helped off your horse. Allah only knows when last you slept. No! I, myself, gave the order that you were not to be wakened. There was very little digging to be done during the night. Field generators and portable floods are only now beginning to arrive." Shoja's deep, rich voice, as he found another packing crate to sit on, made Alan feel like a temperamental kitten being stroked into submission.

"But, dammit! It's been daylight now for almost three hours and there are hundreds of your people still trapped out there." He was not about to be put off that easily.

"Ah, but thanks to the aid of your UN and our own good soldiers and citizens, we are now more than adequately supplied with workers," Shoja smiled disarmingly as he shrugged his shoulders.

"Manpower and time wasted in random search. My instruments can show them exactly where to dig." Alan paced back and forth several times in hurried impatience.

"Of this I have no doubt, Haji. Still, of what help could you be to us should you collapse from fatigue and hunger? Your heaven-sent services would then be lost to us for days, weeks, perhaps." The defense minister's smile was disarming, his logic incontestable. "Even one as truly blessed by Allah as you, must rest once in a while."

"Blessed by Allah?" Alan's nose wrinkled in annoyed amusement, recalling now, in retrospect, the words the crowd of soldiers and civilians had greeted him with on his arrival yesterday. Roughly translated, they had been shouting something like, "Blessed of" or "Sent by Allah!"

"Praise be to Allah! Not here in Iran. But there are small, radical Islamic sects who proclaim you to be al Mahdi, 'He Who is Guided Aright,' the spiritual and secular leader who, prophesy claims, will one day unify all of Islam under his benevolent rule." Shoja smiled with amusement at Alan's discomfort. "After all, it is well known that even though your father was, The Benevolent One forgive me, a Jew, your mother was a daughter of Islam. It is rumored she came from a desert tribe whose lineage traces back, in unbroken line, to the Prophet himself."

"Al Mahdi!" Alan spat under his breath. Damn! Why did people have to persist in elevating him to the impossible role of savior and messiah? Everywhere he went they projected their fantasies, pinned their hopes on him. Why in hell did they all, the African especially, have to look to him as their champion, the paladin who would go forth and, in one sweep, slay War, Famine, Pestilence, and Death. All four of the fabled Horsemen. It was not his fight; it was theirs. Something they should be doing for themselves.

"Few here in Iran hold with such spurious prophesies as that of 'al Mahdi.' Yet there are many sects in other Islamic lands who do. Most, however, also believe that only one who is a faithful follower of Mohammed may claim such a holy title." Shoja's tone grew pensive, hopeful as his dark eyes bored holes into Alan's. "Though it is not the wish of my superiors, to whom I owe first allegiance, still, I do feel in my secret heart that it would be wonderful if all who follow the Prophet of Allah were united: one people, one Truth, under one Leader. Finally at peace among each other. We would then, indeed, be a force to reckon with. They would no longer refer to us as 'Third World' countries. You, my young paladin, despite your father's regrettable ancestry, could conceivably become such a leader."

"Dammit, man! I'm not al Mahdi! So don't start entertaining any notions about finding some way of using me for your precious unifying catalyst! I'm just me. Myself. Alone! No special dispensations from Upstairs; and furthermore, even though I was obliged to study them all, at one time or another, as a child, I don't follow Judaism nor Christianity; nor have I any intention of embracing Islam. I follow the path of logic, of science and technology. The jury's still out on anything else." Alan cursed silently, his eyes rapidly scanning the area for something he could use to change the subject. There was not much to see. Someone had partitioned off this corner of the tent. Probably Shoja's bright idea. The "Blessed of Allah" needed his privacy. There was only the packing crate chair Shoja was sitting on and the "bed stand" crate between the cot he had slept on and the one they had put little Hassan in last night.

"Hassan! The child I brought in with me. Where is he!" Alan demanded.

"He woke several hours ago. The nurses had a dreadful time convincing him to leave without waking you. They had to promise he could see you as soon as you were up. The boy appears to have become extremely attached to you," Shoja smiled sadly, his zeal mellowing somewhat.

"Shoja! I want the truth! What are his chances for adoption?" Outrage washed from his spine. The authoritarian bark in his voice rapidly melted into concern.

"Not good at all, I fear, Haji. There have been so many little ones orphaned by this terrible disaster." Shoja's smile warmed like the morning sun. "Ah! I see you also have become attached. Perhaps..."

"I only wish I could take him, Minister Shoja; but..."

"Yes, I understand. You are seldom permitted to remain in any one place long enough to oversee the needs of a child."

Alan managed the lie with an affirmative nod. He knew the old couple he still lived with would have loved nothing better than another child to fuss over. But he found himself still afraid to love, and lose again. Perspiration beaded his brow as he recalled a long-ago camping trip on horseback into the mountains with his adoptive father, one of many back then. A rabid grizzly had charged them without provocation. Panicking, he had instinctively loosed a blast of PK, unintentionally, but instantly, killing the beast.

From what he had seen of love and hate, different sides of the same coin, they meant emotions out of control; and emotions out of control meant psychokinetic "static." Someone could get hurt or killed in the backwash. The episode with the grizzly had pounded the lesson home. Despite the cost, he had schooled himself with steel cold discipline, imposed on himself the icy control necessary to contain the psionic demon that dwelt within him. It was difficult enough suppressing affection around the professor and Gertha, the old couple who had adopted him after the deaths of his parents. It would be far more difficult with a child like little Hassan, and altogether impossible with a woman. Never having dared, he could only imagine the terrible consequences to his partner, the uncontrolled discharge of PK in the mindless abandon of sexual release. Despite ever-present temptation, he had never allowed himself the luxury of bedding any of the hundreds of nameless women forever offering themselves to him. No! He must not permit any further closeness with little Hassan. No one else must die on his account. It was enough, it had to be enough, that the child was now alive.

"May I offer, then, some small comfort?" Shoja placed an understanding hand on his arm. "I called my wife yesterday when the children started being brought in. We are childless and she was delighted with the prospect of adopting several of them. We all owe you so much. Would it ease your mind somewhat if I made certain that Hassan is one of the children that my wife and I take? That way you would always know where he is, should you ever wish to look in on him."

"I would then be in your debt," he smiled gratefully.

"It is done then. Now come. We can visit with the boy over a belated breakfast before returning to our separate duties."

As Alan emerged with Shoja into the sunlight it seemed as if the entire population of the now-teeming tent city was waiting to greet him. Cries of "Blessed of Allah!" and "Praise be to Allah!" repeated over and over, rivaled in decibels the thundering incredibly painful echo inside his head. So much raw emotion. So many undisciplined minds beating against his unshielded brain like a thousand battering rams.

The emotional tidal wave was overpowering, threatening to drown him in its wash. He dreaded what would happen if the people of other Moslem nations also caught the fever and began seeing in him a banner under which all of Islam might rally. He knew Shoja would not long remain silent; and there is nothing so persuasive as a man who believes, truly believes, in what he is proclaiming.

CHAPTER II

Aᴸᴬᴺ Kᴏʟᴋᴇʏ sat beside M'Butu Moshey as the presidential limousine threaded its way through the cheering, crowd-choked streets of Manhattan. The ride toward the UN Complex was a silent exercise in self-control. Thousands more would be gathered in the UN plaza when they arrived. Eyes closed against the pulsing waves of low level pain, he silently began steeling himself for the even greater assault on his unshielded hyper-sensitive brain when they arrived. Today's special session of the General Assembly had been called at the behest of the Iranian delegation. They wished to publicly honor the paramedic rescue teams and especially the man who had commanded them during the Tabriz crisis.

Sweat beaded on his forehead as he silently struggled to tune out the African's endless stream of small talk and the equally persistent battering of worshipful enthusiasm from the crowd outside. For the thousandth time, Alan wondered how he had ever allowed himself to be suckered into this impossible role of hero-at-large. Despite himself, he had grown to like and respect the balding diplomat with his crown of nappy gray hair and his shining, impossible

37

dreams. Someday his precious UN was going to grow beyond the constant state of emergency imposed by Kali to govern a world finally at peace under one permanently unified federation of nations. Alan had heard the liturgy recited almost daily ever since UN President M'Butu Moshey first entered and took over his life. Right now, he silently cursed that meeting and the man himself. He saved his darkest thoughts, though, for whoever had suggested to the African that the private-sector experimental interplanetary ship Space Tech was building might offer a second chance after all the nuclear warheaded missiles they had sent up had failed to budge that stubborn mass of ice and rock the tiniest fraction of a degree from its original trajectory. Inexplicably, most of them had exploded prematurely, failed to explode on impact, or went sailing blindly past to God knows where in the universe. It almost seemed as if there had been some infernal intelligence behind it all, plotting to entangle him in all this.

"I'm truly sorry about this, Alan; but after Tabriz, there was no way the Iranian people, or their delegates here, would be put off," Moshey fidgeted uncomfortably next to Alan. The limousine seemed to be crawling across eternity on the back of a snail as it winded its way through the crowd-congested streets.

"Sometimes I wonder whether you cast a spell and called up that damned comet," Alan grumbled, looking out at all those cheering people. He desperately wished the huge black presidential limousine were as well insulated against their painful onslaught of thoughts and emotions as it was against the ear-shattering roar of the crowd monster. "The only ones Kali has blessed are you and your infernal UN. The constant state of emergency she maintains keeps you in almost absolute control—control over me as well. I'd give anything to be able to tell everyone to go to hell, except that it was my ignorant miscalculation, my damn fault she's up there at all. It just doesn't make any sense. Why must everyone persist in treating me like some sort of demi-God when they should be cursing me instead?" Alan looked up, then tried to look away again, but Moshey's eyes locked onto his and refused to let go.

"Because, my young Achilles, the people need a champion right now. To them you are a demi-God, whether or not you like it." Moshey shrugged resignedly and offered his most palliative smile. "Look at it from their point of view, my boy. How many millions of people now owe their lives to you? You are always there at every natural disaster, helping transport equipment, supplies, personnel, the wounded, and digging out alongside the victims. Your presence, your continued visibility alone, reassures and heartens them," he continued, placing a paternal arm around Alan's shoulder. "Naturally, they're going to plant you up there on a pedestal. You appeared just when this tired, technologically jaded old planet most needed a champion. You added a little romance and hope into their lives. Now, like it or not, you belong to them."

The African's voice now grew sterner. "For the sake of your precious privacy, you have unwittingly thrown up an aura of mystery around yourself. It has grown into a public persona that has fleshed itself out on the need of people everywhere for the culture hero that technocracy has for too long stripped them of. Unfortunately for the real you, that persona has now taken on a life of its own. To the French you have become 'le Paladin,' to the Spanish, El Cid reborn. Some Buddhists, I'm told, even have you down for sainthood. The more radical right-wing Christians go them one better, claiming you are either the Second Coming, or Satan incarnate. Apparently, they have difficulty differentiating between the two. Then of course we have the Hindus. Many of their learned scholars have pointed out the similarity between your surname: Kolkey, and that of Kalki, the Tenth Avatar of their God Vishnu. They have been even more vocal since you were photographed riding that white mare at Tabriz. Pandava tells me that kalki means "white horse" in Sanskrit.

Alan brushed the older man's arm away like an annoying insect, wishing fervently that he had never allowed Moshey to cajole him into making this appearance today. The damned African was almost as hard to refuse as his adoptive parents.

"Then, of course, there are the Islamic nations," Moshey persisted, grinning wickedly. The bastard was enjoying this. "It is well known your biological mother was Arabic and embraced Islam. Ever since Tabriz, there are those who are more convinced than ever you are their promised 'al Mahdi.'"

"My biological father was also a Jew," Alan shot back with bitter humor. "You'd think that would cool their ardor somewhat. At least to most Iranians and the more conservative sects, I'm only a hero: someone handy to have around in a pinch. Shoja tells me they've even been able to forgive me for being American."

"Just the same, your having come from two such mutually hostile cultures, might be perceived by many as an omen that it is time to stop the killing, that we can all learn to live together, in peace at least, if not in love." Moshey had never been one to surrender an argument without fighting to the last drop of blood.

"They might also decide to split me up the middle, like a wishbone," Alan spat back. He hunkered lower into the plush seat, as though this might lessen his visibility to the crowd on the other side of the bullet-proof windows. "Racial hatreds go deep and die hard. I ought to know.

After my parents were killed, I was raised by a black woman who told me stories about growing up in the south that you wouldn't ever want to tell a child at bedtime."

"All right! What about your birth date: February 2, 1962, Alexandria, Egypt. Two o'clock in the afternoon, I believe?"

"Which makes me thirty-eight, and five months ago we moved into a new century. Other than that, so what!" Alan shot the older man a contemptuous glance.

"So Blavatsky! So Dixon! They were both famous psychics and still have large followings. Each of them have popularized that date and that general area for the birth of another messiah; and while we are on that subject, again, I'm told even Judeo-Christians have some sort of prophecy, as well, about their Savior returning on a white horse," Moshey continued, apparently oblivious to the younger man's black mood.

Alan's nerves had been rubbed raw by now. His patience was growing dangerously thin. "It was a white ass, not a horse. What a shame I wasn't born in Bethlehem, or that the nearest thing they had to a star was a comet you would have needed a very good telescope to see. We could have really given those Fundamentalist Christians one hell of a 'Second Coming' to buzz about."

"Please, Alan! Son..." Moshey suddenly turned a pleading face as he rested his hand on top of Alan's. "Try to understand how very important this is for global unification to solidify beyond the temporary glue that Kali has provided us. Give me permission to name you as my political successor. I am black in a world where white still controls the balance of power. I am president by chance alone. I just happened to be in the right place at the right time, as they say. All I can hope for is to give the UN a few more teeth. But..."

"And I'm white," Alan cut him off. "There are also a lot of blacks who hate whites. With damn good reason."

"True enough! But, with my endorsement and knowing that you were raised by a black woman…"

Alan bared his teeth in a menacing smile "I said forget it, Mr. President! People don't want a world government. It interferes with them killing each other. Don't you know? It's one of their favorite games. Homo un-sapiens have been playing it for thousands of years. The Crusades, the Inquisition, Witch Hunts, Holy Wars: all fought in the name of religion." Alan's expression softened slightly into a bitter smile. "So, no thank you! I think I'll pass on the opportunity to get into the God business. I don't have the qualifications, the pay's lousy, and I'm really not sold on the retirement plan. Besides, the job's already taken.

"I still mean what I said, Sir," Alan continued after a long pause. His head ached fiercely and he was wishing passionately that Moshey would finally get the message and drop the matter for good. "It was a verbal contract, but I'm still holding you to it: after today, I don't want to hear from you unless there's some sort of Kali-spawned disaster where I'm genuinely needed." Here was something he had no trouble refusing the gentle old diplomat, even while watching disappointment once more extinguish the fires of idealism from his dark eyes.

Alan pulled his cloak of gloom closer about him to dampen any further attempts at conversation. He tried blotting out all awareness of the African's presence only to find himself wandering back to the day their paths first converged:

•••

Alan Kolkey grumbled angrily under his breath as he shut down the main computers. Slamming his fist down hard on the desk top, he turned his back on the work he had unsuccessfully been trying to lose himself in. Reluctantly, he started walking back toward the empty shuttle dock. Why had the old professor gone behind his back like that? His time was too valuable right now to be wasted on explanations to narrow-minded politicians. Twenty years of grinding work and unflinching dedication to a dream! Finally, his newly christened *Peregrine* was almost ready for her maiden shake-down voyage to test the off-planet, fusion-plasma drive. Her decks and bulkheads were still nothing more than naked metal partitions. Ship-wide life support had yet to be installed. The main sensor array and navigational instrumentation were operational. With down-loading to the on-board computers almost complete, her bridge would soon be fully functional. He had trained for years in preparation. Now, only a few more days and he would be piloting her himself through the first series of exhaustive test runs scheduled for next week.

Space Tech's Research and Development department had developed a comfortably efficient, self-contained internal environment "spacesuit." The prototype had already been custom fitted to conform to his own body measurements. It was all the life support he would need for now. And dammit, he was ready to go! What he was not ready for was any interference that might spell more delays.

Their work shift had ended over an hour ago. His hand-picked tech and support crew had long since left the underground final assembly hanger, either for living quarters topside, or for Sonora where most, mainly those with families, lived. It was Friday, so many of them, he knew, would be taking advantage of the weekend Tahoe/Vegas jet-chopper shuttle run that Space Tech provided for its on-site employees.

For a few minutes, at least, he could be blissfully alone. Once more Alan paused briefly and turned to admire the sleek beauty of the "someday starship." She was as much a work of art as she was a work of technology. She was his creation. He had been her chief engineer and architect. Although a major stockholder, he left corporate administration to administrators. In charge of Research and Development, he was free to concentrate on evolution of the incredibly complex, radically new technologies on which the building of an interplanetary and, eventually, interstellar vessel would depend. It had been his dream since childhood and the driving force during his entire adult life. Alan had cause to be doubly proud. The *Peregrine's* graceful lines, the crimson translucence of her plasti-metal hull made her look like a jeweled teardrop stolen from the tiara of some titan sky Goddess. Nestled among the gantries and ladders, still needed for last minute adjustments on her external sensors, she slumbered and dreamed with him of glorious journeys soon to come: journeys that might now never happen.

Dammit! So close to completion! Why had that blasted comet chosen now, of all times, to make its grand entrance? Its member nations had wasted no time looking to the UN. A state of planet-wide martial law had been declared, delegating to it temporary emergency power to commandeer materials and resources and to coordinate joint efforts for dealing with the situation. The office of secretary general had suddenly been upgraded to that of president. Secretary General M'Butu Moshey, former delegate from a small, Third World African nation, suddenly found himself the first, if only nominal, temporary president of the "United Nations of Earth."

Four months ago, the interim coalition had somehow pooled together sufficient monies, hardware, and expertise to launch a nuclear war-headed fleet of missiles. Yesterday, news of the mission's failure had sparked hundreds of public demonstrations.

For months, the old professor, Alan's adoptive father, had pestered and pleaded with him to get involved, to come forward and offer Space Tech's assistance. As though the bastards would ever give serious consideration to someone crazy enough to have invested twenty years of his life and billions of corporate dollars building his own spaceship! Granted, most of those billions had been generated from the sale or leasing to private industry of new technologies that were the byproduct of the *Peregrine's* evolution. The ship had been paying her own way now for years, almost from her very inception. As soon as he was finally able to buy out controlling interest in Space Tech, Alan had turned all its resources to the task of designing the tools to build the even more radically different tools of the revolutionary new technology on which the realization of his dream depended.

Really, he had argued, as much to himself as to the old man, what bureaucrat would even consider listening to one lone Don Quixote on another impossible quest? He would have had to submit to the humiliating indignity of being grilled over flaming coals by half-educated morons posing as experts. He did not at all relish the prospect of coming, hat-in-hand, only to be brushed aside as just another crackpot billionaire. And for what: to save a world filled with tyrants, murderers, thieves, deviates, and self-deluded dreamers? These were the sort of human flotsam he always encountered whenever he braved the casinos and illegal back street games, searching for winnings to help feed the insatiable appetite of research. That had been his rationalization, before finally acquiring the last controlling shares of Space Tech. Actually, those early expeditions had provided only a small fraction of the needed revenues. At least now he was able to admit to himself that back then, just as now, they had been nothing more than emotional outlets for bottled up anger and frustration. Those occasional excursions helped keep his martial skills and his psionics honed to razor sharpness. And kicking butt, literally, was often still the most satisfying way to deal with the pressure. The human refuse out there on the streets deserved what they got when they came after him. He never initiated those brawls; but he certainly knew how to end them.

Alan had stepped up the pace of his work after news of the comet first started making headlines. Just in case. He wanted to be ready to ferry his adoptive parents and their families off-planet until the earthquakes, volcanoes and other geological aftermaths of impact quieted down. They were the only ones he really cared much about saving. There were, however, a few members of his R&D team, and even several techs from Final Assembly, he had to admit, that he would hesitate leaving behind. There was no time for fruitless doodling around trying to save the world.

A signal sounded from the underground shuttle that ran between the hollowed-out subterranean hanger and the house, several miles away, where he still lived with his adoptive parents. A small personnel carrier whooshed to a stop. Reluctantly, he stepped forward to greet his unwelcome guest.

"Son, I'd like you to meet UN President M'Butu Moshey," the white haired and mustached old professor offered apologetically, as Alan grudgingly helped him out onto the passenger dock.

The black man climbed out unassisted. He straightened himself gradually, to full length, a rather impressive height for a statesman, Alan thought, rivaling his own six-foot-three. Looking up, the African also revealed a disarming smile and a balding head that wore a crown of nappy gray hair.

"Humph!" the African snorted with a sly grin as his gaze traveled from Alan's head to his feet, and back again.

"You certainly do look amazingly athletic for the scientific wunderkind I was given to expect. So young for all I'm told you have accomplished!" His engaging good humor made it impossible to put the trespasser in his place.

"May I say the same for you, as well, Mr. President." Accepting his visitor's extended hand, Alan found himself smiling despite having already decided that he was not going to like the man. He consoled himself with a hasty scan for reassurance that, if nothing else, the old professor had at least not spilled the whole can of beans about his psi talents. "Neither are you quite the pot-bellied old mustache I would have expected of one who pilots a desk all day."

"Touché!" the African laughed. "We do love to play with our stereotypes, don't we? It's so much easier than forcing ourselves to re-think." Then, the African's wandering gaze was captured by the sleeping *Peregrine*, "Oh my! Doctor, please! Accept my humblest apologies! When you first described this young man's prodigy, I was convinced you were... well, to phrase it as delicately as possible, prone to exaggeration. Thanks be to all the tribal Gods of my childhood I took Secretary Nunzio's advice and listened to you!"

Frowning sternly, he turned back to Alan, impaling him on a finger. "Why, in the name of all the Gods, didn't you come to me sooner? Yourself!"

"And be laughed out of the building for a lunatic with delusions of grandeur?" Alan snapped, following impatiently as President Moshey almost ran for a closer inspection of the giant, five-hundred-foot vessel. "Despite security around this project, it's been common knowledge for years what we were working on down here. Even hidden away among these mountains, this complex has become rather a tourist attraction. We have to maintain a small army of security police, topside, just to control the steady stream of visitors. I'm certain your learned cabinet of advisors was equally aware of our existence."

"Had you come to us in this magnificent bird-of-space, young man, you would most certainly never have been perceived as anything but the incredible genius you most certainly are." The African emphasized his pleading remonstrance with outstretched hands. Looking around him once more, he shook his head in total awe at the towering skeletons of gantries that dwarfed them all to relative insignificance.

"Impossible! She's not flight-ready yet."

"How long?" Moshey demanded, his gaze still devouring the translucent beauty of the *Peregrine*.

"Pushing hard, as I already have been these last months, a week, barring snags. And that's without life support."

"But she will be able to navigate across interplanetary distances?"

"I believe so. I'll know more certainly just how successful my design and engineering is after her first shakedown flight."

"What speeds do you think you'll be able to pull out of her? How long would you estimate in travel time to rendezvous with MP2000CC$_3$: Kali, as everyone seems to be calling that demon-spawned comet, lately?" The African turned to fix his commanding gaze on Alan once more.

"After all the bugs have been worked out, eventually I hope to crank a quarter light speed out of her. But that would really be pushing her to the limit. I'm playing around with a few theories on inter-dimensional warp—bending space, so to speak, between two distant points—to create a short cut." Alan shrugged, smiling indulgently as he tacked on a simplistic description that Moshey might comprehend. "But that's all in the future, still only Fantasy Island. Right now, in the real world, I project a comfortable two-, maybe three-hundred thousand kilometers per hour cruise speed." Alan frowned suspiciously as he unconsciously backed away. President Moshey was leaning too close and he didn't like that hungry gleam in the African's eyes. "At its projected distance from Earth, for the earliest feasible launch date, figuring in acceleration and deceleration time, planetary motion, etcetera, a rough, head calculation would suggest six or seven days. Why?" The question was rhetorical. He already damn well knew why.

"Dammit! Billions of dollars, a cooperative of the best technologies of all our member nations, and most of the missiles we launched never reached their target. The surface detonations of those that made it were so scattered, apparently they managed only to cancel each other out. They didn't deflect that comet one measurable inch from its present trajectory." Moshey cursed angrily as he paced back and forth between Alan and the old professor. "One might almost think they had been deliberately sabotaged.

"By the way, it is now official," he added despondently, "on Kali's present trajectory, she will impact in six months, plus or minus several days, hours, and minutes, from today. I don't recall exactly. Long before it gets here, though, that damned dirty snowball is going to be putting on one hell of a show for us. For several weeks before impact, they say the tail will fill up the entire sky, even during the day. It will give new meaning to that American cliché about going out in a blaze of glory.

"Please, Mr. Kolkey, can you... Will you help us?" President Moshey was a proud man. It would have been obvious even to a non-esper how difficult that final entreaty had been to utter.

Alan found himself snagged on the man's pleading gaze. What for, he wanted to shout as he turned his back on the two older men. Why should he waste his time trying to rescue those miserable miscarriages he always encountered on his for-aging safaris out into the urban jungles of the world. Despite the emotional release it provided, his often violent encounters with them depressed, disillusioned, and occasionally left him worse than useless for several days afterward. Something about this particular old diplomat, however, stayed his tongue. Curious, he sent out a probing tendril of mind to explore the African's deeper, hidden motives.

Moshey, he quickly learned, was one of those rare hybrid crosses between statesman and humanitarian ideal-ist who sincerely believed in the importance of this new global federation. He was praying for a miracle to sustain it beyond the temporary unifying crisis created by Kali, pro-vided of course there was anything left afterward. His thoughts were also very much with the plight of the poor, the ailing, the starving millions of the world. Was this because of, or despite very humble beginnings in his own poverty-stricken nation?

Through the eyes of Moshey's vivid memory, Alan found himself witnessing the murder of innocent villagers by the followers of regional mini-tyrants, children dying by slow and painful degrees from starvation and disease, simple country folk losing all to wars, their own governments, and a plethora of natural disasters. Through the big black man's pain, Alan felt an awakening awareness to the subjective as well as objective aftermath of collision with Kali. What would it add up to in terms of death and suffering? Human beings, not statistics! The destruction, utter annihilation, not just of civilization, but of people everywhere. Perhaps the entire race! Until now it had merely been abstract geo-logical statistics: climate, tectonics, volcanic activity, proba-bility factors: action-reaction calculated on a global scale.

What if he refused to lend such aid as was his to ren-der, no matter how minimal or ineffectual it might prove to be? Could he endure even the silent accusation, the disappointment in Gertha's and the old professor's minds? Ever since his parents had died, they had been his only family, the only friends he had ever permitted himself.

"All right. What is it you want of me?" Turning back to face the African, Alan took a deep breath and surrendered to the only course of action he could comfortably live with. Certainly, he could spare a few months out of his life. What better way, also, to test his *Peregrine* than on an actual mission?

"I want your ship! You! Any alternative strategies you can come up with!" Moshey's face lit up as he almost leapt forward, throwing his arms around Alan in an impulsive embrace.

Embarrassed, Alan awkwardly disengaged, almost tripping over himself, trying to regain the safety of distance between himself and this disconcertingly demonstrative man. He pretended deep absorption, pondering over the problem, while he composed himself. When he was able to think and speak coherently once more, he turned, facing the general direction of the older man. "Right now, without any precise data as yet on the comet and the missiles you sent up, I can only conjecture." He riveted his gaze to the floor for added support as he fumbled for a semblance, at least, of scientific detachment. "However, I suspect the answer lies in an on-site, strategic placement of your nuclear devices for greatest control over the direction of thrust from their explosive energy. Not in bombing and strafing runs."

Alan looked up to see how the African was receiving his suggestions before continuing. "Your best chance might lie in setting down a honeycomb of deep shafts, like rocket tubes, in the solid core under the ice layer. They'll need to be located, angled, and timed for simultaneous detonation of the nuclear devices planted at the bottom of each shaft. Everything has to be carefully computed to provide the maximum angle of orbital deflection."

"The question as to whether or not such a plan would succeed, is purely academic, I'm afraid," Moshey replied. He was on the serrated edge of utter frustration. His arms, hanging at his side, were lead weights dragging him to the ground. Rekindled hope had once more been dashed to shards like a shattered light bulb. "Even if we had the equipment and trained manpower for such a task, it would take months. We just don't have the resources, much less the technology. Or that kind of time."

"Not necessarily," Alan smiled, feeling a bit smug. "I hollowed this entire area out within a 48-hour period, and not by digging." He made a proud, sweeping gesture that took in the enormous expanse of the hanger dome. "I employed a process of molecular compression. By mounting that same generator on the *Peregrine's* prow, it could be aimed precisely, not unlike a laser cannon. I can melt through the ice layer then have your rocket tubes excavated in hours, not months, Mr. President. Not only that, but the walls of the shafts will be composed of densely packed molecules that will make them so super-hard, so highly reflective that the entire force of the explosions will be focused in a single, pre-determined upward direction. Given enough mega-tonnage, we ought to be able to jar your dirty snowball sufficiently away from its present trajectory to assure a clean miss with Earth."

Moshey's expressive features registered amazement and relief in such rapid succession that Alan almost laughed out loud as he added, "I can supply the ship, the molecular compression cannon—and me, Mr. President. You'll have to provide the nuclear devices and a team of technicians, outfitted and trained for extra-vehicular null-gravity activity, to help me plant them."

"You have only to ask, young man." Moshey wiped his forehead with a hastily materialized handkerchief. He looked as though he were about to once more throw his arms around the source of his resurrected hope. "Is there *anything* I can..."

"Yes," Alan replied as he quickly stepped back to discourage a repeat performance. "I want your assurance that during our collaboration, and especially after this mission is accomplished, I will not be subjected to the media or the pointless babblings of bureaucrats and other such non-essential personnel! My privacy is to be protected at all cost! That will, of course, also include not being forced to endure interviews, public appearances, and, most especially, all manner of official and social functions." The last vestige of a smile vanished. Alan was deadly serious now. "Also, when the job is complete, you and your precious UN go your way, Space Tech and I go ours. No more favors! No more convenient emergencies! This isn't a request. It's a demand, in payment for my services. Do you agree to my terms?"

"It shall be as you wish." The African looked away, his enthusiasm severely dampened by these obviously unwelcome restrictions.

Needing assurance that the man's word could be trusted, Alan probed below the surface noise of the big black man's mind. He did not at all relish the conditions just imposed on him. The African had been playing with the idea of offering the people a global hero around whom they might all rally in continued unity—if the public relations and the media were handled correctly. He had just begun savoring his new toy when, just as suddenly, it had been snatched away. He was definitely not happy with the terms, but he held honor and the sanctity of his word above all. He could be trusted.

"A truly splendid vessel, my boy! I pray she flies as beautifully." Moshey smiled sadly, turning to console himself with another glance at the *Peregrine*.

Moshey's features once more realigned themselves into a mask of diplomatic composure, camouflaging his still befuddled amazement as he turned and started walking back toward the waiting shuttle. The old professor followed like a silent satellite in his long-strided wake. He had not spoken since first introductions, but now, as he withdrew, Alan caught his sly wink and felt the warm glow of pride. The old man was projecting with such force there was no way he could have been ignored. Despite himself, Alan warmed to the approval.

He had spent years carefully schooling himself toward complete emotional detachment, trying to dampen the curse of his psionics. He lived in constant fear that they might some day prove as much a curse to his adoptive family as they had been to his natural parents. He may not have been the direct cause of their deaths, but they were no less dead. Nor was he any less the agent of their deaths. So long ago, and yet it still held sway over his soul as though it had only happened yesterday. As diligently as he had always striven to prevent himself from caring too much, from allowing them too close, it was still as nearly hopeless as ever to refuse anything to either Gertha or that impossible old man.

Moshey and his adoptive father, perhaps they had been right. His involvement might spell the difference between millions, perhaps billions of people living or dying. A successful mission also meant that Space Tech, as well, would survive and his work could continue with only minimal interruption. His *Peregrine* would yet have a chance to some day test her wings in interstellar space. Reason enough for upping the wattage to his polite smile.

"Don't forget, Mr. President, there won't be time to install the *Peregrine's* life support. So you'll have to make certain the personnel assigned to me are outfitted and trained accordingly." Alan hurriedly retreated to the relative safety of business-at-hand as he began skillfully herding the two older men onto the underground shuttle dock.

"Once the General Assembly sees your ship for itself, I should have no trouble allocating funds to cover Space Tech's cost for this expedition. That would, of course, also include installation of a temporary life support for your ship's bridge. We are, after all, looking at a journey of three or four weeks. You certainly can't all live in pressurized clothing all that time now, can you? Even I can see that." Stopping in front of the waiting passenger car, Moshey chuckled with amusement as he turned toward Alan one last time. "Perhaps, in gratitude after this crisis is past, we might even be able to allocate additional funds to defray Space Tech's costs for permanent ship-wide life support. Interior fittings and furnishings, as well." Moshey offered a mischievous wink as he increased wattage to his own smile. Apparently, the ultimate success of this mission had become a foregone conclusion in The African's mind.

"Tell me!" He suddenly grew serious once more as he rested an unwelcome hand on Alan's shoulder. "Will you be able to get this glass slipper of yours airborne by the middle of next week? As I mentioned earlier, seeing you ride to the ball in her would be all the argument I need to push every one of your recommendations and demands through during next week's General Assembly. The sooner we can wade through all the political mud, the sooner I can get you and your people closeted with our own technical experts."

"I can make it," Alan nodded, knowing he would have to push himself and his people harder than ever now to honor his new commitments.

"Good!" Moshey caught him in a vigorous handshake. "I'll begin making the necessary arrangements for air clearance from the FAA so your own Air Force doesn't start using you for target practice.

"Now! I'd best get back before my security people decide to storm the poor doctor's house. They were more than a little upset over my insistence that they wait for me there." Climbing into the small car, the African extended a steadying hand for the old professor. Wincing with a slight twinge of arthritis, he accepted the assist, then braced himself for the rapid acceleration as he activated the console.

•••

The limousine finally came to a halt, snapping Alan's awareness back to here and now. It was immediately surrounded by UN security guards brandishing expressions as menacing as the weapons they carried. Alan waited while the African stepped out ahead of him, then followed behind, wincing in anticipation of the rapid escalation from just-barely-tolerable to overwhelming pain. Wave upon escalating wave of seething, churning emotion erupted from this cheering ocean of humanity, pounding against the unprotected beachhead of his brain. If only he could escape! Ahead of them lay their destination: the UN's General Assembly building. The glass-walled expanse of the towering adjacent executive structure gleamed molten gold in the morning sun. It rose like a fairy tower out of this boiling, semi-sapient sea of humanity.

Alan's head was throbbing unmercifully now. Moshey looked as though he were about to resume the discussion as their anxious security guards started nudging them gently, but insistently forward. Their roped-off path was being maintained by New York City police who were stationed on each side every few feet along the way. Suddenly, an island of calm appeared within a cocoon of soft blue that gently pulsed in a soothing rainbow heartbeat—a haven too inviting to ignore. It came from somewhere up ahead, from someone in the crowd close by the rope barrier. Grateful for even so tenuous a sanctuary, Alan allowed his consciousness to slip inside this unexpected refuge of auric light, for only a moment, he promised his nagging conscience.

Even having telepathically locked onto his unwitting host, it took several moments to locate him—no her—visually. She was a small, seemingly unimpressive girl with mousy brown hair pulled back in much too severe a style for one so young. She wore extra pounds and baggy clothes like camouflage, with unconscious deliberation. There was no hiding the excellent proportion, the classic lines of her delicate features. Despite the distraction of ugly over-sized glasses, her large almond shaped eyes, dark as moist rich earth, were hypnotic and hauntingly familiar. They were the eyes of the dying priestess in the recurring dream that had taken possession of his nights ever since Tabriz! Even with minimal attention to hair, clothing, and whatever it is women do to their faces, she could so easily have been a truly stunning beauty. Why then had she chosen to live out her days hidden away within such homely and unassuming armor?

Guided only by what she allowed the world to see, he doubted he would ever have noted her existence, even had they been introduced. Yet, here he was snagged and now trapped by an incredible inner beauty that she had so carefully locked away from the rest of the world.

So alike, and yet so unlike, his dying priestess! Curiosity leapt over the barrier of conscience as he probed deeper.

Her name was Dawn LaSarde, a graduate student at Merrimack University in southern New Hampshire. She was assigned on work-study to the small campus parapsychology lab headed by Dr. Rama Mishra, an East Indian physician-turned-parapsychic-investigator. That was him standing next to her. His professional training was Western, but his manner and philosophy were unmistakably Eastern. He was teaching his graduate assistants many of the ancient, yogic meditative disciplines. That may have been why this young girl's mind was so quietly centered, so serenely comfortable, save for that one painful pebble, that one irrational phobia he could not quite yet put a name to. She was probably as paranoid about being considered beautiful as he was on the subject of being an esper. He could almost laugh at the bitter irony of their parallel predicaments.

Alan's focus shifted momentarily to the girl's companion, Dr. Mishra, probing after a sudden ray of hope. His aura was as soothing as the girl's; and yes, he was much more than merely a researcher into paranormal phenomena. He often counseled those who claimed to be psychics, with problems similar to his own. Turbaned, dark-skinned, not much taller than Dawn, and with eyes as piercing as polished obsidian, Dr. Mishra perceived ESP as a blessing. Though not without its attendant pain, it was a gift from the Gods to be treasured above all else. Peering through a crack in his carefully cultivated cynicism, Alan wondered if this man might be able to help him. Thus far, the only others he had met with any experience in the parapsychic, had been charlatans—self-deluded housewives who greatly exaggerated their modest gifts and researchers wrapped-up in numbers, tests, and statistics. Obsessively locked into hypotheses and data gathering, they were still too busy arguing the existence of ESP, or cataloguing it's various aspects, to even acknowledge the possibility of problems in the management of such wild talents, much less offering any solutions.

Hope burned brighter as he probed deeper. Damn! The man was no better than Pandava, the UN cabinet minister he so closely resembled. Both men were unswervingly convinced that he was Kalki, the prophesied Tenth Avatar of Vishnu the Preserver. In this future incarnation, according to Hindu legend, he was supposed to return one last time to save the world. How could two such otherwise sane and highly educated men allow themselves to subscribe to such superstitious drivel!

Angry, disillusioned yet again, he withdrew his consciousness back within the safe harbor of the girl's auric field. She was no telepath, and yet she could shield to a certain extent. Her emotions were more like the ebb and flow of tides in a sheltered lagoon when compared to his own storm-ravaged coast. Perhaps she could help him. She was, admittedly, in some awe of the media-hyped mystique surrounding him. But she was accustomed to working with Dr. Mishra's psychically gifted subjects. Certainly, she could cope with the less threatening persona of Alan-Kolkey-in-jeans-and-work-boots walking in off the street like any ordinary person, the *Peregrine* and his ever-present attendants nowhere in sight. He promised himself time off for a visit.

Prodded along by Moshey and the press of security guards eager for relief from the heavy responsibility of protecting two such valuable charges, Alan drew closer. More naggingly insistent than before, he was once more assailed by the perception of a parallel oneness between the two images: the dying golden-haired divinity of his recurring dream, and this child, so fearful of being found attractive by men. Had her beauty, in some ancient lifetime, been the source of her undoing, her fear spilling over into the present? Had they known each other then? Loved, perhaps?

Logic stepped in, pushing aside such foolishly romantic metaphysical musings. Imagination stuck in overdrive. This was all nothing more than an externalization of his suppressed need for a mate, a lover who could understand, and knowing what he was, remain unafraid and accepting. Perhaps she was only needing the same understanding herself. Perhaps if he stopped, spoke to her. Did he dare?

"So what does he think he is, the National Anthem?" The harsh, high-pitched male voice came from Dawn's left. Another of Mishra's aides. He was tall, ostrich-thin, with a nose like a parrot's beak, and lack-luster sandy hair that looked as though he had just come in out of a wind storm. He resembled the Disney cartoon rendering of Ichabod Crane Alan had once seen as a child.

"They ought to perform an autopsy on that space cadet to find out how his personality died." The voice was persistent, even though its audience-of-one was making every effort to ignore him.

Dawn knew him as Reggie Hastings. Until a few moments ago he had been gloating over the marvelous ploy he had just pulled off to get them, as well as two other members of their party—that young couple standing directly behind them—through this apparently impenetrable crowd. Dr. Mishra did indeed bear an even more startling physical resemblance to Pandava than Alan had previously noted. Shouting for people to make way for the UN president's chief cabinet minister, and dragging his embarrassed employer in his wake, Hastings had plunged imperiously into this boiling cauldron of humanity. They would have made it all the way into the General Assembly Building too, he was complaining to himself, if only Kolkey and the African had not arrived quite so soon.

Dawn knew, as Alan now did, after scanning a bit deeper, that the young man's wisecracking bravado was little more than a smokescreen. He did not want to admit, to himself much less to others, that he was as mesmerized as everyone else.

The overpowering persona of the conquering hero the media had manufactured out of whole cloth was being wrapped tighter and tighter, suffocating, threatening to destroy him.

"You know, he doesn't look a bit like his stamp," Hastings was blustering to conceal his mounting discomfort. He was becoming increasingly aware of Alan's proximity and the intensity of attention being focused on all of them.

For several awkward moments, Alan half-expected Mishra to prostrate himself. That would really have been embarrassing for him, and demeaning to the good doctor. Thankfully, he did not. Releasing the air trapped in his lungs, Alan turned his attention back on the girl. An amused smile tickled the corners of his mouth as she squirmed uncomfortably under the burning lamp of his scrutiny. Self-consciously, she began playing with a comic mental caricature of him standing astride the roof of the fictional Daily Planet building. Look! Up in the sky! It's a bird! It's a plane! No, it's the Scarlet Pimple!

Ouch! He winced at the stabbing thrust of her silent satire. The girl's caricatured portrait of himself as a caped and costumed comicbook superhero had pricked his fragile ego. He had not realized until now, but yes, the protective crimson plasti-metal environment suit he always wore when piloting the *Peregrine* and his almost paranoid insistence on privacy, they certainly would lend themselves to the persona of the tragic super-hero, a cage of illusion that people were forever trying to lock him up inside of. The girl was providing a mirror for him, and the image she was showing him, though painful, was nonetheless funny.

Despite all efforts at maintaining his stern shroud of decorum, he began chuckling out loud. It felt surprisingly good to be able to laugh at his own absurdity.

Suddenly, she was meeting his gaze squarely. There was dawning recognition in her eyes. The feeling was there for her too—not unlike childhood friends meeting for the first time after years of separation. It could not be merely imagination or unconscious wish projection if she was feeling this way as well, he assured himself. The girl's—Dawn's—amazement over the emotions he *was* evoking in her was compounded by the sudden realization that her previous suspicions had been correct all along: he was a telepath! She had correctly guessed that his quiet laughter had indeed been in response to her silent caricature of him. There was astonishment, awe, yet wondrously, no fear, and thank God, no hero-worship! He stared in almost rapturous wonder as she made yet another quantum leap forward. She understood what his esper curse must be costing him: the isolation and pain it imposed. She too had been something of a square peg, herself, growing up. She understood the reason for his cloak of secrecy, empathized with his dread of being labeled a freak, an outcast, an object of fear were it known what he really was. Smiling gently, Dawn LaSarde was projecting a silent invitation of friendship.

Ecstatic, and to hell with scruples, he plunged deeper into her mind, gathering in all he could learn of her as he went. Those wondrous eyes were the legacy of a great-grandmother on her father's side, the mandarin bride of a sea-faring captain out of Gloucester. The girl was equally proud of her Native American ancestry. Alan smiled grimly. Like himself, she was the product of several widely divergent cultures. Like himself, too, she was proud of her roots. And again, like him, she had buried a large portion of herself away from the scrutiny of the outside world.

Overcome by the myriad conflicting emotions warring within him, all thought for past vows of self-denial were suddenly forgotten in the delicious joy of discovery. He plunged through the last voluntarily lowered barrier. She was inviting entry! Hungrily, he raced along the convolutions of her brain, searching, praying for clues that might hint at any latent or developing esper talents of her own.

Too late, he realized with what excess of force he had driven past her trusting vulnerability, how deep he had thoughtlessly, impulsively plunged. The raw, emotion-charged power of his mind, running unchecked, had disrupted the autonomic functioning of the primitive brain centers that controlled respiration and heart rhythm. Before he could regain control of himself, and reestablish normal functioning once more, Hastings had swept her into his arms and was diving into the startled crowd. Though all color had drained from her, and each breath was a desperate battle, Alan could feel her fighting the friend who sought to rescue her. She was still struggling in his arms, calling out silently for him to follow as they disappeared, swallowed by the ravenous crowd-monster.

Alan was fighting his own desperate battle to maintain a slender thread of connection with her. Not too overpowering this time, sufficient, and long enough only to assure himself that heart and lungs were beginning to pick up normal functioning. If not, he would have to give chase, force his way through crowd and friends to undo the damage he had unwittingly done, even if it meant blowing his cover.

Satisfied at last that she would be all right without necessity of direct intervention, Alan withdrew completely. He was sick to the core of his being with the realization that he had come too close to killing this small girl who had touched him much more deeply even than little Hassan, back in Tabriz. He must never allow himself to see her again! He had been a fool to have forgotten his parents or the time he had panicked, killing that charging grizzly with an unconscious blast of PK. These, and so many more were irrefutable reasons why he must never permit himself the warmth of a woman's arms. Calm, emotionally detached, he could wield his PK with the delicacy of a surgeon's knife, but cornered or in the heat of emotion, Lord knows what havoc he could wreak! From now on he must remain on perpetual guard, constantly reminding himself what almost happened just now, simply because he dared, for one brief ecstatic moment, to hope that he could love as other men were free to.

"Alan! Son! Are you all right?" Moshey's voice intruded itself into his private hell. "Come along! You've been dragging your feet the whole way. Everyone is waiting for you inside.

"Oh, that young woman, over there?" Moshey offered an understanding smile and a paternal arm around Alan's shoulder. "She must have fainted from the heat and excitement. Her friends are with her and there are ambulances and emergency medical personnel stationed everywhere. I'm certain she'll be fine. Now, come along!" That paternal arm now became insistent, dragging him along.

Alan offered no resistance.

"My boy..." Moshey paused, invading Alan's thoughts as he once more returned to his favorite topic of discussion. "Is there nothing I can say to get you to reconsider and..."

"Nothing at all, dammit!" Alan snapped angrily.

"Nonetheless, I refuse to abandon hope that you will eventually come to your senses and realize how much the people need and want you. There is so much more you would be able to accomplish for them as president of the

United Nations of Earth." Moshey caught and held on to Alan's gaze. He could be as determined, as resolute as any true idealist, and he would not be denied. "I am little more than a figurehead, my boy, I hold a transitory office at the helm of a ship of state that will sink the moment that Kali ceases to be an ever-present global menace. You have it within your power to solidify the necessary public support behind you to transform all these squabbling little governments into a true federation of interdependent states. With you at its head: the first true president of a stable and permanent United Nations of Earth.

"Until that time, Alan, my beloved heir," Moshey continued, his features hardened to stone with the force of new-found resolve, "I swear this oath: that I will do all within my small power, sacrifice all, if need be, to retain and maintain the power of this office until the day I am finally allowed to turn it over to you. May the ancient tribal Gods of my ancestors hear me, lend support, and punish me if I betray this trust!"

Alan's rage burned inward, leaving behind a surface ash of cold despondence. Dawn LaSarde, like little Hassan, had to be filed away as just another hopeless dream. For her sake especially, for her very life, he must not ever seek her out. Dawn, little Hassan, his adoptive parents, for all their sakes, he had to maintain the safe distance of icy detachment.

The only path left open to him lay along a tightrope. He could not simply walk away. After all, it was his own damnable blundering miscalculation that had transformed Kali into Earth's second satellite, disturbing the planet's delicate geological equilibrium. It might be years before that equilibrium re-established itself once more. It was bad enough now, his unprotected esper brain constantly battered by every stray thought and emotion around him.

What would it be like totally immersed in the daily bedlam of global politics? How long could his sanity hold out against the constant onslaught of so many minds?

Sullenly, defeated, like a prisoner taking that last long walk to the gallows, he allowed himself to be herded along toward the great glass-walled embryo of the African's dream.

CHAPTER III

"MORNIN', GLORY! Man, it's hot out there for October! The weather fairy must be running a fever," Reggie chirped in an annoyingly cheerful voice as he burst in from the outer office, like a trailhand entering a saloon in a vintage western.

"Oh! Hi, Reg." Dawn LaSarde looked up momentarily from the mountain of books periodicals and scribbled notes in front of her. She was trying for academic detachment but never made it beyond the boundaries of the depression she had fallen into. The reclusive Alan Kolkey had touched her, far more deeply than she had realized last week and life would never be quite the same for her again. Masking a sour mood behind pretended absorption in her research, she hoped Reggie would take the hint and leave her alone. She had been staring at the notes in front of her for hours already and was still unable to recapture even the remotest semblance of the enthusiasm with which she and Dick Dion, her partner in the project, had begun this project several weeks ago. The harder she tried to concentrate, the more she found herself drifting back to last week and the lab team's trip to New York City. She breathed relief as

Reggie wandered across the room and began occupying himself with the morning coffee ritual.

As head of Merrimack's small but prestigious parapsychology department, Dr. Rama Mishra had been appointed to represent the university, delivering this year's application for UN sponsored research funds in person. Several weeks ago, as he finalized plans for the short trip, he had suggested that his research team join him for an impromptu weekend holiday. Reggie had in turn suggested leaving a day early, on the off-chance of seeing Alan Kolkey in person. He was scheduled to arrive on that date for the special session being called to honor him and the paramedics who had helped at the Tabriz disaster.

The volatile temperament of Space Tech's guiding genius was legend. If only they could all somehow manage to get into the council chamber on Dr. Mishra's pass. The trip had promised to be well worth fighting through the heavy crowds that always turned out for Kolkey's rare scheduled appearances at a convening of the General Assembly.

Dawn closed her eyes, once more seeing him in front of her. Alan Kolkey's heavily-muscled frame had towered above the security guards surrounding him and President Moshey. That great black lion's mane of hair, those eyes, cold as ice-forged steel, set deep beneath heavy brows, the powerful set of his jaw, features chiseled from living stone. If such were possible, she had found him even more disturbingly familiar in person than she had on television. Imposing and somber, a majestic black-crested mountain of a man, he had stood there, casting a giant shadow over all those lesser hills surrounding him, smoldering, a dormant but rumbling volcano. Dawn cringed. Oh Goddess! Was that pseudo-poetic drivel really coming from her? All right, she admitted, so he was gorgeous. So what! So were a lot of other men she had met before. She had always been able to appreciate their questionable attractions from the safety of distance without spouting such sophomoric drivel. Why now? She assured herself again: it was only the pain, the loneliness reflected in those haunted eyes that was stirring maternal instincts. Nothing more. After all, she and Rama had an understanding, of sorts. He had spoken, on more than one occasion, of taking her to India to meet his family in Benares. They would have to wait, though, until he had saved enough money for the trip and for the down-payment on a home. Despite her loyalty and deep affection for him, the gentle Rama's image could not exorcise Kolkey's ghost. She wondered again what could possibly have caused him to single her out in that huge mob of people, all screaming and waving in competition for the tiniest shard of their hero's attention.

She recalled again the heart-stopping moment when he had come to a sudden, dead halt right there in front of her. He had appeared totally unmindful of his entire entourage, unaware of the hush that had fallen over the crowd as wild cheers gave way to whispers of speculation. Her entire universe had suddenly centered on the enigma of this strange man and now irrefutable confirmation of what she had for so long suspected: he was a telepath. The first *true* telepath she had ever heard of. The deep sorrow, the isolation he always wore tightly wrapped around himself like a shroud had suddenly enveloped her as well. Somewhere, some when, there must have been a shared karma. It had to have been much more than a telepath in pain, attracted to parapsychic investigators who might be able to help him deal emotionally with the burden of his gift.

She had known, even then, that Kolkey had not deliberately sought to harm her. The moment he realized what was happening he had pulled back. He had not withdrawn completely, however, not until fully satisfied she was breathing on her own once more and her heart had returned to its own natural rhythms. With every fiber of her being, she had also known that if anything had gone wrong, he would have fought his way to her side pouring his own strength into her failing body, just as his mind had earlier flowed so forcefully into hers. Why, then, had his sense of guilt been so out of proportion to the situation? She had never been in any real danger.

A week had passed. Dawn was beginning to lose the last remaining thread of hope that Kolkey had heard her call out to him, and would eventually respond. And yet she still felt the same pressing need to find him, to convince him he was not the psychic vampire he apparently presumed himself to be.

Perhaps he was staying away for fear that a second encounter might prove more dangerous than the first. Certainly it was not a matter of being unable to find her. He had hiked around inside her brain, deep enough and long enough, to have extracted a complete biography back to the moment of conception.

Dammit! She needed to talk to him, as much, she was certain, as he needed to talk to her. There were questions on both sides wanting answers—uppermost, for her, the origin of this unrelenting feeling of recognition. Certainly he must realize they could never be free of each other so long as there were unresolved karmic knots binding them together lifetime after lifetime. It was unfair to him, to her, and to Rama as well. How could she think of marriage now? So long as the specter of Alan Kolkey was not laid to rest, how was she ever to reclaim the tranquil order of her life before his coming? Serenity had been a hard-won skill taught by the placid physician-turned-psychic-investigator. Now, in just one brief week her world had returned to the emotional chaos Rama had found when first they met and which he had worked so long and diligently with her to overcome.

"Hey, Toots! You still alive in there? Remember me? Reggie Hastings, everybody's favorite boy-wonder."

Reggie! Dammit, was he back again? Dawn crumpled the paper she had been scribbling doodles on and looked up to find him hovering over her like an overbearing nanny.

"Don't tell me you're still brooding over Superfreak," Reggie teased. He planted a mug of steaming fresh coffee in front of her, then collapsed like a bundle of sticks into an adjacent chair. Taking a long, pleasurable sip from the coffee mug he was still clutching, he planted an elbow on the table, propped a supporting fist under his chin, and leaned into his words. "C'mon, kid, he nearly cashed in all your chips for you. I used to think he was just Macho-Man, off on some out-of-this-world ego trip. But now, after doing what he did to you, after being able to do what he did to you, man, I'm spooked." Reggie shook himself like a dog coming out of a river. His words were almost as irritating as his high-pitched voice, so different from Rama's soothing, almost musical speech. She never tired of listening to the gentle parapsychologist's soft, cultured, Asian accent, of drinking in the quiet strength that comforted and inspired.

Dawn was beginning to grow annoyed and started riffling papers to convey the fact. "Honestly! Alan Kolkey is nothing more than a very highly developed telepath."

"'Nothing more than...', she says!" Reggie grunted in disbelief. "Isn't that sort of like saying the Titanic's a little behind schedule?"

"Cut the clowning, Reggie! Alan Kolkey is an esper and he's in trouble. He seems to be in full control of his special—talents, except when intense emotions interfere. Apparently, he has trouble juggling both at the same time. No doubt, being as sensitive as he is to the thoughts and emotions of the people around him is probably what's made him so reclusive. He must have to be, just to survive. You've commented yourself about it. In fact, just this week on "Boston Beanpot," Dan Alexander was pointing out the same thing. Whenever anyone finally manages to corner him into attending some official function, he's never there one second longer than is absolutely necessary. He always manages to find an excuse for leaving almost as soon as he arrives."

Dawn took a long, thoughtful sip from the mug in front of her. Staring into the steaming liquid as though she might find insight reflected there, she rambled on, "I'll bet he's never learned how to shield properly, or gear down on his level of sensitivity. He's probably stuck on permanent overload, and if something isn't done about it soon, he's liable to burn out. Dammit, Reggie! I wish he'd quit playing ostrich and give Rama a call." Dawn punctuated her impatience by slamming the reference manual in front of her closed and giving it a shove to the far end of the table.

"Crazy as it sounds, you might have a point there," Reggie agreed, donning the mantle of a scholarly frown. "An esper in trouble would tend to home in on a parapsychic research team like us. It sure as hell wasn't your breath-taking beauty that grabbed him," he grinned, reverting to his favorite pastime.

Dawn pretended not to have heard, but he persisted, leaning into his words like her father's champion Clydesdales leaning into their harness at a county fair. "Look, you can't kid a kidder, lady," he began, stabbing an accusing finger at her. "There's a real pretty lady locked up inside all that camouflage; only you're keeping it the best kept secret since the Manhattan Project. And I'd sure as hell like to know why.

"C'me on, girl," he softened to a more supplicating mode. "Why not let Paula have a go at you? You've got all the right equipment. You just need to advertise it better. I bet inside of a month, if you listened to her, you'd have Doc on the scent and breathing fire. If he's too numb to budge, after all that, then you come and see ol' Reggie here. My heart may belong to my computers, but the rest of me's up for grabs."

"Why don't you try out for Professor 'iggins in *My Fair Lady*? And leave me alone, Reg," Dawn snapped back. "Did it ever occur to you I'm the way I am by choice: so clowns like you will stay the hell off my case?" For Goddess' sake! Couldn't he, Dick, and Paula too for that matter, accept the fact that she did not want to be made over? She was secure, safe, and perfectly content the way she was. Being found desirable by a man only meant being staked out as someone's property, a possession to be controlled, manipulated, stolen, fought over, even killed for. No matter which way she looked at it, it spelled disaster. Better to be free and in charge of her own life than target practice or an ornament in someone else's gilded prison. If it had been anyone other than Rama, the thought of someone trying to corner her into marriage would have sent her screaming for the security of the mountains that surrounded the New Hampshire home where she had grown up. Was Rama as hesitant as she, Dawn found herself wondering. Were financial considerations only convenient excuses for him to hide behind as well?

Even as a small child, freedom had been her most sought after prize, open sky her favorite cover, mountains and forests her first choice for walls. For as long as she could remember, she had been outdoors and gone whenever she could steal time from school or chores. Before they had all grown and left home, whenever her brothers could be bribed or blackmailed into dragging baby sister along, she had been off with them and Dad on their perennial camping trips.

Dawn was comfortable with the status quo of the relationship she and Rama had. He was so much more than merely supervisor of her work-study program. He was her closest friend and confidante as well as her own personal guru. He gave her room to breathe, to just be herself. The yoga and meditation techniques he taught had helped quiet the perpetual conflict of running away, perhaps from the very thing she was at once so restlessly and hungrily searching for. Whatever that was. She had finally almost succeeded in detaching herself from that frightened inner-child when Alan Kolkey came plowing through last week, undoing in one sweep, all the good work she and Rama had so painstakingly accomplished.

"By the way," Dawn offered a polite smile as she reluctantly returned to the ever-present problem of Reggie, "Dr. Mishra wants you to enter the data from the Carmichael-Delaney tests we ran yesterday." It was a coward's retreat into a neutral work-related corner, but, 'she who fights and runs away—may succeed in not killing her meddlesome co-workers,' at least for one more day. "Oh, and Dick wants to see you about some questions you raised concerning our format for the crystal grid telepathy study. We need to have all the bugs ironed out as soon as possible so we can get going on the pilot study by next month."

"Jeesuscrise, woman! You guys have me doing the work of three men," Reggie complained. Draining his mug, he slowly rose to his feet.

"Yes, I know: Chico, Harpo, and Groucho," she grinned, relishing the chance to give him a dose of his own caster oil.

"You could slice baloney with that tongue of yours, Toots." Reggie was still muttering under his breath as he vanished into the sanctuary of his office where the lab's delicate testing equipment was stored under his protective custody. Reg was the psych department's resident programmer and electronics whiz, apparently on permanent loan to the parapsychology lab. The university denied Dr. Rama Mishra nothing. Despite his quiet unassuming nature, the little Hindu physician was a commanding presence in the academic world. His writings on textbook studies he had conducted in parapsychic research were required reading in the field. His books, written in straightforward, uncomplicated English, were also popular among the general reading public and therefore seldom out of print. His name brought in grant money and alumni contributions.

The door leading from the front office opened. "Everybody, it's here! Into my office! All of you!" Dr. Mishra's head poked through for a moment, then vanished once more.

Startled, Dawn looked up. For "the Guru of Merrimack U," as he sometimes whimsically referred to himself, any display of emotion drew attention. It was sufficient to rouse Dawn from the blue funk she had been wallowing in.

"Big deal, it's here. What's here, Armageddon or the Good Humor Man?" Complaining as usual, Reggie reluctantly emerged from his office.

Dick had been talking to Paula at her desk out front at the time. They were already seated on the sofa in Dr. Mishra's office when Dawn and Reggie arrived. She quietly settled herself into the old Boston rocker while Reggie grabbed one of the large meditation cushions stacked in the far corner and took his own customary place on the floor.

"You remember me talking about the work on controlled out-of-body experience being done by Dr. Twitchell in Sedona, New Mexico," Mishra began, arms folded, one leg crossed in front of the other as he leaned back, half seated atop his heavy oak desk. Always impeccably dressed, his idea of casual attire today was gray slacks and a cream colored cashmere sweater worn over a white shirt and maroon tie. "It is common knowledge that sound affects our conscious states. Well, in a paper published by them recently, the Sedona team described how they had mapped the brain wave patterns of test subjects during confirmed OBEs. They were able to identify a specific wave pattern common to most of them. During the next phase of the experiment, they tested various combinations of sound and music to see if any of them could replicate these patterns in other untrained, naive volunteers." He paused, tried on a smile to see if it would fit, looked uncomfortable, then discarded it.

"Employing a computer synthesizer, they finally succeeded in finding a series of sounds and harmonics that could replicate the same wave pattern and choreographed them into a 90-minute tape." Mishra uncrossed his arms for a sweeping gesture that emphasized his words. "Then they tested it out on a new, randomly selected group of subjects who had never received training in any of the metaphysical or religious disciplines. They were rewarded with a statistically significant number of spontaneous, verified OBEs.

"Last month, as you recall, I flew down and met with Dr. Twitchell. He's finally given us permission to do a follow-up study incorporating several additional elements I had suggested to him. I want to experiment with such variables as crystal grids, controlled doses of muscarine and specific training in the techniques of meditation, such as I have taught all of you. Would they be able to subjectively intensify the experience for our volunteers as well as objectively increase the ratio of confirmed OBEs? Might we be able to increase, even further, the statistical level of significance?" Mishra tried another smile on for size. This one fit better, and lasted a bit longer as he picked up an audio cassette from the desk behind him and proudly began waving it back and forth. "Dr. Twitchell has just sent me his signed release, all his data and notes and this copy of their taped synthesizer harmonics."

"I'm a bit confused, Sir." Dick Dion's somber features puckered even further into a puzzled frown as he leaned toward Mishra. His hazel eyes could hardly be seen under an inverted arch of brows that were as bushy and unconfined as his sun-bronzed hair. They were the only things about him that eluded order and discipline. "We've been doing a lot of promising research with crystal-amplified ESP, so I can see why you'd want to include our crystal grids as a variable. But why muscarine? It's a highly toxic mushroom derivative. Whatever reputation it might have for enhancing ESP would be outweighed by its hallucinogenic side effects. No serious research group has touched it for years."

"Congratulations, young man! You've been doing your homework," Mishra smiled approvingly. He had finally found a smile he was comfortable with. "Yes, it's true. The Amanita muscaria can be a potent hallucinogenic when administered orally. However, I've been monitoring the work of a California group which has recently published some very promising results. They have experimented with very small sub-cutaneous injections right at the junctions of the lateral and longitudinal sutures, the so-called soft spot on an infant's head." Mishra paused a moment to settle more comfortably atop the corner of his desk closest to where his team was gathered. "It has been postulated for centuries that the pituitary is the seat of our parapsychic faculties. If there is any factual basis for this, then the longitudinal fissure between the left and right hemispheres of the brain, just under that soft spot, might offer a channel of sorts between the top of the skull and the *sella turcica* where the master gland is located. Granted, the soft spot on an adult is no longer soft, but still may be sufficiently permeable through the fused bone sutures to allow the drug to get through. This extremely unorthodox hypothesis obviously calls for much future investigation."

"Do you plan on combining all three variables simultaneously, Sir?" Interest had begun seeping back in to replace confusion. Dick sat back, leaning closer to Paula, his bride of only two months. She returned his loving glance with an unobtrusive hand squeeze, causing Dawn a twinge of envy.

For just a moment Dawn found herself wishing that Mishra could be as openly affectionate towards her as Dick was to his young wife. Paula was secretary, receptionist, office mediator, and all-around girl Friday. She also broke every stereotype about redheads. Her flaming hair was the only fiery thing about her. She was intelligent, level-headed, practical and a trusted friend.

"Oh, most definitely! I hope to incorporate the variables separately, in varying combinations, and all together, simultaneously."

"Rama, what about us doing a dry run? Today! I wouldn't mind playing guinea pig. In fact it sounds exciting," Dawn said sitting forward, feeling the muscles up and down her spine tensing in anticipation of doing something more than just data-gathering for a change.

"We must plan first. Talk," Mishra dithered. He had been caught completely off guard. This was a spontaneous, unpredictable side of her she had never before permitted him to see.

"Really, Rama! What's there to talk about?" She jumped up to clutch his slender, sinewy hands in hers. Dawn's sudden, undignified, highly unprofessional display ripped through Mishra's quiet protest. "Look! Before we can properly structure even a pilot study, we need some sort of platform to launch ourselves from. We need a test subject who can feed in some first-hand experience to help us formulate the questions around what we're going to have to be addressing. I'm already a trained meditator, Rama, and I know you've already stocked some muscarine. I'm certain you've familiarized yourself with the proper dosages, and you are still a duly licensed physician. I'm strong; I'm healthy; I've got my head screwed on relatively straight. No major hang-ups at least," she hastened to add, seeing the warning glint in Reggie's eyes. "What more do you want? What could possibly go wrong that you wouldn't be able to handle? Besides, if there are any risks, we need to know what they might be before we subject others to them." Dawn looked around. Dick and Reggie were wearing an eagerness almost equal to her own. Paula looked interested, but concern was etched deep into her otherwise flawless features.

Hesitant, reluctant, Mishra's gaze traveled from one face to the other, finally returning to her. "All right. I will allow it," he conceded, his arms falling to his sides in a gesture of outnumbered defeat. Then his right arm came up, jabbing a finger at them all as a reminder that he was still in charge. "But only because this is the first time, since returning from New York, that I have seen our Dawn take an active interest again in what we are doing here. And the points she raised, admittedly, are well taken: the experiment could prove a valuable aid in our research design.

"Dick! If you would. The tape player and headphones in Reggie's office." Loosening his tie and unbuttoning his collar as he stood up, Mishra turned to unlock the refrigerated steel cabinet where anything stronger than aspirin was kept.

Paula ran out, returning with her own small transcriber. Dick arrived right behind her with the larger machine. He set it down on a table next to the comfortable recliner Mishra used for interviewing and hypnotizing test subjects and for counseling the many troubled esper-sensitives who sought him out for help.

Filling a small pneumatic syringe, Mishra gestured toward the tape cassette on his desk. Nodding, Reggie obediently slipped it into the player then adjusted the machine and headphones. Dick started humming the monotonous little tune that always signaled intense concentration. He was already lost in the geometrically precise placing, around the recliner, of twelve large, naturally terminated quartz crystals that were clamped onto slender, adjustable tripod stands. Rama still was not entirely convinced there was anything more than merely a placebo effect in the higher psi scores of subjects tested within various crystal grid patterns. But neither was he ready yet to dismiss them. Much more data was yet needed.

"If you make it out, and you are able to initiate conscious action, go to my apartment. My cleaning woman always brings the paper in before she leaves. Try to notice where she laid it and see if you can describe a photo or read any of the front page headlines. Also, make note of anything Mrs. Simoneau might do sufficiently out of the ordinary for her to recall later when I have a chance to question her. That should be a relatively satisfactory confirmation as to whether this was an actual OBE as opposed to a drug-induced hallucination." Mishra's voice was coldly clinical now as he swabbed the top of her head with alcohol and injected the muscarine. Dawn began drifting almost immediately.

"Take yourself all the way into alpha, now," Mishra instructed. His voice was soothing now, reassuring. Dick adjusted for balance and volume then helped her fit the headphones comfortably in place.

The synthesizer 'music' sounded more like someone stapling cats together; but then, several deep yoga breaths later, as she began slipping into light first level meditation, the computer-composed symphony did not sound so bad after all. In fact, as it started saturating her brain, she began finding it more and more soothing, more and more like a siren song: calling, beckoning, teasing her away.

Multi-hued tendrils of sound swirled and shot through her head, became large rolling waves that sloshed and eddied between her ears. Swooping up and down, they rode her spine and the convolutions of her brain like a rollercoaster traveling through nebulous lightning-shot, cotton candy clouds. The music spiraled in on itself now, shrinking to a white-hot point of light just above her head. The point elongated, grew into a softly lit tunnel that gradually began pulling her up and outside herself. She was floating free now, bobbing up and down in a pool of buoyant air. She looked down and saw her inert body. A lifeless, waxen figure stretched out on the recliner, it was now the center of rapt attention. No one was noticing her up here, and strangely, it really did not matter.

Where was it Rama had wanted her to go? It seemed so unimportant now: something about his apartment. What was it he had wanted her to do there? Oh, it felt so good, no longer shackled to the ground by gravity! She envied the birds. This was their natural element, their birthright: ever free to ride the winds and clouds. With the sophisticated jet-powered backpack developed by Space Tech she had once seen him demonstrating on TV, Alan Kolkey could be nearly as free in the air as his giant ship was in space. Did he ever appreciate what he had? Recalling her meeting with him, and the aura of quiet desperation that hung about him like a pall, she wondered if there was anything in his life that brought him happiness. Once more, Dawn found herself recalling—reliving—those hypnotic eyes, the great sorrow that haunted them, the desperate need he had sought to fulfill in her. The hopeless despair, when he thought he had harmed her, still echoed inside an empty corner of her soul. So many questions his retreat had left unanswered.

Suddenly, her own need became overwhelming. She had to find him, seek release from this strange obsession he had roused within her. According to books she had researched on the subject and interviews with psychics experienced in OBE, once you were out, all you had to do was concentrate and visualize where it was you wanted to be.

OK, then! Engage! She was about to track her elusive falcon to his eyrie. She concentrated, willed herself to be where he was. That should not be too tall an order. Hadn't his mind already once touched hers? Surely some sort of tenuous connection must have remained, a psychic spoor for her subconscious to follow.

She found herself floating up through the ceiling, through the roof of the small one-story research building, as though it had been nothing more than a holographic image. She floated higher yet, till she was skimming the tops of trees as she found herself speeding westward. Faster and faster she flew, following the contours of the landscape below. She dipped and rose across the Berkshires, part of the Eastern Appalachian chain. She hop-scotched over towns and cities, and skip-stoned across the broad Mississippi, delighted with her new-found freedom. She danced across plains and deserts and rode the wild roller coaster of the Rockies. It was delicious! Too soon, she came to a stop, hovering over the westernmost boundary of the great mountain chain. Toward the western horizon, naked peaks were beginning to give way, once more, to tree-mantled foothills that took up the march to the Pacific. As she sensed a familiar presence below her, she began to drift toward the ground, and into it. She found herself sinking through solid stone as though she were slow motion diving into a body of murky water. It should have been utterly dark. Yet, with an inner light that illumined everything around her, she could see the fractures and stress lines in the subterranean granite, like waves in the ocean. She should have been terrified. She had never experienced consciously controlled OBE before, never mind suddenly finding herself swimming in an ocean of bed rock, with no idea where she was. Yet, the powerful pull of something below, Kolkey's spoor perhaps, was a reassuring life line that kept her moving. Briefly the rock became so dense it felt as if she were moving through molasses. She finally broke through into a huge, hemispheric artificially-hewn cavern, coming to rest several inches above a polished, softly glowing floor.

It should have been pitchblende dark, but instead, there was a soft, crimson-textured illumination emanating from the polished rock of this immense dome. The smooth floor emitted the same faint, sanguine radiance. Something that looked like a huge glowing jewel glinted off to Dawn's left. It was Space Tech's now-famous *Peregrine* asleep in her nest, a graceful cradle constructed of the same ruby-like, semi-translucent substance as her hull. Behind her, in sections, towered the exo-skeleton of her gantry scaffolding. Still in use, no doubt, for general servicing, it cast an eerie, distorted, diamond-shaped grid pattern of black metal against the crimson wash of mirror smooth rock. Close by, like a nestling, rested a freight chopper. Large as it was, it was dwarfed beside the massive bulk of the immense ship. Beyond, and just left of the *Peregrine's* shimmering semi-translucent beauty, like petrified monsters standing silent guard, stood great slumbering machines, some almost humanoid in appearance. They appeared to be awaiting, with infinite patience, the magical electronic touch that would once more call them back to automated life. No doubt, they had been employed during the ship's construction and perhaps were still in use for maintenance.

To her right, Dawn noticed a small side cavern where jagged virgin rock was innocent of any sanguine pulse. Only the floor had been worked smooth. It was probably all that remained of the original cavern from which this mammoth hanger-dome had been carved. Illumination, here, came from more familiar, less oppressive sources. Here, too, sprawled an unbelievable laboratory-engineering complex that might easily have accommodated a dozen different disciplines. Off in a far corner stood an elaborate computer complex. If size alone were any gauge, its capacity for memory and complexity of function ought to have been phenomenal. Dawn smiled to herself, thinking how Reggie would have bartered his soul for equipment like this.

Dawn was beginning to wonder if she were only hallucinating. It was all too insane: the Batcave, right out of her old childhood comic books, along with a strange admixture of elements, no doubt, from her recent preoccupation with the mysterious Alan Kolkey. Still, everything felt so real. Not at all distorted the way she imagined it ought to have been in the thrall of a drug-induced hallucination. On the contrary, her reasoning faculties had never felt keener. But, if Batman and Robin suddenly popped up, that would be the final proverbial straw. From that point on, the game would be called: "sit-back-and-enjoy-the-show" while you're waiting for the muscarine to wear off and the tape to wind down.

She was following the strange interplay between light and shadow against miles of glowing granite wall, thinking back to her undergraduate Philosophy 101 and Plato's Allegory of the Cave, when a stern, paternal voice shattered the thrumming monotony of orchestrated electronics. It was coming from the direction of the small natural cavern.

"Young man, do you realize how much Gertha's been worrying about you?" An aging patriarch was looming over a much larger, much younger figure lying on an ancient army cot. "You've sent the entire staff off on temporary assignment somewhere else, and all but buried yourself alive down here for over a week now. You're not answering any of President Moshey's calls and barely eating anything we've been bringing down to you. One would think you were deliberately trying to work yourself into the grave. Please, Son! Won't you tell me what's wrong?" The old man's frown crumbled, exposing deep concern as he set the dinner tray he had brought with him down on a small table next to the cot. So much smaller, and yet, with his magnificent mane of silver hair and that proud plume of a mustache, he cut an imposing figure, commanding the younger man's attention.

"I can't, Sir. Not now at least. I'm sorry I've been avoiding the two of you. I just need time alone to think this thing through for myself. Tell Gertha I promise I'll be all right." As the prone figure planted its feet on the floor and half-heartedly sat up, Dawn recognized the all-too-familiar features of the famous Alan Kolkey. She had found him after all!

"All right, Alan. Whenever you're ready to talk, you know we'll be here. But for now at least, try to eat this lunch Gertha sent me down with. She's been all morning cooking your favorite dishes, trying to tease your appetite back to life. You'd make both of us so much happier though if only you'd come to the house and join us at table this evening.

"You do remember Stan, I hope. You know, Gertha's youngest?" The sarcasm in the old man's voice made Kolkey wince as if he had been stung. "He's here for the weekend with T'shanna and the boys. They're all asking after you. You know how much those youngsters enjoy hearing you and their father 'get down' and jam together?" There was mischief in the older man's eyes as he pantomimed playing a piano and strumming a guitar, while dancing about on slightly arthritic feet. His efforts were rewarded with a fleeting smile from Kolkey.

"They all begged me to make you take a rest break and visit with them this trip. The boys especially miss you so much, Son," the old man continued, coaxing paternally as he pulled up a folding chair and sat down. "And the women. Well! You know how they love your music. I must confess a certain partiality, myself, to the way you render some of the old songs from way, way back, when I was a lad courting my Martha." A nostalgic smile moistened the old man's eyes, making him sniffle in a most undignified way.

"Please, Son," he added, climbing stiffly to his feet after a long pause. "Is there no way I can get you to reconsider? Breaking bread with family, a little music, and a decent night's rest in your own bed, I'm sure it'll help snap you out of whatever's causing this depression."

"I'm afraid it's going to take a hell of a lot more than that, Sir." Alan answered as he stood up also and began gently but insistently nudging the smaller man toward a nearby shuttle dock where a tram car was waiting. "Right now what I need most is time to think my way through it on my own. Aside from getting away, off into the mountains for a few weeks, I always do my best thinking while I'm doing katas or banging away on my old twelve-string. But give my apologies to everyone. Tell them I'm not feeling well and that I'll make it up to the boys as soon as I can."

Shoulders drooping under the weight of defeat, the old man allowed himself to be helped into the tram car. Reluctantly, he reached for the controls and was whisked away down the tunnel in an almost inaudible whoosh of air.

So, this was Alan Kolkey: owner of Space Tech, a research corporation with assets in the billions; the man who had conquered and chained Kali; the UN's favorite trouble-shooter, and "hero-at-large!" As the old patriarch vanished, his shoulders slumped and lost their starch. In that old T-shirt, tired denims, and badly scuffed work boots, suddenly he no longer looked like bullets would bounce off.

Returning to the cavern, he seated himself at the small table next to his cot then lifted the plate cover, setting it off to one side. Picking up a fork, he fidgeted restlessly with his food for several minutes before taking two or three disinterested bites. Finally giving up, he pushed the tray aside and walked over to a large walk-in refrigerator. He emerged with a bottle of beer. Slamming the door closed behind him, he tossed the cap in the general direction of a waste receptacle. And missed. He took a long thirsty swallow, then turned to stare at what appeared to be a perch for a very, very large bird. It had apparently been hewn from the gnarled trunk of some ancient tree.

Setting the bottle down on the table next to his abandoned meal, he pulled off his boots and walked slowly toward a large exercise mat. It was spread out inside an alcove that appeared almost to be a separate chamber. There were large full-length mirrors mounted on the three polished granite walls, interspersed with wide, heavily padded boards. Close by the farthest wall, a heavy punching bag hung from a securely mounted metal overhead frame. Shaped suggestively like a life-size mannequin, it was secured to the floor, perhaps to prevent it from swinging wildly when struck. At the near end of the mat, also securely bolted to the floor, stood a stout six-foot leather padded beam. It reminded Dawn of a silent sentinel guarding entrance to a private dojo.

Closing his eyes for a moment, Kolkey took a deep breath, bowed to no one in particular, then fell into what Dawn recognized to be a basic martial arts defensive posture. For as long as she could remember, while growing up, her two oldest brothers had been enthusiastic students of Oriental martial arts. Determined to teach their baby sister how to protect herself, before going away to college, they had enrolled her in self-defense classes at their dojo. They had even managed to interest her in attending some of the regional competitions. But only when one of them was entered.

As he executed his katas, standardized patterns of practice moves, Kolkey looked as though he were battling invisible opponents. Between each kata, as he progressively intensified his power and speed, he made frequent, increasingly more powerful lunges at the heavy punching dummy and leather-wrapped post as well as the various wall-mounted padded punching surfaces. Spinning and leaping high into the air with the grace of a dancer, he punched, jabbed, lunged, and kicked. Dawn recognized them as exercises designed to toughen the striking surfaces of his hands and feet and to build reflexive patterns. Kolkey's impressive size belied his speed and control.

It felt as though hours had passed before he finally exhausted himself. Breathing deeply, he bowed again to the mat, then returned for the towel at the foot of his cot to wipe away trickling perspiration. Discarding it on the floor, he sat down at the small table once more, and began slowly pulling his boots back on. He picked up an old acoustic twelve-string guitar that had been leaning against a rough wall of virgin granite. Taking another long swallow of beer, he laid the bottle down on the floor close by, then collapsed onto his cot. He propped himself up with pillows against the dark granite behind him, then cradling the instrument like a lover in his arms, he closed his eyes and let it speak to him.

Aimless notes spun out into chords that in turn slowly began weaving themselves into the nostalgic fabric of an old John Denver classic. Slowly the melody merged into another, more lovely and mournful than the first: one that Dawn had never heard before. The manner in which he improvised, experimenting along the thread of the same basic theme, Dawn found herself wondering if it might have been his own composition. She listened, enchanted, as he hummed along and then began embroidering lyrics into the melodic tapestry. They spoke of empty centuries, searing loneliness and longings as deep as the void between the stars. Such sensitivity, such beauty, such a richly expressive baritone to be coming from this somber, brooding, mass of muscle and martial skills! Dawn smiled, shaking her head in bemused disbelief at this complex tangle of contradictions. Which was the true Alan Kolkey? Where did his soul really reside?

The music faltered, fading away as the guitar gradually slipped from his lap onto the cot. Kolkey's head drooped forward into exhausted sleep.

CHAPTER IV

GROWING BOLDER, Dawn allowed her focus of awareness to drift closer. So much power and yet, asleep, he
looked so vulnerable. If only she could have been here in
the flesh; but she did not even know precisely where "here"
was. Impulsively, she reached out trying vainly to brush
aside a stray lock that had fallen across his forehead.

"Wha... Who's there!" he was suddenly awake and on
his feet, his ice-hot eyes searching, piercing the gloom.
Caught off guard, she felt like a trespasser about to be captured. Panicking, she started wishing desperately for the
safety of Rama and the lab.

"No! Wait! Please. Don't leave!" His voice rang out
simultaneously on verbal and mental wavelengths. There
was an anxious desperation to it. All at once he was everywhere, surrounding her, drawing her back inside a net of
thought-form.

"Please! Forgive me, dragging you back like this. I
couldn't let you get away this time without talking to
you." It was a strange sensation, though not altogether
unpleasant, hearing him without actually hearing him.
"You're Dawn LaSarde, a graduate student at Merrimack

University in New Hampshire. I'm surprised. I didn't know there were any other schools in that state, aside from UNH and Dartmouth, large enough to support projects like parapsychic research."

"Oh, hey! We're even big enough to have intercollegiate sporting competitions. At our last meet, in fact, we had this cross-eyed javelin thrower. He didn't win us any medals, but he sure kept the crowd on its toes," Dawn countered, borrowing one of Reggie's defensive strategies to hide behind. It wasn't every day you went for an astral walk and ended up at the Batcave for a chat with Alan Kolkey of all people! She was nervous, more than a little intimidated, and trying very desperately not to let it show.

His laughter, no doubt, was over her pathetic attempt at humor and the futility of trying to mask her feelings from a telepath. The blue fires in his eyes had warmed considerably though sending a disquieting tingle up a spine that was probably thousands of miles away at this moment.

Suddenly speechless, she started fidgeting like a frightened school girl. She felt naked, transparent as glass under the intense scrutiny of his gaze. He looked awkward himself, wearing a smile as if it were unfamiliar apparel. Was he finding himself as tongue-tied as she was?

"And your name, of course is Alan Kolkey!" Space Tech's reclusive young owner was the only subject Dawn could ever recall her employer, and dearest friend, ever losing his cherished objectivity over. She laughed, suddenly, forgetting her fear. "You know, Rama—Dr. Mishra—he's convinced you're..."

"I know, dammit!" His embarrassed smile twisted itself into an expression of disgust. "When I first saw him standing next to you, last week at the UN, I really hoped... I need to find someone who's familiar with esper-related problems. Then I realized he was no better than Pandava and some of those other devout Hindus I've met. You've worked with espers though. Perhaps... I..." He tripped over his tongue, lost his balance, and fell speechless.

Dawn did not trust herself either, for fear of blurting out something school-girlish and utterly parochial. This man who juggles comets, border disputes, natural disasters, all with equal facility; this man who entire nations, even the UN itself, consulted with, turning to her for help? Good grief! If Einstein can't solve the problem, you certainly don't take it to Mortimer Snerd!

He suddenly erupted into laughter. Something warm reached out and touched her like a reassuring hand.

His laughter died too soon. The fire burned cold once more as he said, "The first time I noticed you out there, it was like stumbling onto a quiet oasis; but then, when I drew closer... I don't know, it was as if I was remembering you from some other lifetime. I know it sounds stupid, ridiculous, but do... Do you buy into reincarnation?"

Dawn nodded, recalling that same haunting sensation herself. She realized that she did not have to pattern her thoughts into actual words for him to hear. His eyes told her.

"Mr. Kolk..."

"Alan. Please," he insisted, very softly.

"All right, Alan. Who are you? Really." Without realizing, she found herself moving closer, feeling slightly more at ease in his presence. "What's this place we're in and who was that sweet old man you chased out of here a little while ago?"

"That 'sweet old man' is Dr. Heinrich Zarkov, retired head of the physics department at Berkeley. Now he's liaison at Space Tech, between the executive board and Research: me. He also does PR for Space Tech —whether I like it or not," Alan added with a slight edge of annoyance in his voice as he leaned against a nearby instrument console. "He and his wife, Gertha, adopted me when I was twelve, after my natural parents died."

"Zarkov? Dr. Zarkov?" It was Dawn's turn now to laugh. If she had been here in the flesh tears would have been rolling down her cheeks. "Don't tell me! You're really Flash Gordon! Alan Kolkey is just an alter ego you hide behind for privacy."

"We both joke about that ourselves," He replied, joining his laughter to hers. "It's been a running gag for years. His students used to tease him unmercifully. He still threatens to change his name, at least once a week."

Happy to have once again evoked the healing balm of laughter, Dawn looked up and found him staring with eyes that were seeing into her soul. She hurriedly shifted the focus of her attention to something a bit less emotionally charged, like the enigma of the eerie glow coming from the huge dome's polished walls. Once more she felt like someone trapped in a drug-induced nightmare where the old Batcave of her childhood had been dumped into a kettle full of thirties-vintage "Flash Gordon" pot boilers.

"Alan, how…"

"This?" he made a sweeping gesture, with both arms that took in the entire hanger dome. Once more he was replying before her question could be framed into words. He walked back toward his cot and sat down once more, pushing his guitar safely off to one side. "When I was fourteen, Zarkov and I discovered this place on a hiking expedition into the mountains. It's only a dozen miles from the house. This corner here is all that's left of the original, natural cavern.

"A year or so later, during a month-long camping trip on horseback much deeper into these mountains, we hit on several theories revolving around the dynamics of gravity and molecular cohesion. They're actually interrelated." He paused for dramatic affect.

"When we got back home," he continued, leaning forward and propping elbows on knees, "we built a couple of small prototype test generators. Physicists still don't actually know what gravity really is beyond the laws governing it. We hadn't come up with actual anti-gravity, but we discovered something almost as good: a functional gravitational deflector field, so to speak. We literally just happened on exactly the right combination of molecular manipulations through pure dumb luck. If we'd been searching for it deliberately and systematically we probably would never have found it. It was almost like that cliché muse-telling-me-in-a-dream scenario." He paused to offer her a somewhat self-conscious smile before continuing. "Rather than nullifying gravity or creating a nullifying so-called anti-gravity, we came up with a way of—of bending the flow of gravity around the deflector field, so to speak. Twenty years of refinement, though, and still the damn generator aboard the *Peregrine* takes up almost the entire two lowest decks—a lot of space but not really wasted, considering the vastly increased maneuverability and tremendous savings in chemical combustion fuel we have to burn in a life-harboring planetary environment.

"Creating the technology to build a working generator has suggested so many new applications. Not the least of them is the eventual development of a 'warp' drive that could some day take interstellar travel out of science-fiction and into science-fact. That first primitive little generator we built was what gave me the idea for building the *Peregrine* in the first place." Without rising from the cot, Kolkey managed to look like a strutting peacock in full plumage.

"The first problem I faced was finding somewhere large enough and private enough to build her," he added pensively. "This place immediately came to mind. The original, natural cavern, where we are now, would have been far too small. That's when I struck on the idea of expanding it through molecular compression. After all, molecules and atoms are composed almost entirely of empty space.

"So, I built a much larger version of our first model projector." Alan paused once more to bask in the awe that Dawn was unconsciously broadcasting. He took a long swallow from the bottle on the floor next to him then repositioned the pillows once more so he could lean back against them. "The original cavern was only two hundred feet at its longest spur."

Wondering how the *Peregrine* managed its comings and goings, Dawn looked up. Her attention was momentarily distracted at sight of a narrow, precipitous pathway that meandered up one of the rough-hewn walls of this last remaining section of natural cavern which they presently occupied. It lead to a small dark tunnel, far above, that probably in turn lead to the original entrance that Alan had discovered as a boy.

A clank, followed by a click-groan and then a soft rolling of metal over metal startled her. She had not noticed before, but the entire flattened ceiling of the hanger-dome section was innocent of the ruddy glow that pervaded the compressed walls of the dome. She saw a long sliver of blue appear and begin to grow at the far side of the darkened area. As the aperture slid open, daylight flooded through, revealing a sapphire expanse of cloudless sky.

"Answer your question?" Alan was grinning with smug pride.

Dawn frowned, seeing no visible controls in his hands or within reach. "Don't tell me! Let me guess…"

"Right! Psychokinetic: PK com-link through my computers," he volunteered, again rushing ahead of her unvoiced question. As soon as he had spoken, his features reflected regret, perhaps over having demonstrated this even more awesome aspect of his esper talents.

Dawn understood what it must have been costing to admit this hidden aspect of himself to an almost total stranger. He was testing the waters, perhaps, to see how far in he could safely wade. She had to swallow hard on this even more incredible dimension of the man. Frowning, she gathered her own courage around her and waded further in herself.

"Alan, how close are you to the San Andreas? How secure is this place against earthquakes," she asked, casting a nervous glance around. The millions, billions perhaps, that had been invested in this hanger dome, the ship that slept here, the lives of all the people who worked here. His especially!

"Don't worry, little mother!" His grin was just a bit condescending; but Dawn felt an underlying warmth that resonated to her concern for his safety. "The compressed granite of this dome could take an eight point 'quake with no structural damage at all.

"I'm feeling some concern from you as well over the glow emanating from the walls and floor of the dome section." His smile was warm now, almost affectionate. "No big deal either. Really. It's caused by the abnormally dense packing of molecules that excites them into emitting a constant, very low-grade radiation. It's almost entirely within the visible and near infra-red spectrum. Well within even the strictest safety limits. Not much light to work by, but it provides enough warmth to drive the chill and damp out of the air. And no, there was never any danger of the molecular compression touching off a fusion reaction. That would require a great deal more compression than I've created here. As I said before, well within safety limits. And yes, I brush my teeth every night before I go to bed."

"Smart ass!" she muttered to herself, causing him to chuckle softly.

"Alan, earlier, when you were doing your katas, I couldn't help noticing how beautifully they were executed. I don't recognize the style though. But then, I really don't know that much about martial arts," she added apologetically.

"Thank you, pretty lady," he nodded, graciously accepting the compliment.

Dawn had never been called pretty anything before. She teetered briefly, precariously balanced between taking it as well-meaning tribute or a sexist slur. Thinking better of both, she scrambled for the safer ground of academic curiosity. "I can't quite picture someone, with the extraordinary empathic sensitivity that must go along with being a telepath, taking up such a violent sport. How do you manage? And how in the world did you ever get involved in the first place?"

"My father studied martial arts himself during his college years. He didn't want me turning out all mind and no muscle, so when I was seven, he started me out in judo. By the time I was nine, I had won my first junior black belt. When I was old enough to be accepted by his own dojo master, he switched me over to Shotokan. It's a Japanese form of karate. My esper sensitivity wasn't the constant problem for me back then that it is now. Until I was twelve, I couldn't do much more with PK than move a few pebbles or toy soldiers around, and my telepathy was hardly more than a frequent and annoyingly involuntary occurrence. Something that happened to me, rather than me making it happen.

"After my parents died," Alan continued, his eyes emptying as they lost focus, "I wasn't handling their deaths very well. So Zarkov decided that physical activity, something I was familiar and comfortable with, would help. He found a small Shotokan dojo not too far away from here. I fought against everything Zarkov or Gertha tried to do for me back then. I suppose I still do. Here, at least, their strategy worked. For a while, I even participated in some of the regional competitions.

"Eventually, training in just one style got a bit boring. I was fourteen when I began studying Kung Fu. It's much more popular than karate on this side of the Rockies. Since then I've also mastered Chinese Kempo, a Burmese style called Bando, and a less well known Japanese style called Atemi-waza."

Dawn knew about Karaté and Kung Fu, but those other exotic styles Alan mentioned were nothing but Eastern gibberish.

"By the time the empathic factor became an issue," he continued, pausing to flash an amused smile in her direction, "I didn't want to give it up. You're right: feeling the pain you're inflicting on an opponent in actual combat situations is decidedly not pleasant. I've long since become painfully aware of that fact. Fortunately, during the intense concentration of fighting mode or moving through a kata, I seldom feel my own pain, much less my opponent's. Still, the sooner I can render him unconscious, the happier I am."

"This place. That ship of yours," Dawn frowned. "It seems they'd tax the resources of an entire nation. How did you ever manage the financing? And how in the world, with all this, do you still find time for your music and your martial arts training?"

"I make the time. The mind works only as well as the body that houses it." Alan paused to try on a smug expression. "I insist that everyone working at Space Tech be in some kind of medically supervised fitness program. Luckily, a dozen or so of my people here in R&D are also into martial arts. Working out, sometimes together, sometimes in occasional sparring matches helps us all cut through the tension and mental fatigue that's part of the job description around here.

"For me, it's the only time I can effectively block out the noise. For the sake of my sanity, I work alone and as isolated as possible. I coordinate through Zarkov, memos, phone, video com-link. Still there are a lot of times when I have to be here with my tech people. Especially during the *Peregrine's* final assembly. That's the reason for the mat over there.

"Martial arts and my old twelve-string, here," he paused to give the instrument, still lying next to him, an affectionate pat. "They help block out the background noise, keeping me sane and functional. So, like I said, I make the time for both of them. Damn! If only I could block all the time!" There was a deep intake of air, then a pause for another long swallow of beer.

"Financing all this was actually the least of my problems—more time consuming than anything. PK does have some very interesting and profitable applications." Alan leaned forward, resting his elbows on his knees. "Several years before launching myself on this project, Zarkov and I were on one of our camping trips. It was something my father and I used to do before he died that the old man tried, as best he was able, for as long as he was able, to continue. Experimenting with a PK technique similar to dousing, I located a rich gold vein very close to the surface and less than fifty miles from here. Even though most of what we mined was eventually used in compounding the plasti-metal alloy of the *Peregrine's* hull, it contributed a nugget or two to the kitty."

Alan's smile suddenly grew cold and hard as polished steel. "There was another minor source of revenue that my esper skills also made available to me. It's not really gambling when you're a psychokinetic telepath, so I concentrated most of my attention on rigged and illegal games. There was a certain poetic justice in taking the takers and using their money to help finance research that may someday take us out to colonize other worlds in other star systems. It may seem like rationalizing to you. Maybe it is. But that's how I felt about it at the time. To a certain degree, I still do."

"You must have some kind of death wish," Dawn said, frowning. "Esper faculties and martial arts: even so, you don't take on your friendly neighborhood Mafia for very long and live to brag about it!"

"Oh, but I did! "Alan winked. The glint in his eyes was ice-hard. This was a facet of his dark, shadow side that Dawn did not feel she was quite ready to deal with. It toppled the romantic monument to the tragic, self-sacrificing champion of the people she had erected in her mind.

"Actually, I'm not too proud of that part of my life either," Alan admitted grudgingly, "I did what I felt I had to at the time. I've never made excuses for myself. I am what I am.

"My real source of start-up money was a 30 million dollar trust fund set up for me by a distant relative after my parents died." Dawn felt a great deal of anger behind his reluctance to specify which relative. "With Zarkov's help," he continued after inching his way around to the other side of his emotional discomfort, "we invested all of it. It had grown considerably by the time we decided to buy into Space Tech. The revenue generated from royalties or the outright sale of whole new technologies and processes that were the by-products of our research was reinvested to buy more and more shares in Space Tech and to fund more and more of our research. By the time I was twenty-six, Zarkov and I controlled over 90 percent of the corporation.

"We contracted out most of the *Peregrine's* actual construction to a lot of small companies that have grown much larger because of us. Some were even launched into existence because of us." He was beginning to sound like a corporate, public relations tour guide.

"Alan, if you had all that money to begin with, what was the purpose of prostituting your esper gifts looking for back alley games?" Dawn challenged. She was more than a little uneasy. Certainly the relatively small amount he anticipated netting had, by no means, been sufficient motivation for putting his life at peril. "You were out there deliberately inviting contracts to be put out on you," she accused. "I'll bet you even hung around, deliberately leaving bread crumbs that even Hansel and Gretel could have followed. Either you have one hell of a death wish, or you were out there trying to justify your need to act out violent urges by baiting criminals who 'needed to be put out of action anyway.'"

She was on a roll now. Heck, might as well go for broke and get it all said and out in the open. "I wouldn't even be surprised if you greased your way to almost total ownership of Space Tech with your esper manipulations: read a mind here, plant a thought there. It would have been so easy to eliminate anyone who got in your way." Dawn was outraged now, and yes, just a little frightened. Where does someone with so much power to manipulate the lives of others draw the line? "Is that all most of us are to you: puppets to pull strings on and then cut when we get in the way? Why go through all that bother! Why not just walk into Washington and take over completely! Tell me: which one is the real you, Alan? 'Flash,' or 'Ming the Unmerciful?'"

"Shut up! Dammit! Not you too! For God's sake, not you," he shouted, holding his head as if he were in physical pain. "Now do you see why I never wanted anyone knowing what I am?" The pain subsided leaving him stranded in the puddle of self-pity he had fallen into.

Oh damn! She had gone and shot her mouth off again. In her response to his honest disclosures, Alan's worst fears were being realized. "Now do you see why I decided to go into research instead of clinical work?" Dawn recanted guiltily. "I do too much of my thinking with bile and not enough with brain.

"Look," she began again, trying a more rational tack. "Manipulating the free will of other people, even when you're certain it's for their own good, can bring down a lot of heavy karma. Cause and effect. The Law of Threefold Return. Simply stated: What you send out bounces back like a boomerang. Or, as Reggie would put it: 'garbage in, garbage out.' There are no angry Gods out there pulling strings to punish their naughty children. Only us doing to ourselves. Cause and effect, action, re-action: 'the psychics of metaphysics,' Rama likes to call it. Okay, I apologize. You've been playing God games, but that doesn't automatically brand you a blood-thirsty, power-hungry tyrant. No, I don't at all like that side of you; but have you seen me shrieking in horror as I stampede for the nearest exit?"

"You probably wouldn't have succeeded had you tried. I've still got you pretty firmly anchored here," Alan reminded her. He was wearing an expression that vacillated between gloating and contrition.

"You mean you'd actually hold me here against my will?" she challenged in total outrage.

"Well, uh, no. No, dammit! I'd probably hold you long enough though to try to change your mind," he dithered, squirming uncomfortably. He was not at all happy with the defensive posture she had maneuvered him into.

"No doubt a very simple matter for so accomplished a telepath," Dawn fired back.

"Good grief! Not that way! Never you!"

"Oh, but others maybe?"

"Dammit, woman! You're impossible to reason with." He was beginning to look tired and beaten.

"Look, why don't we call a truce and find something a little safer to discuss?" Dawn offered. She was suddenly afraid that he might retreat back into his shell, never daring to trust her, or anyone else, ever again.

He swallowed a deep breath of relief. Looking into the mirror that Dawn had been holding up to him had been a visibly painful ordeal.

"Why have you allowed this ship to become such an obsession, Alan? You have no social or family life to speak of, and you act like you resent anything that pulls you away from it." Resurfacing concern was helping to crowd the outrage from her voice.

Picking up his guitar again, he plucked aimlessly at the strings for long moments before finally looking up. "I certainly couldn't be any more isolated out in space than I am down here. At least out there I'm not constantly reminded of what I can never have, what I can never be part of. And who knows, perhaps some day during my explorations, after I've developed a workable 'warp' drive, I might even find a race of espers like myself." The tired smile on his face told her he knew he was piping fairy tales. "Enough of me for a while! It's your turn now. Tell me something about you," he added.

"Why bother! That walk you took through my head last week ought to have given you more than anyone would care to know of the boring little particulars that comprise my life." Dawn shot him an impatient, self-conscious frown. She was not at all eager for her turn on the hot seat.

"So pretend I'm the big bad mutant-ninja-esper-tyrant who'll destroy the Earth if you don't tell him what he wants." He was smiling again, but this time there were too many teeth showing and his voice had a cutting edge to it.

Dawn was not frightened really, but she did have to confess to being distinctly uneasy. She began talking, hardly knowing what she was saying until she saw him relax once more into the pillows he had propped behind him for a backrest. His guitar was still on his lap, one arm affectionately wrapped around it. His right foot rested on the floor, his left, up on the cot. Gradually, it became a pleasant, rambling journey back to her childhood in the tiny central New Hampshire farming community where she had grown up. Her father was a lawyer, specializing in medical law. He was on staff at Dartmouth. He occasionally taught and lectured to medical students, but served mostly in the capacity of legal consultant to the college. He also maintained a small, select private practice and did some pro-bono work for humanitarian and ecological causes. He had always been able to provide a more than comfortable subsistence for his wife, four sons, and only daughter; but he loved rural life. The farm she had grown up on, the magnificent Clydesdales he bred and trained as much for love of the regal and powerful animals as for pride at show. They were as much a part of him as his family.

She told Alan about school, her friends, Rama. Especially Rama. And of course, Reggie! Her stories of his insane antics that always kept things jumping around campus made Alan laugh again. Once more, his laughter made warm, funny things happen inside her.

"I wouldn't be too quick to uncork the champagne when you get back, Dawn," he cautioned, after she told him of the impromptu experiment that had unexpectedly landed her here, and how happy Rama and the team would be. "Experiments in crystal amplification of ESP have dangled some tempting carrots. But most of the promising data are probably only the by-products of placebo effect. They work because, with all the New Age hype, they're expected to work. Everyone possesses at least some degree of esper talent; but in most people it's dormant, only surfacing on rare occasions and very sporadically. Granted, the *Peregrine's* grav-shield is a specific grid layout of natural and synthetic crystals tuned to resonate back and forth along a very narrow, very specific band of harmonics, but ESP's a whole other ball game.

"God, after last week! After the telepathic mind overlay I impulsively initiated, that inexplicable bond we both felt back then is so much stronger now. That's why it was so easy for you to find me and why we're sitting here so casually, sharing everything but tea and cakes."

"Alan, I know you only grudgingly buy into this idea of reincarnation," Dawn conceded, recalling the hypnotic attraction, that haunting feeling of familiarity at their first meeting. "But there have to be some pretty hefty karmic ties as well dragging us together like this, almost in spite of ourselves."

"I'm forced to admit, the theory's becoming increasingly difficult to refute when I keep tangling you up with the girl in a recurring dream I've been having ever since the Tabriz earthquake," he added eagerly. His eyes sparkled as he leaned forward in pursuit of the idea. "I can't help feeling as if there's a connection. In fact, all the while we've been talking, I've been seeing her image overlapping yours. It's almost as if she's the real you. And the way you appear to others now is only a mask. Like the one I'm forced to wear.

"There's no denying the muscarine, the crystals, the music, they all provided the catalyst, the extra push that got you here." As he spoke Alan was visibly struggling to reclaim his own lost clinical detachment. "Without your own latent psi talents, without these psychic/karmic bonds, and especially without the esper force I've been exerting to help anchor you here, this little impromptu experiment of yours might never have worked to, at least not to anywhere near the extent it has. Just how successful Dr. Mishra's study might prove though, under normal test conditions, with 'normal' subjects, is still up in the air I'm afraid."

Dawn nodded, fell silent a moment, then spoke hesitantly. "Alan, my skills as a counselor are so minimal, as I've already rather graphically demonstrated more than once today. That's why I chose to specialize in research. I can hardly help myself much less others. You must have realized that the first time our minds touched. How can I possibly help someone like you?"

"When I first discovered you last week…" It was his turn now to struggle for words. "At the time, what I needed most was someone to talk to who wouldn't run shrieking in horror or, worse yet, fall to his knees, pronouncing me some sort of messiah. I needed someone familiar with esper-related problems."

"At the time?" she probed, puzzled by his deeper, unspoken meaning, and more than a little concerned over the tortured expression he now wore.

"Did you ever read about 'Superman' when you were growing up?" he suddenly challenged angrily.

"Yes, but what's that got to do with…"

"OK! Suppose there actually were such a person, and he actually was that powerful. If he and Lois had ever actually tried to make love, just picture what he could do to her, forgetting himself even for an instant, in the heat of passion. Well, Babe, that's me! Look what I nearly did to you just getting excited over the prospect of finding a sympathetic friend!"

"But Alan," she protested, "You were always in control. You stopped the moment you realized what was happening, long before I was in any real danger. If I had, I knew even then, you'd have been right there beside me till I was all right again."

"That may have been true then, but what about next time? You might not be so lucky. That's why I don't want there ever to be a next time."

"Look, you need someone to talk to. I want to listen. You need a friend. I want to be one, very much so. That doesn't mean we have to jump into the sack together."

"Are you kidding?" His features were drawn tight with an inner rage that was almost palpable. "After what's happened between us just passing in a crowd, do you honestly think we'd be able to keep it strictly clinical when we're finally face-to-face in the same room. When I can finally reach out and actually touch you?"

Dawn, totally flustered, was thrown completely off course. The nearest any male, hot-blooded, blind, or otherwise, had ever come to losing his 'cool' over her had been Reggie, earlier this morning. She could not, in her wildest imaginings, visualize anyone, especially someone like Alan Kolkey finding her, of all women, irresistible? It was almost laughable.

"Alan, you're dead wrong!" she said, finally managing to retrieve the thread of her argument. "Every instinct in me says that you are no threat, to me or anyone else. It's your emotions, not your psionics you can't handle."

"Fine!" he shouted, jumping to his feet and starting to pace like a caged tiger. "Go tell that to my parents! I should have died with them in that car crash. They were only up here, at the time, on my account. And what about that charging grizzly I once killed, in blind panic, with a blast of PK? I'm not ready, now or ever, to gamble anyone else's life, much less yours, testing out your theory."

"So, how about at least letting Dr. Mishra work with you?" she pleaded, feeling the futility of trying to break through, with logic, such as it was, her only available tool. "He's the best in his field."

"Forget it!" he spat, turning his back to her. His fists clinched till the knuckles went white. "Have you forgotten? He thinks I'm his precious Tenth Avatar. He may be all you say he is, but where I'm concerned, he's got a blind spot in his objectivity that's as big as a baseball diamond. All I'd have to do is come waltzing in and introduce myself: 'Hi! I'm Alan Kolkey, and I'm a psychokinetic telepath.' Then watch the fun really begin!"

He took a deep breath. Trying to compose himself, he turned to face her once more. The anger had spent itself, leaving him drained, despairing. "Honest, I just don't understand any of this. It's global insanity. I've been proclaimed to be just about everybody's religious or cultural messiah: someone who's going to run out and solve all the world's problems in one day. I've got Mother Kali to thank for all these blessings. That blasted comet was well named!"

"Kali is popularly thought of as a Goddess of Destruction." Dawn softened her voice, trying to reach for some deeper, more spiritual level, "Her worship's been terribly corrupted by ignorant followers trying to justify their own lust for bloodshed and violence. In the Vedas, she's more accurately referred to as the Terrible or Dark Savior of Mankind. She's Shakti, the Great Mother, in her warrior aspect. Our new satellite has actually been quite accurately named. By hanging up there, like the sword of Damocles ready to descend on us at any moment, she's become an ever-present global threat that's drawn almost every nation together in mutual cooperation. Everyone's too worried about her, right now, to be thinking of more efficient ways to keep on blowing each other up. She's also managed to flush you out of the hole you were hiding in. She's probably hanging around just to make certain you stay outside, involved. At risk of sounding like Rama, I wouldn't be surprised if The Lady's chosen you for something far more important. Maybe her namesake was only sent as a waking call. Maybe there's something far more important She wants you to do, and everything so far has just been a rehearsal for the real thing."

"Oh really?" Alan sneered as he sat down on the cot once more. "Well, if I'm the best she can do, then Mother Earth's in a whole lot of trouble. Hell, I'm the first to admit it: I've got more hang-ups than a dress factory, and enough problems to keep a Jungian analyst muttering to himself for decades. I think you've been spending too much time listening to your boss and all his 'Avatar' nonsense."

"While you've been generalizing, stereotyping and making value judgements, right and left, based on insufficient and subjectively distorted data: three cardinal sins for anyone who presumes to call himself a scientist," Dawn volleyed back in a passion of indignation.

"And I suppose you aren't, with all that nonsense about Goddesses, destiny, and premonitions?" he smiled ferociously, gesturing for her to continue.

Her indignation was not so easily extinguished. Oh, for solid hands to wrap around his throat and shake some sense into him. There seemed to be a perverse ratio that governs genius: the greater the intellect, the wider the tangents of emotional, illogical rationalizations it could fly off on at any given moment. "Dammit, at least give Rama a chance to meet the real Alan Kolkey, not that ridiculous, intimidating, darling-of-the-UN persona you wear wrapped around you like armor. Suppose you just walked in off the street, dressed, well, like you are now: wearing denim instead of a spacesuit and a jet-pack. And no space ship looming overhead, looking like a demon hawk about to strike down any non-believers. I mean, some of those spectacular entrances and exits you've been known to make, do tend to leave the impression you walk on water."

"Touché!" he laughed. Dawn could see she had finally struck a nerve. He was beginning to feel a bit foolish. Self-consciously, he picked up his guitar and, once more, began plucking aimlessly at the strings.

Dawn's mind drifted back to the lovely melodies Alan's fingers had earlier coaxed from those same twanging strings. She would have liked to hear more, but hesitated to ask. People were forever making demands on him, and already she had begun joining their ranks. Right now he was looking so tired and beaten. Again, thanks to her.

Alan looked up, smiling with a boyish pride that seemed totally alien to him. "Where my music's concerned, ask away. I'm never too tired."

He struck several emphatic chords, then launched himself into the joyous strains of an old country favorite of hers. Dawn followed closely as he once more lost himself within an intricate maze of melody. She was caught up with him, swept away by the magic of his music. As he sang, she felt herself melting, merging with him into oneness with the lyrics and instrument.

The final chord echoed and died, leaving them both with an eerie sense of completeness that neither had ever known before. She could not tear herself from his gaze as they blended into a shared experience that needed no verbal exchange. Once more she felt him reach out in a hesitant mind touch that was an erotic caress. Every atom of her being vibrated in response, then leapt with joy as she sensed the answering thrill that swept through him as well. It was a whole new level of being for them both: plunged into an encounter where feelings were mutually shared in an open merging of minds that neither needed nor permitted pretense on any level. Dawn felt transparent as glass and twice as fragile. She could not believe it was possible for her to be able to give as well as receive such pleasure from a single contact that was so fleeting, so ephemeral. Neither was she prepared for this sudden and total trust, the lowering of defenses that made such a shared experience possible. Like star sapphires in a swirling midnight stream, his deep-set eyes glowed moist and velvet-soft as he gazed up at her with an added intensity that touched every level of awareness.

"Alan," she whispered, when she could finally trust herself to speak. Her voice rapidly gathered strength with awakening hope. "If we were able to reach out as close as we just were, certainly…"

"It's not the same, Dawn. Making love, when it entails total physical involvement, is so intense, so out of control. What we just did was quiet and gentle. It was an irrational impulse, and we were doing it before I could stop myself. But God, it was so beautiful! Even so, we were taking such an awful chance."

"Alan, I don't think I could ever be the same, after that. But I am alive!" Her voice and eyes pleaded with him. If only she could have reached out and touched him, taken him in her arms and comforted him! "If anything, I'm more alive now than I've ever been before. Oh, please believe me! You can love without killing. And you can learn to shield against unwanted transmissions from people around you. Other psychics have done it. You don't have to spend the rest of your life buried away down here. Unless, of course, that's what you really want."

Dawn tried to remember how Rama looked and sounded, the gentle reassurance in his voice, even when he was working with a particularly challenging client. "Have you ever considered that maybe your inability to shield is just an unconscious excuse for avoiding people and emotional situations? I don't think you've ever truly made a sincere attempt to learn. You're evading, even now when the opportunity's being offered to you on a silver platter. You know, one of the first things a student of metaphysical science is taught is how to psychically shield himself inside a sort of cocoon of white light. Sometimes it helps visualizing a brick wall or a circle of parabolic mirrors surrounding you to reflect negative energy back to its source. Thought-forming, visualization, can be a very effective telepathic tool.

"But all of this is so elementary." Dawn slipped, allowing exasperation to creep into her mind. "Alan, I can't believe you've never tried speaking to other psychics or at least read up on it. There are so many good books available."

"The only psychics I've ever met were either con-artists or self-deluded old ladies in long caftans. I never bothered reading the books because I figured they couldn't have been of any more value to me than their authors." He laughed a bit too derisively. "All that nonsense about 'white light' and 'thought-forming' is nothing but voodoo and Witchcraft," he added, assuming the posture of a disapproving parent scolding a superstitious child.

"I can't speak for Voodoo. I don't know enough about it. But Witchcraft I do know about. It's a science as well as a magickal-spiritual discipline. In fact, for quite sometime now, it's been recognized by most states as well as the federal government, as a legitimate religion focusing on nature and kinship with the Earth as our Mother. You could have found that out for yourself, too, if you weren't such a pseudo-scientific snob." Dawn had given up all pretence by now of clinical detachment. Alan was attacking the spiritual path she had been following with increasing dedication ever since she had met the well-known psychic and

and coven leader Vivian Carmichael-Delaney and began studying with her. That was almost two years ago, shortly after joining Rama's research team. Vivian had been—and still was— one of the parapsychologist's favorite volunteer test subjects. They were different, but they liked and respected each other.

"So, for your edification—Mr. Kolkey," she continued, her indignation honed now to dagger sharpness, "Witchcraft has nothing to do with Satan or Devil worship or those crazies who go around getting their jollies by desecrating graveyards. We reverence the Earth as a living entity—the archetypal 'Great Mother'. She is the Goddess worshiped by Witches and most other Neo-Pagans. Before you start hollering about superstitious drivel and self-deluded old ladies you should take a long second look. Modern science is beginning to come around to the same conclusion as our ancient ancestors who were far more in touch with the Earth than we are. They've known for centuries that the planet is a living, sentient being. We still anthropomorphise her into a Mother or Earth Goddess figure because it's an easier reference for us, with our limited senses to relate to. It's no easy task for someone who's been blind since birth to deal with the concept of light and color. Some years ago, James Lovelock, a Nobel Prize winning biochemist, published what he called 'The Gaea Hypothesis,' presenting evidence in support of the same thesis: that the Earth's ecosphere behaves like a single, living, multi-celled entity. Lately, more and more highly respected people within the scientific community are finding credibility in the theory. Honestly, Alan! When it comes to anything pertaining to psychology, parapsychology or metaphysics, you have perfect, twenty-twenty tunnel vision. And as for 'supernatural': there is no super-natural! Everything in the universe obeys Natural

Law. There are just some natural laws even you have yet to discover," Dawn added on a note of exasperation.

"Thank you, Dr. Freud! Or should I say Dr. Jung," Alan said, impatiently slamming his mind shut once more. "If you don't mind, this is all just a little too far out in left field for me. I think I'd rather stick to what I can see, weigh, and measure for myself, thank you."

"Oh good grief!" she sighed in exasperation. "Alan! The only difference between magick—real magick, not stage illusion magic—and what your psionics can do is a matter of definition. There are a whole lot of people out there who would label you a Witch too, Satan himself even, if they knew some of the far out things you can do."

A whistle of air through feathers and the drumbeat of giant wings overhead interrupted Dawn's explanations. She could feel Alan's relief at this welcome distraction. Following the direction of his gaze, she saw a huge spotted eagle, a great fan of tail feathers tucked under and beating the air furiously to break its descent. It settled onto the nearby log perch with a dignified riffle of feathers. Neatly folding its wings,which must have spanned eight feet from tip to tip, it began dancing back and forth along the length of perch, screaming impatiently.

Dawn had heard of such spotted birds before. A rare mutation of the golden eagle, they were larger, stronger and considered by the Plains Indians to be heavenly messengers. Her Uncle Little Bear, a Wabanaki medicine man for her maternal grandmother's tribe, had friends among the Navaho and Lakota. He had told her many stories when she was growing up. A feather fallen from such a sacred animal was considered very powerful medicine. And here, this very reluctant young messiah owned an entire birdful. It was huge, easily four feet, from beak to tip of tail. What little she knew of avian aerodynamics made her wonder how it was possible to get airborne at all, much less fly with such facility. With mischievous glee, she wondered how the Native American community would react if word ever leaked out that Alan Kolkey, owner of Space Tech, had a giant spotted eagle for a pet.

"Don't you dare say a word!" His anger rang inside her head like tolling bells. "They're one of the few ethnic groups that aren't climbing all over me. And I want it kept that way!"

"Hey! Who invited you inside my head!" Dawn blustered to hide the discomfort of once more having her private thoughts intercepted. Friendship with a telepath was going to take some serious getting used to.

"Poor hunting, friend?" he asked, pretending to ignore her as he climbed to his feet and started walking toward the huge bird. She knew he had overheard again, and was feeling a twinge of guilt.

Disappearing inside the walk-in refrigerator, he emerged a moment later with a chunk of raw meat, still-attached to a large fragment of bone. He closed the door behind him with a resounding metallic clank, then hurled the meat into the air. Eyes that were blazing topaz riveted onto the flying provender. With wings fanning for balance, the eagle caught its dinner in one outstretched dragon claw. Laying its catch across its perch and anchoring it down with steel-tipped talons, it began tearing off bits of flesh and gulping them down.

"Oh Alan! He's absolutely exquisite! Where on the Seven Planes did you ever find him?"

"If you tell anyone about him, or me, I'll…"

Dawn laughed uneasily. At best, Alan might best be described as a violent man of peace. Despair, grief, anger, guilt, they were building up to critical mass: an esper about to blow. Would he ever allow Rama or her close enough?

Were their small talents equal to the task of defusing this emotional time bomb?

He sat back down on the cot, tucking his legs under him in a yoga-like style. Appearing not to have intercepted her thoughts this time, he gathered up his guitar, then took a long drink from the bottle on the floor next to him. A momentary expression of displeasure shadowed his features as he mumbled something inaudible about warm flat beer.

Laughter came more easily for her this time and evoked quiet laughter from him as well.

"He was only a nestling when I found him last year, more dead than alive." Alan settled back and into his story. "At the time, I'd been experimenting with techniques for fine-tuning my psychokinetics. I got to wondering if it might be possible to use PK, like a surgical tool, to repair damaged flesh. I had to go into an almost catatonic trance in order to form a strong enough mind link: literally a gestalt mind-fusion. Even with such an extremely limited mind, I was amazed to discover a measurable increase in my own psi potential. But only during mind link. Imagine what that could mean, merging with another human mind! I was even more amazed when I found out I could also focus all the way down into the genetic material within the nuclei of the eaglet cells. And manipulate it! Over the next few weeks I perfected this new skill, literally redesigning him. By increasing the energy output ratio of muscle tissue to body weight, and proportionately increasing the length of the wingspan, I was able to nearly double the average adult weight of his species, without appreciably sacrificing flight capacity, speed or maneuverability."

Alan gestured with unconcealed pride. "What you see there is the result of my psionic bio-genetic engineering experiments. I've seen him snatch up a new-born fawn and carry it for ten miles. Once, he even took on a mountain lion in a dispute over a rabbit. If I hadn't forced him away, he probably would have turned that cat into coleslaw."

"Don't tell me! Along with the rest of it you're a falconer, too," Dawn said with a sly grin.

"Hell! Where would I ever find the time, even if I enjoyed hunting? Actually, he goes out on his own. I just go along, once in a while. You see, I was never able to completely sever the mind-fusion. We're both essentially still separate, independently functioning units. Yet, on certain subjective levels of shared memory and experience, we've become extensions, halves you might say, of a greater whole. There's still a him and there's still a me, but now there's also a we. Merely by shifting levels or mental gears, in a very general manner of speaking, we can merge once more. I become part of him, seeing what he sees, knowing, literally feeling what he does...

"Oh, Dawn." Alan's features suddenly relaxed into an expression of dreamy ecstasy. "If only I could share the thrill and freedom of flight with you! I don't mean walled up inside a ship or with a noisy, cumbersome jet pack strapped to your back, I mean having your own wings, being a creature of the air, totally free, with nothing holding you down. To climb, leap, dive, to soar over mountains so high they poke holes in passing clouds! If making love to a woman is half as..."

"'If?' You mean you don't know?"

"I... I never dared," he cringed, flushing with embarrassment. "Right now... I... Maybe with you." His eyes brightened, became lasers, burning holes through her.

Caught up in the backwash of powerfully projected emotions, she dithered uncomfortably, making him smile. If she had really been here, the whole package, she would have been in a lot of trouble with Rama about now. Looking directly at him, meeting his gaze with equal honesty and intensity, she silently confessed—to herself as well as to him—that it was trouble she would have welcomed with great enthusiasm.

Now it was his turn again to squirm. Perhaps it would be better leading them both back into safer waters. "Alan, when I first arrived, there was something you were terribly depressed about, something you didn't want to share with your father. Did it have anything to do with last week?" Too late, she realized that was not the wisest choice of directions to lead him in.

"What I almost succeeded in doing to you was only part of it." He hesitated as storm clouds gathered once more, almost blotting him out. Obviously, it was going to be painful for him to speak. He sucked in his breath and found the courage. "Handling heavy equipment, under the best of conditions, carries certain built-in risks. More than once, Gertha's nursing skills have seen me through some pretty bad times. Her comments about how incredibly fast I always mended, and never with any scarring, was what first made me wonder.

"I finally decided to run some tests on myself several weeks ago to find out why. I wish now I hadn't. Sometimes ignorance *is* bliss. Last week, while I was hiding out down here, I finally ran my data through computer analysis."

"And?" Dawn prodded impatiently after an uncomfortably long silence.

There was another eternity of silence while Alan clutched his guitar the way a child would hug a teddy bear. When he finally spoke it was a cold computer-generated response. "Given the extreme flexibility of my metabolism, the abnormally rapid rate of tissue regeneration, when compared with norms for my age group, all the way back to intra-uterine fetuses, the most conservative projection gives me a life expectancy of at least four to five hundred years."

His voice became barely audible now, brittle and cracking in places. "I'm more anxious than ever now to see the *Peregrine* completed and with a functioning interstellar warp drive. I don't want to be around watching everyone I know age and die on me. Dammit, Dawn! Why did you have to remind me about that. For a few minutes, a little while ago, I was actually crazy enough to think that maybe … Oh, what the hell's the use!" He slammed his right hand down flat against his guitar, making the strings shriek in angry protest.

Dawn's soul rebelled against such a bleak outlook. The last thing Alan needed was to be preached to by somebody who could only guess what life must be like for someone like him. She wondered which was worse: passing barren centuries without friendship, without love, or time and again, suffering the pain of loss. What special dispensation gave her the right or wisdom to advise? All she had any right to do was listen and share his pain as best she could.

Once more, she looked up to find him staring at her with an expression she could have poured on her Sunday morning waffles. Whoops! Time to alter course again. Fine counselor she would have made! Every time things got intense, she found herself playing dodge 'ems as fast as he was. No, faster.

"It's all right to talk about something else. I'm not up to any more deep catharsis, myself, right now." Alan leaned forward, smiling sadly as he laid his guitar aside.

"I guess. OK. Uh, your pet eagle: what do you call him?" That seemed a safe enough topic.

"He's hardly a pet. He's so much a part of me, I never really thought about tagging a name on him. But if you'd like to, I'd be happy to acknowledge any name you choose."

"Well, you could name him Wambli Galeshka after the Great Spotted Eagle of the Lakota. Or, since your name is Kolkey and you've already been accused of being the final Avatar of Vishnu... Why not call him Garuda, after the giant blue eagle the Preserver is supposed to ride around on in Hindu mythology?"

"Yes, 'Garuda's' a bit less of a mouthful. All right, 'Garuda' it is! I think..." Alan stood up, abruptly losing the warm smile he had only just rediscovered.

"What's the matter?" She asked, suddenly aware herself of the problem.

"I was just noticing the progressively larger amount of energy I've been having to expend anchoring you here."

"Maybe you'd better let me go," Dawn suggested regretfully, yet feeling a pang of guilt. She had completely forgotten the experiment, her friends, even Rama. "Dr. Mishra's astral tape and the effects of the muscarine must have run out hours ago. Everyone ought to have been long past worry, and well into the panic zone by now." She could feel Alan's reluctance echoing her own as he slowly released his hold on her.

"Alan?"

"Anything, Dawn."

"Promise you'll visit the lab. I know Rama can help you. If only you'll give him a chance to know you, *the real you*. Maybe he could do some hypnotic regressions on both of us, too, so we can find out if we actually did know each other in some other lifetime...

•••

"Promise me! Please, Alan..." she was almost shouting as she opened her eyes. Four very worried faces were hovering above her. Reggie's features were cast in gray slate as he and Dick worked furiously over her, slapping her face, massaging arms and legs. Rama was just lifting a pneumatic syringe from her arm.

"By the blue throat of Shiva!" His normally soft voice was strained to the breaking point. "Young lady, you had us worried out of our minds. What happened? Are you all right? Can you recall anything?" It was the first time Dawn had ever seen him so completely lose his legendary composure. Pushing panic buttons was supposed to have been Reggie's department.

"I got side-tracked, Rama," she replied, shivering with cold. Somehow I managed to find Alan Kolkey instead of your apartment." She knew she was in for some heavy debriefing. All she could do was grit her chattering teeth, beg for some coffee, hot as Hades, to flush the ice water out of her veins, and wonder whether this had all been real or merely a muscarine-spawned dream.

CHAPTER V

A s Dawn walked silently beside Rama, her mind ran far ahead of the Munson children. It was Saturday and she had promised to take them to McDonald's and a movie. She enjoyed the children and looked forward to Saturdays and occasional evenings, babysitting for the Munsons, who were close friends of her parents. They had opened their home to her when she first arrived, almost six years ago, as a homesick freshman.

Rama had come along today to "keep her company." So far, like her, he too had been walking in silence, wearing an autographed rain cloud over his head.

"I fear for you, Beloved," he announced, finally climbing over the wall that was growing between them. His voice was soft but heavy with concern. "He is an eagle, that one, and flies too high for the small wings of so tiny a sparrow. You will end up dashed to the ground, or consumed in the flames of the sun."

"Oh Rama," she sighed guiltily, "how do we even know I didn't just hallucinate it all, yesterday. After all, muscarine is a…"

"When—alright, if he shows up, then we will know for certain that this was a genuine OBE. Still, in your heart, do you honestly believe that is all it was?" He leveled his dark gaze at her like an accusation.

She found herself unable to reply. Alan Kolkey had been real enough. Now she was trapped, caught between the powerfully hypnotic attraction of that brooding man and the deep affection, the loyalty, she felt for Rama. She owed him so very much.

Maureen's impatient squeaking called Dawn's attention back to the children. Seven-year-old Matthew was teasing his younger sister with a ball, jumping and dodging her frantic efforts to wrest it away from him.

"I found it, Aunt Dawn. Make him give it back!" she squeaked. She always squeaked when she was upset.

"Matthew! Stop that! Both of you share and play nicely or we're going right back home!" Dawn tried to look stern and annoyed, but she was grateful for the distraction.

"Oh, all right. Here, Brat, catch!" he pouted, throwing the ball too high and too hard for the tiny five-year-old to intercept. Before she could be stopped, Maureen was in the street, running after it. Shouting her back, Dawn gave chase.

The dirty blue Chevy materialized out of nowhere, baring down on the little girl. Tires shrieking, the frantic driver was desperately attempting a dodging maneuver that might have succeeded, but for an oil slick that sent him hopelessly out of control. Once more, he was aimed directly at little Maureen. No time for anything but to launch herself in a head-first football tackle. And pray the child would be knocked clear of the car's sideways skid path. She was still airborne when she felt the sickening shock of impact. Her nostrils were assaulted by the suffocating stench of burning rubber, her ears battered by the angry protest of screaming tires as her universe exploded into a million multi-colored stars.

•••

Dawn LaSarde swam upward through a sea of obscurity that percolated and melted like vaporous phantoms of a sick mind. Far above, a tunnel of light. Soft pulsing blues and golds tantalized and beckoned her. And sound: incredibly sweet, like the Gregorian chants of monks at worship. Thrumming like some giant, invisible heart, the tunnel called to her, promising rest from pain and conflict. Her path was suddenly blocked by a group of shadowy figures. She recognized her long dead Wabanaki grandmother among them.

"Go back, child!" The old woman's voice was a soft caress, a gentle nudge in the direction she had just come from. "Your time is not for many, many years yet. You are sorely needed back there. Much pain and hurt that you alone can heal!" Recalling Alan, Dawn let go and allowed herself to be drawn back down.

•••

The light was gone. Blackness engulfed her now on all sides. She was aware of lying in a bed, felt the crisp coolness of clean sheets. She reached out an exploring hand and felt metal bars, like the sides of a crib. Her fumbling efforts were rewarded by awareness of stiffness and pain: head-splitting, wall-to-wall, ear-to-ear pain. And voices.

"Beloved! Praise be to Vishnu! We thought we had lost you." It was Rama's voice, bleached by pain and fatigue.

"Hey Doll, how ya' doin'?" That was Reggie. His voice was coming from the other side of the bed. One or both of them was holding her hands.

"Maureen. Is she all right?" The words came out dry with sandpaper edges. Even her throat hurt.

"She's fine, Dawn. Just a slightly skinned knee."
Paula. She was here too. Dawn felt better knowing her
friends were with her.

"It really doesn't matter whether the rest of this crazy
world knows or cares. To us, and especially to Maureen's
family, Lady: you're the hero of the century. They sent all
kinds of flowers, but the damned nurses here in ICU
bitched about them being in the way. They couldn't get rid
of us so easily, though." That was Dick's anxious tenor trying to fake reassuring nonchalance.

"Yeah! Doc, here, belongin' to the union like he does,
gave us some drag." A more accomplished actor than Dick,
Reggie sounded convincing, but there was a slightly higher
pitch to his voice that communicated his concern as well.

"Oh, by the way, we got hold of your folks. They'll be
here sometime late tonight. Your Dad said to tell you he's
not worried. You're too contrary. The Devil would never
have you." Paula again. Her voice sounded much closer
this time.

It was good knowing her parents were coming. She
would have enjoyed seeing her brothers too, but they all
either lived too far away or had families to worry about, more
than over a few bruises and some silly bump on her head.

"Rama, could you pull the shades up or turn some lights
on? It's pitch black in here." Dawn was beginning to wonder
why everyone was standing around in the dark like this.

"Dr. Greg!" Rama's voice was velvet soft, as always,
but there was an unnerving urgency to it.

A shuffle of feet as bodies exchanged places, and then,
"Miss LaSarde, can you see anything now?" An unfamiliar
voice accompanied fingers pulling at her eyelids. Silence.
Then, "Nurse, pull the curtain please." Metal dragged
against metal, and then she heard the sides of her crib clank
down, and felt the covers being pulled away. "Can you

move the fingers of your left hand? Now the right. Fine! Now the toes of your left foot?"

She tried, but nothing below her waist wanted to move. "Can you feel this?" The quiet, clinical composure in Dr. Greg's voice was vaguely reminiscent of Rama's. Still nothing. She was beginning to feel fear, however. Like a multi-legged insect, it crawled up and down her spine several times before nesting in her stomach.

Damn! If only the hammers in her head would quit pounding for a while so she could think clearly. They even managed to drown somewhat the pain in her chest, arms and upper spine. Almost, but not quite. She had to bite her lip to keep from crying out.

"What in hell's going on out there? Don't people know this is a hospital zone?" Dr. Greg. What was he complaining about? Then she heard it too: The sound of horns honking and people shouting. She heard footsteps rushing to the far side of the room, felt bed linens being pulled back up, and then the clink of metal sliding against metal, once more, as her crib sides were pulled back up and the bed curtains were drawn back. The air felt a bit less close about her.

"What in blazes is going on out there?" Dr. Greg repeated himself. His outraged voice came from close above her where he still hovered like a guardian angel.

"I don't believe it!" came an awed female voice that Dawn did not recognize.

"Reggie, Dick, you don't think…" Paula now.

"Hell! Why not! Didn't Dawn say he was a bloomin' telepath? If the bastard is, he must really be tuned in on her wavelength." This time Reggie's flippancy was a poor disguise for the tension in his voice.

Filtered through a closed door, Dawn heard a flurry of excited voices down a distant hallway, the sound of metal utensils dropping, glass shattering. Heavy-booted footsteps were running up a corridor, rapidly approaching.

A door opened and then silence, broken only by an exploding breath of air from someone in a far corner of the room.

"Oh, my God! Please, not again!"

Thank heaven, it was him! "Alan?" she called hesitantly, fearing it might only be illusion.

A crib side came down and then he was sitting beside her, gathering her into his arms. Suddenly she was no longer afraid. His strength was hers as well. She was a storm-tossed ship finally home in safe waters. She felt the cold, metallic bulk of tools and instruments around his waist, the sharp pressure against her chest of the steel collar his breathing helmet clamped onto. His hands were still heavily gloved. She felt the barely perceptible shape of a medallion, of some sort, through the plastic-alloyed fabric of his controlled-environment suit—his space suit. She had seen him wearing it often enough on news broadcasts.

"How… How bad is she?" His rich baritone cracked and dropped several registers.

"About as bad as you can get without ordering the cof… Ugh!" That was Reggie with his usual lack of diplomacy. The grunt of pain must have been the result of a badly kicked shinbone, administered no doubt by Paula. Dick might otherwise have punched him outright. Rama's reprimand would have been silent, but lethal.

"Just couldn't resist one of those spectacular entrances of yours, could you, Flash?" she whispered, trying hard not to sound—or think—frightened again and worry him even more.

"What do you mean? I thought I restrained myself quite admirably. I'd much rather have come crashing in through that window, over there, and saved a few minutes.

Not to mention a lot of useless arguing with staff and security people downstairs." His reply was obviously casual and flip for her benefit.

"You know, I was feeling so good after you left, I went back to the house for dinner. I played requests for the women and horsed around with Stan's boys. This morning I even called The African and let myself get suckered into playing chauffeur to a bunch of physicists, geologists and astronomers who wanted a hands-on look at Kali," he continued. "We were just suiting up for EVA when that car hit you. Almost blacked out, myself. I piled on g's so fast, getting back, they're all probably changing underwear, about now. You want to see a scared bunch of scientists, go take a look down at Canaveral, where I dumped them. They're lucky; I almost dragged them right straight here, with me.

"Now, what's..." He made a gurgling, half-choking sound far back in his throat. "Oh, my God! You're blind! Your legs too? Why the hell didn't you say anything?" Laying her back down very gently, he leaped to his feet.

She heard a sound like plastic or rubber being peeled back. The other crib side came down. Her bed clothes were pulled briskly aside and then she felt the naked heat of powerful hands against her bare flesh.

"Sir! Mr. Kolkey! Unless you have a license to practice medicine in this state..." Dr. Greg's voice broke in mid sentence.

Dawn wondered how Alan had silenced him.

"If looks killed, as they say, he'd be a dead man. That's all," he replied grimly. His hands confidently, unashamedly, began exploring every inch of her body. She sensed, rather than felt them, traveling up and down each leg, and wondered that she could have been aware at all of his touch. Blinded, lacking all sensation in her lower extremities, yet she knew when and where he was touching her. Could he have somehow been tapping her into his own sensory awareness?

"A torn muscle. Dislocated right humorous. Some badly bruised ribs. Small hairline fracture of the left tibia …" He was muttering out loud to no one in particular. "Good job setting the bone! Multiple bruises and abrasions, all well tended to. No spinal injury or serious internal trauma." Lovingly, ever so cautiously, Alan rolled her onto her left side, facing her away from him. He brushed aside the scant gown. Slowly, with a touch that was whisper soft, his hands began tracing the length of her spine from buttocks to the base of her skull. "Several areas of abnormal nerve blockage: some old, some very recent. Aside from that, nothing to account for. Wait! There's blood in the spinal fluid."

Once more, ever so gently, ever so lovingly, Dawn was rolled the rest of the way onto her back. She felt the weight of him as he sat down again beside her. His hands burned hot as they pressed her temples then explored the entire geography of her skull. "Here's something. A large subdural hematoma pressing hard against both cortical hemispheres into the region surrounding the junction of the longitudinal and both central fissures. That would account for the sensory-motor loss. Hematoceles also present and still enlarging in the striate areas of both occipital lobes. Again, possibly accounting for the blindness. No irreversible damage as yet, but unless the pressure is relieved, and damn quick, it will become permanent. Wait! There's massive hemorrhaging into the ventricles surrounding the thalamus. Unless it's halted and the pressure relieved here too, immediately, she could…"

"Dr. Greg!" Alan's outrage was fierce, a tangible, ominous force. "Why hasn't she been prepped for surgery yet? You can't possibly have been unaware of this!" Dawn could almost hear teeth rattling in the small room, even through the pain and fear that was rapidly drowning out all other sensation.

"S... Sir." Dr. Greg's voice cowed. "I... I've already consulted with several staff neurosurgeons. Lord only knows how you could just touch my patient, here, and immediately arrive at the same diagnosis it took us hours to reach." The professional starch was beginning to seep back into his spine, offsetting somewhat the awe that still trembled just audibly at the very edge of his voice. "I don't know how, but yes, you are right on target. We could operate on the hematoma and the hematoceles. The surgical field would be extensive, however, necessitating entry from at least two different locations, obviously with greatly increased risk of death or permanent damage. The odds for this alone are frightening, and would be cause for much cautious deliberation, whether or not to risk surgical intervention. The hemorrhaging into the ventricles around the thalamus, however, is from at least two or three different locations. Virtually inoperable. We'd have to cut through too much healthy tissue, killing her ourselves, or at the very least, reducing her to the level of a vegetable. I... I'm afraid, under the circumstances, the only cure we can offer would be worse, perhaps, than the disease. I'm truly sorry. However, there is medication to keep her comfortable and life support to see her through any crises. The body, of course, has a miraculous capacity for healing itself, sometimes under the most impossible conditions. Perhaps..."

"Thank you, Doctor." Alan was having trouble swallowing something large that had lodged itself in his throat. His voice, hardly more than a rasping whisper, had lost its authoritarian ring. Defeat and utter helplessness were all that remained. Dawn once more felt the weight of him next to her. His hand stole about hers, squeezing, not quite painfully, needing rather than offering comfort now.

She had traveled to the portals of the Lord of Death's domain and caught a glimpse beyond the boundaries of that far country. Promising a peace that was to be sought rather than dreaded, her only real fear for herself was that she might get trapped between floors, not quite there, yet not really here. A carrot caught in limbo. If that happened, she prayed Alan could find the courage and compassion to release her.

"Oh Babe, please, don't ever ask that of me," he pleaded silently, inside her head, as he wrestled with his own private pain.

Ignoring the agony that movement caused, Dawn reached out with her free hand to caress long fingers that dwarfed her own. Her second, and suddenly far greater fear was for him now. He had yet to resolve the guilt over his parents. She was as certain as death itself that he was going to find some way of blaming himself for this too. How would he be able to handle this added burden?

She had to live! She had to make it back all the way! She recalled the vision of her grandmother. "Many, many more years," she had promised. Hope was a fragile seedling, at best, but watered now by a sudden inspiration, it took root.

"Alan, remember Garuda?"

"Dawn! You can't be serious!" His voice fell and nearly broke, then jumped several octaves above normal. He was way ahead of her.

"Why not? If you did it for him, you could certainly do it for me too."

"I know what you're trying to say, but that was something else entirely. I was playing around with the cell structure of a dying animal. I could kill, or…"

"What other option is anyone else offering me?" she asked, looking up in the direction of his voice and digging her nails into his hand for emphasis. "All Dr. Greg says is lay back and hope for a miracle while I slowly disintegrate. Alan, at least with you I've got a fighting chance. So what's there to lose? Dammit! What is there to lose?"

"I suppose," he sighed, sounding almost relieved to have lost the argument. He wrapped his free hand around hers reassuringly. Now there was something they could do instead of waiting around with only pie-in-the-sky prayers to sustain them.

But Goddess! What if they lost? What would it do to him? It might prove to be the final proverbial straw that could destroy him altogether. Did she have the right to ask so much of him on the tenuous assurances of a wraith who might only have been the construct of a traumatized brain?

"Girl, you have every right," he whispered close to her ear, with a finality that lost her the round.

"Dr. Greg, there's a chance. Granted, only a slender chance, but it just might work," he began, preparing to bend the truth somewhat. Dawn felt his weight vanish from the bed, next to her. She heard him moving in the direction from which she had last heard the physician's voice. "There's an experimental technique I've tried successfully on animals. Granted, it's never been tried on a human volunteer before, but since you and medical science can offer nothing more than some elusive hope for Divine Intervention…"

"My dear Mr. Kolkey! I bow to your very obvious engineering and technological genius, but you are not a physician. I would hazard that you are not licensed to practice medicine in this, or any other state, for that matter. I'm afraid I simply cannot allow…"

"Why don't you go sit on it, Dr. Greg!" Reggie's voice was angry now, deadly serious as he stepped out from behind the shelter of his clown act. "Look, if Alan Kolkey here says he can offer us even a whisper of a chance, for chrise-sake, man, let's go for it!"

"Fine! You can 'go for it' to your heart's content. But not in this hospital, and most assuredly, not with my blessing! I bid you good day, gentlemen. Please call me as soon as you've returned to your collective senses and are willing to leave the practice of medicine to qualified practitioners." Dr. Greg's outrage was punctuated by the emphatic opening and closing of a door.

"Hey, how about that, Mr. Kolkey! At least someone around here doesn't hold a charter membership in your fan club. Too bad it had to be Dr. 'Do-right'." Reggie was back in his clown suit again. His concern for her, however, was still apparent, despite the smoke screen and a throbbing headache.

"Shit! Who needs the bastard anyway! Doc, here's an M.D. And a damn good one, too. I know he'll back you up." Dick said, rediscovering his voice.

"I fear that will be of little practical value." Rama's voice sounded awed, almost reverent, yet planet-bound by the gravity of the situation. "I am not affiliated with this hospital. Even were I presently connected with any other, to move the poor child right now would almost certainly prove fatal."

"Dr. Mishra," Alan's resolve had firmed up. He was beginning to sound like Space Tech's guiding genius once more, conqueror of Kali and advisor to UN President M'Butu Moshey. Again, he was the man who could tell heads-of-state to go to hell and not give a damn what they thought about it. "Just say you'll back me up, and not only will I get this institution's blessings, but their complete cooperation as well, whether they like it or not.

"Good," he thundered, in reply no doubt to an affirmative nod from Rama. "Nurse, call down for the administrator of this great stone placenta. Tell him Alan Kolkey wishes to speak with him. Here!"

"Yes Sir." Dawn heard movement close to her head, the flipping of an intercom switch, then a brief, subdued exchange.

"Dr. Perrault is just down the hall, Sir. He'll be right in."

"Thank you, Nurse," Alan replied, his tone of voice dismissing her.

There was a barely audible sound of timid rubber-soled footsteps retreating to a respectful distance. The awkward silence that followed was finally broken by the hesitant sound of a door opening again.

"Dr. Perrault. You must have spoken to Dr. Greg before coming in here." The entire room vibrated to Alan's impatient authoritative baritone. "I trust you won't prove as unreasonable. I'm certain you've been told there is little conventional medicine can do for Ms. LaSarde. However, there is a chance I can help." His voice eased into a slightly more conciliatory mode. "Look, if it will make you feel any better, Dr. Mishra here, will be in charge. You'll have yourself a licensed M.D. Right now this girl's life is in question. We need the use of this hospital and its facilities. Now!"

"Really! I don't..." Dr. Perrault's voice flustered uncomfortably.

"Doctor, I have never before taken personal advantage of this role the public and the media have cast me in. However, were it to leak out that you had refused me your help trying to save the life of someone very dear to me, well ..." Alan's voice grew softer, hissing and coiling like a serpent about to strike. "I am not without a certain influence, as well, with the UN's Grant Appropriations Commission, and through them, your AMA. Need I continue?"

"No. No need at all, Sir. Rest assured, you will have the full cooperation and resources of this entire institution at your disposal." Dr. Perrault's voice was subdued, chastened.

At that moment, he would probably have acquiesced to any demand Alan Kolkey might have made.

"Good! Now listen carefully. The technique I'll be employing is still experimental, so I don't want anything of what's being done in here leaked out of this room. I want strict security. Only the people here now are to be allowed in or out. You will post guards at this door around the clock. Understood?"

"Understood, *Sir*. Will there be anything else, *Sir*?" Dr. Perrault's voice was beginning to grow new horns.

Dawn wished that Alan would have been a bit more diplomatic, but tried to understand his impatience with bureaucracy. She sensed an amused acknowledgement from him at the outer fringes of consciousness.

"Yes! We'll be needing another bed in here and an IV set up. Also, would you make certain there's a steady supply of serum glucose and saline?" His voice was less authoritarian now, but he was still the general, issuing commands to an insubordinate underling.

"Fine. We'll get them to you right away." Dr. Perrault's reply had lost some of its cutting edge. He sounded slightly more willing to cooperate. "Notify me through the nurse's station down the hall if there's anything further you require. Until I see you again, I wish all of you all the luck you are desperately going to be needing." The sound of the door opening and closing once more signalled his departure.

"Sir? I wonder if I might be allowed to remain." The nurse's small voice had to fight for acknowledgement. "It would be a great honor assisting on this case. I'm certain you and Dr. Mishra could use the services of a good R.N."

"You're quite correct. Yes, you are most welcome. But only on condition that what all of you see here remains here, in strictest confidence."

"Oh yes, Sir!" the nurse's voice bubbled and gushed with almost worshipful enthusiasm. Sickening, in fact downright nauseating, Dawn decided, and heard Alan's answering chuckle of amusement. Apparently, he was in total agreement.

"Since you're all very possibly going to be spending the next several weeks together here, I suppose formal introductions would be in order." Alan was finally managing to sound less intimidating, less imperious. Well, at least it was a step in the right direction. Dawn could not quite picture Alan ever becoming drinking buddies with the gang down at the neighborhood pub. She would, however, have liked to see him more relaxed around people, and a whole lot less imposing. If only he could just loosen up a bit perhaps, then people might be a lot less prone to measuring him with an Olympian yardstick. Once more she felt his esper touch as he acknowledged her editorial observations. She wondered that he was so closely attuned to her, then suddenly realized that he must have been the reason why the pain, especially in her head, had so greatly diminished during the past fifteen or twenty minutes. Somehow, he was blocking for her. She sent him a silent bouquet of gratitude. His reply was an almost tangible psionic caress. Odd, no muscarine or other aids, and yet she was still so completely tuned to him that she could hear his silent communications as easily as if she had been a telepath, herself.

"Nurse Susan Hammond," he began, hastily retreating to the business of introductions. "Dr. Rama Mishra, Mr. Richard Dion, his wife Paula, and last but by no means least, my most loyal advocate, Mr. Reginald J. Hastings." Had she actually detected a faint note of affection and satirical good humor in Alan's voice? Perhaps there was hope after all.

"I don't understand. How did you know my name?" The nurse sounded puzzled, and just a bit anxious.

Gently, Alan! She's going to have to know, but please, don't make it sound like you're delivering the tablets from Sinai, Dawn warned silently.

"The same way I knew everyone else's names here. I'm a telepath." The news was direct and to the point, but delivered with a quiet warmth that must have been completely disarming to everyone present.

"I don't get it. You said we'd be spending a couple a' weeks together here. Where are you gonna be?" Reggie asked, breaking a long breathless pause while everyone was struggling to digest the reality of this pronouncement. He sounded surprisingly composed. Dawn glowed with silent pride. She felt Alan's answering glow, like a warm sun, within her.

"I'll be unconscious. My body that is. So will Dawn. It's necessary in order to create the mind fusion necessary for me to effect the necessary psychokinetic repairs." That was going to be an even bigger bite to swallow.

"Oh shit!" That was Reggie.

"Uh… Yeah…" Dick's barely audible response.

"Oh my!" Paula.

A very nervous giggle came from Nurse Hammond's last noted location.

Rama's conspicuous silence was loudest of all.

The unnerving quiet was punctuated by the heavy clank of a large, metallic object striking the floor. The image of Alan's jet pack flashed into Dawn's mind. Another smaller, rattle-clank, and she 'saw' his bulky utility belt falling to the floor beside it. He was sharing his eyes with her, as best he could under the circumstances.

Under these circumstances, it was amazing that he could project anything directly into her mind. She remembered Garuda, what Alan had told her about the huge eagle. Dawn had a strong hunch, after this mind fusion to repair her broken body, there would no longer be any problem whatsoever telepathically sending and receiving between them. Once more, feedback: the vague tickle of a sly, knowing grin.

"Will you be wanting to get out of that bulky space gear, Sir?" The nurse's voice registered reaction to the bomb Alan Kolkey had just exploded under her. She was recovering her professionalism quite rapidly, however, and was trying to prove herself worthy of his trust. "I can get you a johnny to slip into, if you'd like."

Dawn's sometimes too-vivid imagination was painting a portrait of the mighty Alan Kolkey, parading about in one of those rear ventilated hospital kimonos. The image was something less than heroic. If anything could lay to rest all illusions of him as Earth's savior, that would do it. She felt the prick to his ego.

"I, uh, really don't think so," Alan mumbled, struggling to hold on to his crumbling dignity. "I'm afraid a bed sheet would be more in keeping, Ms. Hammond. Any hospital issue you could provide, on me, might prove a bit too revealing. There are ladies present," Alan chuckled, almost good naturedly. False modesty was not to be counted among the chinks in his armor. Certainly, there was no reason to fear offending Dawn, or the nurse. It had to be Paula.

If he had been reading her at all, he would immediately have recognized her for the small-town, puritanical New England, sexual prude she was. Dawn and Reggie had teased Dick unmercifully for months after their marriage, wondering out loud if he had as yet seen his bashful bride naked—skyclad, Lady Viviane, would have more poetically phrased it.

"Dr. Mishra!" Alan cleared his throat then shook his composure and dignity back into place. "I don't want you giving me any nourishment or fluids through esophageal tubes or intravenously. My metabolic rate will have lowered itself sufficiently to not need any supplemental nourishment. It would only prove a dangerous distraction, sidetracking energy for digestion or processing that should be going to the work at hand. However, Dawn will be undergoing a vastly accelerated period of tissue regeneration. She'll definitely be requiring a continuous IV drip containing a high concentration of serum protein and glucose. No esophageal feeding, for her either! Digestion, here especially, would be diverting the blood supply from where it's going to be far more urgently needed. We'll both be under very deeply. and will need constant monitoring of vital signs."

The door opened again, accompanied by the rattle-clang of something large being wheeled in—the other bed, by the sound of it.

"Dr. Mishra, while I'm in the bathroom changing, would you order a mild tranquilizer? One of the amytol derivatives ought to be sufficient. Psionic inter-phasing will go faster if Dawn's a bit less anxious."

He was right! With so much going on around her, she had not realized how many knots her stomach had twisted itself into. It was a tremendous relief when Alan was finally close beside her once more. A bare arm lifted her head, ever so gently, ever so slightly. His breath was warm against her face.

"I bet you look like a Roman senator getting ready to make a speech." She tried to smile as Rama injected something into her arm with a pneumatic syringe.

"I want you to know, I cut quite an impressive figure in this crazy toga," he whispered. His lips were scant inches from her ear.

"Alan," she reached out, her fingers brushing his cheek, "If anything happens, you've got to promise me you won't manufacture some crazy excuse to blame yourself. Remember, we're going into this at my insistence. We both know the enormous risk and the stakes we're playing for. We're gambling, nothing more. No blame, no self-recrimination! Agreed?"

"Agreed," he conceded softly, cradling her a little closer in his arms. "Remember, Dawn, when this is over, I may not be able to completely dissolve the mind link. There's a small piece of me still tangled up inside that over-grown canary of mine, back home."

"MMMMmmmmm, sounds delicious! I'd looooove to go flying with you and Garuda, sometime." She was already beginning to feel woozy from the amytol.

"Don't forget, I'll never be further than the bed next to you," he assured her. "My body will be in that other bed, that is. I'll be in you, around you, part of you; and you'll be part of me, part of us: fused into a single entity. It's actually going to be that combined entity doing the work."

"Super! Sounds like part of a verrrrrry far-out wedding ritual. I hope no one sneaked in a priest while we weren't looking." She felt giddy and silly. It was getting very hard to talk and make sense at the same time.

"In a way, perhaps it is, Dawn." His barely audible voice was an almost erotic caress as his fingers tangled themselves in her hair. "We may come out of this bound together tighter than any vows or documents could ever accomplish. You're not afraid, are you?"

"Of you, Flash? Never! How 'bout you?"

"Yes! Shitless. But not for myself."

"Guess I trus' you more'n you trus' y'rse'f." She decided to end any attempt at further dialogue. Her speech was sliding all over the place. She was feeling more and more disoriented, like a balloon filling up with nitrous oxide.

Alan's lips brushed lightly against hers and then he was gone, but only for a moment. He returned on tickling, probing fingers of sensation inside her head. There were the burrowing ants, again, that she had experienced when Alan first probed her mind just a little over a week ago. They were gentler with her this time, so much gentler, melting into her, merging with her: becoming one. This time she ran to meet him, to welcome him. She opened herself fully to him as she had never been able to with Rama. Slowly, she found herself submerging into a strange new sensation, an awareness that she and Alan had only been halves of something so much larger that was only now being born.

Vaguely at first, she became aware of the physical extension of her new self, the part that once had been him. She saw his heart beating, slower and slower. His blood, once a raging torrent, was tamed now to the slow meandering of an ancient woodland stream. From chamber to chamber, she wandered through his private universe, losing her way in a seething whirlpool of searing memories.

CHAPTER VI

ALAN KOLKEY was the product of a union between a beautiful Arab princess and a Jew bastard. At least that was what his father had told him once, because it annoyed his mother. Actually, the princess, whose name was Aisha, was the once-favorite daughter of an oil-rich desert chieftain, disowned after she had married the cursed infidel.

Dr. Daniel Kolkey, Alan's father, had been orphaned at an even earlier age than his son. Too young, in fact, to remember his own natural parents. He had been adopted by an Orthodox Jewish couple. The family name had been Kolkovitch before the elder Kolkey Anglicized it "for business purposes" after emigrating from Russia.

•••

Alan was sitting cross-legged on his bedroom floor, surrounded by an army of toy warriors from his favorite TV show. He was angry. Why were his parents insisting on sending him to school? Kindergarten was for babies, and he was not a baby. Babies can't read. It had been more than a year since he had needed to have his mother read to him. He could do other things, too, that babies couldn't, like

making that alien monster over there trample the warriors.
Without having to get up and reach for it.

A stifled scream came from behind. He looked up in
time to see his mother drop the tray of milk and cookies
she was carrying, and run from the room, calling out for
his father. Frightened because she was frightened, he
started crying.

•••

Alan tried to rub the sleep out of his eyes, enough to
make it to the bathroom. The sound of the front door
opening made him turn and head toward the living room.
He was hoping it was his father.

"Dan!" Aisha Kolkey angrily accosted her husband as
he walked in the door. "You must speak to your parents,
and while you are at it, to your son, as well." Even agitated,
her voice was deep with its warm, rich Arabic accents. Alan
had lost count of the times it had soothed and comforted
him through the panic attacks accompanying his recently
emerging telepathic and psychokinetic esper faculties.

He was eager to greet his father. There was so much to
tell him about school today and his talk with Dr. Pickering
at the psych lab. He was also feeling a bit guilty, eaves-
dropping. He had promised to try not to listen in on their
private thoughts. Curiosity over whatever was upsetting his
mother, however, kept him hidden in the shadows of the
unlit hallway.

"Why? What's the matter now?" his father replied,
hanging his coat in the closet. He took a deep breath, steeling himself for the inevitable, then turned to face his wife
once more.

"Your parents! Every time I turn around they have
Alan at Temple school. They insist on having him bar

mitsvahed next year." His mother's voice jumped an octave with exasperation.

"And you want him raised to follow Islam," Dan grinned.

"If you had your way, he would grow up Godless, worshipping only computers and splitting atoms." She walked toward the small portable bar at the far end of the living room. Alan heard the clink of ice cubes dropped into a glass and the sound of his father's favorite scotch pouring over them. Returning, she handed the drink to her husband.

"At least the poor kid wouldn't be so confused, worshipping science instead of the fabricated deities of some ancient, self-deluded prophets," he snapped back, taking a large swallow. "My folks shoving Jehovah down Alan's throat, and you with your Koran. You may have left the desert, Sweetheart, but the desert sure isn't done with you.

"Look, Princess, we have a very special son and a very, very special problem. Hon, remember old Dr. Zarkov?" Dan added, appearing to his wife to be conveniently changing the subject.

"How could I ever forget, Dan?" A nostalgic smile sneaked past her guard.

"I'll never forget that first day you walked into the Physics 101 class I was teaching. Or your father's bodyguards waiting outside the door," he grinned, leading her back into the living room. "Dr. Zarkov was my department head at the time, and my doctoral thesis sponsor. I'd never have made it through those difficult times without him."

"We would never have found each other as well, but for him, my husband," Aisha smiled demurely, allowing herself to be pulled down on the couch next to him.

"Remember how many times he ran interference with your chaperone and all those bodyguards? Just so we could have a few hours alone together." Dan placed a tender arm around his wife, drawing her close.

"Then, when you stole me right out from under their noses, that dear, sweet old man hid us for weeks out at his summer camp. Thank Allah Father finally stopped hounding us once he realized we were married and I would never willingly leave you."

"Actually, Princess, it was a lot longer than that. I never told you, but twice, your noble sire tried to have me killed. It wasn't until Alan was born that he actually gave up and settled for just disowning you. You don't regret having married such a Godless infidel, do you?" he added. A shadow had fallen across his wife's delicate features.

"I miss my mother and sisters, and yes, I miss the closeness that few daughters of Islam are privileged to share with their fathers. It would give me much pleasure if, some day after he has grown into his manhood, Alan were to distinguish himself, do something so outstanding, so heroic, that my father could no longer deny us."

"His half-Jewish grandson?" Alan's father sneered.

"Oh, he'll do it, Dearest. I know he will. Remember what Mrs. Carmichael-Delaney predicted for Alan the day he was born?"

"Good grief! That Park Avenue Witch?"

"She prefers calling herself a follower of the 'Old Religion'," Aisha corrected, indignantly squirming out of her husband's embrace. "She's a famous psychic with a large following and an excellent reputation. She's also a very dear friend. You can't deny that she has been right, so far. She said he would be gifted with great psychic powers. He's only twelve years old. Conscious control over his esper gifts has only just begun emerging. And, my God, Dan! Look what he can already do!

"I can still see her standing over his crib as though it were yesterday," she smiled wistfully, forgetting her indignation. "I remember every single word she said, just as if she had just spoken them: 'He is an ancient soul, this one. He will suffer great loss and know great sorrow, but great also will be the love given and received. He bears the mark of the Great Mother and her consort, the Lord of Death and Rebirth, in whose service he has chosen to return. One day, when he has shed the last of his chains and comes into his own, the Old Ones will once more speak through him. They are the Soul of this Living Planet and their power, his birthright, already flows through him. Our paths will cross once more after he is grown. I will be twice honored by the Mighty Ones: Once, for having known the child; and again for having known and aided the man he will become.'"

"She said all that, and there were no claps of thunder? No wise men or shepherds? And no star," Dan laughed sarcastically. "Hey, if you really bought all that, I've got a great story about little green men in flying teacups with a couple of bridges for sale."

Aisha's eyes flashed with blue lightning. Her long black hair whipped across her face, half concealing it for a moment as she jumped to her feet and spun around to look proudly down on her husband. "Allah, give me patience! Dan! She was only speaking metaphorically. If an Arab and a Jew can live in love and harmony, at least most of the time, perhaps it is an omen of what their son might some day accomplish."

"I love you with all my heart, Princess." He offered a placating smile as he pulled her back down beside him. "But even so, I think I'd rather consult the wisdom and judgement of someone like Dr. Zarkov than read Alan's future in tea leaves. I want to know we're both doing everything we should to prepare him for what's ahead. Being an esper as well as a child with an IQ Pickering has yet to find the upper limits of is one hell of a load for such a little man to bear.

"Look," he suddenly brightened, "next week's the symposium in Sacramento. We're both going to be on the west coast anyway. I'd like to take Alan along with us and leave a day or two early. Zarkov accepted the physics chair at Berkeley after his wife died. He's been living out in the foothills of the Sierras, near Sonora, ever since his heart attack forced him into semi-retirement last year. It's not that far from Sacramento, sixty, eighty miles, maybe. We can rent a car after we've checked into our hotel and drive out there. We'll visit a while and introduce him to Alan. See what he thinks. How about it, Princess?" Dan held his breath, anticipating an argument.

Aisha only smiled sadly as she nodded reluctant assent.

•••

Alan sat in Gertha's kitchen, licking frosting from the bowl she had given him to stir. Her cheerful, rambling words melted into a distant monotone as his mind listened in on the conversation in the professor's living room. He knew he was the main topic on the evening's agenda.

Dinner over, Dr. Heinrich Zarkov had led his two guests into the spacious living room where a fire crackled and spat in a granite fireplace that dominated the entire area. Settled into his favorite recliner now, he freshened the tobacco in his pipe. Balancing it between his teeth, he took several drags, still unlit. His ample gray hair and mustache were showing signs of going completely white.

"Well! Good dinner, coffee's coming, and Gertha's keeping Alan occupied in the kitchen, helping her make dessert. Never met the child yet who could resist her Boston cream pie," he chuckled. "I assume it's Alan you came all this way to talk about." His grey eyes twinkled mischievously under a mantle of bushy, grey-white brows as he gazed in the direction of the nervous young couple seated on the couch in front of him. They both nodded in unison.

"I must admit, your son certainly is a most prodigious child, to say the very least. He must present some equally prodigious problems." Zarkov cranked up the voltage on his smile to give the conversational ball another nudge and start it rolling in the proper direction.

The young woman signed for her husband to start first.

"Sir! I want to apologize again for the imposition, barging in on you like this; but you see... Well, yes. You're right. We did come about Alan. He is, most definitely, a very exceptional child." Dan Kolkey poured a glass of wine for himself from the crystal decanter on the coffee table in front of him, then took a long sip. Retrieving his misplaced composure, he settled into his story.

"We first started noticing just how exceptional he really is when he was three and talking about the 'pretty colors' he saw around us and other people. A psychic Aisha knows said he was seeing auras. That was the same year he started hounding us to teach him how to read. At four, he was handling ninth-grade level books with ease, and by the time he was six ... Well, you know how word gets around a university faculty community. I hold a research fellowship at Columbia now. The psych department there got wind of Alan's scholastic prodigy and begged us to let them run some tests. We finally caved in. At the time, Alan's psychokinesis was weak, sporadic. The most he could handle were pebbles and toy soldiers. He'd long since gotten bored with the game and we'd all but forgotten about it. It really wasn't until six months ago, when he turned twelve, that the telepathy and PK really began developing.

"Well, they had their fun. Gave him all the tests. Finally had to use a revised Adult Wechsler and then a whole battery of tests designed by Mensa for children like Alan. And still they're a little gray about where to set the upper limits of his IQ.

"As if that wasn't enough," Dan Kolkey continued, throwing his arms up in a gesture of wonder, "Now the boy reads minds as easily as a deaf person reads lips. And his PK's beginning to handle a lot more than just pebbles. So far at least, he's only demonstrated minimal precognitive skills. That much, at least, he's been spared. Alan's in total agreement with us not to share this part of him with Dr. Pickering and his team. If they found out, they'd have him under their microscope twenty-four hours a day.

"My God, Sir!" Dan Kolkey looked up pleadingly after a long, introspective pause. "My son's a psychokinetic telepath with an IQ nobody's got a yardstick long enough to measure. And he's only twelve years old. Now, dammit, how do we handle it!"

"How have you been handling it so far?" Zarkov countered, still puffing on his unlit pipe while his fingers matter-of-factly plucked at a piece of lint on his chair's upholstered arm.

"Well, Doctor," Aisha had finally found her courage and her voice, "at first we had some strong differences. Perhaps, we still do. I don't believe the arts, the humanities, especially religion, can be stressed too strongly. Without a healthy sense of values and perspective, without a carefully cultivated appreciation for the sanctity and rights of his fellow beings, it frightens me to think what someone as powerful as Alan might some day be capable of."

"Yes, but in the process of protecting the world from the future 'Dr. Doom,' she was turning my son into a damn sissy." Dan countered impatiently. "She had him studying philosophy, taking ballet, and learning to play exotic Arabian musical instruments with names no one can pronounce."

"So what did Mr. Macho here do?" Aisha cut in, frowning as she gave her husband's hand an impatient shove. "He started dragging that poor baby off with him on camping and fishing trips. Mind you, he was only six at the time. Mercifully, he was a few years older at least by the time Dan had the child enrolled in a martial arts school." Aisha switched back to quiet indignation.

"Hey, and has he ever made me proud! Sir, by the time Alan was nine he had a junior black belt in judo. By then he was old enough to enroll in Shotokan karate, the discipline I studied during my college years. He's at the same dojo, working under my own master. Just last week he earned his junior black belt in Shotokan as well. Alan is one hell of a scrapper. No one is ever going to accuse my son of being a wimp."

"Dr. Zarkov, 'scrapper' isn't the word for it." Aisha's indignation was turned back up to full volume once again. "Only last week he tried cutting his steak with a karate chop. He smashed a plate from my best set of china and put a crack in my new dining room table. I'm still washing grease stains off my carpet and ceiling.

"Dan," she added, aiming a baleful glance in her husband's direction, "you're turning our son into a half-pint storm trooper."

"If you had your way with him, Princess, he'd probably end up a monk, living in a cave on top of some mountain in Tibet. I have nightmares of him dancing with the New York City Ballet and playing an oud at some Near-Eastern restaurant on Thursdays and Fridays for a bunch of belly dancers."

"You probably won't believe it, sir," Dan continued, smiling now as he turned to face a vastly amused Zarkov once more, "but we did finally call a truce, a couple of years ago, and managed to work out a compromise of sorts that, so far, all three of us have been able to live with. Alan is still studying religion and all that other artsy philosophical religious crap, but he's also getting a good healthy background in the physical sciences. He enjoys his martial arts training, so we haven't pulled him out, but I place a great deal less emphasis on it, now. And I still take him with me on camping trips. It gives us time for father-son talks. Best of all though: no more belly dance music. I bought him a beautiful twelve-string acoustic guitar—a man's instrument."

"Have you ever seen a twelve-string guitar, Dr. Zarkov?" Aisha laughed. "He had only just turned ten at the time. It was almost as big as he was. I hung it on his bedroom wall, then went out and bought him a smaller, more sensible six-string instrument that his little hands could manage."

"Ah, but three months ago, on his twelfth birthday, he took it down from its peg, restrung it, and played for us such a concert." Dan grinned, expanding his chest to its fullest. "My folks went home in tears, blaming us again for robbing the world of a great cantor by refusing to have him bar mitzvahed."

"He does have a beautiful singing voice, Dr. Zarkov," Aisha admitted, as proud of her son as her husband was. "Alan's music has always been a very important part of him."

Dan Kolkey leaned forward now, his hands out in supplication, the anxious frown he now wore suddenly made him look years older. "Dr. Zarkov, which of us is right? Am I wrong to want my son to grow up unafraid: a man's man? Aisha would have him a poet and saint. And how do we help a young psychokinetic telepath grow up at least reasonably secure and happy in such an intolerant world?"

The old man closed his eyes in deep thought and puffed on non-existent smoke. After long moments swimming in silent, amused deliberation, he surfaced once more. Leaning forward in his recliner, he turned to face his younger colleague. "Actually, you are both right. The sciences and the humanities should receive equal billing. It's the only way to provide the balance necessary, not only in his education, but in his emerging manhood as well. That way too, when the time comes, Alan will be able to choose more wisely for himself what he will do with his life. It is, after all, his decision to make. It is for us only to guide and arm him with the knowledge he will need to steer the wisest course.

"Aisha is right to insist on religion and philosophy," he continued. "If the child is as powerful an esper, and as intellectually prodigious as he already is, think what the man will be. He needs values to guide him. As she pointed out, he needs an awareness of the sanctity of Man, indeed, of all life. Or would you have him growing up in intellectual snobbery, looking down on the rest of us as little more than insects to be ignored, or stepped on whenever we get in his way?

"From what I've been able to observe, the both of you discipline with love, and he responds with love, wanting to please. That is good. Each of you has been focusing on different facets of the same diamond, but on your own, you have already found peaceful compromise. Aisha, don't begrudge the martial arts training. The discipline, the focus it offers will be invaluable, in later years, for one as powerful as your Alan seems destined to become. Your instincts thus far have been good. Beyond that, there isn't really much more I can advise that you haven't already done, except to continue as you have been. Your son is a delightful child. He'll make you both very proud some day."

"Oh, he already has," Dan smiled, sitting up straighter and placing an affectionate arm around his wife.

"Yes, he has. A thousand times over," Aisha crooned, cuddling closer to her husband.

"If the three of you are finally ready, there's coffee and Boston cream pie on the table," Gertha announced from the dining-room archway. She was a handsome black woman, well into middle age, and proud, in floor-length paisley caftan, of her African origins.

Blue eyes, set deep into an impish grin and crowned with a mass of black, loosely curling hair, poked through between her arm and ample skirts. "Hey, Ma! Guess what. I helped make dessert."

"My son baking cakes now!" Dr. Daniel Kolkey laughed in mock despair as he rose to follow his wife and the old professor. "This is the great future leader of Earth's teeming billions you were promising me, Aisha?"

•••

"Dan, please! Won't you reconsider and spend the night? It's terrible out there, and threatening to get much worse," Dr. Zarkov pleaded as he reluctantly helped Alan's mother into her coat. "These mountain roads are treacherous at best in weather like this."

"I don't doubt it, Sir," his father apologized, "but I'm first on tomorrow's agenda: a little surprise they had waiting for me when we checked in last night. But I promise to be especially cautious. I'll have to be. I've got my family with me."

Alan endured quietly as Gertha and his mother fussed over him. His father picked him up, and then Gertha was there again, wrapping him in a blanket against the drenching rain outside. It was humiliating being treated like a baby, but he was too sleepy and too full of Gertha's good food to complain.

"Oh, by the way, Sir," his father laughed, "you might try putting a match to that pipe of yours, once-in-awhile. Makes it a lot easier to smoke."

"Can't, you young smart-aleck! Doctor's orders. Heart, you know," the old man chuckled, opening the front door.

The two women hugged briefly. His mother kissed the old professor's cheek, and then they were out the door in a mad dash for the shelter of their rented car.

Alan was lying down in the back seat, still swaddled in Gertha's blanket, and listening to the hammering rain slamming against the metal roof over his head. Suddenly sleepless, despite the almost hypnotic swish-click of the windshield wipers, he listened to his parents, talking up in front. He never tired of hearing the warm liquid notes of his mother's voice or his father's quietly assured baritone.

Thunder rumbled angrily as it slowly stalked the racing lightning in endless marathon among the surrounding foothills. Occasionally, a nearby bolt cut a jagged wound across the night sky, to be followed close after by thunder that sounded like giant redwoods crashing to earth.

A nagging premonition, more insistent than the penetrating wind outside, made sleep impossible. A shaft of lightning hit very close by and thunder boomed louder than ever. The car suddenly skidded sideways, throwing Alan to the floor.

"Dan! What happened!" his mother's voice, octaves higher than he had ever heard it.

"Oil slick! Out of control! Get your heads down!" his father shouted over the roar of the storm and shrieking of brakes.

"Dad! Don't use your brakes! We'll skid worse!" Alan shouted, trying desperately to make himself heard. He felt his father's panic merge with his mother's, amplifying his own.

The car went into a spin, hit an embankment, and rolled end-over-end. There was a sickening crunch of metal and bone, mind-curdling screams, landing upside down.

And then a return to the relative silence of rain pounding its staccato rhythms against metal.

Blood! The smell of it, mingling with the stench of burning rubber, penetrated every fiber of Alan's being, threatening to suffocate him.

"Mom? Dad?" No answer.

"Mom! Dad!" Still nothing. Alan bit down hard against the fear, finally managing enough focus to reach out hesitantly, uncertainly with his mind. He had promised not to invade the privacy of their minds without permission, but he had to know. First Dad. Nothing. No breathing. No heart action. No cerebral output at all. Mom? Here the life force was weak, yet still palpable.

No time for tears! Grief would have to come later. Right now his mother needed him. Fuel was leaking out and the up-ended car might explode at any moment. Both rear doors were jammed shut. He kicked out on the passenger side to loosen the last fragments of shattered glass then crawled out.

His mother's door was jammed also. He couldn't kick glass in on her, or risk injuring her further trying to pull her through the small opening left by the caved in roof. No! He couldn't lose her too! Panic and anger fused into deadly determination. Something within him whispered that childhood was over. If he was a man now, then he needed a man's strength. He called and muscle tissue responded, transforming itself into fleshed steel. The car door came away in his hands with an ease that would have shocked him had there been time for reflection. With cautious desperation, he managed to dislodge his mother's body, then lifted and carried her to the questionable shelter of some thick underbrush and an outcropping of rock. Not much, but still better than being exposed to the full fury of wind and rain. And it was a safe enough distance from the car. Remembering the blanket he had been wrapped in, he ran back and grabbed it. He was halfway back when another lightning bolt hit, closer than all the others, touching off a trickle of gasoline.

He was not sure whether it was the shock wave from the explosion or the piece of flying shrapnel lodging itself deep into his back, or both, that knocked him down. As if it mattered! All that really did matter was holding onto consciousness. He willed his eyes open. Focusing on the dim outline of his mother's body in the darkness, he forced himself back onto his feet. The chunk of metal was just large enough for him to reach back and grab a firm hold of. Pulling it out from such an awkward angle necessitated tearing more flesh, but it had to be done or it would work its way in deeper. Whether, or how much, it bled was immaterial. No time now to think or feel. The blanket, mud-drenched by now, was still better than nothing.

The smell of roasting flesh, his father's flesh, made him vomit as he crawled back to his mother's side. He wrapped the wet woolen fabric about her body, not much larger than his own, then positioned himself as an added windbreak.

Force of will and his desperate need called her back to consciousness. She was bleeding from ears, nose, mouth, even her eyes! As he pillowed her head in his lap, she tried reaching up in a token attempt at wiping the blood, mingled with mud and tears, from her son's eyes. The driving rain, accomplished the task for her.

"My medallion. The one I always wear. Take it!" Her hoarse, choking whisper was barely audible above the angry outcry of the elements. "Put it around your neck! It is your heritage, the symbol of your mother's lost people. Wear it with pride, my son! Bring to it so much honor that the day must come when my father—your grandsire—can no longer deny you. Do this for me! Swear it, by Allah!"

The child, still dwelling within, cried out, protesting bitterly. "I swear, Mother. By Allah and Jehovah!" he finally managed. The medallion was silver and gold, a lunar crescent embracing a solar disk. An intricate overlay of gracefully curving, geometric shapes abstractly suggested a winged steed in flight. The image was recognizable, yet still within the strict Islamic injunction against the depiction of people or animals in art.

"Go back… Dr. Zarkov… Get help!" They were the last words she ever spoke to him.

Her body was cold, beginning to grow rigid before Alan was finally able to tear himself away and climb back up to the road. Only blind obedience to his mother's last wishes kept him moving. She had wanted him to find Dr. Zarkov.

Alone, with only thunder to console him and lightning for a lamp to lead the way, he began his lonely climb. A distance that had been covered by car in less than twenty minutes, now, uphill and on foot, took hours.

Numb, only half conscious, he was almost past the old professor's house when a familiar memory of warmth and acceptance turned him around and up the winding drive.

He was vaguely aware of pounding feebly on the door. A well of light and then large brown arms swallowed him up. It was a bad dream, badly distorted, and only dimly recalled from moment to moment. Gertha was there, pulling off wet clothes and shoes. He was vaguely puzzled by her horrified gasp when she looked at his naked back. The wound couldn't have been all that bad. He hadn't even felt it, pulling out the imbedded fragment, or much else for that matter, since abandoning his mother's body.

He was forced to submit to the woman's gentle ministrations while Zarkov hovered like an avenging angel, prodding, questioning, and then making endless phone calls.

•••

Lying in bed up in Zarkov's guest room, Alan fondled his mother's medallion as he strove vainly to numb his aching soul in the opiate of sleep. Weeks had passed. His back had long since stopped hurting. The numerous glass cuts had all healed. Yet he still found it impossible to close his eyes without reliving that horrible night: the shrieking tires, the screams of his parents, the bone-wrenching crash, the explosion. His mother dying in his arms. He had no right to be alive when they were now both dead, on his account. They would never have been out there traveling that road but for him. Why had he survived? Why couldn't he have died with them?

The sound of the back door opening and closing signaled Zarkov's return from nearby Sonora. Desperate for any distraction, Alan tightened the focus of his mind, aimed it in the direction of the kitchen below and listened in.

"How did the hearing go, Heinrich?" Gertha asked as she poured the old professor a cup of coffee and then sat down with him at the kitchen table.

"It could have gone a lot better. I was more surprised than the judge when we were informed that Dan and Aisha had actually gone ahead and named me as Alan's guardian in their wills.

"We had talked about it, years ago, before I moved out here. The boy was only five at the time. It was just after I lost Martha. I couldn't understand why he wouldn't have preferred a young couple, or at least a younger man, should something happen to both of them. He only said that Alan was very special and he couldn't think of anyone else who wouldn't be afraid to allow him to develop his unique gifts to their fullest potential. Well, I was puzzled, at the time, by his choice of words but I agreed, then promptly put the matter out of my mind. Who'd have ever dreamed I would outlive them both?" The old man paused to stare out the window with vacant eyes.

"So what happened?" Gertha reached out a compassionate hand to bring him back.

"Oh! Forgive me! I was just reliving happier times." A sad counterfeit of a smile was the best he could manage. "Judge Santiago has agreed to let Alan stay with us until she's made her final decision. She wasn't too encouraging, though, about my petition to adopt the boy: my age, my heart, especially the fact that I'm alone. After the trauma he's suffered, she feels the boy needs a mother more than he needs a surrogate grandfather."

"Did you tell the judge I'd be willing to stay on for as long as the poor child needs me?" Gertha asked. "And that I'm a registered nurse? You didn't forget to point out Alan's very special educational requirements, did you?"

"Yes, I covered all that territory, and it did cut some ice with her. She's already studied the test findings from Columbia and the transcripts from the school for exceptionally gifted children that Alan was attending back in New York. She was most impressed with my credentials, and admits I'd be eminently qualified to supervise the education of so prodigious a young mind. As far as my age, I finally persuaded her that it shouldn't be considered too great a liability. After all, Alan's already half-grown.

"There's one point, at least, in my favor," he continued, after pausing to take a sip of coffee. Frowning at its bitter potency, he quickly reached for the sugar bowl and creamer. The embassy in Saudi Arabia finally got a message out to the old sheikh. He sent an army of lawyers to represent him at the hearing. Islamic law had decreed punishment for the dishonor Aisha had brought on her family and people, they told the court. By rights, the sentence should have been death for an adulterous female. Yet, the old sheikh, in his 'infinite wisdom' and for the sake of the 'love' he still felt for such an 'unworthy and disobedient daughter', had 'compassionately' decreed only banishment.

"Still, news of Aisha's death, we were told, had left him devastated. He couldn't bring himself to legally recognize the son of that 'accursed Jew who had so corrupted his once-obedient daughter,' she who had been the sun of his days and the bright moon of his soul.'" Zarkov indignatly elaborated his quote with exaggerated, baroque gestures. "No less could he bring himself to take the boy into his household. But, 'Allah forgive him,' the boy was still Aisha's child, and he couldn't allow her son to be raised in poverty or on the charity of strangers. His solution was to turn over to Alan the money he had long ago set aside in a special investment account. It was to have been Aisha's dowry, had she married the man her father had chosen for her. We were told the present balance is 30 million dollars. And still growing.

"So, Alan is now a rather wealthy young man," Zarkov sighed, "and the question of custody is now pretty much between me and Dan's family. They're old too, but they're a couple. And legally, they're blood relatives."

"But Heinrich, there's also two of us." Gertha reminded gently, reaching out to touch his outstretched hand. "And you have the mandate of the child's natural parents."

"Gertha! That's too much of a sacrifice to ask of you. Your family, your friends are all back in New York," Zarkov protested.

"Oh, it is! Well, why don't you go take another long hard look at how badly our little Alan is hurting. And then you tell me it's too much to ask!" Gertha stood up, looming over him threateningly. "My God! That poor baby's gone and convinced himself he's to blame for his mamma's and daddy's death. Dear Lord! If only he'd let us get closer. If only he'd open up and talk to us."

Zarkov nodded in sad agreement.

Gertha collapsed back into her chair.

"And another thing:" she persisted, not wanting to waste an advantage, like this, for winning her point, "how long have we been friends?"

"We lived next door to each other for years. Our families grew up together," he conceded.

"And how many times were you and Martha there to keep me from falling apart after my Rafe died, leaving me alone to raise four small children? Well, Martha died, you ran off to the west coast, and last year my youngest fledgling left the nest. Nobody back there needed me any more. I was more alone than ever. Believe me!" She laughed, a husky, deep-down-from-the-heart laugh. "Coming here to take care of you, after I heard about your heart attack, would never wash as an act of selfless charity. I was packed and gone so fast I almost landed before my plane did. Now, once again, I'm needed. I have the chance to be part of a family again. And you call this too great a sacrifice to ask of me?

"Heinrich!" She suddenly brightened with inspiration. "If we were to marry, would it help your… our chances for permanent custody?"

Zarkov frowned losing himself in deep concentration for several moments.

When he finally looked up, a relaxed smile lit his face. It was the first he had worn in weeks. "Well, it certainly wouldn't hurt our chances. And it just might help, especially if they try to make an issue out of my health."

"You don't think they'd try to rattle the old racial skeletons, do you?"

"Believe me, I know Judge Santiago. She would never allow that in her court. Besides, she's had nothing but praise for the way you've held that child together through this whole mess."

"We're going to win, Old Man, I just know it," Gertha smiled encouragingly as she rose to begin preparing the evening meal.

"Lord, I hope you're right! I've met the elder Kolkey. He's a good man, but dogmatic. Set in his ways. Not at all the best influence for a very impressionable young telepath."

"You didn't tell the judge about that, did you!" Gertha cringed, almost dropping the bowl she was carrying.

"Good Heavens, no!" Zarkov snapped back. "No one must know that! I've already cautioned the boy. I won't have his life disrupted any worse than it already is by scientists trying to use him as a guinea pig, or the public turning him into a circus side show!"

•••

Dawn was herself once more. Alan had opened himself completely to her, sharing his deepest pain, his most private memories, in the most personal way possible—by allowing her to relive them with him, through him. He had stepped back now, long enough to remind her it was time to sleep and merge with him, totally in preparation for the work ahead.

Suddenly, he was everywhere, melting, merging, becoming—an ecstasy of oneness. There was not an atom of being that escaped the searching scrutiny of this newly expanded self. Like a dream, so much happening, a universe of reaching out for knowledge, exploring, questing for answers within silicon memory. From somewhere just beyond the outer limits of conscious awareness, the shining image of Grandmother radiated wisdom and assurance like a living sun. Everything was going to be all right now. The passing of moments, hours, days. Years? Time held no meaning here.

•••

Certainty dissolved into confusion as the Alan half of her severed its connection, leaving her lost, utterly alone in an ocean of nothing. Far above glowed a tiny pinpoint of light, beckoning like a candle flame atop a distant mountain. Frantically, she swam toward it, somehow knowing he was there, waiting for her. Again, was it hours or only moments before she finally broke surface into consciousness?

Dawn found herself once more the sole lonely tenant in her body. Her eyes opened slowly, reluctantly, protesting the painful assault of filtered sunlight. The shades were drawn, but the diffuse room light still hurt. What matter! She could see again! Turning her head to the left, in the direction she recalled having heard them set up the other bed, she found it untenanted. The only activity in that direction came from an IV unit hanging from a metal stand next to her own bed. It was slowly dripping its contents into an arm that was strapped to a board. Odd! The first time she had regained consciousness after the accident, it had been her right arm, with the dislocated shoulder, that had been immobilized. Now it was free, Neither was there a cast on the leg they had said was broken. She could see the smooth natural outline of both legs quite clearly under the light bed linen.

She was beginning to think she was alone in the room when her free arm brushed up against something. Turning her head, she found him in an armchair that had been pulled up hard against her bed. Alan's upper half, head, arms, and chest, were spilled out onto the bed, next to her. Eyes closed, hair a mad tumble of raven curls, he looked more at peace with himself and the world than she recalled ever having seen him. Cautiously, not wanting to wake him, she reached out her free hand to touch the rumpled mane of her sleeping lion.

Opening his eyes, he raised his head slightly and smiled. A window shade rolled up with a snap. Sunlight suddenly flooded the room, so bright it made her eyes water. She fought down tears that backed up, filling her nose and forcing her to sniffle a most undignified noise.

Alan's quiet smile exploded into a loud grin. "So, that's what it feels like to be a woman!" he laughed softly as he reached out to cover her hand with his.

"So, that's what it feels like to be a man. To be you!" she countered, returning his smile as she repositioned her arm so her fingers could give his a loving squeeze. "You're dressed!" she suddenly noticed. He was wearing a black turtleneck shirt, tucked into belted, black slacks. She wondered where they had come from. "How long have you been back?"

"Six or seven hours." Stretching, he fought back a yawn, then shook the hair out of his eyes. "I really wasn't paying much notice. Your friend, Reggie, had these for me when I woke up. He said he thought they'd be more comfortable than climbing back into what I arrived in. They are.

"You can see again!" he announced redundantly. His smile flipped over into a concerned frown. "How are the legs? Feel like wiggling a few toes for me?"

"Whatever turns you on, lover." She managed to jack her head up high enough to see where her feet lay under the covers. They moved. Thank the Goddess, they moved! Exhausted from even so slight an effort, she let her head fall back against the pillow and closed her eyes.

"Where are Rama and the others?" she asked around a tired yawn.

"Mishra's sacked out in a room down the hall. Reggie's out on an errand for me and I chased Dick, Paula, and Nurse Hammond down to the cafeteria for a decent meal and a break," he replied.

Despite every effort to hang on to the joy of the moment, she drifted back to sleep.

•••

The sound of a door opening woke her. The room was a bit darker than before, making her wonder how long she had been sleeping this time. Alan's hand was still closed around hers. His eyes were shut and his head was slumped onto the pillow, next to her. He must have fallen back asleep right after she had. She looked toward the door and saw a young nurse smiling at her.

"Excuse me! I'll be right back. I think Dr. Mishra will want to know you're awake." Her gentle smile radiated quiet jubilation as she disappeared once more behind the closing door.

"Alan! What happened to you!" Her voice was a breathless whisper of shock as he stood up on somewhat wobbly legs. The lean powerfully muscled body she remembered was now almost emaciated. He must have lost at least fifty or sixty pounds during their shared ordeal. Why hadn't she noticed earlier how gaunt his features had become? The hollowed cheeks, the sunken eyes frightened her. "Why, in the Lady's name, didn't you tell me it would take so much out of you?" she demanded, feeling at once horrified and guilty.

"Sorry, I really didn't know, myself. Not that it would have mattered. It took a bit longer than I anticipated. Actually, we've both been… gone… for over four weeks. We had rather a long repair order."

"Oh, but Alan, you're so thin!"

"Hey, didn't your mother ever tell you: There's always a sunny side to every tombstone. Just think of the fun Gertha's going to have scolding and fattening me back up again," he laughed, bending to kiss her on the forehead.

Mishra burst into the room. "Beloved! You have been returned to us. Made whole, once more, Nurse Hammond tells me." It was good to see the relief in his tired eyes as he leaned over to kiss her.

"Hey, Dawn, Light-of-my-life...and all that other good stuff! It's all over the hospital: you're finally up and on the mend." Reggie loped into the room like a galloping giraffe, Dick and Paula hard on his heels.

"Oh, my baby! My poor baby!" The familiar voice came from the back of the small crowd that was beginning to collect out in the hallway.

"Mom?" Dawn called out to the slender woman squeezing through the door. She was tastefully dressed in a gray pantsuit, her silver-shot hair twisted into a braided bun at the back of her head. "Where's Dad?" she laughed and wept, as they embraced.

"Right here, Kitten." Her father, loud and loving as ever, was shouldering his way through the door and the pile-up collecting now around her bed. He gave her one of his infamous bear hugs. This one, though, was a whole lot gentler than she was used to. His hairline had receded a bit more since the last time she had seen him, accentuating his prominent widow's peak. He had also added a few extra pounds to his mid-section, she noticed. And the Holidays were still weeks away.

"Say, young lady, why didn't you tell us you'd finally taken our advice about doing something with your hair? Only isn't it a bit short? And... uhh... you haven't gone and had plastic surgery, or some such nonsense, have you?" he asked, donning a puzzled frown that added more wrinkles to his weathered features.

"Don't be foolish, Papa! It's just all that weight our little girl's lost, makes her look so different," Mrs. LaSarde scolded, giving her husband a love tap on the top of his head.

What were they talking about? Where was Alan? Her head was beginning to spin.

"You're right, Mama," her father conceded with a good-natured grin. "You just ignore your Papa's ramblings,

Kitten. It's only that we've been so terribly worried for so long. Every day, waiting downstairs for any bit of news, wondering if you'd live or die. It's got us all acting a bit foolish. But that's in the past now. We called home the minute we heard you were all right. The whole family will be here tomorrow, and probably half of Grafton County, too. Our girl's suddenly become something of a celebrity," he puffed and preened, peacock-proud.

"Miss LaSarde! I'm Dr. Perrault, hospital administrator. This is Dr. Greg, neurosurgery." Two more faces now hovered over her bed, grizzled, dignified, and wearing their best bedside manner. "We are indeed most gratified, and most relieved to learn that you are still ali … looking … so well."

Above the rising bedlam, Dawn could feel the gathering storm of Alan's outrage, his sense of trespass by all these strangers. She was his! After all, hadn't he saved her life? Now this babbling bunch of baboons was endangering it, once more.

A deluge of roses suddenly rained down on her from out of nowhere.

"Hey Dawn! Remember me, Gil Markey? Advanced Tests and Measurements, last semester? I told them I knew you, so the Graduate Studies Department sent me with these posies to extend their best wishes." The voice sounded vaguely familiar, but she could not find its owner in all the confusion now engulfing her.

Someone broke through the bottleneck of security guards at the door, struggling vainly to restore order, and shoved his way to the front of the tight knot gathered around her bed. "Smile!" he shouted. Something flashed close to her face, blinding her once more. Her heart began fibrillating wildly, like jello in an earthquake. Suddenly, she could not catch her breath. Her head swam in crazy spirals and dives as panic moved in, taking control.

She heard something smash against the floor, and then Alan was there, hovering protectively over her. Propping one knee up next to her on the bed for balance, he swept the loose clutter of flowers away, onto the floor next to a smashed camera. His large, deep-set eyes caught hers, commanding her attention. Easing himself inside her once again, he quieted the vortex in her head. Her heart slowed down, tripped, caught a strong beat. Repeated it. Again. Then it steadied itself back into a normal, more comfortable rhythm that finally permitted breathing to resume once more. As he loosed his grip on her wrists, Dawn threw her free arm around his neck and buried her face in his chest, feeling like a very frightened little girl trying to crawl inside him.

"All right, that's it!" Alan snarled ferociously, easing her gently back down onto her pillow as soon as he was able to loose her hold of him. "Everybody! Out of here!" His voice boomed like human thunder as he spun around to challenge the small mob. His rage was mighty and magnificent to behold. Before it, the crowd melted, cowed into submission.

"Dr. Mishra! Mr. and Mrs. LaSarde! We need to talk." Alan called after them as the room rapidly began emptying. His voice was softer, gentler for them, but still commanding.

"Look," he began, shutting the door behind the last unwelcome visitor. "We have a serious problem. Dawn is conscious now, but only just barely. She's far from fully recovered. Her entire metabolism is still focused strictly on massive cell-regeneration. She's in a very weakened condition. We almost lost her again, just now."

Arms folded across his chest, his manner resolute, his voice commanded with steely authority, "I realize everyone means well and only wants to help, but this place has become little better than a circus side show. And it's only going to get worse. Meanwhile, Dawn will be needing four or five weeks more of absolute quiet and rest—plenty of rest—to build her strength back up. There's no way in hell that's going to happen here."

"We could take her back home with us, Dear, and hire a nurse to help me look after her." Mrs. LaSarde glanced imploringly at her husband as she tightened her grip on his arm.

"Don't I wish we could, Mama. Our little girl would be even worse off there than she is here, though. We'd have the entire county camped outside on our front lawn her first night home, and half of New England inside of a week.

"Meaning no disrespect, or ingratitude, Mr. Kolkey," her father continued, apologetically, as he turned to address Alan. "Lord knows we owe you more than we could ever hope to repay for saving our baby, our only daughter. But by doing it, by singling her out for your special, very special attention—I'm not even going to ask how it is you came to know each other—you've made her a celebrity. She's trapped out there now, under an awfully hot spotlight with you. Hard enough to deal with, when you're healthy and strong, but in her condition ..."

"For Godsake! Don't you think I'm aware of that?" Alan's expression was fierce, bitter. "I have family too. I know what it's like for them, despite around-the-clock security."

"What about my cousin, Daniel Little Bear, Papa? He lives up in Canada now, practically in the middle of a wilderness forest. We could send her there. You know how much he's always loved..."

"That self-appointed medicine quack? Don't get me wrong, Dear. Your cousin's a great guy. Even if he is only rowing with one oar. He's a terrific drinking buddy too, with those wild stories of his. But I wouldn't trust him to treat a hangnail." Leaning now toward Mishra and Alan, as if confiding in them, he added in a dramatic stage whisper, "The man claims to heal with crystals, herbs, and the help of spirits. Fine, over a couple of beers, but not when my baby's life is hanging by such a slender thread."

Dawn caught her mother's secret grin. Uncle Little Bear had seen her and her brothers through more childhood illnesses and traumas than Dad or the family doctor could ever have suspected. She remembered vividly the bitter taste of his medicines and the healing touch of his hands. It was the magick and the power of the man that had first interested her in parapsychology then later in the Craft, the Old Religion of the ancient Celts.

"I fear there is little else I, myself, may offer. But for the typhoid epidemic now raging in Benares, we might have sent her to stay with my family." Mishra wore an expression of philosophical acceptance, so familiar whenever he was forced to deal with unpleasant, unalterable facts.

"Doctor, Mr. and Mrs. LaSarde! With your permission, may I offer a possible solution?" Alan looked as if patience was beginning to fray at the edges. He had their immediate attention. "The elderly couple who adopted me after my natural parents died I know they'd love to help out. Gertha's a retired nurse who never really retired. The house is isolated, way back in the mountains. As I already mentioned, there are plenty of our security people patrolling the grounds. I can also arrange with President Moshey's office staff to patch your calls directly through on our hot line so she can stay in touch with all of you."

There was an anxious, whispered conference between her parents. Slowly, their shocked expressions melted into resignation. Her father looked up, finally, nodding his reluctant approval. He looked as if he was about to say something.

"Good!" Alan barked, cutting off any further discussion. "Now let's get moving. The natives are getting restless and the sooner we're off this island the better for Dawn." He was looking out the window, his features frozen into granite.

"The corridors must be as mobbed as the streets down there." Mr. LaSarde's face darkened by degrees as he joined Alan at the window. "How can we hope to get my daughter out of here still in one piece? My God, you'd think it was the Fourth of July out there!"

"I know I'm going to catch hell from Dawn for this, but there is a way." Alan turned briefly to offer her the small compensation of a grim smile, then opened the window as wide as it could be coaxed. The reaction from the crowd below was deafening.

"Dr Mishra, would you prepare her while I get my gear together?" He pulled his utility belt out of a large burlap bag somebody must have provided, and buckled it on. As he wrestled with the jet pack that had been leaning against the wall next to the bag, her father hurried over to assist.

"My Ushas, the morning of my days, is no more. Transformed, she now soars on the golden wings of Lakshmi, reborn to be consort and shakti of the Incarnate God." Mishra whispered the words like a benediction. There was a deep sadness moistening his large, obsidian eyes as he worked to release her from the restraints of board and needle. "Only remember that I was ever your servant." It sounded so final, as though he expected never to see her again.

Leaning precariously far out the window, Alan hurled the burlap bag into the air with great force, apparently aiming at something waiting up above. Whatever his target, he must have connected, because the bag never came down again. Then he was back beside her, scooping her up, bedclothes and all, into arms that were still powerful, for all the weight he had lost.

"Just a minute, Flash! What, exactly, did you have in mind?" She was beginning to worry and wished fervently for the strength to have raised a more persuasive objection.

"Merely planning one of those melodramatic exits you were objecting to so pointedly the day we first met." He took the time to soften his manner and smile reassurance down on her, like manna from heaven. "It looks like I'm going to be trapped in the messiah business a little while longer."

"A little while longer, you guess?" Dawn laughed. "Oh Flash, you are in deep trouble! I can see the headlines now: 'Dateline Manchester, NH: Alan Kolkey, guiding genius of Applied Space Technologies, Inc., saves life of local damsel and flies off into sunset with same.' That's got to be good for at least another year of media hype. Maybe two even. The human race does love its living legends, doesn't it." She was building another Reggie-style smoke screen to hide her fear, but Alan saw through it and laughed. Holding her a little more securely, he sat down on the window sill and swung his legs over.

"Are you ready?" he grinned, obviously enjoying her discomfort.

"If you plan on waiting around till I'm ready, you'd better break out the trail mix," she complained. Reggie had the right idea. Sometimes a little bravado, no matter how transparent, helps you face down the fear and wrestle your anxieties to the ground. Looking up, she saw the *Peregrine* hovering, motionless, above them. It was no more than thirty feet away, but still, one hell of a jump, even for Flash Gordon. And it was three floors down to the hard asphalt of the crowd-congested parking lot below. "You mean this is the least traumatic of the alternative escape routes? Dear Lord and Lady! Those others must be real killers."

Dawn looked up and the expression in his eyes melted away all fear. She turned around for a last look at the people she was leaving behind.

"Please, call home often. Let us know how you're doing and if you need anything." There were tears in her mother's eyes as she leaned across for a last hug and kiss.

"Try to be home for the Holidays , Kitten. Folks in New England are pretty level-headed. I'm sure the novelty will have all worn off and it'll be back to normal by then." A quick hug, a paternal kiss planted on her cheek, and then her father moved back to stand beside his wife. Behind him, Dawn could see Mishra standing silent and alone, already light years away. Had he been right? Was this the last time she would ever see any of them? Why were all these farewells feeling so final? Even if Alan was her present and future, she would never willingly close the door on her past, on family and friends who meant so much to her. Certainly, no matter where life took her, she would always find her way back home.

Alan kicked off over the edge. People directly below them cried out, scattering in all directions. They were in freefall for only a moment before his back-mounted jet-pack kicked in, slowing and halting their fall. Gradually, they began to regain altitude as the surprisingly silent jets angled to aim them in the direction of a large gaping hatchway in the Perigrine's aft starboard section.

Dawn's stomach made a few editorial comments on this unscheduled flight that almost drowned out the "Oooh's" and "Aaah's" from the crowd surging back, below them.

CHAPTER VII

Alan sent out a mental command to the ship's on-board computers and the huge freight bay slid open. He was in no mood for playing around with airlocks in mid-flight right now. As they entered, he cut their speed by half and angled his jets to fly them to the forward section of the empty freight deck. Landing in front of the newly installed lift, he blessed the timing. He would not have enjoyed having to carry Dawn, light as she was, up two decks of steep ladders in his presently depleted condition. Nor would she have borne the ordeal particularly well, herself.

"When do they send the rest of the pieces to the kit?" Dawn smiled weakly and relaxed her strangle-hold around his neck, as she snuggled more comfortably into his arms. The warmth of her body, the heady softness of her cheek, pressed against his, made him dizzy with a hunger he had never before felt so intensely.

The lift hatch slid open. Entering, he used voice-command to get them to the bridge. A moment later he was reluctantly surrendering his precious cargo to the bucket acceleration seat in front of the computer console. As he knelt to strap her in, he looked up, snagging himself once more on the velvet warmth of those large brown eyes. Unconsciously, he reached out a hand to touch again the incredible softness of her cheek and then to brush back a wisp of the short blonde hair that had just begun growing back in.

How could he ever have allowed himself to do this, he asked himself in a wash of guilt. What demon had possessed him, that he should have presumed so much? He only vaguely recalled the overpowering impulse that had suddenly obsessed him to start juggling with her DNA in order to "set things right once more," the way she should be again. At the time, it had been only a dream superimposing itself over conscious action, yet somehow, unconsciously, he had acted on it. What right had he, he asked himself again. It was one thing manipulating the genetic material within the cells of a dying eaglet, but quite another when it came to playing around with that of a fellow sentient. How in hell was he going to tell her what he had done? Would she understand, forgive, or would she finally have reason enough now to run screaming from him, as others would, if they ever found out what he was?

He was going to have to tell her soon enough, but not now. She was not strong enough yet to be faced with such news, and selfishly, he wanted these few remaining moments alone with her to bask in the heady intoxication of fantasy. While she could still look up at him with such love and trust in her eyes, he desperately needed to pretend, for this little while, at least, that she was his alone, forever, and that there was a future where such miracles might yet manifest. He tore himself away and, needing what slight distraction the activity might offer, strapped himself in at the navigation con to pilot his ship manually.

On a whim, he touched the control panel to his left. Instantly the *Peregrine's* bridge became a transparent sun deck, suspended between sky above and the small New

Hampshire city below. Laying aside his guilt for the moment, he reached out to share her joy and amazement.

Not wanting to tear his eyes away from her, he switched back to psionic mode, controlling the images surrounding them through PK com-link. He watched through her eyes and emotions, savoring her excitement, her pleasure as he magnified portions of the projection, focusing on the crowd. He smiled with her when she recognized the faces of her friends. They were waving frantically in the direction of the ship, as though they knew she was watching. Those wondrous eyes turned to look at him, reflecting gratitude for this last look back. He shared with her the accompanying sadness of separation that suddenly began welling up within her.

Eager to provide a pleasant distraction, he altered his flight plan slightly. The ship nosed upward and began its homeward journey—with a slight detour programmed in. The panorama projected around and under them began dwindling to doll-size, then to indistinguishable geometric patterns, and yet again to cloud-covered splotches of color, suggesting gentle but constant acceleration. This was no time for piling on G's. His cargo was far too fragile and precious.

Clouds replaced ground below them, and still they climbed. The blue of the sky darkened into star-spangled black. Behind and below them, the earth's horizon had taken on a very noticeable curve. Ahead, the moon was a majestic golden crescent, swimming in a sea of spackled light.

Something warmed by several degrees within him as he watched wonder radiate like an aura from Dawn's exquisitely delicate features. Spoken language was superfluous. The psychic bond was functioning far more efficiently than he had feared. Now, more than ever, he would have to master the shielding techniques he had learned from her during their time mind-linked together. She needed the privacy of her own thoughts as much as he, or anyone else did. Far more urgently though, for her safety, he had to harness the powerful longings she had begun arousing in him. War had formally been declared between his dread of the harm his unleashed psionics might cause and his rapidly escalating need for an intimacy with this small girl: a closeness he had never permitted himself with family, friends, not even poor little Hassan, much less a woman. Look what had already happened to Dawn since their first meeting outside the UN when he had very nearly killed her. History was too closely repeating itself. An oil slick on a street in a small New Hampshire college town was echoing a night, long ago, that would haunt him forever. It had almost accomplished what he himself had failed to do. And now this! If an uncontrolled blast of PK did not finally succeed in killing her outright, the curse that accompanied his esper "gifts" certainly would. He could see the wreck it had already made of Dawn's life. To feel her so much a part of him. So close. Yet, each time he reached out, if only to touch a petal soft cheek, he was inviting Death, his constant rival. How could he bear to endanger a life that had already become dearer to him than his own? For the sake of that life, he had to find a way to shield completely, to totally shut her away from him once more.

"Oh Alan, it's incredible! It's soooooo beautiful!" The warmth, the gratitude, the love radiating from those magical eyes melted his resolve and drew him back under their intoxicating influence.

"I knew you'd love it as much as I do," he smiled, wondering if drowning men ever smiled as they went under for the third time. "I bring the *Peregrine* up here often when I have to fortify myself for another day of the UN, the African, and my 'worshipping public.'" He had to swallow hard now to get around the growing lump in his throat "Sometimes I go outside where it's only my spacesuit between me and all that and just float around, wallowing in it. Or I'll go up to the observation bubble, above the bridge here, and just sit. For hours. I'll bring you up there as soon as you're well enough. Naked, with only a bubble of colorless plasti-metal that's so transparent you hardly know it's there, it's as though there were nothing at all between you, the universe, and the Goddess." Good Grief! When did he start perceiving deity in terms of 'the Great Mother'? Dawn! Some of her perceptual biases had apparently transferred over to him. He wondered what idiosyncrasies the poor girl may have picked up from him in exchange.

Dawn's eyes were glowing with anticipation of seeing the universe with him through the *Peregrine's* observation bubble. Basking in their warmth, he was drunk with the wonder of her.

Reality suddenly came crashing in, imposing instant sobriety once more. How could he dare to bring her up there? That was definitely the one place where well-intentioned resolve would never have a prayer. He had already done enough to her to last a lifetime. Gloom descended like a black curtain, cutting off any more foolish fantasizing as he struggled vainly once more to lose himself in the manual piloting of his giant ship.

"Alan! Something's wrong. Please, if I did, or said something I shouldn't have, please let me know." Dawn's pained voice cut through his self-imposed isolation like a scalpel.

"It's not you. It's me. Oh Dawn, I'm so sorry!" Suddenly, the cork was off the bottle and everything had to pour out. From somewhere he found a store of courage to tap into. Returning control of the *Peregrine* once more to her computers, he unstrapped himself and began pacing nervously. Sweat beaded his forehead like a crown of thorns. Arms across his chest, he began fiercely kneading strength back into his biceps.

"When you're under as deep as I had to put myself to form our mind gestalt," he proceeded hesitantly, "sometimes it's impossible to separate wants from shouldn'ts, objective from subjective, dream from reality, what exists now from what's long dead and gone. Dawn, remember me telling you how my perception of you gets so tangled up with the image of the dying priestess in that recurring dream?"

"Will you please quit agonizing and cut to the chase! What you're trying to tell me: does it have something to do with Mishra's weird behavior and my father's even stranger remarks? It is, isn't it? Alan, what did you do to me?" She reached up to tug at short, loose ringlets, managing to pull one lock far enough down in front to catch the warm glint of honey and gold. "Oh Goddess! What did you do to me!"

He swallowed hard, turned his head, and tried to close his eyes so he would not have to see the accusation in hers. "After our bonding, I did an intensive scan of your whole body, all the way down to the intra-cellular level. I discovered a number of defects. Naturally, the most serious damage was related to the accident. There was other damage resulting from earlier traumas that hadn't healed completely and congenital imperfections as well. I wanted to correct as much damage as I could. I, or more accurately, the expanded I that was the both of us, psi-linked with the *Peregrine's* on-board computer, and through it, with the Berkeley and UN com-links, I was able to access just about every database I could possibly need for another crash course in genetic engineering. And did I ever get one! I felt like a computer, myself—on overload and dangerously close to system crash...for God...dess only knows how long afterward. With all I was finally able to assimilate though, I was able to correct pretty nearly all the damage, genetic defects, blockages, and imbalances I found."

He suddenly stopped pacing and forced himself to look directly at her. "Honest, Babe, I don't have any conscious memory of ever having deliberately tampered with the DNA strings that determine hair color. I only know what I was told when I woke up. They said your hair fell out completely the second week into our... experiment. It had them scared shitless until it started coming back in, a few days later. Except now it was growing back b...blonde. Mishra said he nearly called it quits at least a dozen times.

"Dawn," he pleaded, kneeling and reaching out to cup her small hands in his. "I'd never have done something like that if I'd been functioning on a rational, conscious level. But look: at your temporarily accelerated rate of cell regeneration, your hair will be almost as long as it used to be inside of two months. Then you can have it straightened, and dye it back to its original color, if that's how you'd feel more comfortable." Alan cringed at the thought. Granted, she could have come out of this looking like Gravel Gertie and it would not have changed the way he felt about her or the way he saw her, really saw her, with the eyes of his soul. Still, there was a part of him that vibrated to the symphony of honey-gold and sunlight, that played such perfect counterpoint to the earthy umber highlights within those large magnificent eyes. They sent delicious, unfamiliar shivers down his spine every time he lost himself inside them.

"Well, Mr. Alan of the Ritz!" Each sarcastic word cut like the barbed tail of a scorpion. "While we're chugging right along, why don't you tell me what other wonders your sculptor's mind has wrought on this too, too fragile clay of mine."

Aching to pull her into his arms, he had to wrestle again with the fierce emotions warring within him. "Uhh... I vaguely recall a few chromosomal and somatic adjustments that ought to significantly enhance learning and cognitive skill, and to some degree, your already high esper potential, as well."

She stared up at him in open-mouthed shock, waiting, knowing there was more. He closed his eyes again, tasting his need for her. Better she remain angry with him. It would make separation easier, for her at least, when she was well enough and he had to return her to her own people where she would once more be safe from him.

"Well, some of the adjustments to your metabolic 'thermostat' controlling the rate of cell regeneration will be permanent. That, along with some of the hormonal and electro-chemical imbalances that were ironed out, will all add up to a greatly increased life expectancy."

"How... much of an increase?" she challenged, looking as though she immediately regretted having asked.

"Four, maybe five centuries—like myself," he mumbled almost inaudibly. He had visited his curse on her on a far grander scale than he had earlier realized. Focusing on the memory of what had happened to his parents because of him, he found the will power to keep from throwing his arms around her and pleading for her forgiveness, her understanding, her love.

Returning to the bucket acceleration seat in front of the ship's navigational console, he riveted his eyes to the closest instrument panel. Suddenly realizing, he cursed himself for the bungling fool he was, not to have made an attempt at least at shielding his thoughts and emotions from her. Dawn was reading his pain so clearly right now he might as well have posted it in neon lights. Dammit! When was he ever going to learn!

The sound of a body slumping to the deck spun him around. In the space of another heartbeat, he was kneeling beside her, gathering her up, and propping her head inside the crook of his arm.

"...saved my life... endangering your own... thank you by acting like a perfect bitch." Her sentences were chopped to almost unintelligible fragments between deep gasping swallows of air. She paused for several more deep breaths in feeble attempt to rally nonexistent strength. "... felt you... hurting so badly...tried... your attention.... wouldn't listen..."

"Well don't try that again," he scolded, knowing what she could have done to herself in her still dreadfully weakened condition. "At least for another couple of weeks. My Yiddish grandfather is stronger than you are, and he's been dead for ten years. Your entire metabolism right now is geared for tissue replacement only." His fear for her was momentarily sobering. Momentarily.

"Alan!" Her breathing had slowed to nearly normal once more. "Why did you have to make me like you?" she began sobbing as she buried her head in his chest. She was remembering her own grandparents, how alone they had been during their last years. Everything they had known and loved gone, they had become strangers in the very town that had birthed and nurtured them for so long. As he held her, gathering her even closer, he could feel her thoughts spinning: Was she only rationalizing, reading into his actions what she wanted to see? Had extending her life expectancy to match his own been a declaration of love, of wanting her to remain a very close part of him from now on, or had it merely been a panicky knee-jerk reaction to the prospect of facing the centuries ahead totally alone?

She looked up, a lost and frightened little girl, needing assurance from him. With a single wet diamond glistening in one corner, her eyes glowed moistly, catching the light and making magic with it. As he bent closer, reason suddenly surrendered to rampaging emotion. His mouth on hers was hard, unbending. She was all: woman, lover.

Mother! It was as though he were madly racing through her, searching for the source of his being, retracing the same route he had taken years ago coming into this world. And beyond, to the safety of non-being, once more within the Womb of the True Mother.

Desperate, frightened, angry, driven by raging hunger, the unchecked power of his embrace drove the air from the lungs of the small body beneath him. The wildly intense kaleidoscope of conflicting needs pouring out of him was suffocating her mind as well. He felt her feeble struggling. She was almost unconscious before he was able to will himself back to sanity.

Horrified awareness of the violation he had almost committed against her, again, became a floodgate slamming shut on the raging torrent within him. Her eyes were open now. As she began breathing more easily, his own breaths started coming in great racking sobs.

"Again! I almost did it to you again! Damn! Do I have to destroy everything... everyone I love! He climbed back to his feet. Still cradled in his arms, ever so gently this time, he brought her back to her seat and strapped her in once more. The bitter gall of new forged-steel resolve had silenced his tongue, freezing his features and his soul into lifeless marble.

With his back to her, desperately trying to lose himself in the manual operation of his ship, he was only marginally aware of Dawn's losing battle with exhaustion as she slipped into uneasy sleep.

Alan agonized over this new-born sexual urgency. He had felt its powerful stirrings with his first sight of her that day at the UN. Before then, there had been occasional desire and, he was certain, the functional capacity for copulation, yet now, all of a sudden, the sight, the mere thought of this one small girl started a desperate, painful throbbing in his groin that set his whole body aching.

Was it karmic magick wrought through some ancient past-life connections, recalled now only in hauntingly persistent dreams and flashes of déja-vu? Yet, from a far more rational perspective, based on his recently discovered, greatly extended life span: perhaps he had only now finally come into full sexual maturity. Dawn had merely been the needed catalyst, at the right time, to rouse his dormant manhood. If so, then Nature had sure as hell picked one damn lousy time to trigger the onset of this second puberty. More than ever, he must avoid this woman-child he had so quickly come to love and now needed so desperately. At all cost to himself, he had to get her as far away from him as possible, back within the shelter of her family, her friends, and to Mishra, just as soon as she was strong enough.

As the *Peregrine* dipped her nose back into the ocean of atmosphere, Alan started reviewing all the techniques he had pulled from Dawn's mind on the forging of psychic armor. She had learned them from Vivan Carmichael-Delaney—Lady Viviane—the woman who had brought her into the Craft. She was as loved and revered for her wisdom as Dr. Mishra had been. The name was disturbingly familiar. As a child he had known a Carmichael-Delaney, but that had been so long ago back in New York City. It was extremely unlikely they were the same person. In the crisis of his present emotional turmoil, he dismissed the matter as irrelevant.

•••

A faint rose-tinted light tiptoed across the quilt covering her. Dawn found herself lying in a large bed in a cozy bedroom that was comfortably furnished and wallpapered. Looking out the two large side-by-side windows, through filmy chintz curtains, she watched the bright birthing of a new day that was full of pastel pink and gold-shot promises.

"Liar!" Dawn whispered hoarsely as she watched the sun's disk appear and begin to grow up out of a mountain-jagged landscape. The closer slopes, marching right up, almost to her window, were green-mantled in pine and vegetation. They were smaller, gentler, than their more distant cousins crowding the horizon. Those far-off peaks were real mountains. Naked and cragged, they thrust themselves skyward: raw saw-toothed angles that menaced the very dome of heaven. In ermine robes of eternal snow, several reigned supreme, towering over their lesser subjects, who crowded close as though kneeling to pay homage.

Somewhere close by, Alan was also waking up. She could feel his unguarded, half-dream thoughts. On that unending spool of his, he was again reliving the stormy night his parents had died, the memory revived and intensified by similarities and associations he had made in his mind with her own recent accident. Exactly as feared, he had managed to hammer some more nails into the cross he was building for himself: a hobby he could well afford to live without.

Slowly, as he began practicing the techniques he had pirated from her mind, a wall began to materialize, effectively blocking him off from her. She felt it growing increasingly stronger, resembling the stone dungeon of some ancient fortress, rather than the simple shield it should have been, for filtering out unwanted transmissions and negative psychic energy. Once more his old fears and manufactured guilts had risen up to condemn him to his lonely prison of self-imposed isolation. She wanted to scream, beat fists against it, force him to listen to reason, but he had succeeded most admirably in laying the granite walls of his cell. He would no longer allow himself to hear her.

"Hush, hush, child! You'll hurt yourself." The voice was female, but deep, rich, and strong like fresh-brewed coffee. Looking up, Dawn met the concerned gaze of a black woman, smartly dressed in a floor-length yellow pais-ley caftan. Anxiously, she crossed the room, setting the breakfast tray she was carrying on the nightstand. "Perhaps I should call Alan. He'll…"

"No! Don't! I'll be all right." She did not want Alan to see her this way, to lose what little was left of self-respect beating on dead horses. The vines that were choking the life out of him had deep roots, and no amount of tearful pleading was going to dislodge them. She had worked long enough as a counseling intern, before switching over to research, to know that it would probably require some-thing measurable in megatonnage to free him.

Alan's stint at playing Pygmalion had robbed her of identity and autonomy. She had to preserve at least the outer vestiges. She took several deep breaths to help cen-ter, then willed full attention onto the woman who was now sitting on the bed next to her, squeezing her hands almost painfully, and forcing reassurance through them. If this was Alan's adoptive mother, Gertha, she ought to have been somewhere in her mid or late sixties, at least. Yet this magnificent lady sat tall, proud, unconquered by time. The dark umber skin was firm and unwrinkled, except for what people might prosaically have called char-acter lines that were lightly traced into classic Afro-Amer-ican features. Her salting hair was cropped close, following the graceful curves of a well-shaped head. Her gait, as she approached the bed, had been smooth, rhythmic, reveal-ing a full figure that was softly rounded, almost but not quite plump. Smiling maternally, she lifted Dawn's head, propping it up with extra pillows that had been stacked on a nearby chair.

"Not much of a breakfast, I'm afraid," she apolo-gized. She reached toward the tray on the nightstand for a glass of something that was pale orange then wedged the flexible straw between Dawn's lips. It tasted like orange-flavored water.

"Never mind. Drink it anyway. You need the fluids." She flashed a momentary smile, followed closelyby a reprimanding frown. Her face finally settled into an expression somewhere between the two.

"My Alan tells me you've both been unconscious for nearly four weeks, so we'll have to reintroduce solid food very gradually. I promise, there'll be a little more juice in your juice tomorrow." She propped several more pillows under Dawn's head, easing her into an almost-sitting position, then urged a bit more of the all-but-tasteless liquid down her throat. It was wet at least, and managed to water the cotton beginning to grow in her parched throat. That was the best she could have said for it. Despite an all-consuming lack of appetite, the older woman's gentle scolding finally succeeded in coaxing down several spoonfuls of a very soupy, also very-nearly-tasteless oatmeal. At least the coffee tasted like coffee. It was hot, black—and strong!

"I know," she laughed at the face Dawn was trying hard not to make. "Alan complains that my coffee's so strong it keeps the neighbors awake, and they live five miles down from us."

"That's usually the way I like it myself," Dawn managed a weak smile, "but it's been a while, I guess. It sort of snuck up on me from behind."

"Now listen, child. I'm going to leave this glass of 'juice' here next to you." Gertha paused to flash a mischievous smile. "I want it empty by the time I bring you some vegetable broth and more 'juice' for mid-morning snack, hear?" Climbing to her feet, she gathered up her tray and disappeared.

As though Gertha's departure had been his cue, an elderly gentleman entered. She remembered him from the

Peregrine's hanger/assembly dome. With that great halo of silver hair, bushy white brows, and full mustache, he reminded her of a gentle albino lion. He made a dramatic counterpoint to his adopted son's somber black mane and dark fiercely angular features. The old man's gaze also had a leonine intensity, like his son's, but mellowed by the wisdom and humor of years gathered in and aged like good wine. Aside from being approximately the same general height as Mishra, there was no physical resemblance at all; yet something about this very dignified old gentleman reminded her so much of her former teacher, guru, and very dear friend: the man she might eventually have married if Alan had not suddenly exploded into her life, ruining everything.

"Good morning! I'm Dr. Heinrich Zarkov." His smile warmed the room as effectively as the bright morning sunshine. Pulling up a chair, he sat down, taking her hand the way her father used to when she was a child. "Alan is our adopted son. He told us what happened on the way here. I fear it's our fault, in part at least, for the way he handled the situation. We should have pushed him out of the nest, forced him to learn how to survive in an over-crowded, non-esper world, to learn to use his gifts—his curse, as he insists on referring to them—out in the so-called real world. Instead, we felt with him the magnitude of his loss: a loss he still hasn't stopped grieving over. We tried to make up for it, I suppose, by overprotecting, overindulging, perhaps even encouraging his reclusiveness. I regret, now having permitted him to drop out of school and complete his education through computer link with Berkeley. Gertha used to drag him off to church on Sundays, when he was a boy. Don't ask me how, but she even managed to badger him into singing lead in choir. Boy still has a damn good voice! Outside of that, and us of course, the only personal contact Alan ever really had, growing up here, was from friends of mine on the Berkeley faculty. At first they came down to help tutor, and then pretty soon, to consult with him on sticky technical problems they needed help with.

"Alan's never allowed himself any closeness with people." The old man shook his head despairingly. "Even us. So he never had to develop the social skills so necessary when interacting with others, especially with women. All the more so, one as lovely as yourself. I daresay, the lad isn't a total waste: at least he has exquisite taste in women," Zarkov added with a sly wink.

Either the old scientist had been sniffing too many of his own chemicals, or Alan had gone even further than he had already confessed to. It was a train of thought Dawn was not yet up to pursuing.

"Please, child," he continued, "don't let him chase you away with all his foolish fears. I saw the look in his eyes when he was carrying you into the house. With you, at least there's a chance of breaking through that titanium shell he lives inside of. Lord knows, we've both tried." The old gentleman pulled a pipe that looked even older than he did from an inside pocket. Filling it with aromatic tobacco from a worn leather pouch, he wedged it between amazingly white teeth, and began sucking on it as though it were lit. "You know, you're probably the best thing that's ever happened to that young man."

"I... I'll try." Dawn found herself responding like a contrite child. "He builds such high walls though. And they keep getting higher all the time." She wanted to offer more assurance, but she would only have been deluding them both.

"Don't I know! Well, before I exhaust you completely, young lady..." He gave her a sly wink as he rose stiffly. Pulling the extra pillows away, he fluffed the remaining one before easing her back down. "Alan says you'll be needing a great deal of sleep during the next few weeks. Almost as much as a new-born. We'll have some much longer visits as you start recovering your strength though. Meanwhile, Gertha's got her work cut out for her fattening the two of you back up. You both look like flesh painted over bones. That old woman is never happier than when she's got something to scold about. And she's got fifty, sixty pounds worth of scolding and fussing ahead of her, just on Alan alone. You look like you could stand an extra fifteen or twenty, yourself. Oh, Gertha's going to be ecstatic!" He stretched, yawned, then resumed sucking on his unlit pipe.

"Oh, my old brier?" he chuckled. He must have noticed her staring over-long at it. "Heart, you know. Doctors won't allow me to smoke. Poor substitute, but it pleasures me some having it in my mouth and smelling a good, fragrant tobacco. Sometimes I light up, though, when the warden's not around," he whispered, feigning concern at being overheard.

After the old man left, Dawn fought to stay awake. She needed to think. So much had been happening, and so fast. Lately, it seemed as though everyone else was making her decisions for her: Reggie and her parents telling her how she ought to make herself over. Alan actually doing it: according to his own blueprint. Mishra had decided she now belonged to Alan. As though she were property that could be arbitrarily transferred over to someone else! And then this decision to bring her here, wherever "here" was. It seemed as though everyone had been given a vote but her. Alan had now suddenly switched the rules, now deciding she would be safer anywhere else other than here with him. Through all of this, no one, not once, had consulted her on how she felt about any of this. And now Dr. Zarkov and Gertha were jumping on the bandwagon, playing matchmakers to save their adopted son from the hell he was carving out for himself. She saw herself becoming their reluctant pawn as well. Again without regard to her stand on the matter.

There was a dresser with a mirror on the other side of the room. If she could just make it there to see how far Alan had actually gone! Why had her father thought she'd had plastic surgery? Why had Mishra suddenly waxed poetic, equating her with Lakshmi, the Hindu Goddess of love and beauty? And Zarkov's disquieting observations just now concerning Alan's "exquisite taste" in women.

She tried prying herself up onto her elbows only to discover that Alan had also stolen the calcium from her bones, and transmuted muscle tissue into silly-putty. Weeping in frustration, she collapsed back down onto her pillow.

•••

Dawn opened her eyes to warm sunshine bathing the room. She was grateful Gertha wasn't one of those compulsives who always insisted on drawing shades simply because night had fallen and someone might be peeking in. She wondered if it had been three days or three weeks since having been brought here. All she could remember were the ceaseless rituals of feedings, bed pans, baths, massages, alcohol rubs, and sleep. Especially sleep. Dr. Zarkov's frequent brief visits had lengthened, however, as she was able to stay awake for increasingly longer periods. Her annoyingly frequent "feedings," too, were growing progressively more substantial. They were gradually beginning to take on the character and substance of actual meals, and between-meal snacks.

Occasionally, Zarkov would read to her. Was it yesterday he had begun teaching her the basics of chess? During all this time, Alan had not once come in to see her. Whenever she had asked after him, Gertha or Zarkov would mutter some evasion about an epidemic in India, then scurry for cover behind a safer subject.

It was earlier than usual when Gertha suddenly burst into the room, still in bed slippers and robe. Something filmy and pink was draped over one arm, fresh towels in the other, and she was carrying her ancient porcelain wash basin. She was not usually quite so cheerful this early in the morning. Today, she was actually singing as she washed and groomed with a positive vengeance. The "something-pink" turned out to be a silk and lace-embroidered night-gown with matching peignoir.

"I had the old man go into Sonora and pick up a few necessaries," she explained as she pulled the gown over Dawn's head and eased her arms into the flowing sleeves of the almost transparent peignoir. "Soon's you're strong enough, we're all taking a drive up to Tahoe for a week or two of vacation and shopping for proper clothes. I have a son who's a faro dealer up there. He's promised to introduce you around. So you won't be long wanting for male companionship. Enough, I hope, to make that young boo-head sufficiently jealous to get off this latest tear he's been on, and stay home once in a while, where he belongs." She flashed a wicked grin as she tied the last bow on the peignoir.

Dawn's hair had grown another six inches since coming under the ample umbrella of Gertha's care. It was already reaching her shoulders, she noticed, as the older woman started brushing it. A pink ribbon materialized and was employed as a decorative headband. A little lip gloss was touched up with a pinky finger; a final fluff was given to the pile of pillows that were now propping her up into a comfortable sitting position. Several careful redrapings of the peignoir and bedclothes, and then Gertha stepped back to survey her masterpiece.

"There! Very pretty!" Gertha laughed, applauding herself. "Now I admit, it's not really the right look for you, but we'll take care of that in Tahoe, won't we, child."

"Gertha! What's going on? What in hell's all this nonsense about?" She was being treated like an overgrown Barbie doll, and it was beginning to rankle.

"Company! You're having company this morning, child." She winked as she threw a pair of dainty pink slippers down on the floor next to Dawn's bed. She hummed a lively melody as she hurriedly straightened the room. Gathering up the wash basin and used linen, she disappeared in a flurry of activity.

It was obvious: Gertha was brewing more than coffee in her kitchen this morning. Dawn was certain of what was going on down there and wished fervently that Alan would not have had to be manipulated into coming upstairs for a visit. She regretted having overslept and missed the sunrise convention of colors on the horizon. Sunrises and sunsets, here, were so much more dramatic than the ones back home. The show would have been some compensation for this morning's ordeal. She would have to settle for the quieter display of the sun's stately procession across a razorback line of mountains in the distance.

A hesitant knock was followed by the sound of the door slowly opening. Gertha, no doubt, with breakfast.

"Have we made it all the way yet to straight unwatered down orange juice this morning?" she asked, not wanting to turn her head and lose this hard-won moment of forgetfulness.

"I doubt it. She's doing cranberry today." The sound of Alan's voice made her start. He looked so different. The mighty tamer of Kali, demi-God to millions, the driving force behind the United Nations of Earth, standing before her now in a stained T-shirt, threadbare jeans, badly worn work boots—and carrying a breakfast tray! Thank the Goddess and Reggie too, for this vividly perverse sense of the ridiculous that now permitted her to hang onto perspective, and a semblance, at least, of pride!

"Gertha's scolding appears to have paid off." She tried to sound casually matter-of-fact, even though she knew she was just about as transparent as her peignoir to his esper senses. Old habits, and behaviors too, die hard. "It looks as though you've recovered a few pounds since you last blessed me with your presence." She could not resist injecting a bit of sarcasm.

His ice-hot eyes devoured her as he made his way to her bedside. "You don't know how determined that woman can be." He was proving equally proficient at playing let's-pretend. He must have studied patience under Job himself, she decided, as he laid the tray across her lap and sat down near the foot of the bed. "I wasn't home two days before they were calling me about that epidemic Mishra was talking about. It was getting out of hand and they needed whatever technical aide and public morale boost Space Tech and I could lend.

"Gertha had Moshey on the hot line before I was out the door," he grinned, forgetting himself for a moment. "She told him I'd lost far too much weight and he'd better see to it I ate well and properly while I was about his business. You know, the bastard actually had a dietitian and a Black Hat master chef assigned just to me! I suppose I should feel honored." Alan paused to display the watered down smile of a martyred saint. "They say there are less than a dozen chefs in the world who hold the honorific title of Black Hat. Every time I opened my mouth to say something someone was trying to shovel food into it. I have to confess, though, the meals weren't half bad. Almost as good as Gertha's."

"Speaking of Gertha, how did she ever con you into coming up here this morning?" She shoved a piece of bacon into his mouth when he tried answering, and laughed out loud at the incongruity of Earth's celebrated Savior/Messiah running room service. Only the tiniest solar flare in his eyes told her he had intercepted her thought.

"It was late when I got back last night," he managed with difficulty, between swallows, trying to get the bacon down, "and I overslept this morning. She caught me before I could leave again."

At least the bastard was being honest.

"Along with double helpings of everything on her breakfast menu, she fed me a line about her arthritis kicking up and what with being so busy… It was a crock of shit," he added, after gulping down half her juice to clear his throat, "but she yells a lot, and this was the easiest way to keep her quiet. Anyway, here I am; there's your breakfast, and now I'm gone. Moshey and half his cabinet are waiting for me right now."

"Please, Alan don't leave so soon!" Dawn called out as he rose and started heading for the door. She was immediately angry with herself for begging him to stay. She made a futile attempt at camouflaging her humiliation behind an exploration among her eggs for some small remaining tidbits of bacon. Alan had grabbed the last of it as he was leaving. He had also finished the last of her cranberry juice.

"How long before I'll be able to get out of this bed?" she asked, grabbing for small talk, like a life-preserver, while she worked up the courage to confront him.

"Another week. Two at most." His eyes were still burning holes through her like the blue flame of a welding arc.

"Alan! What else exactly have you done to me? I mean besides what you've already owned up to." She washed a mouthful of eggs down with Gertha's coffee. It was so strong today, it would have been declared lethal if the FDA had intercepted it.

"OK. Tell me. How clearly are you able to see me from halfway across this room?" He answered her question with another, as he continued inching toward the door.

"Fine. Why?" she replied, somewhat puzzled. And then, "Oh!" as she suddenly realized she was not wearing her glasses. In fact, the Goddess, alone, knew what had happened to her coke-bottles since the accident.

He grinned nervously and then, emboldened, continued. "There were about ten teeth, also, that had either been filled or needed work. They'll be falling out in a few months, and new ones will be growing in to take their place."

"Alan, help me over to that mirror!" She was strengthened by a burst of new resolve. She shoved her tray onto the nightstand, brushed aside her blankets, and swung her feet over the side of the bed. Alan made a quick leap-and-grab just in time to prevent another crash landing. With his arms supporting her, she was able to navigate across the room to the dresser.

A stranger stared back at her from the mirror. The features were essentially her own, but subtly altered. Her cheekbones seemed higher, more defined, accentuating further the slight oriental slant to her large brown eyes, lending them an almost mystical aura. Her hair was the color of honey, fresh from the hive, falling in rippling cascades to her shoulders. Alan had been a consummate artist, sculpting in living flesh and bone.

"Dr. Zarkov was right. You do have exquisite taste." Her voice was a half-choked whisper as she turned away from the mirror and looked up into his eyes "Oh, Alan! Please, can't you put me back the way I was?" The tears would no longer be contained as she buried her head in his still-ample chest. "Maybe I wasn't anything anybody would have wanted to write home and tell Mom about, but back then, at least, I knew who I was, and it was me, not everyone else, making the decisions in my life.

"That face I just saw in the mirror, it's beautiful, but it isn't real. It isn't me. It belongs to the priestess in that recurring dream of yours you're always tangling me up with. I'm not a dream, Alan. I'm only me. For better and a whole lot of worse. I'm not property. I'm not a house or a suit of clothes to be sold, redesigned, or dumped when I'm no longer comfortable. That's the way women who look like this are treated by men. Take you, for instance. You're a perfect example. When I was plain, just an astral visitor, a disembodied voice, we were fast on the way to becoming bosom buddies. But after I woke up from the nose job you gave me and was suddenly the center of attention, I felt your reaction. They were trespassing on your property. But then you did another flip-flop and now your emotions are so knotted up, you can't wait to get out of here and as far from me as possible. Please, Alan! Don't leave me in limbo like this where we can't even be friends! Put me back the way I was. Please!"

"I can't! I don't dare!" He shook his head and swallowed hard against what must have been a watermelon lodged in his throat. "The first time was risky enough, but there was a death sentence hanging over your head at the time. We beat Murphy's Law once. Any more monkeying around with your DNA, and... No! It would be too dangerous!" He gathered her closer into his arms, trembling almost imperceptibly. "Honest, Babe, except for the hair, outside of losing an awful lot of weight, like me, I did nothing to alter your appearance. What you saw in that mirror was always there: you, minus a lot of weight and those ugly glasses. Only, for whatever reasons, maybe as crazy as you think mine are for hiding my esper curse, you'd chosen to conceal the fact. I'm not the only one around here who's mixed up," he added emphatically, and with a twist of irony.

"Why did you let this happen to us, Alan? Why are you shutting me out? It's almost as though you can't wait to finally be rid of me for good." She cradled her head under his chin and wrapped her arms imploringly around his neck as he lifted her and carried her back to the bed.

"Want to be rid of you? Are you kidding!" he laughed bitterly as he eased her head gently down among the pillows. "Dawn. I want you so bad it's a fire in my gut and a taste I can't get out of my mouth. Only, can't you see? I mustn't ever let myself.

"Remember what happened outside the UN? Then the accident? What I did to you in the hospital and, Goddess forgive me, later on the *Peregrine*? Can't you see? I'm your worst nightmare come true." Alan's expression had grown fierce as he sat beside her on the bed. "My parents died because of me. I don't think I could handle it if anything happened to you too. Especially by my own hand.

"Dammit! This power, this curse, I can't control it. It controls me." He had her by the shoulders, now, as though trying to shake sense into her. Suddenly horrified at what he was doing, he shoved her back onto the pillows, and retreated to a safer distance, close to the door. "My whole life is nothing but one long prison term in solitary. It's too painful to live among normal people. Being an esper has robbed me of all the ego defenses. I always know what other people are thinking or feeling about me, about everything. What do you think would happen to all that wonderful hero worship if my adoring public ever learned what sort of freak I really am? Man, they'd break speed records, running for silver bullets and wooden stakes. And maybe they should. When my emotions run wild, this demon inside my brain: Lady, it can kill! Look what nearly happened to you! I bring you here to protect you from the mob, then fifteen minutes out, and I'm worse than anything they could have done to you." Unconsciously, he had been inching closer to her as he spoke, until he was hovering over her once more.

"You jackass! You didn't kill your parents. That 'demon' also saved my life. Remember?" Dawn was almost shouting as she reached up and grabbed his wrists, digging her nails into the tender flesh. "It also made me so much a part of you that trying to go our own separate ways again would be like separating Siamese twins who share the same lungs and heart. I need you now as much as you claim to need me."

"Not claim, dammit! I do need you too. But there's a fire inside me I don't dare let out of control again. My parents, that rabid grizzly, back when I was a kid. I haven't killed since then, but..."

"Don't the hit-men your gambling syndicate victims sent after you count? No matter what else, they were human, and you admitted to me, even bragged, how you'd deliberately set them up," Dawn challenged angrily. "Tell me, by what divine authority do you set yourself up as judge and jury to decide who'll be permitted to live and who's OK for a little target practice when you're feeling out of sorts?"

"I only mopped the streets with them," Alan snapped back defensively. "The few who left me no other option, well I was only exterminating vermin!

"You're right though," he added more contritely after a long agonizing pause. "I've asked myself that same question dozens of times since then. But even if it weren't a moral issue, I don't think I'd ever voluntarily put myself through anything like that again. Each time left me sicker than the time before. All the filth: the hate, fear, perversion! Opening up for a blast of PK to another mind, even when there's no deliberate contact, you get caught in a mental backwash. It left me feeling as though all the water in the world wasn't enough to wash me clean again. Thanks, but no more!

"Some day, though, I might involuntarily kill again. Innocent people this time. And God, I don't want it to be you! Not you!" He reached out hesitantly, cradling her cheek in the palm of one large hand.

"No, Dawn. It's settled!" The fire in his eyes had turned to blue-gray ash. His features had frozen over into unreadable granite. Unbending steel had replaced the calcium in his spine. "As soon as you're well enough, you're going back where I know you'll be safe. I promise, though: the moment I can either bury this demon for good, or at least get it under complete control, I'll be back for you so fast." The intensity of the emotions he was struggling to suppress momentarily softened his features.

"Right! By that time I'll be an old memmay with dozens of great, great grandchildren."

"Believe me, you are not 'memmay' material!" he smiled grimly, "At least not any more. Not since…"

"That's another thing!" Dawn sat up, reaching for as much height as possible, then leveled her most disparaging frown at him. "Look how much you've changed me, all the way to the roots of my soul. I'm no longer the same little fish you pulled out of my home pond a while back. You tell me I'm going to outlive my family and all my friends now, by centuries maybe. Do you honestly think all you have to do is throw me back, and I can just pick up where I left off at intermission? You have got to be kidding!"

"At least you'll be alive—and safe from me." His blind obstinacy was glacier-hard and ice-cold.

"Dammit! You stubborn, pig-headed mule! It's my life! I'll choose how I spend it, where I want to go, the risks I want to take. Not you! Now do me a favor... and get the hell out of here before I regress to some embarrassingly juvenile behavior and... and start throwing things at you!"

As he left, his silent desperation enveloped him like a cocoon, shutting him off from her more effectively than dungeon walls.

●●●

Alan was worried as he raced outside to the garden patio. The golden afternoon drifted, warm and lazy, suggesting a peacefulness that belied his inner turmoil. Only a waist-high stone retainer wall separated the tiny garden from the sharply dropping slope of the worn old mountain stump the aging professor had built his wilderness retreat on. His eyes searched the heavens anxiously, expectantly.

That damn UFO! For weeks now, ever since he had first sighted it near Tabriz, it had been growing increasingly bolder: following, circling, venturing closer and closer. Teasing. It beckoned like a coquette, yet was unwilling to initiate even limited radio communications. Persistently and silently, it continued poking at him, perhaps only interested in seeing how the rat in its maze would respond.

With equal tenacity, Alan had ignored, testing in turn how far they were willing to push, to provoke. The game had proven both annoying and intriguing until today when the uneasy stalemate had suddenly broken. It was the first time they had followed at such close range during a homeward trip. It was enough they knew home for him was somewhere on this west-jutting limb of the Rockies, without following him right down his rabbit hole.

His sudden about-face maneuver must have been as much of a surprise for them as it had been for him. A

180- degree turn at an almost vertical angle of ascent had brought him close enough to have shouted across to them. A moment later, having recovered from their surprise, they were gone and out of scanner range. He immediately ducked under the holographic camouflage Space Tech maintained over the landing access to the underground hanger dome, part of its elaborate security system.

The moment the *Peregrine* had settled into her docking cradle he was out and running for the waiting tram, panicking and nearly trampling the few technicians on duty at the time. Arriving back at the house, he had taken the basement stairs two at a time. Now, from the vantage of the patio, he scanned the skies overhead and in the direction of the assembly site, some ten miles distant, to assure himself all was still secure. When naked vision could find nothing, he closed his eyes and probed for Garuda. Happily, the great bird was circling in toward the original entrance to the untouched, natural portion of the cavern. Adequately concealed behind boulders and brush, it had been left open for Garuda's comings and goings.

Alan had seldom ever done more than passively ride along, observing, enjoying flight and the strangely altered state of dual awareness. Now, he moved in deeper, his own consciousness merging with, becoming the eagle. He caught a strong updraft, and on mighty pinions soared higher and higher, to altitudes seldom frequented by any save the giant condors and man. The sky was cloudless above and below him, visibility high, as he searched the empty heavens through eyes that saw a rabbit darting between cover, from nearly three miles up. As he withdrew, allowing Garuda to dive for his prey, he breathed more comfortably. There was a peppering, though, of disappointment at having found no trace of his erstwhile pursuers.

Alan opened his eyes and turned back toward the house. As he passed under the old apple tree, he felt something tugging at his hair. It was Dawn, perched like a small bird, on a lower limb. Reaching down with one bare foot, she was grinning as she continued teasing locks of hair between her toes and tickling behind his ears.

He could see Gertha's hand in this. One reason for the two-week stay in Tahoe, that they must have just returned from, had been to shop for decent clothes. Although it was late into November, the weather had been unseasonably warm and "decent clothes" today still meant a ruffled halter top that teased suggestively and shorts that disturbingly called attention to her long, shapely, newly tanned legs. He forced himself to focus on the image of his parents and the dying priestess of his recurring nightmare, that Dawn now, more closely than ever, resembled. It helped somewhat in shoring up his staggering resolve. Even so, he had to dig nails into tightly clinched fists to keep from reaching up and plucking the forbidden fruit from this tree. He had been having daily talks with himself to buttress his soul for the ordeal of returning her to the safety of Mishra and her family. No longer to feel her close by, no longer to snatch stolen moments of guarded conversation and furtive glances with which to feed his hungry eyes, if not his aching loins. The mere thought of it tore at his innards. Yet he had no right loving her, or any woman for that matter, so long as loving meant the remotest chance of harming the victim of that love.

"How long have you been there?" he challenged, trying to conceal his agitation behind a mask of annoyance.

"How long have you been out here?" Her mischievous grin grew teeth that cut into him as he watched a soft breeze tangle itself in the liquid undulations of her long honey-colored hair.

"When did you get in from Tahoe?"

"Last night. It was fun. You should have been there with us." The casualness of her reply and that wicked smile were calculated to disquiet, and, oh, she had succeeded so admirably.

With masochistic curiosity, he lowered his shield and shifted levels sufficiently to tap into her surface thoughts. As though anticipating him, she began replaying the entire trip, for his sole benefit, no doubt. He wanted to pull back out, but concern for her welfare—Oh shit! Call it by its real name: Jealousy—would not permit.

Zarkov and Gertha had both badgered for several weeks, trying to get him to come along, but he'd had a legitimate excuse to hide behind. The UN was finally addressing itself to the problem of the expanding Sahara. They had commissioned Space Tech to come up with some solutions, and Moshey, as usual, wanted immediate input.

Dawn had agreed to the shopping expedition only after the old people had worn her down with assurances. If they had the means with which to build a ship like the *Peregrine*, they could certainly manage a modest wardrobe for one small girl. She had fought for her usual shirts, jeans, and sack dresses, several sizes too large, as always, to hide away inside of, but she had been hopelessly outclassed by Gertha. Now, sitting there like some mythical tree sprite, the hidden beauty that first had won him was given an outer expression for all to see.

"How was 'D'? Did he get a chance to show you around at all?" Next to Stan, of course, 'D' was the only other, among Gertha's and Zarkov's rather large broods, Alan felt comfortable with. A moment of nostalgia tugged at the corners of his mouth as he recalled his eighteenth birthday and his near-initiation into manhood. 'D' had kidnapped him for a Vegas weekend of drinking, gambling, and general rowdiness. Alan had sabotaged the elaborate arrangements for getting 'baby brother' deflowered, however. Paying the girls extra to report back with a falsified mission-accomplished had proven the simplest solution to his problem. After that, three or four stiff drinks, followed by many others, that weekend, had succeeded in sufficiently numbing his psionics so he could enter into the spirit of the celebration, sufficiently to have kept 'D' purring with pride for weeks afterward. Alan's nostalgic smile suddenly inverted itself. What if the bastard had tried to do the same for Dawn!

"Oh, 'D' was an absolute sweetheart!" Dawn crooned. "I'm afraid he must have found me rather... uhh... square." She offered her editorial postscript with a contrived little pout. "He and his friends decided to rescue me from myself and volunteered to put me through 'cool school'. They taught me how to dance, play poker. You know, vodka isn't so bad if you mix it with a twist of lime and a lot of tonic water.

"Oh, and you should have seen the tennis pro at the hotel. He was gorgeous!" She gushed like a lovesick teenager. Again for his benefit. "I met a real movie star, of sorts, too. He had me up on stage with him, almost every night we were there. I even got to sing some duets with him. 'D' had to pump a couple of drinks into me before I could work up the courage, the first time, but after that...

"Crash told me, if I ever changed my mind, he'd have his agent waiting with a contract. What do you think about a career in show biz, Alan?" Her tauntingly lecherous grin curdled his insides.

Suddenly, desperate to find out what really had happened, he probed deeper, breathing a little easier as he went.

The tennis pro had tried teaching her more than just tennis, but thank Goddess, unsuccessfully. Like the "movie star," she had convinced herself his sole interest was only the face, the body, and a couple of rolls in the hay. So, when he had tried waxing poetic, suggesting, "Come fly with me," all that had flown was one small fist, shattering his macho image, along with a glass jaw. Alan could not suppress a smile of relief—and admiration too. Dammit! If he was cringing now over such meaningless incidents, how the hell was he going to be able to handle dumping her back into Mishra's arms?

"Alan! Not to switch tracks on the train of this scintillating conversation, but something must really have been on your mind for a telepath, of all people, not to have noticed me up here. And for so long! Worried about Kali falling into the Pacific, or an invasion from Mars?" Dawn asked tauntingly.

"Hardly!" He took a deep breath, and then told her about his most recent encounters with the UFO.

"And you just ran off?" Disillusion and outrage gave her voice a sharp, grating edge.

"Well what the hell did you expect me to do, wait around for an invitation to tea and crumpets?"

"Why not!" she snapped back. "Best way I know to get acquainted. They must have been tailing you for a very important reason. Maybe they were trying to make up their minds whether or not to open up communications with Earth and wanted you to mediate. Or maybe they were testing Earth's defenses, using you as a sample guinea pig. Whichever, you should have hung around long enough to find out."

"I did!" Alan frowned. He did not at all enjoy being put on the defensive, or being forced to have to look up at her. Massaging the crick out of his neck, he backed away and sat down on top of the nearby picnic table, before continuing. "They're definitely human, but of extra-terrestrial origin. Their interest in us is purely academic: something to do with searching for evidence of a common ancestry and the planet where the parent race is supposed to have evolved. They kept me too busy playing hide and seek to find out much more."

"Terrific!" she challenged, unwilling to surrender her advantage. "Only, what about all those reports of people abducted by aliens and then later returned with great big holes in their memories? Dead animals found surgically dissected…witnesses, close to the scene of landings, suffering from radiation burn?"

"And the moon is made of green cheese." Patience was beginning to wear dangerously thin. "Look, there have been records alluding to sightings that go back to paintings in caves, and in all that time none of them have come down collecting slaves or with plans of conquest…"

"That we know of," she impatiently completed his sentence for him.

"How about making up your mind, Babe. Are you advocating for or against them?" Alan chided. She did have a point, he forced himself to concede. Both arguments had to be considered and properly weighed. "The reports of most sighting incidents are greatly distorted or made out of whole cloth entirely. At worst, the most any of them may be guilty of is treating us like laboratory specimens," Alan continued. "We've been equally guilty ourselves with species and cultures that we consider inferior or expendable. We're probably as primitive to them as Bushmen appear to us. But that's all strictly academic, as far as I'm concerned. Whether or not they're planning on coming out of the closet, let someone else crowd the hero's bench for a while. I'm tired."

"Such mighty logic leaves not room enough for reason." Dawn plucked a shriveled, mimmified apple and made ready to hurl it at him "Stop me if I'm mis-remembering, but wasn't one of the rationalizations you once dumped on me for building the *Peregrine*, so you could go out on a 'voyage of exploration,' searching for other civilizations out there?" Dawn paused for an over-dramatized gesture that took in the entire firmament. "Races that might, perhaps, be espers like yourself? Well, here's one of those super-races, now, knocking at your own back door. A golden opportunity, wouldn't you say? So what does my big, brave hero do? He prods them with a stick, and then runs like hell when they poke their heads out. If your common sense ever catches up with the rest of you, Flash, you're going to be a real world-beater."

Storm clouds, black as Gertha's coffee, were percolating within his brain. The girl was stepping on some sore toes.

"I'm sorry, Alan," she persisted, her mood as dark now as his own, "but this whole argument of yours is nothing but a threadbare fabric of rationalizations pinned together with all those carefully nurtured phobias of yours. They're almost, but not quite, as dumb as that crap you've been trying to force-feed me about why you have to send me away—'for my own good.'"

"Babe!"

"Knock off that 'Babe' nonsense, too! I'm tired of it. For future reference, my parents gave me a perfectly functional name. Use it!"

"Dawn…"

"That's better! See, you're getting the hang of it now."

Dammit! He was not going to let her get to him! He took several deep breaths, and set his jaw for control. "Dawn! Stop it, and listen, will you! You know I love you: enough to want you to be free, of me and of my esper curse… before it kills you too. For Godsake, girl! Where you're concerned, I'm a hurricane, a flood, name your disaster." He was up and pacing now, knowing too well how a caged tiger must feel.

"Great! Some more shit to dump on the compost pile." Dawn sighed, looking up to heaven as though needed strength might be found there. "Then again, maybe you're right. Hanging onto an irrationally negative attitude like you are, could turn any day into Friday the Thirteenth.

"Alan, please!" She took a deep breath and looked down, extending her right hand to him in a gesture of pleading. "Try thinking with that fantastic brain of yours, instead of your spleen, for a change! After what you've turned me into, the chains we've already forged between ourselves, how can we, either of us, ever truly be free of each other again? We both knew the price when I badgered you into doing for me what you'd done for Garuda.

"You know, you'd be a Jungian analyst's idea of paradise," she laughed bitterly, changing tack once more. "Imagine, a patient who can literally mold the likeness of his anima, the archetypal Eve—his feminine ideal—out of living flesh! Hey, did you ever consider going into production? You wouldn't have to worry then if one of us broke on you."

"I keep telling you, Dawn, other than the life threatening injuries we were dealing with at the time, except for your hair, I only worked on functional problems like eyesight, teeth, hormonal imbalances, recent and old traumas…" He hated the way she kept him on the defensive.

"With apologies to ol' Doc Jung," she persisted angrily, seeming not to have heard a word he said, "we may finally have dug down to the root of your problem, Flash. You're a latent human being, lost in a world full of overts." She lost her hold of the branch she had been sitting on, and started falling. Catching her just barely in time, he suddenly found himself with an armful of wounded fury.

"Dammit, Alan, get off it! I'm not made of glass!" she complained with furious indignation. Her small fists were pounding his chest, trying to drive her point home. "I'm not going to break! Honest! I've been climbing trees all my life. Believe me, I know how far it's safe to jump!"

As her anger found fuel, his was cooling. Shielding was already becoming an automatic, unconscious function, growing stronger and more efficient with practice. He suddenly realized how solidly they were up right now. Even such powerful emotion as she was hurling at him, and from such close range, was bouncing off. "Dawn, you were right! Sonnovabitch! Those thought-forming visualization techniques of Mishra's and your Lady Viviane really work." Laughing out loud, he hurled her into the air, hugging her fiercely as she came down. "Come on, Babe, do your damnedest! Think all the anger and all the hate you can throw at me!"

"Alan!" She pulled back from him with worried suspicion in her eyes. "I think you'd better start adding fluoride to your shampoo. You're developing a cavity in your brain."

"Oh relax! I'm not slipping my gears. Well, not completely anyway," he amended. "It's only that those shielding exercises are working so well, right now, that if I taped your mouth shut and closed my eyes, it would be totally, blissfully quiet out here."

"You don't have a split personality, wasoochie breath; it's completely shredded." Dawn complained angrily, borrowing a favorite expression from Uncle Little Bear as he threw her into the air, once more, caught her, then spun her around.

"Honest, Lover, I..."

"Honest, you're not. With me or yourself," she cut him off, spitefully. "As for being your lover, you won't let me. If you were honest, and I was your lover, it might solve a lot of problems... for both of us." Her anger suddenly melted into a hopeful smile. Her arms wrapped themselves more possessively about his neck as she looked up imploringly. Her moist brown eyes were piercing his soul once more exposing a need he dared not allow expression. "If you can block out that well, maybe you can block in also. Then you wouldn't have to..."

"Forget it! You're still going back. At least until I know, with absolute certainty. Today, in fact." He set her back down, peeling her arms from around his neck. "Now go pack while I find Zarkov and tell him."

"No need. I'm here." The old man's voice came from behind, sounding stern and patriarchal. His teeth were clamped tightly around his ancient pipe as he stood motionless, framed by the sliding glass doors that let out from the spacious living room. "I'm afraid you're going to have to postpone Ms. LaSarde's departure for at least another few weeks, young man. I've had about all I can stand of painting still-lifes and mountain landscapes, and I have quite exhausted the patience of colleagues, friends and family. The dear child has graciously consented to sitting while an old mustache indulges his favorite pastime. Isn't that right?" His stern expression melted into an irritatingly impish grin.

Dawn's stoic smile in reply, as she turned her back on him, was even more infuriating. "Of course, Sir. But really, you're only prolonging the agony. I could talk to The Old Man of The Mountains, he's only made of New Hampshire granite, and get more response. Come to think of it, though, there are millions of women who think he's the greatest thing to come along since indoor plumbing. Perhaps, in the interest of science, I ought to hang around for a while and try to figure out, for Goddess' sake, why!

"Alan!" she suddenly spun around, addressing him directly once more. "Millions of devout worshippers have you on the ballot for Godhood—or at the very least for canonization. The scientific world community holds you in absolute awe. You can all but command entire nations and they'd probably obey without questioning. People either love you with blind loyalty or fear you as the Devil incarnate. But, you know, Flash, I can't, for the life of me, think of anyone who likes you, who considers you a friend—me included.

"Dear Heart, I love you more than words could ever express. I don't think there's anything that could ever stop me from loving you. But. Alan, as a human being, you're nothing but a self-castrated social eunuch!"

Another crack in his fragile armor! It turned out not to be quite as strong yet as he had thought only moments ago. The little Witch could still find the right buttons to push.

Defeated, for the present at least, Alan made a brisk about-face and stormed back into the house, wearing his black shroud of anger wrapped tightly about him for added protection. The next few weeks that Zarkov had purchased so dearly were going to be hell, not only for him, but for all of them.

CHAPTER VIII

DAWN STRETCHED, catlike, and yawned as she stood up trying to work the stiffness out of her limbs. She had spent the last two weeks here on this small garden patio, parked on Dr. Zarkov's stone retaining wall and posing for him. It was amazing how exhausting sitting and trying not to move could be.

"You mean you're finally done? Which did you run out of first, paint or patience?" she asked, dancing to nonexistent music to speed the sluggish return of life into her numb and aching body.

"Both," he smiled sadly as he beckoned her to take her first look at his completed masterpiece.

Half anticipating the usual crude product of most amateur Rembrandts, she was amazed at the bold strokes, the life that vibrated out of the canvas. The golden features were a study in rose-highlighted perfection, framed in long, softly flowing, honey-colored curls. It was the same sulky brown eyes and flawless face that had been staring back at her from the bathroom mirror these past two months, ever since coming here.

"Why so sad, child?" Zarkov looked up. Fatigue had stolen the luster from his gray eyes as well. "Is there something you don't like about the portrait?"

"Yes! It's beautiful. But it's not me," she smiled sadly, turning away to stare off into the distant mountains. "Oh, it's not your fault. You only painted what you saw. This face is really Alan's creation." Even the white dress with plunging neckline, billowing sleeves, form-fitting bodice that made her look more bosomy than she really was, and yards of skirt that made it look disturbingly like a wedding dress was Gertha's choice. Not hers.

"Ah, but the eyes!" He smiled at her, the same way her father used to when she was a little girl and he was trying to console her. "The sadness in those eyes, the gentleness of expression, they are most certainly a very important part of you, and this portrait."

"Oh, Dr. Zarkov, I've tried, but I can't get used to not being me. Not belonging anywhere any more. Alan robbed me of what I was, and now he's rejecting what he's made me into. I'm caught between worlds. I can't go back to what I was and he won't let me be what he's turned me into."

"Perhaps not entirely, but I think I may have at least an inkling." He offered her a knowing glance as he gave an extra roll to the sleeves of his old painting sweater and started cleaning his brushes. "After my Martha died, for months I grieved too much and ate too little, until one day I looked in a mirror and saw a stranger staring back at me too.

"Listen, child! With advancing years, the beauty steals inward if it's to survive at all. It has to; there's nowhere else for it to go." He looked up to throw her a sly wink. "That's why I suppose I'll always find Gertha a most handsome woman." The old professor paused for a moment to refill his pipe before continuing with his brushes. "You already possess that inner beauty. Alan only reversed the process, bringing it up to the surface for everyone to see—a bit prematurely perhaps. Neither of you were prepared to handle it. Remember, it isn't Alan alone who's wanting in the wisdom of maturity.

"Oh, Dawn, dearest child, go slow! You're still, after all, as much a child as he. Be patient with yourself—and with Alan! Seeing the two of you constantly hurting each other pains us, as well."

"I want to, Sir." She breathed a despairing sigh and wilted into one of the cushioned patio chairs. "But he's hardly ever home; and when he is, he spends nearly all his time down there in Space Tech's answer to the Bat Cave. If he isn't counting test tubes or chatting with his computers, he's off somewhere squaring the cube root of pi just to keep busy. When I do finally manage to corner him into a conversation, he gets all bent out of shape, telling me about his favorite phobia-of-the-month. All I hear, most of the time, is what he's going to have to do to protect me from the Big Bad Alan Wolf. He never has any time left over to hear what I'm saying.

"I got so fed up, the other day," she continued with an exasperated smile, "I asked him if I should start wearing garlic and locking him up during full moons. You wouldn't want me to repeat what he answered."

Caught off guard, the old professor laughed so hard he almost spilled the jar of turpentine his brushes were soaking in. Only a quick save prevented an even bigger mess for them to clean up.

"If only Alan would quit treating me like he was the bull and I was the china shop!" Dawn complained as she grabbed a rag to help Zarkov daub at the few small puddles of turpentine that managed to slosh over the rim of the jar onto the small table. "I grew up with a bunch of older brothers who used to throw me around so much I thought

I was a football. And surprise! Here I am, still in one piece, and a whole lot stronger for the experience," she added as she started capping tubes of paint and returning them to their box.

"After all, it is my life we're debating. I should have some say as to where, and with whom, I want to spend it and the risks I'm willing to take. I know the danger is all in his imagination, Dr. Zarkov." She looked up in the vain hope she might find answers in his eyes. "It's his emotions, not his psionics that need schooling. Even if there was a chance the danger were real, though, it'd be worth anything to share even one night of loving him.

"Life itself is one gigantic gamble. Why can't he gamble just a little for me too? When we first met, I couldn't shut him up. Now, I'm Virus X. It's weird. The more deeply I care for him, the further he retreats inside himself."

"Try to understand, Dawn!" Zarkov laid his cleaning rag and brushes down, and returned his brier to the pocket of his painting sweater. Taking both her hands in his, he lead her out of the shade cast by the house into a patch of sunshine near the retaining wall. "Ever since the tragedy that brought him to us, Alan's whole life has held nothing but the isolation imposed by his psionic hypersensitivity. Then, on top of that, discovering he's also possessed of a life expectancy that alienates him even further from those he cares most about. Think, girl! What a daunting prospect that must be! He knows no rest, except in work.

"But you, young lady, your major field of study was psychology." The old professor's manner grew sterner, more reproachful. "You should know better. Alan is a very angry young man. Anger when it's turned inward against itself manifests as depression. When it starts going sideways, as it's been doing lately—with the both of you, may I add— then words become weapons as you tease and tear at each other. Children! Both of you! Nothing but savage, destructive children!"

Zarkov closed his eyes for a moment and took several deep ragged breaths. His exasperation cooled once more to gentle scolding. "I'm well aware how hard it's been for you. But it's been far worse for Alan. He walks the narrow edge between two worlds—the higher worlds of a powerful, but vulnerable esper, and the dark, narrow world the rest of us inhabit. The public is amazingly tolerant. It can forgive almost anything except genius. And this young genius is also a powerful psychokinetic telepath. If this were found out, as quickly as he was made a hero, that's how quickly he'd also become the target of a modern day Witch hunt. You already know how painfully aware he is of that fact. While his amazing intellect is aimed toward the stars, he's at the mercy of all the potholes in the road."

"I don't know." Dawn stared at her fingernails with vacant eyes. Her own despair was beginning to suffocate. "Maybe it was the wisest move I ever made, switching over to research. I'd really have made a lousy therapist. I know Alan has problems. But every time he comes around and starts laying that same old line on me, I turn into his worst problem yet. He's always angry lately, too, and getting worse every day. This morning he was storming and thundering as if it was next month.

"You were buying time, these last few weeks, painting as slow as you could possibly get away with," Dawn sighed deeply. She could no longer deny the utter futility of it all. "Face it! All we managed to accomplish was to keep knocking brick walls into each other. You and Gertha have tried so hard to help, and believe me, I appreciate all your good intentions. But enough! Let it go, please! I can't take any more. If you wouldn't mind driving me to the airport in Sacramento, I can be packed and out of here by tomorrow.

The next time he passes through, tell Alan he won."

"Not on your life!" Zarkov snapped indignantly as he returned to his clean-up chores. "That stubborn idiot brought you here. He damn well can take you home! If he persists in this ridiculous behavior, it's his problem. From now on he can clean up his own messes. No one is going to do anything around here anymore to encourage his insanity." He closed the lid on his paint box with an emphatic thunk. "You know, you just might be on the right track about leaving. Sometimes the best way to convince a fool of his folly is to stand back and let him have his own damn way. But don't you worry, child! I don't plan on making this any picnic for him. Your portrait is going to be hung where he can't help seeing it whenever he's home. I've watched how he looks at you when he's too preoccupied to notice me noticing him.

"Dan's son can be as obstinate as his father was," the old man winked with a sly grin that reminded Dawn of an overgrown leprechaun. "But give him a month, tops, maybe two, and I guarantee he'll be climbing over all of his foolish little phobias, and out of his skin. I know that boy, far better than he realizes. Sooner than he thinks, he'll be coming after you, even if he has to swim to the other side of this galaxy to do it." Chuckling to himself, he retrieved his old pipe, jammed it between his teeth, still unlit, then picked up his paint box and vanished into the house.

Dawn looked up toward the sun. It wasn't quite noon. Intending only to reassure, the old professor's words had fallen far short of their mark. It wasn't her, but the image he had molded her into, she was certain, that Alan was obsessed with. It wasn't her, but the dream she symbolized that drove him. Ghost from a past life or dream fantasy, it mattered little which. Neither was her.

She should have been heading upstairs to pack. The prospect, however, of gathering up all that was her in this house, and then waiting around with nothing left to do but sit and watch her depression grow thorns was not at all inviting. Long walks had always proven therapeutic in the past. Perhaps, right now, a brisk hike would be the best medicine for what ailed her. The more exhausting, the better.

On the other side of the retaining wall, there was a rough path, about a hundred feet down, that had been cut into the gentle, grass-covered slope of the old mountain. She had gazed down there often during the interminable hours of posing while Zarkov painted. It appeared to have been carved out, over the years, by the steady traffic of horses and dirt bikes. She had watched their occasional passing, wondering where the path led and wishing she too might have been on it. Well, at the moment, there was nothing but hell and gravity holding her back. Certainly it had to be better than sitting around, the only guest at her private pity party. She was not about to let any man, not even the Mighty Alan Kolkey, himself, reduce her to that.

Climbing over the wall, she picked and skidded her way down toward the path. As she started walking east, in the direction of the higher peaks she heard the sound of the security chopper heading toward her. It paused to hover so close above her head that she was momentarily caught in the prop wash. It was making its routine pass over the house and grounds. Waving energetically, she put on her friendliest smile to let the pilot and guard, riding shotgun, know that all was well. Recognizing her from several occasions when she had been allowed to ride along with them for the afternoon, sharing conversation, sandwiches and thermos coffee, they shouted greetings down to her over the roar of the whirling blades and a warning not to wander off too far. She was relieved when the chopper finally vanished over the far side of the slope and she could once again hear birds and insects going about the more important business of living.

As Dawn followed the narrow pathway, almost nonexistent in some places, her mind traveled backward in time, reliving everything that had happened since Alan's "conquest" of Kali. For so long now, it had been a permanent resident in both day and nighttime sky. In truth, it had been Mother Kali who had conquered Alan Kolkey.

She tried to make sense of it, to find some purpose behind it all, and some logical reason for Alan's paranoid fear of his esper 'curse', as called it. What was it, specifically, that he really feared? And for Goddess' sake, what the hell was she doing here, in the first place? She was New England. She was country. Her only legitimate claim to fame was being the prosaic research assistant of a very caring, very brilliant parapsychologist. She was not made of the fabric from which the consort of Earth's misanthropic young champion ought to have been cut. She would have been content to have spent the rest of her life in meditative obscurity, seeking peace and inner wisdom, with Rama as her gentle guru, and perhaps, some day, husband. Instead, here she was picking her way along a mountain path, while desperately clinging to what precious little sanity and self-respect remained in the wake of her frenzied encounters with a man who could control the destinies of nations, but not the giant surge of his own emotions. Whether or not she liked it, whether or not they remained together, their paths were forever bound up in this hopeless tangle. After having altered her so drastically, having giving her a life expectancy as great as his own, Alan had slammed forever the door that lead back home. What had been, no longer existed for her.

The path began leading upward at an increasingly noticeable incline, though still meandering in a generally eastward direction toward who-knew-or-cared-where. Dawn tried to cheer herself by focusing the spotlight of memory on those few and far between moments when Alan was home and had forgotten himself enough to share a confidence or a respite of quiet conversation. By then she had learned a lesson or two and had been especially careful not to break the fragile spell by further confrontation or demands.

One of the happiest of these had been two weekends ago when Stan came up with his family for a visit. Alan had surprised everyone by joining them at the table. He had even stayed for after-dinner coffee, thoroughly enjoying himself when Gertha's grandsons started climbing all over him like fleas on a dog and dragging him down onto the floor with them. Laughing and pummeling in playful abandon, they had refused to allow him up until he promised them their long overdue family concert. After a heated debate over whose turn it was, eight-year-old Jared, the younger of Stan's two boys, had been appointed to run and fetch the guitar that Alan kept in his room, upstairs. He had warmed up on some traditional country and gospel for Gertha and T'shanna, her daughter-in-law. He played a few of the old favorites that were guaranteed to bring tears to the old professor's eyes. Then, finally, the highlight of the evening: what the boys had been screaming impatiently for all evening. With Stan on piano and Alan on Guitar, they offered their "infamous" laundered-for-young-ears rendition of "The Dozens." Their musical salvos, back and forth, of insults set to rhyme and meter had Gertha and Reverend Haley, their dinner guest every Sunday, muttering in pretended outrage, while the boys urged them on with laughter and verbal challenges as they clapped in tempo to the music.

Later, ganged up on by Stan and his two sons, Alan had rendered several contemporary rock favorites that had Gertha and Zarkov up on their feet, trying to dance along. Jesse, Stan's eleven-year-old swinger, had come close to tripping them several times in his eagerness to demonstrate how it ought to have been done.

Dawn had never seen Alan so relaxed, or so full of laughter. Badgered into it by Reverend Haley and the boys, he had even danced with her. She had found it amazing that someone so large, so heavily muscled could also have been so gracefully well-coordinated.

"Would you prefer me swinging from a tree with a banana in one hand, and shouting like Tarzan?" he had grinned, replying to her unvoiced commentary.

"Don't they make a lovely couple?" she had overheard Gertha asking her daughter-in-law. How many times had those same words been said at Bluebeard's weddings, she had thought to herself. Suddenly, she had looked up to find Alan scowling bleakly down on her.

That night she had seen a side of him that had made her love him more than ever. If only she had been able to inspire the freedom and spontaneity in him that children or his music could, perhaps she might not have been leaving tomorrow. Or ever.

He had warmed to her so encouragingly that evening. She had even dared to dream of a fresh beginning, to hope he might at last be outgrowing his irrational fears. He had been gone, though, next morning when she got up, and this time it was more than a week before she saw him again. That was when he had begun growling at her. And everyone else as well.

She had been walking for almost two hours when exhaustion finally overtook, quieting the bedlam in her aching brain. She found an inviting patch of grassy incline and collapsed onto it. The sun was warm, soothing her protesting muscles. Closing her eyes, she slept her first untroubled sleep in weeks.

"Damn! If that ain't the purtiest sight these here sun-parched eyes ever seen!"

Startled awake, Dawn found herself looking up at a wire-thin young man, seated astride a well-muscled bay gelding. Horse and denim-clad rider both wore the dust of several days riding. Bedroll, rifle and laden saddlebags completed the impression of an Old West trail hand, fresh from a cattle drive.

"You all right, ma'am?" The wide-brimmed hat he wore hid his features in shadow but there was no mistaking the broad, boyish grin he flashed in response to an answering nod of her head.

"What in blazes you doin' way out here, all alone an' dressed like that!" He climbed down and unfastened a canteen from the saddle. "You must be a might thirsty 'bout now." He unscrewed the cap and sat down as he handed her the container.

"Thanks." She forced a smile and sat up to accept his offering. The water was warm, but clean and sweet, trickling down past painfully dry lips. "I… I'm staying with friends," she managed to explain after several more swallows made speech a little less of an ordeal. "They live several miles west of here, along this trail. I'm really not sure how far, or how long, I've been hiking. I was upset about something and needed to walk it off. I guess I overdid a bit."

"I hope to tell you! Nearest place I know of here 'bout's a six, eight mile hike down that path. That there was one hell of a stroll for ground like this; 'specially dressed like that. " He chuckled good-naturedly as he removed his hat to wipe away an accumulation of dust and sweat with a large blue-and-white handkerchief dug out from a back pocket. "Yes sir! That there's a mighty nice dress. But not 'xactly what I'd recommend for this neighborhood or fer nappin' out here in the sun. It's a wonder you ain't all burnt up and sunstroked. Them sandals are mighty pretty too, ma'am, but they ain't 'xactly hikin' shoes neither.

That's fer damn sure! Yer feet must really be talkin' back at you 'bout now."

"Oh, don't you know it!" She winced in pain as she tried to stand, gave up and sat back down.

"I think ye'd best accept the hospitality of me and my pardner, Ben, over there, for a lift home," he laughed. "You stayin' at the ol' professor's place?"

She offered an affirmative nod as she brushed grassy debris out of her hair and clothes.

"Raised quite a ruckus round these parts, some years ago, when he married hisself a nigger lady so's he could 'dopt the son a' some friend who'd jest died." The boyish grin melted into self-contrition. "I shouldn't ought'a call her that. Folks used to think a' her that way. But when someone's ailin' an' can't afford no hospital, she's always there, helpin' ol' Doc Brewster take care a' them. She saw my ma through her last sickness. Towards the last, she hardly left her side. No! Ain't no one gonna' say bad 'bout that fine lady while I'm 'round.

"But Al, now! Ain't got no problem sharin' stories 'bout him." He laughed, screwing his face into a comical half-frown. "Tell me, is he still as tetched as folks 'round here say he is?"

"I don't know. How 'tetched' do folks say he is?" Dawn shrugged and tried not to laugh at Alan's expense.

"Well, they say he ain't been right since livin' through the crash that took his ma an' pa." The young "cowpoke" frowned as he returned his hat to his head then adjusted it for more shade before getting into his story. "When we was kids together, we both sang in Reverend Haley's choir at church. The girls'd all drool over him like he was candy or such. But he never had no use for 'em. Er any of us kids, fer that matter. So, we finally jest decided he was queer er tetched. Er both. An' then left him alone too. He dropped out'a choir when we was both 'bout fifteen. Then gradually, he jest quit comin' t' church altogether.

"We see the Professor an' Gerth… Miz Zarkov in town often 'nough. But after Al bought inta Space Tech, an' then gradually started takin' over, he set up that security compound a few miles from here…" Dawn's rescuer paused to gesture in an easterly direction. "All that heavy security and umpteen skillion guards 'round the compound an' house, 'bout swallowed him up better'n a grave, until that 'Kali' thing suddenly shook 'im loose an' made 'im famous. Still don't hardly socialize with no one, far as I can see. There's the reverend though. Has dinner there every Sunday. There's ol' Red an' Hey-suus, too. They're dep'ties. Patrol the roads 'round here. Ye must'a met 'em both by now. They're always checkin' on folks when they're out on patrol: seein' they're all right, an' tradin' gossip fer coffee an' eats. All they'll ever say is, yeah, he's alive. If you wanna call that livin. Yeah, he still lives at home. An' yeah, he's still mighty unsociable.

"Read a while ago, too, where Al still ain't got no use fer the ladies. But after savin' yer life an' then takin' you back home with him… You *are* the lady all the newpaper an' TV reporters are still writin' 'bout, ain't you? It kind'a puts the lie to them stories. You bein' up there, livin' with him an' all. He sure has got hisself one mighty sweet filly!" He looked up, a disappointed smile tugging at the corners of his mouth.

"Correction: Alan doesn't have me." Dawn tried to hide her bitterness behind a busy pretense of draping her skirt more modestly over her knees and searching for bits of grass to brush away. "He finds computer chips and space ships a lot safer than people."

"You mean a powerful purty gal like you, right there under his nose, an' he ain't never tried to put his brand on you!" Her companion looked dumbfounded. "Somethin's gotta' be ailin' that boy, even worse'n we thought," he added, shaking his head in continued disbelief.

"Hey! Look at me!" He suddenly brightened, trading the frown for his boyish grin once more. "Here I am, gossipin' like an ol' ranch wife 'bout the people you're takin' hospitality from, an' I ain't even innerduced myself! Name's Beau. Beau Reynolds. Me an' Pa, we own a small ranch down the valley." His features were angular, his skin nut-brown and weather-toughened, almost the same shade as his matted hair and the three-day accumulation of stubble on his chin that gave him a wild, vagrant look. His hazel eyes were warm though, with a quiet humor that had put her off guard from the moment she had first seen him.

"And I'm Dawn LaSarde. I come from back East, New Hampshire." Managing to climb back onto her feet this time, she brushed grass and wrinkles from the back of her dress once more, then walked over to stroke the muzzle of the bay. "Beautiful animal! Looks to be part Morgan and Quarter Horse."

"Say, you know your horseflesh!" he laughed, pleasantly surprised as he secured his canteen behind the saddle once more.

"I ought to," she smiled back. "I grew up on a farm, myself, in New Hampshire. Dad's a lawyer, but his first love is horses. We've always kept three or four for riding, along with the Clydesdales Dad used to breed and train for show. They've won him a lot of ribbons—and beer—over the years. There's a brewery not too far from us that uses the breed as their trademark."

"Now ain't that a coincidence!" he clucked, checking the saddle and girth straps. "Ol' Ben, here, his dam's a Morgan we bought, 'bout five years back, on a trip to Vermont. Got relatives on my ma's side up there. That ain't too far away from you. We bred her to a champion Quarter Horse a friend of ours lets out for stud. But there are times I'd swear Ben's sire was a mule. He can be that ornery. He's great company out on huntin' trips like this though."

"Oh! I was wondering how come the heavy artillery."

"Yeah. I needed a couple days away from Pa, an' figgered, while I was out here, to bring back some venison fer the freezer."

"Any luck?"

"Ain't really been tryin' yet. Still workin' on unwindin' an' jest havin' me a good ol' time knockin' 'round the high country." He flashed her a brief grin, that turned to squint as he gazed briefly in the general direction of the sun. It was hanging threateningly low on the western horizon. "Say, it's gettin' on. If you don't want'a be stuck campin' out with me all night we'd best be on our way.

"Ma'am?" he suddenly grew serious. "I was wonderin' if I might have permission to come callin'. I know I ain't tall or good lookin' like Al. An' I sure as hell ain't as rich, but cleaned up an' in my Sunday clothes, I really ain't too bad. Ain't never been a real ladies' man, neither. But Pa taught me how to treat a lady like she oughta' be, an'..."

"That's awfully sweet, Beau, but I'm going home tomorrow," Dawn smiled politely, hoping to discourage him.

"No you ain't, Ma'am! Not if I can convince you to stay on, between here n' the professor's place," he announced with confident sincerity. Both hands, resting firmly on her shoulders, commanded her attention. "Like I said, you are one awful purty lady. You got a whole lot more educatin' n' me. An' I know you deserve a whole lot better. But our spread gives us a real comfortable livin'. You'd have to go a hell of a ways to find anything finer than our valley or grander than these mountains. An' Ma'am, if you'd jest gimme a chance to prove myself, I could give you all the lovin' an' cherishin' you could ever ask for."

Dawn was trying to free herself from Beau's impulsive embrace when a high-pitched scream from above ripped through the silence of the wilderness. Wings folded back in a power dive, a spotted eagle, so huge it had to be Garuda, was aimed directly at her gamey, trail-worn Galahad.

"Get back a' me, ma'am!" he shouted, yanking her to the ground behind him as he unsheathed his rifle and aimed it. Before he had time to get off a shot, the weapon went flying out of his grasp, as if wrenched away by invisible hands.

The sound of deep baritone laughter echoed above them as Garuda pulled himself up out of his dive, inches away from Beau's head. Eyes wide, teeth clenched firmly, Beau looked almost as frightened as Ben, as he leapt for the reins to keep the terrified horse from bolting.

Searching the rocks overhead, Dawn spotted Alan standing smugly on an outcropping, looking vastly amused.

"Ma'am, quick!" Beau shouted, reaching down. Somehow he had managed to climb into the saddle and was holding his mount reasonably steady next to her. Irate at Alan's juvenile display, Dawn decided to let Beau 'rescue' her. As she reached out to take his hand and grope for a foothold in the stirrup, Garuda wheeled and dove once more, cutting a feathered arc between them and knocking her down.

Eyes ringed white with panic, the horse reared, screamed, and bolted. Beau was a helpless passenger as Ben tore eastward, crazed with a madness Dawn suspected was far more than merely the animal's instinctive response to Garuda's attack.

"That old plug won't stop till he bangs into a mountain." Alan laughed and jumped down to offer her a hand climbing back onto her feet. "It's Sunday. No one else around. Lucky for you, I happened to be here working on the *Peregrine* today."

"Oh good grief! Will you please pull your head off and screw it back on straight!" Dawn indulged herself in some well-deserved outrage as she ignored his outstretched hand and climbed to her feet unaided. "Who did you think you were rescuing me from, 'The Mad Rapist of the Rockies'? The 'Sonora Strangler'? Come on! You knew damn well the poor guy was only trying to give me a lift home. So, big deal, he got a little carried away. Nothing I couldn't have handled on my own. Surprise! I'm a big girl, now. I have four older brothers and a father who all ganged up to make sure I learned enough judo and karaté to keep any man in line. You, of all people, ought to know that. We've been sharing each others' memory engrams for over two months now.

"Damn! Wouldn't you know!" She complained, shifting from outrage to exasperation as she brushed grass from her hair and clothes for the third time. "I walk for miles trying to get you out of my head, for a little while at least. And where do I land? Right smack on top of the old 'Bat Cave' itself. How's that for a lousy run of luck!"

"Well… Not exactly right on top…"

"Oh, for the Goddess' sake: give it a rest, will you!" She was almost screaming now. "What the hell are you doing home, anyway? No world-shattering crises to run off to? How about that. The UN must have had an open date on its disaster calendar."

"No," he dithered, not appearing to know what to do with his hands as his eyes devoured her hungrily. "Actually, I—had to lay over for a while to repair a bug in the *Peregrine's* computer system software."

"What happened? Did some of the beads get stuck?"

"Dawn!"

"Oh, go back and fix it, will you, so you can fly back out of here! I'm sure President Moshey can't wait till you go up and find out what's inside the Big Dipper."

"Dawn!" he shouted her down, grabbing her arms so she could not back away from him again. Silent, unmoving now, he stood there, hovering, staring at her with the penetrating intensity of x-rays. Gnawing at his lower lip, his face registered intense pain, as though some giant conflict were being waged within him. Hesitantly, he reached up to brush the tips of his fingers across her cheek. The fierce gaze of his cerulean eyes followed, as his hand traveled down her neck to touch her left breast, awkwardly caressing and tracing its contours. His breathing grew shallow, forced, wrenching an agonized whimper from his throat. The last of his 'noble' resolve crumbled, as he pulled her into a vice-strong embrace. His taut lips, against hers, were hard, hungry, painfully demanding.

How many times, since meeting this mass of contradictions and conflicting emotions, had she dreamed of this moment when his need for her would consume all else. How many times had she wakened in the night, wanting the taste of him so desperately that she would have bargained for him on any terms; when, but for the fear of humiliating rejection, she would have thrown herself before him, a naked, living altar, in the Great Rite of the Goddess, Herself. Now here he was, a slave to Eros, in abject surrender. But was surrender what she really wanted? And just who the hell was he surrendering to?

Certainly not her! Dawn LaSarde had never moved any man to uncontrolled passion in her entire life. Perhaps a little interest, now and again, but never passion, controlled or otherwise. Not even Rama. Especially not Rama! No, it was not her who had inspired such uncontainable desire in Alan, but the image of the dying priestess in his dream fantasy, a woman he had convinced himself, from the beginning, was her, reborn from some ancient shared lifetime.

To simply lie back and passively allow him, even fumbling his way through a first attempt, was unthinkable. It was like being a captive voyeur, forced to watch from behind a one-way mirror while the man she loved made love to another woman. She wanted to pound his chest and scream for him to find her, to let her out and make love to her. The real Dawn LaSarde. Before she ceased entirely to exist.

Furious, resentful, she managed somehow to break free of his painfully clumsy embrace, then ran, cursing him with every colorful invective she could wrap tongue around.

Her lungs were screaming their message of agony along every nerve fiber in her body before she allowed herself to stop. Half hoping for, half dreading pursuit, she ducked for cover behind an elbow of rock. It was such a childishly futile gesture. If Alan truly wanted to find her, an entire galaxy would not be enough to lose herself in. The world had time to grind to a halt, and creation begin anew before she could breathe comfortably once more.

Cautiously, she peered out from behind her rock, again half certain he would be waiting to pounce on her. There was nothing out there other than her own tracks in the trail dust. She heard nothing, other than the echo of her despair floating on the silence of oppressively still air. Relief turned to disappointment. Perhaps, if he had followed, overtaken her, perhaps if they had gone at it fang and claw, in open confrontation—got all their shared hurt and anger outside where it could be examined—she might have reached him, forced him to find her. To make love to her this time.

Dawn looked up at the sky. It was rapidly darkening as a molten cauldron of black clouds seethed in to block the late afternoon sun. She could feel the mounting static of an approaching storm crawling over her skin. Nature was recreating, on a far grander scale, the storm already raging within her.

She recalled little of her journey back except the rapidly coalescing resolve to return home alone. Tonight, if the old professor or one of the security people would be willing to drive her down to Sonora, she could grab a bus the rest of the way into Sacramento. As soon as she had a flight schedule, a call home would have her father waiting for her at the airport in Lebanon, New Hampshire. No need to waste time packing. There was nothing Alan's money had bought that she wanted to bring back.

School would have to be a thing of the past, now. There would be too much notoriety attached to her from her connection with Alan Kolkey—something neither the university nor Rama needed. It would also be too cruel a hypocrisy to go back to Rama. How could there ever be room enough for any other man when she knew her universe would always orbit around Alan's, forever chained to him by the bonds forged during the psychic "surgery" that had soul-welded them into one single entity. Why even try! She would only end up hating, pitying, resenting any man who tried to take his place. She had been too changed by Alan. She was too different, too like him now, to belong anywhere else but at his side.

No! Despite all he had done to strip away her identity, her individuality, she had always been—would always continue to be—a survivor. Perhaps never again a happy survivor, but a survivor, nonetheless. Somehow, despite her altered appearance, her abnormally expanded life span, the notoriety now attached to her name, she would endure! With her father's help and his connections, she could change her identity, adopt a reclusive lifestyle similar to Alan's. She would become a nomad, a drifter, never putting down roots, never allowing herself the luxury of any but the most superficial attachments. Alan's cowardly betrayal was more than enough pain for several lifetimes.

She would never again leave herself so open, so vulnerable. Perhaps, in years to come, when the tedium of life finally became too much to endure there were ways to court the healing embrace of Herne, God of the Wild Hunt and Lord of Death and Regeneration.

•••

Night had almost completely taken over. A cold wind had whipped up, driving a stinging rain before it by the time Dawn finally limped through the patio doors into the old professor's living room, somehow touching off all the alarms in the house.

"My Lord, child! Where on Earth have you been!" Gertha came at her like an avenging angel. "For Heaven's sake, Old Man, turn off those alarms and let Security know we haven't been invaded!" she called out above the din, as she began stripping off drenched clothes. Removing her own terrycloth robe, she hurriedly wrapped it around Dawn's shivering naked body.

The brain-blasting symphony of sirens and shrieks had died down. Zarkov reappeared, pushed a soft armchair close to the fireplace, where a log was cheerfully crackling and shooting sparks up the chimney, then swaddling her in an afghan coaxed her down into it.

He pulled up a straight-back chair for himself and started massaging her icy fingers. "We were so worried! Gertha doesn't think as much of Space Tech's own security people as she does Red and Jesus. When we called down to the sheriff's office, half an hour ago, they were just coming on shift. They should be here any time now. They'll certainly be relieved to see you're all right."

When she had first met them, Red Phillips and Jesus Mendez had proven a bit too macho for Dawn's taste. But, then again, how much more macho could anyone get than wrapping himself inside the persona of the infallible hero, advisor to nations, needing nothing and no one save himself? Yet somehow, she had managed to find the hiding place for Alan's humanity, even if he had not been able to.

Just so, she had peeked around the official badges and found two new friends. The frequent, though brief, visits of the Tuolumne County deputies who patrolled this area, trading coffee for local gossip, had always been pleasant evening diversions. Gertha was skilled in plying them with bribes of fresh-baked temptations to coax out the lurid details of a recent scandal or some local crime the Department was investigating. Dawn knew she would be in for rough indoor weather too, after the initial relief had worn off. Red's temper could be as blustery as Gertha's. He would be uncompromising as he read her the Riot Act for such irresponsible behavior. Running off into the mountains! Alone! Telling no one! Not even dressed properly for the terrain and the unpredictability of the season!

And Jesus! Not much older than she, he could be counted on to smother her in blankets of paternal advice. Still, if she could only survive this next ordeal and somehow manage to look appropriately contrite, perhaps the two deputies might be prevailed upon to give her the needed lift into Sonora, sparing Dr. Zarkov the imposition.

"Here, child, wrap your hands around this. It'll warm your fingers as well as your belly." Gertha reached out a steaming mug of chicken soup, then pulled up a chair. "Now! What happened? You look like death warmed over twice."

She was putting the finishing embellishments on her story when she heard the heavy pounding of boots on the basement stairs. Alan was standing motionless in the front hallway, staring at her, when she looked up. His features were distorted into a mask of rage, his fists clenched white with nervous kneading of sweating palms. Storm clouds were gathering behind his eyes, readying themselves to loose their thunderbolts. He was the Great God Wrath, incarnate, Lord of the Tempest! Outside, lightning and thunder acknowledged his rule. A shudder, like the vibrations of a tuning fork traveled through the length of his body.

Let him loose his bolts! Dawn sat up straighter in her chair and refused to be intimidated.

"Here he is, world! Champion of Justice, Defender of the Downtrodden... and if you scratch his tummy, he'll roll over and play dead." The open sneer in her voice brought Alan's head up with a jerk.

"As always, touchy as a misanthropic cobra," she loosed a second verbal arrow." No response. Again. "Oh for Goddess' sake, say something, will you!" she set her mug down and struggled out of the afghan, and onto her feet. They were scratched, bruised, and painfully swollen, yet only a minor discomfort compared to the invisible wounds Alan had inflicted, deep within, where blood would not flow. "Ever since you brought me here, I've been trying to light a fire under you. But all I've got, so far to show for it, is a soggy log and a fistful of wet matches. Honest, Flash, you are so mixed up! I swear, they could stick you inside a Waring blender and you'd never know the difference."

"Dammit, woman! What the hell more do you want from me?" His voice was hoarse, and cracked several times under the strain of emotional overload. "You won! You had me exactly where you've been angling to get me ever since I brought you here. And then you ran away!"

"That's odd! Nobody told me this was supposed to be a contest. I won? What is it I'm supposed to have won?" She was standing close now, poking an angry finger, like a drill bit, into his chest. "Near as I'm able to figure it, any man who thinks letting go and allowing himself to love someone else is losing the 'good fight' —is just plain sick.

I'd be tempted to call Uncle Little Bear, except I'm afraid, if he tried to heal you, his fingernails would probably fall off.

"Dammit!" She was almost shouting now. "I'm not a toy. I don't break that easily. I'm no one's possession, either. How dare you, or anyone else, presume to tell me what chances I may and may not take with my life, or where and with whom it's safe for me to be. Ever since I met you, nobody even bothers asking 'May I' any more; they simply go ahead and do with me anything they like. For my own good, of course.

"And another thing, while we're on the subject, ever since we met, all I've been hearing is this endless breast-beating diatribe over your esper 'curse': how you 'killed your parents' and how you're so afraid you're going to kill me too." As she continued jabbing her finger into him, he backed away. Pressing her advantage, she continued goading him. "Did it ever occur to you, if I really was the priestess in your dream, I died back in that other lifetime because, for some unknown reason, you had abandoned me? Now you're doing it again. Your specialty seems to be stirring up the pot, then, when it gets too hot to handle, running like hell. Apparently, that's how you handled it then and that's how you're handling it now. Karma isn't Someone upstairs who punishes when we've been bad little girls and boys. We have to keep doing it and doing it... and doing it... until we finally get it right. So for Goddess' sake, Alan, grow up and quit dragging us through this, lifetime after lifetime!

"I loved you, you asshole! I really loved you!" She was calling up all the vitriol now that had so long been suppressed. "But right from the first day at the UN, it was the priestess in that recurring dream of yours that you were really in love with. Only you couldn't have her, so you made me over in her image. It may have been me, back in some other lifetime, but it isn't me anymore. You don't even know I exist. And you'd rather suffer alone in stoic mega-macho silence than to face up to your problems, much less let anyone far enough in to help."

"Right, dammit! You're right!" he erupted, a human volcano, as he rammed his fist through the wall sending a spray of plaster and dust in every direction. "Can't you see? You'd be better off mated to a king cobra. For Godsake, get out of here before I end up killing us both. Get out!" His eyes flamed red as molten lava. His words burned deep.

She looked up at his fiercely handsome face, distorted now by almost maniacal rage. All the grief and pain, dammed up since coming here, suddenly transmuted into a fury of her own. It could no longer be contained. "You yellow-bellied bastard! You bet I'm leaving! But it won't be back home where you found me. Or to Rama. Because of you, I'm a stranger and a liability now to my own family; and I hurt the kindest, gentlest man I've ever known. I can't go back to him. Or to any other man for that matter. You've seen to that too. Not so bad for a few month's work, is it?"

Bolting for the front door, Dawn dodged his first attempt to grab her. She ducked around him and was halfway down the hall before his second grab connected.

"You little idiot! Your brain must have warped out in all that rain. It's dark and it's storming out there. Get upstairs and pack! Tomorrow's soon enough."

"The hell it is!" she screamed over the thunder and pounding rain. "And what's to pack? I came here with nothing; you gave me nothing; now I'll leave with nothing. You created your own very private little hell, and you've made it abundantly clear there's only room enough for one. So cherish all those insane little phobias of yours! Hold on tight! Because, Mister, pretty soon, they'll be all the friends you have left. Gertha, Dr. Zarkov, even President Moshey, they've all tried to reach you. How much longer before they give up on you or you end up chasing them away, too?"

Alan's grip on her arms grew fiercer, but the rage rising up within her finally went critical and exploded. Turning the force of her nuclear blast on him, she sank her teeth into the flesh of his left wrist and bit down till her jaws ached and she drew blood. She could feel his startled disbelief as he momentarily loosed his hold on her. Wheeling about once more, she slapped him with all the force desperation could muster. The sharp blow left a scarlet handprint on his cheek as he backed away from her. The emotional gratification was almost compensation for the white hot pain that shot through her hand and all the way up her arm.

Startled by the chutzpa, the sheer effrontery of her little mosquito bite, he hesitated. Just long enough for her to make it to the front door. Opening it, she bolted outside, quickly losing herself under a blanket of darkness and driving rain.

CHAPTER IX

THE RAW mountain wind whipped about, stinging Dawn's face. Tears that would no longer be contained poured out and mingled with the rain pelting her cheeks. Her bare feet slipped on a patch of mud. She went down, picked herself up, and continued running down the road. She slipped and fell again.

Headlights coming up and around a turn pierced the near-total darkness sandwiched between flashes of lightning that intermittently ignited the sky. The path of light traced by them slowed then came to a full stop hard by where she lay struggling to rise. Another moment and then two uniformed men were stooping over her, scooping her up, and carrying her to their car. Shivering uncontrollably, she was deposited into the back seat. A blanket was dug out of the trunk and she was wrapped in it like a caterpillar in a cocoon, her head barely poking through. Hot coffee poured from a thermos was gently coaxed down her throat.

"You? Damn! What in blazes you doing out here, girl? Doc and Gertha are half sick with worry fer you." It was Red Phillips, growling as he and Jesus Mendez climbed back into the front seat of the cruiser. He could scold more effectively than even Gertha and was the older of the two deputies. Even though his hair had long since gone grey, he held title to the appellation by virtue of his still-fiery temperament.

"Ignore him, Dawn! He had a fight with the sheriff and he's got a hair across his ass tonight. You OK?" Mendez' eyes communicated genuine concern. She knew Red liked her, but Jesus never had the problems he did expressing his feelings. Jesus was short, dark-haired, with large glowing eyes. His youthful features had access to an entire library of dramatic expressions. He always seemed to be in the middle of some project, always had something newsy to chat about.

She offered an affirmative nod, biting her lip in an effort not to behave foolishly in front of them.

"Good!" Mendez took the empty cup and screwed it back onto the thermos as Phillips released the brake. "Now, let's get you back home. You can tell us what happened later when you're up to it."

"Please, Red! I don't want to go back there." She reached around the bucket seat in front to touch his shoulder imploringly. "Could you take me into Sonora instead? I can grab the next bus from there to the airport in Sacramento."

Red stepped hard on the brakes, bringing the car back to an abrupt stop. "Did Gertha or Doc say something? I can't believe..."

"Oh no!" She hurried to correct his misapprehension as she struggled to retract her arm back inside the warmth of the blanket.

"Al, then! I should'a known! What'd that bastard do to make you run like that!" Red was full of righteous wrath as he turned around to look at her. "The way he constantly avoids everyone, I always figgered he wasn't wrapped too tight. But... Look, we'll take you down to the Sheriff's office and patch in a call on the way to let Doc know you're all right. You can dry off there, call for flight schedules, make whatever travel arrangements you need to. Then we'll drive you to the airport ourselves. And if you want to press charges..."

"Oh no, Red! It was nothing like that. We had a pretty serious fight, but... I mean he didn't beat me or try to..." Dawn protested, shaking her head. She didn't want the two deputies thinking Alan was some sort of monster, even if he seemed to think he was.

"What was it, then?" Mendez frowned. "It had to have been a lot worse than a lover's spat to send you out into a night like this."

"It was," she admitted, unable to explain further. Sniffling unbecomingly, she tried to control another bout of shivering.

"Maybe leaving's the best, Dawn." Mendez offered one of his paternal smiles as he reached for the thermos, poured another cup of coffee and handed it back to her. "I mean it! If rudeness were snow, that *hijo de cabrone* would be a blizzard. Sometimes I wonder if the best part of him didn't leak down his father's leg."

"Hay-suus's right, Dawn," Phillips agreed, turning the car around and aiming it back in the direction of town. He always deliberately exaggerated the Spanish pronunciation of his partner's name. There was a friendly rivalry between the two deputies that always made conversations between them both lively and entertaining. "The guy's smart, all right. Jeeze, is that bastard smart! And I know none of us would be here tonight if he hadn't stopped that runaway comet the way he did. But still, Al's personality is way too far off plumb. Even a darlin' like you ain't ever gonna' penetrate that elephant hide he wears for skin. You'll find someone else a whole lot better. Wait and see!" Dawn caught the flash of his reassuring smile in the rear view mirror.

"Oh shit!" Phillips swore, slamming on the brakes again. "Was I sniffin' glue, or were you barefoot and wearing only a bathrobe five sizes too big when we picked you up?" he asked, frowning at her over the head rest of his bucket seat. "We're gonna' have to go back to the Doc's. Don't worry! We'll be waitin' right in earshot while you put on some clothes for traveling and pack a bag. We'll make damn certain Al don't hassle you one bit. I promise! Then, like I said, we'll take you directly to the airport ourselves. OK?"

"Not OK!" she persisted. "Please Red, I can't go back to that house again. When you call to let the old people know I'm safe, ask if they'll bring me a change of clothes."

"Dammit! What the hell did the bastard do to make you feel that strongly!" Phillips grumbled as he shifted the car into drive and started, once more, for Sonora. "Dawn, you sure you don't want to file a complaint?"

The windshield wipers maintained a monotonous rhythm barely audible over the roar of prowling thunder and rain slamming against metal. The patrol car's headlights hardly pierced the drenching downpour ahead of them. The air was heavy with the astringent smell of ozone as jagged lightning intermittently turned night into day. Between each bolt, the darkness that poured back in took on tangible weight and substance, making it feel as though they were moving in slow motion through thick black soup.

As she sipped hot coffee, trying to warm the icy cold spot at the pit of her soul, Dawn listened with half-hearted interest while Mendez patched a call through the switchboard back at the sheriff's office.

"No answer. They're probably out searching for you themselves by now, along with Space Tech's entire security staff," Red supposed. "Don't worry though. We'll keep trying until we get through to them."

They had been traveling for nearly a half hour when a fork of lightning arced across the sky, frighteningly close. For an instant, obscured in the downpour, she recognized a familiar blood red silhouette hovering above them in the distance. The sky darkened and then it was gone.

The heavens lit up once more, ripped open by one bolt fiercer than all the rest so far. She saw it smash into something that looked like a saucer-shaped craft, not too far from where she thought she had seen the *Peregrine*. The vessel shuddered, tilted drunkenly and was beginning to plummet toward the ground just ahead of them when the sky closed up once more.

"Whatever that damned thing is, it looks like it's gonna come down near Fitzgerald's farm. We better investigate." Phillip's foot hit the accelerator—hard, knocking Dawn back into her seat.

A sharp swerve, and then they were headed uphill on a narrow side road. They turned again, this time onto a dirt side road full of corkscrew turns. It had been reduced by now to little more than a muddy cow path. Then she saw it: a huge ship, larger even than Alan's *Peregrine*. It reminded her of a giant frisbee. Apparently, it had managed a semi-controlled landing that had dug a nearly half-mile-long furrow across a pasture. Before coming to a complete stop, it had plowed half-way through an old wood-frame farmhouse, setting it afire. The area was illuminated by the rapid play of lightning across the sky and flames that were beginning to shoot from several windows. It provided tortured, distorted images one might see during a particularly bad acid trip. The vessel appeared, at least, to have suffered no external structural damage.

"*Madre de Dios!*" Mendez whispered, crossing himself.

"Shut up and let's go!" Phillips shouted, jumping out as the patrol car skidded to a halt behind the cover of several fruit trees. A brisk radioed report, and then Mendez followed. Dawn heard them fumbling around in the trunk. Wriggling free from the restraint of the blanket, still wrapped around her, she turned to watch the two deputies running toward the house. They were carrying high-powered rifles.

A hatch had opened in the side of the ship, spilling out a dozen or more strangely uniformed, helmeted figures. Some of them appeared intent on putting out the blaze while others were concentrating their efforts on effecting exterior repairs of some sort.

Phillips and Mendez were joined by an older bearded man in badly worn denims and a boy still in his teens. Both were armed with smaller hunting rifles. There were exaggerated gesturings pointing toward the house as they spoke. Then Mendez, following the older man, ran toward the house, climbing in a window on the side furthest from the crippled UFO. Phillips and the boy, weapons aimed, were covering them.

The idiots looked like they were about to open fire at any moment. Common sense, comprised of a little intuition a large measure of logic and an understanding of behavioral psychology, told her there was no hostile intent on the part of this strange craft's crew members. They were as much victims of elementals on a rampage as were the people whose home they had crashed into. It should have been obvious to anyone with a brain, who was not also totally blind, that they were as intent on putting out the fire in the house as they were on protecting and repairing their ship. Why couldn't the deputies and the Fitzgeralds see this too and back off a little?

She was asking herself a foolish question. Uncle Little Bear had certainly impressed her enough, growing up, with first-hand accounts of situations that too easily had gotten out of hand: where unreasoning fear had turned neighbor against neighbor, friend against friend. He had also taught her that weapons held at the ready always spell trouble. Goddess! Why didn't Alan shake the lead out and get here! She was certain now she had seen the *Peregrine* earlier, and that he too had witnessed the crash-landing of this UFO. Incapable though he may have been of handling emotional encounters of the intimate kind, this type of close encounter, she was certain, he was up to. She had to get out there, run interference. Somehow, she had to prevent the situation from exploding into a shooting match until Alan could land and take over.

As Dawn climbed out of the car she saw fiery blossoms sprouting from a window at the rear of the house, dangerously near where Mendez and the older man had entered. Three crewmen from the alien craft had separated themselves from their fellows. Armed with heavy equipment strapped to their backs—obviously intended for fire control—they ran to engage battle at the new front. Phillips and the boy were standing between them and their objective. Cautiously Phillips backed away but the boy stood frozen to the spot. Succumbing to unreasoning terror he suddenly opened fire, downing one crewman and scattering the other two.

"No!" Dawn screamed, heedlessly running to stop him before anyone else was killed. The freezing wind-driven rain slapped against her cheeks stinging her with cold. Her small voice was lost in the surge of thunder and confusion all around her.

Mendez emerged from the house carrying two small children. The farmer, close behind him, was leading a woman and several other older children. Without questioning, he followed his son's mindless lead and started shooting blindly as he ran. The crewmen fighting the blaze scattered, regrouping around those who were occupied with repairs on the crafts exterior. They were employing their extinguishers now to create a smoke screen to hide behind. Choking on the fumes, the boy and the farmer continued firing into the dense chemical mist.

The cloud and parts of the ship still visible behind it caught the yellow-crimson glow of the flames, reflecting them back like some demon-possessed nightmare. Rain, transformed into steam by the leaping flames, created a fiery halo that heightened the hellish illusion. Leaping into this thick soup of smoke, mist, and chemical fog, Dawn groped her way in the general direction she last recalled having seen Phillips and Mendez.

Confusion rapidly escalated into fear as she lost her bearings. Thunder rolled overhead, lightning crashed to earth somewhere close by and bullets ripped the cold-hot air. A helmeted head pierced the mist, shouting at her. The words were unintelligible but the body language frantically signed danger and a command to get down. Disoriented, unable to respond, she was only vaguely aware of the metallic head launching itself in the general direction of her mid-section. Like a quarterback caught in a flying tackle, she went down. Her head thunked against something hard that sent a galaxy of stars splashing in a million directions. Something warm and sticky ran down her face mingling with the mud and rain as she lost herself in an ocean of darkness that lapped over, in tiny waves at first, then totally engulfed her, in one final tidal surge.

•••

Several moments ago when Alan Kolkey was climbing the basement stairs, he had been furious, a rampaging wildfire out of control. The little Witch had finally worked her magic, winning complete and unconditional surrender. At that moment, he would have done anything, sacrificed anything, to have possessed her totally, to have finally fulfilled himself as a man. Every other consideration had suddenly lost all meaning in the screaming hunger of his need for that one small woman-child. And yet she had run from him, not once but twice, leaving a pain in his gut and an aching in his groin worse than anything he had ever experienced. Why! Wasn't that what she had been wanting all along?

Now he stood at the open door shouting Dawn's name, eyes straining to pierce the black curtain of rain. Lightning walked the earth again tonight. Roaring with a voice of thunder that raped the screaming wind, it forced him to relive, more vividly this time than he had ever dreamed possible, the incredible agony of that long ago night and his mother dying in his arms. He could not lose Dawn to this storm, as well! He wanted to run after her, bring her back, but the monster of hysteria had possessed his soul, paralyzing his limbs. Reason and sanity were crowded out by the replay of that long ago night, the endless walk back to this house, with only driving rain and thunder to echo his loss.

"My boy, when are you ever going to master the gentle art of keeping your heart open and your mouth shut!" Zarkov's voice came from behind, harsh and brittle as dry winter leaves. The old man was right. He had missed a golden opportunity to stay his tongue. Anger always governs things abysmally. That was a lesson he should have digested years ago. Tonight he had been shouting too loud for the dying voice of reason to ever have been heard.

"All right young man, enough is enough!" the old professor had taken charge. His words cracked like a bullwhip. "You've been having your way around here for too long. My patience is finally exhausted. No more trying to understand! You've gone too far this time. So get out there! Now! Find that poor child and bring her back. Or don't bother coming home at all!" Zarkov's angry shove had caught him off guard, sending him stumbling several steps out into the full fury of the night. "Gertha, get our coats! I'll call Security, then we'll take the car and search too." The front door slammed shut behind him with forboding finality.

Heart pounding in his chest and throat simultaneously, ears ringing, he sent out a hesitant tendril of thought, trying to pinpoint the direction she had taken. His mind finally managed to touch hers, stopping him cold. The hurt, the utter despair he had caused her was like the raking of claws across his brain, sending him reeling backwards into the door. If he could only collect himself, beat down the panic, rein in his runaway thoughts! If only he could quiet his mind, concentrate sufficiently to tighten the focus, he might be able to smash his way through the barrier of seething emotions around her. And probably fry her brain in the process, he hastened to remind himself as he hurriedly withdrew altogether.

The few scattered visual fragments he had managed to safely glean from Dawn's mind told him she was on the road, heading west, and that she had just fallen. There was also the fuzzy impression of a car pulling up beside her. Perhaps if he focused on the passengers inside, once more only marginal success. It was Phillips and Mendez! They had her with them now and were heading back toward town.

Praying for the thunder to lend him strength instead of sapping it, he conjured up a wild courage from the pit of his despair. Somehow, he managed to focus his mind long enough to program a psychokinetic command into the *Peregrine's* on-board computer. Her sensors fed back response as the grav shields kicked in and she began floating upwards several feet above her docking cradle. She paused, waiting momentarily for the giant roof-mounted hanger bay to slide open. Then, angling her nose thirty degrees skyward, she glided up and outside into the storm.

Buffeted more by his own emotions than by lightning and wind, Alan only barely maintained his weak connection. Finally, after what felt like an eternity, he managed to bring the huge ship safely down on the small mountain road. The psi-link had been weak, muddy. His focus and concentration were bad, his energies scattered, ineffectual. It would be a relief to be at her manual controls.

Damn! If only there had been time for his people to have completed that small shuttle flyer! It would have been infinitely more maneuverable, in tight quarters like these, than this great space-going arc, and infinitely less conspicuous too. But the mother ship, herself, had yet to see completion. Other priorities were always diverting his energies.

Strapped into the acceleration seat in front of his navigation con, he switched over to manual then took his ship up to a thousand feet. Perhaps if he followed safely out of sight, Phillips and Mendez might stop someplace where he could land safely. He might have a chance then to talk some sense into the girl, to get her to come back with him.

Ordinarily, flying through such turbulence would have been a simple matter of minor stabilization and inertial-grav compensations—something the computers would have corrected for automatically, had it mattered enough to initialize the command. As if anything would ever again matter should any harm come to Dawn, on his account. The girl had wakened a desperate longing within him that only she could satisfy. All he wanted, all he dreamed of day and night, was to be lying atop her, spilling his love into her warm, naked body. She had become an obsession that had not been allowed expression, until today. Animal instinct had finally won out over his conflicting need to protect her from the danger of his esper curse. To have indulged the demands of his body, his manhood, might have condemned to death one who was so very literally the most vital part of him. The prospect of life, devoid of the sparkle and magic her mere presence lent to it, was equally unthinkable. By either path, holding on or giving her up, he was condemning them both to a life devoid of warmth and meaning.

Tangled up in self-condemnation, he was drowning in the realization that what had so long ago happened to his parents was once more being reenacted with Dawn: the violent storm, the racing car on the road below. His mind sped ahead of him, conjuring images of the cruiser skidding off the road and exploding in a ball of flame. He had allowed the controls to slip, and was nearly hurled from his seat by a fierce gust of wind. Almost as uncoordinated physically as mentally tonight, it felt like another go-round with eternity before he was finally able to steady his bucking mount once more and relocate the patrol car on his scanners.

His port sensors began screaming warning of a fast-approaching vessel, half again larger than his own. Suddenly, one Herculean lightning bolt, worthy of Father Zeus himself, ripped apart the sky, turning the cosmos into a gigantic light show. In that moment of blinding daylight, Alan made visual contact. Gauging distance by sight alone would have been grossly deceptive, but his instruments told him it was only several miles from him and had abruptly slowed to a near-dead halt. Apparently struck by that last bolt, the unidentified ship was listing drunkenly and beginning to lose altitude as darkness closed in once more.

Following the vessel's descent by instrument, he knew that a crash landing was imminent. Immediate assistance would be needed. He had to collect himself and act swiftly. His own problems had to wait. He schooled his mutinous emotions back in line, consoling himself with a quick check on the progress of the patrol car. He would report the approximate crash site to the local authorities, then get down there himself to do whatever he could until help arrived.

That same lightning bolt had apparently also taken out his radio antenna, forcing him to waste precious minutes programming a temporary computer-linked connection to his hull-mounted sensor network. More valuable minutes had to be eaten up trying to convince some thick-headed deputy down at the Tuolumne County Sheriff's office that this was no crank call and, yes, he was indeed *the* Alan Kolkey. His report was acknowledged only after Mendez was overheard reporting in with the same information. He and Phillips were already at the site: the Fitzgerald place. The UFO had crash-landed into the family's big farmhouse, setting that ancient pile of kindling ablaze.

Alan was forced to identify himself again, for the record this time, then promised to lend whatever aide he could until they arrived with emergency fire-fighting and paramedic equipment.

There was no longer any need for an instrument search. The fire, clearly visible through the heavy rain, was all the beacon he needed. Dawn would be there too. The existence of deity by any name or in any form was purely conjectural. Yet, when he could not make telepathic contact with her at all, he found himself offering up a silent prayer to the Goddess she had sworn allegiance to that he would find her unharmed. His inability to touch her mind, he assured himself over and over, was merely due to extreme anxiety that made it impossible to concentrate or focus properly. Perhaps she had merely fallen asleep. Still, he was unable to shake the feeling that something was dreadfully wrong.

The *Peregrine* had hardly settled to earth before he dove through the opening hatch and started running for the parked patrol car. He suddenly felt the dizzying sensation of ground coming up and smashing him in the face. Impact with something hard and sharp sent him grabbing for his head in agony. On the level of awareness mutually shared with Dawn, a remote part of him blinked out. The pain was suddenly gone. When he opened his eyes he was surprised to find himself still on his feet, propped against the abandoned patrol car. Dawn! Something had happened to her. The rear door hung open, the back seat tenanted only by a damp blanket. Frantic now, he ran toward the blazing house shouting her name over and over.

Horror laid its icy grip around his heart as he recognized Fitzgerald and that equally trigger-happy son of his. They were shooting into the chemical smoke screen thrown up by guards trying to protect a team of workers who had been clustered about a damaged section of hull-mounted instrumentation. Abandoning tools, they were swarming up a ladder now, diving for the safety of the ship's interior. It was obvious none of them were armed with anything more lethal than fire extinguishing apparatus; and yet these homicidal lunatics were expending bullets as though their targets were ducks in a shooting gallery.

Already one of the alien craft's crew members lay dead nearby. Dawn was lying unconscious out there, lost somewhere inside that cloud of smoke, steam, and chemical spray. He had to stop them.

Desperation drove him at the pair like one of their own bullets. Before they were aware of him descending on them, he had ripped the guns from their hands. Splintering them against a nearby tree, he hurled what remained at their feet.

"You lunatics! They were only putting the damn fire out for you," he shouted. Off to the right, the wind was beginning slightly to dissipate the overcast. Several anxious moments passed before he was able to distinguish a helmeted figure carrying a small body. Wearing protective clothing of some sort, similar to his crew-mates, he was handing the unconscious body up to another crewman above him on the ladder.

"Dawn!" he shouted. Hysteria once again claimed victory over sanity as he recognized the slender shape of the girl.

"Don't worry, Al! I'll get the bastard." Phillips called out from behind.

Alan spun around in time to see the deputy squeeze the trigger of his high-powered weapon, but too late to stop him. Looking back, he saw the crimson wash where the bullet had smashed through the spinal column of the crewman carrying his woman and felt a searing, white hot pain as it ripped through her heart. Reaching out from the shelter of the open hatchway, disembodied hands caught hold, pulling her inside. Other hands were grabbing for her falling abductor—or rescuer—and missed! He pitched to the ground and lay still in a pool of blood-tinted muddy water.

She had been dearer than life itself, dearer even than the precious memory of his own parents. Alan watched, paralyzed by a steely hand that dug razor-tipped nails into his own heart, as the body of his woman was pulled inside the alien ship, her life gushing out in fountaining spurts of blood.

The finality of it hit like a neural explosion inside his brain, ripping a scream of uncontainable rage from his throat. Rage suddenly found focus on the deputy he had known for nearly ten years. Grabbing his weapon, Alan's fist slammed, out shattering bone in the man's jaw and hurling him several yards backward into the air. Clutching the rifle in both hands, once more he bellowed out his agony as he pounded it, over and over again, on a nearby outcropping of rock until the barrel bent and the polished wood of the stock was reduced to splinters.

Through the scarlet surge of inner torment came vague awareness of a hatch closing and the alien craft rising into the air. It hovered, motionless for a moment, then vanished, an immense discus hurled skyward by some giant invisible hand. Like cold water hurled in his face, sanity, or at least its specter, returned once more to whip him into action. His feet hardly touched ground as he bolted for his ship. Belting in, he opened her up, acceleration pressure be damned! Mushrooming g-force sent a shudder of protest through every beam and girder, threatening to cave-in his chest. Outside, the ruby hull flamed an incandescent red from the tremendous friction of air screaming past. The *Peregrine's* fragile life support was unable to keep pace with mounting internal temperatures. Her bridge had become a large oven by the time she finally climbed above the last layer of atmosphere and out into airless space. Obediently, she answered when he called for yet more from her already straining chemically-fueled engines. At last it was safe to fire up her plasma-fusion reactors. Now he had a chance of closing the rapidly widening gap between himself and the escaping alien vessel.

Still, as he crossed the boundary traced by the moon's elliptical orbit, he was hardly able to keep within scanner range. Another hour out and he had lost all trace of his quarry, entirely. One moment, by upping power to his forward sensors, he had re-established a fairly definite fix, and the next, it had suddenly winked out like a closing eye.

"Love knows not its own depth until the hour of separation." Words Alan had read once, long ago, came back now to haunt him with infinitely deeper meaning. Tendrils of despair crept like jungle vines from his brain, coiling and tightening around his heart.

Dawn was dead. He had driven her to this. Because of his blundering stupidity she was lost, beyond his reach now forever. And he had never once told her how much she truly meant to him. Until this moment, he had never taken the time to realize how much more, how far beyond merely the hungering after her flesh his need actually went. Yet lately, it seemed, the more he had denied his body its own need for her, the more obsessively demanding that need had become. Goddess, how he had loved her! With a love that was so much more than love. Ever since the mind fusion he had never been able to completely dissolve, she had become an actual tangible extension of his own being.

Cutting himself off from her had been like depriving himself the use of an arm, a leg, and half his soul. Still, he had been able to draw a certain limited comfort from having her close by where she might be seen, spoken to, occasionally touched as their paths collided in Zarkov's small house. Though he had chosen, for her sake, for her very life, to send her back to her own people, he had known she would always remain a very real extension of himself, a subtle, but steady source of strength. And always, there would have been the hope to hold onto, that one day he would have... Oh who the hell was he kidding! Dawn had been right all along. Yes, he had been afraid for her, but even more, scared shitless of her.

Casual encounters were difficult enough, but he simply had not been able to handle the feeling of vulnerability, the fear of impending loss that came with intimacy. Nor had he dared permit himself to grow any closer to those he already loved, in spite of himself: Zarkov, Gertha, the African, Little Hassan from earthquake-ravaged Tabriz. Most especially, Dawn. Now she was lost to him, beyond all recall. It was as if a large chunk of himself had just been brutally ripped away, leaving him clinically alive yet no longer among the living. Only awareness of transcending emptiness remained to let him know he still existed. Like a rapidly spreading fungus it grew around his soul, deadening all pain and sealing it off from the rest of him.

Mechanically, functioning now on automatic like his own ship, Alan's hands slowly checked the *Peregrine's* wild flight. He reined her in like a runaway mount, and gently brought her about, till her prow once more pointed the way home. Home. He could not go back. He could not face Zarkov and Gertha. No less could he bear the constant reminders of Dawn, of things that no longer were, and worse: things that might have been, but for his blinding stupidity and the violence of his temper.

Alan Kolkey had to die too! He no longer had the stomach for being Moshey's glorified errand boy. The world had gotten on quite nicely without him, before. It would again. He had already paid his dues a dozen times over. No one was indispensable. All that truly mattered right now was to find some place, some balm, to help him forget. Perhaps the ultimate forgetfulness might be found, following the siren call of oblivion into the silence of dreamless dust.

It would be so simple to cut power and let the *Peregrine* plunge unchecked into Earth's ocean of air. An oversized comet had, in essence, given birth to the popular heroic persona of Alan Kolkey. What could be more fitting than ending his brief career by completing the fiery odyssey he had interrupted more than a year-and-a-half ago. If his recurring dream had been more than merely a dream, if there actually was something to all the hoopla throughout the centuries about life-beyond-death, then perhaps Dawn would be there, waiting for him on the other side.

Earth's blue-white mantle grew until nothing else was visible on his forward view screens. Anxiously kneading the palm of his right hand, he reached out and cut power. Freed from the restraint of her braking thrusters, the *Peregrine* leapt forward into the waiting arms of the planet below.

Her sensors were beginning to register a dangerous rise again, back into the red zone of outer hull temperatures. Suddenly, possessed of a will of their own, his hands shot out to power up once more. Still eluding conscious control, they carried out the necessary re-entry sequence to guide the ship through safe planet-fall. Something echoed sternly inside his head, like a wordless reprimand from an angry parent, letting him know that any further such foolishness would also be doomed to failure. If there were any such things as guardian angels, or spirit guides, Alan suspected his had kicked in: introducing themselves, loud and clear. That, or a very insistent, incredibly lucid attack of conscience.

The lights of San Francisco lay sprinkled below, like countless gems scattered across a black velvet cloak. Alan was once more in control of his body and his ship. Leveling off at five thousand feet, he replied to a radioed ground control challenge to identify himself, then coasted until he spotted a deserted stretch of road a dozen miles northeast of the city. Locating a relatively treeless strip large enough to accommodate his ship, he set her down.

Unbelting, he climbed to his feet, and was about to leave when he noticed the leather carrying case secured in its safety niche. It contained the old twelve-string guitar his father had given him so many years ago. It was still his favorite. Memories flooded his mind as he opened the case and caressed the satiny veneer of the beloved instrument. He was remembering his twelfth birthday when he had taken it down from the wall peg where it had hung, waiting until he had grown enough to handle such a large instrument. Fitting it with new strings, he had given an after-dinner concert that night for his parents and grandparents. His grandmother had wept and his father had patted him on the head proudly, calling him "a man now." Oh yes! He was a man, all right! A gold-plated winner! He laughed bitterly as he donned his black leather jacket that had been secured in an adjoining nitch. Snapping the guitar case closed, he slung it across his back by the ornately embossed leather carrying strap. One last look around the bridge and he was in the lift and headed for the forward cargo hatch ladder.

Outside, he turned to hurl a mental command to PK com link that would put the *Peregrine* on automatic, taking her back to her cavern eyrie. Nothing happened. He tried again, more slowly and deliberately this time. He tried visualizing a finger, step-by-step, spelling out his commands through the miniature electromagnetically-modulated voice box that allowed almost instantaneous inter-communication between himself and his ship's on-board computers. Still nothing. Comprehension, like the dancing head of a cobra, began insinuating itself into his awareness. He cautiously essayed moving a small pebble at his feet with a psychokinetic nudge. It was a kindergarten trick he might ordinarily have performed while simultaneously juggling tools and balancing an equation. Once more, nothing.

The comfortable cocoon of protection Dawn had taught him how to spin for himself had suddenly solidified into the dark image of a prison cell, invisible, intangible, yet very real. It had suddenly coalesced into indiffusible, solid walls that were now unscalable. Narrowing drastically the boundaries of perception, they blocked out all the white noise. He was deaf to it. At last, blissfully deaf to all but the senseless, contradictory verbal sounds that esper-blind humans call language. His curse had been lifted at last. Too late, however, to help him save the girl it had finally succeeded in killing.

He walked slowly back to his ship. Once more back on her bridge, he programmed her computers manually. This time, as he stepped out onto the exit ramp, he gave her ruby hull one last farewell caress, then leapt to the ground. Several hundred feet away, clear of her grav-deflector field, Alan stopped and turned to watch the landing ramp retract. Her forward hatch slid shut, ringing down the final curtain on a very badly staged play; and then she was airborne, floating skyward. At three-hundred feet, the *Peregrine* oriented her prow in an east-southeasterly direction, and vanished.

It was dawn now. The rain had ended. The sun was coming up to take charge once more of a rapidly clearing sky. Only the black clouds of despair remained to darken all light in his soul. The vivid hues of breaking day on the eastern horizon went unappreciated. They seemed only to mock him as he turned his lead-weighted steps toward the distant city. A chill early morning breeze stirred the grass and was gone, leaving behind only an icy echoing indifference. There was nothing left within him that cared to question why he had been saved or why his feet should choose this particular direction over any other. Nor did he question why, when he would have stopped, something from deep within, manipulating him like a puppet, continued driving him relentlessly on. To where?

PART II:
THE SUIT
OF PENTACLES

CHAPTER X

A LAN TRUDGED across the grass of the city's largest park. The noon sun, riding leisurely across a flawless sky, warmed his skin but was unable to penetrate the arctic chill that had settled around his soul. He recalled little of the past days, nor could he have said how many had passed since Dawn's death. Even had he wanted to, only a hazy collage of memory fragments could have been accessed: waiting out an afternoon rain in an abandoned shed, facing down an angry pack of stray dogs. And endless, aimless walking, sometimes in open country, occasionally suburban and sidewalked, but most often along canyoned urban streets, paved with concrete and faceless strangers. Dreading the wasteland of ceaseless nightmares his country of dreams had become, he slept only when exhaustion could no longer be denied. He could not recall when he had last eaten, or cared to. All that body and soul now craved was tomb-like isolation, some deserted corner, eons and light years distant from any other living thing, a place that would finally allow him to stop moving, to stop being. Yet each time he found a quiet hole to crawl into, some restless spirit took over. Animating his body when he would have lain there, it kept him moving, searching, driving him on with an unrelenting compulsion that only his music could briefly silence.

The ancient Greeks used to say that when the Gods are angry with a man, they grant his prayer. He had prayed to be rid of his psionic curse. He was. He had prayed for Dawn to be free of him. She was. And now, he walked the earth utterly alone and lost in a limbo of sensory shut-down. He was half blind and all but deaf now without his esper faculties. Two prayers granted. He guessed the Gods were angry with him.

Earlier today his override pilot had led him to this park, past an ancient grist mill, in the direction of the bay. Finally able to stop, he had found a spot under a tree, on a knoll overlooking the water, and sat down to rest. A City park crew worked in the cold January air dismantling a creche. Christmas had passed and Alan had not even noticed.

He was pouring out his pain and despair through the strings of his guitar when something, an overshadowing awareness, forced him to look up. A graying, elegantly-dressed gentleman was hovering over him, a luscious young woman hanging onto one of his arms. Eyes glowing moistly, the stranger dabbed at them with his pocket hand-kerchief and sniffled once or twice as if struggling to contain some deep sorrow of his own.

"You're wasting a precious talent playing alone out here where only the birds, and a few fortunate passers-by, like myself, can hear you, young man." He stuffed something into Alan's coat pocket. "Go down to the Suit of Pentacles. I wrote the address on the back of my card. Tell Harry Costanza that Winthrop Hayes says he should listen to you. Don't thank me!" He raised a gloved hand in remonstrance when Alan tried to object. "This isn't charity. You'll be doing both of us a favor. The warm-up group he booked for this month was supposed to open tonight. I'm told only the keyboard player showed up." Then he was gone.

Alan dug into his pocket, pulling out a hundred-dollar bill and a business card ornately lettered in black and gold. An address had been hastily scribbled across the back. Again that same damnable something stopped him when he tried tossing the card and money to the ground. Disgusted, he shoved them back into his pocket and stood up, brushing grass from his badly soiled pants. Returning the guitar to its case, he slung it across his back once more.

As he started walking once more, he reached up to brush a hand across his face and laughed bitterly. Dirty, disheveled, his once proud mane of black curls was now matted and snarled. The days-long growth of stubble could already be called a beard. Several weeks ago he had been petitioned to mediate an upcoming series of Arab-Israeli talks. Today, taken for a derelict, he found himself the unwilling recipient of a handout. Seeing in it a vicious brand of masochistic irony, he started laughing until tears burned his eyes and passers-by gave him odd looks and plenty of room.

Walking in his usual apparently aimless pattern, he suddenly found himself facing a pretentious replica of a Venetian palace. A large Renaissance sign colorfully proclaimed the building in front of him to be the Suit of Pentacles. A pair of gilt doors, painted with themes from the ancient Tarot deck, caught his eye. On the right door was an almost life-size representation of the Magician, his right hand holding up the wand of will and power, his left, pointing to earth in a gesture of creation, typifying potentiality. On the other door was the Priestess with the solar cross on her chest. She was seated between two pillars that symbolized positive and negative life forces. Exemplifying the balance of those forces, she represented spiritual enlightenment and inner illumination. Surprised, Alan wondered where he had learned all this. Before meeting Dawn, he had always steered clear of metaphysics and mysticism. They were games for bored housewives and eccentrics with nothing better to occupy their time. Then he realized: he had unconsciously been tapping into Dawn's memory engrams once more. At least this much of her survived within him, he consoled himself—unsuccessfully.

The Suit of Pentacles was one of San Francisco's most popular and fashionable clubs, offering gambling, food, and live entertainment in its casinos and huge dinner theater. Alan had heard of the place often when his "gambling" expeditions to help finance the building of his *Peregrine* had brought him into the area. Somehow, he had never gotten around to including the place on his itinerary. A pity too. It was said to have an excellent casino and many smaller, very intimate, very private upstairs gaming rooms.

A perverse whim curled up the corners of his mouth. He was thirsty, he decided. He needed a drink. Now! Here! Let them refuse him entrance. Clothing filthy and torn, several weeks, perhaps, of beard and road dirt concealing his features, his self-loathing had been bottled up inside him for too long now. Suddenly, it craved something, someone, to vent itself on. He had often wondered how well he would fare in battle without the enormous advantage his esper faculties had always given him. Now seemed as good a time as any to find out. He would not be going in totally unarmed, however. He still had his size, backed up by steel-hard muscles, cultivated and maintained through the regular practice of his Katas and frequent sparring matches with some of his tech and engineering people back home. His martial skills had been honed to an even sharper edge during his endless battles with the aftermaths of Mother Kali's hell-spawned disasters.

Finding the doors surprisingly easy to open, despite their deceptive mass, he passed through a small foyer into an immense, richly-appointed lobby. At the far end, hanging from the ceiling, two floors up, was a great globe of a chandelier made up of hundreds of crystal disks, inset with glittering gold pentagrams. Directly beneath it, an equally spectacular staircase spiraled up to a second floor mezzanine that looked down on the lobby from three sides. The stair banisters and balcony guard rails were all of richly carved black oak. The steps were fabricated from some translucent acrylic material. Illuminated from within, they glowed blood-red, melting like a sanguine waterfall, right into the plush, deep red carpeting of the main lobby. Just in front of the row of ornate ebony columns that supported the rear mezzanine section, where the winding staircase eventually connected with it, was a line of small fountains. Each was shooting a pencil thin stream high into the air where it caught and danced with the green magic of hidden spotlights. Trained on the bubbling fountains below, they transformed the playing waters into pools of liquid emerald. Under the rear mezzanine, behind the columns and the curtain of playing water, the cashier's cage and a foyer leading to the public rest rooms could be seen. They were set into a wall that was one immense mirror which gave them the appearance of surrealistic stage props standing in the middle of a forest of columns and fountains. The curved base of the stairs was also paneled with mirrors. Looking like a huge faceted diamond, it heightened even further a surrealistic forest-maze effect. Behind as well as to left and right of the ornate staircase, columns, and fountains, other oversize paintings of cards from the ubiquitous Tarot hung from mirror-paneled walls, seemingly suspended in mid-air.

At Alan's right, a gilded sign boldly announced entry to the gambling casino. Below it, on the far wall of the entry way, rather appropriately, he thought, was a six-foot-tall painting of the Wheel of Fortune, another card in the major deck of the Tarot. On Alan's near right, close to the entrance to the casino, was a cloak room, barren but for a few coats, and presently unattended. It was, after all, only mid-afternoon.

To Alan's left, at the front of the lobby and directly across from the cloakroom, was a counter where a computerized register waited to begin ringing up the evening's dinner receipts. A small girl, costumed scantily and most suggestively, was organizing her station in preparation for the impending dinner rush. Above her head hung larger-than-life-size murals of The Emperor and The Empress, again from the Tarot's major deck.

Beyond the register, another elegantly wrought sign pointed the way into the dinner theater. Beneath it, on the far entry wall, was the Hermit, his upheld lamp lighting the way into the dimly illumined interior. Below the painted flame of his lamp was the Maitre d's station, and the Maitre d' himself, looking like a gorilla trying to pass for a penguin.

Alan grinned with evil anticipation. They would certainly never grant him entrance into such opulence, dressed as he was and in such a grimy state of disrepair. That muscle-bound Maitre d' looked like a worthy adversary. With shoulders back and chest puffed out in wordless challenge, he walked boldly toward the watchdog posted at the entrance to the dinner-theater.

"Pardon—Sir! Do you have a reservation?" The Maitre d' reminded him of an exquisitely attired dropout from Saturday morning wrestling, who had been given a quickie course in diction, etiquette, and snobbery.

"No. But the bar will do quite nicely," Alan decided to play along with the charade for a while.

"I'm afraid all our tables are reserved—uh—Sir. And there are no unoccupied places at the bar. Perhaps you might be more comfortable at—Skinny's Leaky Bucket. It's only five blocks down, by the waterfront."

"Oh no! I'm certain I'd be far more comfortable here." Alan was enjoying the man's discomfort. He was also beginning to rankle somewhat. He planted his feet more firmly and silently dared the man to make the next move.

"Please. I must insist!" The Maitre d's white-knuckled fists hinted that he wanted to do a whole lot more than merely insist. His cultured exterior was obviously a thinly painted-on veneer.

"What seems to be the problem, Malgrove?" A dark-complexioned man with a coldly polite smile intruded himself between Alan and his intended victim. He was impeccably attired in dark suit and ruffled wine-colored shirt. Though lacking mustache or sideburns, there was a distinct flavor of nineteenth century riverboat gambler about the man. Hovering close behind the intruder loomed the menacing hulk of a bodyguard. Alan curled his lips back in dark anticipation of two additional victims on whom to vent his rage.

"This—'person'—seems to think…"

"This 'person' only came in to warm himself over a drink." The venom-dripping sarcasm in Alan's voice was a deliberate goad.

"I trust you realize the Suit of Pentacles isn't exactly a neighborhood pub. Drinks here are—rather expensive," the riverboat gambler smiled with oily diplomacy. His bodyguard inched closer, leaning toward Alan like a hungry vulture.

Glaring back in open provocation to this mindless mass of muscle, Alan reached into his shirt pocket. As he pulled out the hundred-dollar-bill to wave in their faces, his benefactor's business card fell out onto the floor.

"Hey! What're you doing with this?" The intruder bent over, picking it up before Alan could retrieve it. "The address of the club on the back is in his hand. Did Hayes send you here?" His eyes narrowed to suspicious laser slits as he looked up.

"He heard me playing in the park, earlier. Said to tell you to give me a listen," Alan replied with a disinterested shrug, hoping he would not.

"It's gotta' be a joke, Mr. Costanza."

"Hardly, Malgrove. When my not-so-silent partner is joking, you bleed, only you never see the blade go in. Besides, where'd the humor be for him, sending a big mother, like this, who looks like he's itching for any excuse to tear the place apart. Remember, he has as much of his own money invested in it as I do.

"OK! Hayes sent you; so you can go in," he added, turning to level his frown in Alan's direction. Then, jabbing a finger for emphasis, he added, "But only for an hour. I want you out of here before the dinner rush. And, for chrissake, sit somewhere in a dark corner! There aren't that many people here this time of day, but still, they're paying customers, and the economy's not so great I can afford to chase them away. Malgrove will send a waitress to get you whatever you want. If I have any free time before you leave, I'll come give you a listen."

"Sure! And if I have any free time, I might even play. I plan on being pretty busy, myself." Alan returned a caricature of Costanza's patronizing smile, then walked into the huge lounge. He felt cheated, but consoled himself with the thought that a hundred dollars could buy a lot of pain killer. While he waited for his eyes to adjust to the dim lighting, he listened to Costanza, still talking to his Maitre d'.

"Since when does Hayes go for constitutionals in the park this time of year?"

"Since his latest shack-up, sir. This one's a little teenie-bopper type. Has him on a fitness and nature-appreciation kick."

"Last month, it was that leggy gymnastics freak from the chorus line, with her ridiculous ambitions of becoming a circus trapeze artist. I still have the swings and bars he put in for her cluttering my private gym upstairs. Why do I always get caught in his fallout."

Too far from them now to hear the Maitre d's reply, if any, Alan traveled down the center aisle, between rows of tables, toward the stage at the far end of the room. A lone figure was seated behind a large concert grand, pounding out an emotional interpretation of Chopin's *Polonaise*. Alan found a front row table almost directly below the pianist. He rested his guitar case on one of the chairs, and was just collapsing onto another, when a waitress in almost no costume at all appeared to take his order.

"Whiskey! Make it a triple with a tall beer chaser. I don't want to have to wait around all day for the message," he added in reply to her raised eyebrow.

The pianist was wading into a particularly moving rendition of Beethoven's *Moonlight Sonata* when the waitress returned with his drink. He gestured for another triple, then turned his attention back to the music. His adopted brother had never played this well, although once in a while during a reflective mood, he could display a surprising understanding of the old masters. Thinking of Stan reminded him of home, Gertha's cooking, and the way she always used to fuss over him whenever he was troubled or tired. This pianist, also being black, only intensified the sudden wave of homesickness that now washed over him. He was tall, like Stan, and slender too, but big-boned with a frame that would have looked better carrying more muscle, and a bit more flesh to soften the sharp angles in his face. His cheekbones stuck out too far; his mustache and brows were too bushy, and his close-cropped hair was not quite full enough to balance the weight of features that were far too prominent. A quiet good humor though and a genuine love for the music he was making danced together in his dark brown eyes and somehow managed to soften most of the sharp angles.

"I can't believe a place like this is paying for that kind of music." Alan could not resist giving voice to his cynicism. The chill of death had frozen down to the marrow of his soul. He downed the triple in one swallow. It burned his shriveled stomach, but the momentary pain would be worth it to warm him slightly, even if only for a short while.

"Believe me, they aren't," the pianist paused and looked down to grace him with a slightly patronizing smile. "I'm on my own time right now. Management said they didn't much care what I played so long's it don't chase the afternoon customers away, and I give the evening crowds what they want to hear.

"Looks like I'll have to be playin' solo tonight, too," he added with a stoic shrug. "Our lead man OD'd and the rest of the band stayed on with him in Denver. They won't budge till he's outta' danger and his folks arrive. They sent me on ahead to try and salvage the gig. We're billed as Wild Hunt, by the way. Least we were. Costanza's threatenin' to have us blacklisted if the others don't show up in time for the first show tonight," he added with a gesture of resignation as he turned attention back to his music.

"You play like that and you're working with a rock group? My God, you should be on the concert stage." Alan smiled fleetingly at the bitter irony as he recalled how often Dawn had scolded him for withholding and wasting his own talents, such as they were.

"Maybe so, man." He stopped playing again. This time his expression broadcast a frustration whose roots ran very deep. "But there still ain't much call at the Big 'C'— that's Carnegie Hall, mister—fer black dudes from the Detroit ghettos. I know. Believe me, I tried."

"So you simply gave up and settled for a rock band that plays jungle sounds for a bunch of sweaty customers jumping around on a dance floor, like they're trying to kill snakes." Alan's sneer was one of self-accusation. If anyone was guilty of running away it was certainly himself.

"Hey, man! I didn't 'settle' for nothin'." Venom ran from his words as he impaled Alan on his finger. "There's a lotta' serious rock music out there. Today's popular rock; country rock too, like ours: tomorrow's classics. Ol' Beethoven, he was the rocker of his generation. Started a whole new trend in music, an' raised a lotta' eyebrows doin' it."

Alan smiled with malicious glee. He had managed to singe some tail feathers.

"By the way, honkey," his 'victim's' features lit up with an evil grin of his own, "how well d'you play that guitar a' yours? Or d'you just tote it around as an invite for free drinks?"

"A lot better than you play that tired piano—Boy," Alan shot back contemptuously. He resented being called "honkey," especially in that tone of voice. The waitress returned with his second triple. Once more he drank it down in a single swallow, eager for any anesthetic relief, no matter how slight, or how brief.

"Hey—honkey! Ain't you heard? You can't drink your troubles away."

"Maybe so. But I'm sure as hell going to make them swim for it. I came here because of the condition of my liver: it's healthy and I want to do something about it."

"You drink enough of that stuff, guaranteed, mister: it's gonna' set you free. Permanently."

"Now you've got it! That's the whole idea, friend." Alan smiled grimly as he toasted with his beer glass before taking a long swallow.

"Sounds to me like you're a dude who's got more problems than a Ubangi with chapped lips," the black man frowned, looking almost concerned. "But believe me, Man, you're only takin' the scenic route to the bone yard, comin' in here to solve 'em."

"Why the hell should I give a damn? I never asked to be born, in the first place." The whiskey was taking hold: he was already beginning to sound like a sulking ten-year-old.

"Lucky thing too. 'Cause if you had, they'd a' said no." The pianist smiled down sadly, shaking his head in disbelief. "Man, oh man! You may be built like a 'mighty oak,' but your brain's still locked away in the acorn."

"Wild Hunt?" Alan grudgingly returned his serve, "I've heard about your band. Club owners say they'd give you longer breaks between sets, if only it didn't take so damn long retraining you each time." Beginning to tire of this infantile duel of tired old one-liners, he tried once more to lose himself inside the foamy fascination of his beer.

"You gotta' forgive him, folks. He's bein' himself tonight," the musician persisted, directing his editorial remarks now in the direction of a couple who was settling down at the next table. Turning back to Alan, he added playfully, "Tell you what. I've got a few minutes to kill. Why don't you tell me everything you know. By the way—honkey; what's your name, so's I'll know who I'm insultin'?"

"Al. What's yours—nigger?"

"Ham," he smiled, showing too many teeth.

"You mean like short for 'Hambone'?" Alan laughed, pulling himself up out of a slouch and sitting forward.

"No, jive-turkey! 'Ham,' like in Hebrew, for 'black,' I'm black, in case you ain't noticed."

"No kidding! I thought you just liked playing in the mud. Hey, I heard how your father proposed to your mother: 'You're going to have a—what?' They say her wedding dress was something else too. The veil was so long it almost covered her jeans. She wore something old, something new, something borrowed, something blue, something lilac, something red, something yellow, something green, something orange..." It was beginning to sound like "The Dozens" Stan and he used to entertain the boys and the women with. It felt like home. It felt good.

"You know what a dope ring is, don't you? That's twelve members a' your family sitting in a circle," Ham shot back.

Alan stood up to pull his guitar out of its case for some background rhythm. Leaning against the table, he thought for a moment, and then set his next barrage of family insults to meter and rhyme:

"His pa's a genius, none would refute.
Ran an elevator, but couldn't learn the route."

Ham broke out in a delighted grin, played some background rhythm of his own, and then countered with:

"Well ding my dong, and light my light.
Saddle that ass! I rides tonight."

Alan's turn again:

"Reincarnation gives a broader view;
So tell me, sir: in your last life,
What part of the ass were you?"

He leaned back and waited for Ham's return volley. It wasn't long in coming. Several deep base chords, a keyboard riff, and then:

"No wonder the fool's got no damn worth:
His ma threw out the baby
an' saved the afterbirth.
But give her credit.
She's sure got pluck:
Wearing that bright red dress,
Makes her look like a bow-legged fire truck."

In spite of himself, Alan began unwinding, the way he always did, doing "The Dozen"s with Stan and the boys, back home:

"Ease off, nigger!
As a beauty you're no star.
There's others handsomer far.
Now your face: you don't mind it,
'Cause you're stuck behind it.
It's us folks up front that you jar."

The next round was delivered by Ham with an even broader grin that displayed twice as many teeth as before:

"Cool it, Dude!
You're in a helluva stew.
My grandpa gets Christmas ties
Ain't half as loud, or useless as you."

Alan found Ham's grin infectious, warming him almost as much as the whiskey:

"Have a good look, folks,
It must be full moon.
Hey, friend, take cover:
Sunsweet's out prowling,
Looking for a new prune."

Ham hit an emphatic chord, and then did a run down the keyboard that sounded like ripples of laughter:

"Talking 'bout dumbbells,
Which really ain't nice,
When his ma gets her mind read,
They only charge her half price."

Alan came back with an elegant guitar riff that won him a nod of approval.

Ham's off-color rejoinder suddenly grew fangs and claws. Playtime was over. From here on in, it was going to get brutal. This was not going to be the watered-down version Alan was used to offering for a living room audience that usually consisted of Stan's two young sons, Reverend Haley, and the old people who had raised him since boyhood—but "The Dozens!"

Ten minutes later, still in rhyme and tempo. Ham called a cease fire with:

"He's really a treasure,
An' a whole lot a' fun.
So you folks take him,
'Cause I'm all done."

The silence Alan had only been marginally aware of suddenly erupted into cheers and applause. Drinks almost as suddenly appeared in front of him and on Ham's piano. The small mob that had materialized out of thin air around them consisted of late afternoon hangers-on and the arriving cocktail hour crowd. Even waitresses and bar attendants had stopped their work, inching closer to listen.

Embarrassed, and fearful he might have been recognized, Alan made a grab for his guitar and a lunge for escape only to find himself hemmed in on all sides by a solid wall of living bodies slapping him on the back, congratulating him, offering to buy more drinks, and pleading for encores. He finally surrendered, taking whatever comfort he could from the growing assurance that no one had thus far recognized Alan Kolkey beneath the grime, dishevel, and facial hair. He took a measure of satisfaction as well in seeing the cause of his present predicament faring no better than himself.

"Say, Bro! What you doin' hidin' out inside that ugly white skin? Where'd you ever learn to 'play house' like that?" Ham had to shout to make himself heard over the loud appreciation of this predominantly white crowd who had obviously never heard "The Dozens" fought before. Not surprising, since, regrettably, it was a dying art form, seldom heard any more, even among blacks. "Never mind! You can tell me later. Right now, let's us show this bunch a' turkeys what a couple a' brothers can really do. Jump in whenever you're ready!"

Reluctantly at first, Alan followed Ham's lead, elaborating on themes thrown at him by Ham, and weaving them into tapestries of melody. Losing himself in the opiate of his music, he forgot the people who were now standing back, listening hungrily. Forgetting himself as well, he began pulling ahead, taking the lead, giving lyric and melody to the pain crushing in on him from all sides. His song became a dirge, a lament. It started whisper-soft, growing in power as he wandered out among the stars with the ghost of his lost love.

Somewhere, from the outer fringes of awareness, he heard Ham calling out encouragements. "I knew it! Anyone who can play "The Dozens" like that has got to have soul. Come on, cut 'em! Make 'em bleed! Sing us a song that'll make us all cry! Break my heart, bro, break my heart!"

Crying out his grief now, he wove his improvised tapestry tighter with brighter, wilder colors. His song finally ended, dumping him back once more into unendurable reality. The crowd surrounding him was hushed now, spellbound. Had someone recognized him this time around and spread the word? The unbearable silence suddenly exploded into wild applause with endlessly repeated calls for more.

Relieved that it was only his music they were screaming for, he gave in to them. His next song was as wild as their enthusiasm, filled with rage, lamenting over life, betrayal of love, betrayal of self.

Still they screamed for more.

This time his music soothed and wounded as he conjured the melody and bled the lyrics of an old country classic that had been one of Dawn's favorites. He was playing now for her and, for a brief moment, she was there with him. Her lovely features, at first as solid and tangible as his own, wavered and blurred with the gathering mist in his eyes. His song cried softly now, piercing the hearts of all his listeners until they grieved along with him. The music finally died, leaving him alone once more, in the middle of this rapidly swelling, wildly cheering mob. While he wondered where all these people were coming from, more drinks began materializing in front of him.

Ham had jumped from the stage, managing somehow to work his way through the insistent press of people crowding around, and was hugging and pummeling him with a ferocity that threatened to shatter his spine. "Al, Baby! You are one bad dude with a song. That ain't no guitar, man: that there's a deadly weapon. An' you just murdered yourself a bunch a' willing victims."

"Are you with this clown, or are you independently insane?" The familiar cultured tones came from behind, oiling their way through the shrill accolades of the people pressing in closer.

"Independently insane. Why!" Annoyed at the man's effrontery, Alan did a quick about-face, cracking his words like a bullwhip.

"Harry Costanza. I own this place." The man introduced himself, taking several nervous steps backwards. "We met back in the lobby. Remember? The gentleman in the park who sent you here is my partner. If you're looking for a job, mister, you found one. Davis here: his band lost its lead man. If they sign you on, they'll still have their four weeks. And more, perhaps, if things work out. We could use a hot new group as our house band: work banquets; private parties; do warm-up for our name acts. Provided, of course, the rest of Wild Hunt is here. Tomorrow! As for tonight, both of you: on time for the first show! Oh, and Davis, see that your new lead vocalist is cleaned up and properly attired. We'll re-talk money and contracts when the rest of the band arrives."

Before Alan could draw breath for a few choice rejoinders, Costanza was gone and he was being devoured once more by the ravenous mob. Logic said minutes, but it felt like hours before the crowd finally began breaking up once more and wandering off.

"OK, Mr. Big-an'-Muscle-Bound, we got us some serious hustlin' to do if we're gonna' get you cleaned up an' back, in time for the first show tonight." Ham flashed a disarming grin over his shoulder as he grabbed Alan's arm and started hauling him away from his table and out into the early evening rush hour streets. The horizon-hugging sun, suddenly visible between several tall buildings, was brutal to eyes adjusted to the dim lighting of the dinner lounge.

"First: its back to my hotel for a shave, shower and a quick meal.

Then we gotta' buy you some new clothes before the Board a' Health catches wind a' you. Literally," he added, fanning the air in front of his nose with his free hand.

"Wait a damn minute, will you!" Alan snapped out of his daze and dug heels in, forcing his abductor to stop. "What makes you think I want to join that carnival act you belong to?"

"You gotta', Al!" Ham pleaded insistently, grabbing him by the forearms in an uncomfortably firm grip. He had surprisingly strong hands, even for a keyboard man. "You're a brother, ain't you? Well, this brother's hurtin'. You heard the Man: without you, we lose the gig. Then the whole band's outta' work. Permanently. Breach a' contract. We'll be black-balled." Taking Alan's momentary hesitation as surrender, Ham started dragging him along once more.

"All right! I'll come quietly if you quit mauling me," he finally conceded, recalling with a bitter taste of irony how vehemently Dawn had complained of his manipulations. Divine justice at work, he decided. The Gods had a knack for making their punishments fit the crime. "A long, hot shower and clean clothes sound wonderful. I don't know if I'm up to handling food yet. It's been a while. But the shave and haircut part are definitely out."

"Hiding? On the lam?"

"In a manner of speaking." He was going to need all the beard and hair he could grow to keep perceptive customers at the club from recognizing him.

"From the law?"

"I almost wish that's all it was. But no, I'm not."

"Personal?"

"Yes!"

"Look! I ain't in the habit a' stickin' my nose where it ain't invited, but you're doin' me a big favor right now." Ham paused, looking into Alan's eyes with a depth of sincerity that did not require his lost esper talents to read. "So, if there's ever anything I can do to help in return, even if it's only just listenin', please, let me know! Man! I got a feelin' it's gonna' be one hell of a story when it finally gets told. You look about five-hundred years old an' beat with a chain. An' your clothes look like they was pulled out'v a snowbank during a spring thaw."

"Thanks, Ham! Maybe someday, when we can both handle it, I'll take you up on your offer." Alan was grateful when Ham ended it there, allowing him his privacy. This time he followed without having to be pulled along. As they walked, he watched faceless people flowing past: busy ants racing at different speeds in dozens of directions. They all seemed so strangely blank and monotone without the multi-hued halos of color he had always seen around them. Auras, Dawn had named them. He'd never read up on the phenomenon before because he'd never known it was one; never questioned it as different. Part of the way everybody saw things. The intensity, clarity and blending of various hues had always told him so much about people: personality, moods, even state of health, without ever having to actively invade the privacy of their minds. The colors had always been there, as natural as his sense of hearing and touch: part of the normal visual spectrum. Nothing he had ever wasted thought on until now, when they were so conspicuous by their absence. Had he doomed himself to spend the rest of his life like this, esper-blind and half dead?

This new career Fate had launched him in was also going to take a whole lot of getting used to. Costanza was going to take even more. He did not like the man. Something about him raised hackles and had Alan wishing fervently for his lost psionics: something more than haughty abrasiveness.

"Ham, do you have any idea what Costanza would be needing with a bodyguard? I seriously doubt the Pentacle caters to that rough a clientele."

"Don't know. Only just got here, myself. But I've been wonderin' about that too. Man, do you believe that dude! Felsh, I think he's called."

"He provides one useful service, at least: he's a constant reminder that Darwin was right," Alan laughed mirthlessly.

"Maybe so," Ham grinned, "You know, if you threw that dude in the bay, I bet you could skim off 'ugly' for a week. I mean, his knuckles rub the ground when he walks. The waitresses say, if he weren't mean, rotten, and crazy he wouldn't have no personality at all. He's on the books as Head of Security. But in my book, that's not all he does around there.

"I'd steer clear a' him." Ham paused for a moment to look back, a warning signal flashing in his eyes. "I seen the way he was eyeballin' you back there. He didn't look to me like he was plannin' on joinin' your fan club. If you ask me, there's more shit around that place than a thousand-year-old cesspool. But dammit, it's a job. They pay their bands real good too. An' it's a chance to settle down in one place for a while. You heard the Man! If the customers dig us, we could be the house band for the classiest club in 'Frisco. Drawin' a steady paycheck ain't gonna' hurt me none either. So, for chrissake, let's mind our own business an' do what we're bein' paid for. Nothing else, all right?

"Honest, Al! I don't know how we're ever gonna' have you ready to go on tonight." Ham had decided it was time to drop the subject. "I've seen 'haggard' before, but right now, your face could hold a four-day rain. I mean it. You look worse'n the inside of a bookin' agent's nightmare. Man, oh man! What have you been tryin' to do, kill yourself?"

That had been the general idea. His failed attempt on the *Peregrine*, and later when he had wanted only to find somewhere to curl up and wait till death finally found him: had they been the intervention of a 'guardian angel,' for lack of anything else to call it, or had it simply been the mechanations of an over-active conscience kicking in? Whatever it was, it had kept him moving, searching, driving him unceasingly, sabotaging every attempt at submission. Ham was beginning to look like another uninvited angel. Perhaps, it was just as well. There had to be a less painful way of checking out than by slow starvation.

Until he could find that better way, well, he had never liked being drunk before, but right now it seemed infinitely more desirable than staying sober and continuing to hurt this way. He suddenly regretted having allowed himself to be dragged off before finishing all the drinks that had been sent to him.

CHAPTER XI

E VEN IN SLEEP, he had to keep reminding himself: he was Al Falcon now, vocalist and lead guitarist for Wild Hunt. Alan Kolkey had only been a bad dream: the ridiculous, mega-macho construct of a legend-starved public, to be sacrificed up to them on a pedestal of hero worship. Nothing more! Al Falcon was all that was left of him, all that was real.

Standing on a sandy beach, he looked up at three moons swimming through a sky as emerald green as the sea below it. Several hundred feet ahead of him, he saw Dawn, ankle-deep in the rushing surf. Her eyes were searching the water and sky with rapt intensity as she slowly waded in deeper. Dawn? Alive? How, when he had seen her die, felt the bullet rip through her heart. Or had he finally died in his sleep? Was this the realm of lost souls? It was insane, yet however it came to be, thank the Gods! He had only to call out, run to her to reclaim once more what he should never have rejected. He shouted her name, again and again, yet all that came out were hoarse whispers, inaudible above the pounding waves. When he tried running to her, he found himself moving in agonizingly slow motion, like a film being run one frame at a time.

He stopped. Watched hungrily once more. Several hundred feet beyond the breaking surf was the object of Dawn's enthralled gaze: the silver-haired warrior of his still-recurring dying-priestess dream. Garbed now in sea-green armor, eyes flashing like living emeralds, he opened his arms, beckoning, drawing her inexorably closer.

As she waded further out, Alan shouted again and again in voiceless whispers. She paused, looked back, saw him at last, and began weeping.

"No, you're dead; you're only a ghost: a bad dream! I mustn't listen! Have to forget!" Tears were trickling down her pale cheeks as she turned once more toward the Silver Warrior and continued wading toward him.

Once he had her, she would be lost to him forever. Shouting soundlessly, Alan ran, frame by agonizingly slow frame, trying to reach her in time. The distance between them only increased as she floated into the sea-clad warrior's arms. Folding her within his all-consuming embrace, they sank together beneath the waves and vanished.

"Dawn! Come back! Dawn!"

"Al! Wake up! Come on, man, it's only another one of your nightmares. Wake up!"

The Earth was shaking again. No, someone was shaking him.

His head ached and it hurt to open his eyes, but the sight of Ham sitting on the bed next to him was consoling. He relaxed slightly and let his head fall back onto the pillow.

"Same one again?" Ham frowned with concern.

"No. Different this time," he mumbled through dry lips as he rolled over slightly to wipe the sweat from his face with a corner of the sheet that was covering him.

"An' I suppose you ain't gonna' say much about this one neither." Anger now bleached the worried concern from Ham's eyes. "Look, Al! For ten months now I've nursed you through hangovers and those awful depressions you fall into, for days sometimes, after one of these nightmares. You never volunteer much of anything about them, and even less about yourself. But I respected your privacy and never asked. Only things are gettin' worse instead a' better. You're gettin' those dreams more an' more, lately, an' dammit, I'm scared for you.

"Outside a' my music, I know I ain't got much polish an' education." Ham sat up straighter, folding his arms across his naked chest in an authoritative pose that commanded attention. "But I don't need to be one of them high priced psychologists, with their fancy diplomas on the wall, to know what I'm talkin' about. If you don't quit tryin' to drink yourself to death, an' start talkin', you're gonna' end up in the rubber room at the palace for peculiars. I've known a lot of alcoholics in my time, Al, an' you're not one of 'em. You don't need booze to survive; you need it to die. I've never seen anyone work so hard, or so deliberately, at trying to kill himself. Now why!"

Ham stood up, hands on hips now, feet firmly planted. The last of his patience had finally been used up. "OK, Al! This is it! I've taken it for ten months, watchin' you die a little more each day. Hey man, we're brothers: helped each other through lots a' rough times. Honest, I wanna' help you through this too. But, outside of a name I know you manufactured, you ain't told me shit about you. This time I really mean it. Either you open up and let me in, or we're history. I can't hang on any more, watchin' you destroy yourself like this." He paused to let his meaning sink home. It did. "So what's it gonna' be, Al, Baby? Do you talk, or do I walk?"

There had been a time when Alan would have felt the powerful projection of Ham's emotions like a blow from a sledgehammer, but right now, what he was receiving was hardly more than a reading in body language, a slight singeing around the edges from the fire of resolution flaming in his friend's eyes, and yes, perhaps just a momentary auric shimmer about him, or was he still slightly awash within the alcoholic aftermath of last night and only wish-thinking?

Whatever it was, he was suddenly very keenly aware, for the first time, of the pain he was inflicting on the only person who had ever called him friend. As suddenly too he was struck by the immensity of his egocentricity. He had been so lost for so long in a wallow of self-pity, so single-mindedly dedicated to the numbing of his own pain, that he had been blind to the pain he was causing others. Creeping cynicism had convinced him that Ham only put up with him in order to ride the gravy-train of his inexplicable popularity as an entertainer at the Pentacle.

Looking back now with suddenly clearer vision, Alan was forced to admit to himself that, from the very beginning, Ham had been far more than drinking buddy or wet-nurse on these increasingly frequent mornings after.

An incident that occurred only last month suddenly came flooding to mind. Starting out alone, after the final show, he had been heading down the pre-dawn streets for his usual walk along the waterfront. The sound of water lapping against shore and pilings, the fairy lights of bridges spanning the bay, and the dramatic panorama of morning spilling up over the city skyline: They were often so much more soothing than anything he could have poured down his throat. He had hardly gone more than a block when an uneasy feeling made him turn around in time to see a gang of skin-heads herding Ham into the alley that lead to the club's rear service entrance. There had been a recent rash of incidents in the city attributed to an unholy alliance between Klan and neo-Nazis. Ghetto-raised, Ham was quite capable of taking care of himself. That night however he had been far out-numbered and in desperate need of an ally. Always grateful for any excuse to vent the anger still raging within him, he ran back and dove in. Then, back-to-back and laughing in vengeful anticipation of their own kill, he and Ham had decimated their enemy's ranks. His friend's hands were bruised and swollen, but several days later he was still grinning like an over-ripe melon about to split wide open, and swearing it had been worth every lump.

Now, looking back across the entire panorama of the past ten months, Alan realized the vast majority of the rescue missions had in fact been run by Ham. Alan's impressive size alone invited constant challenge from bar patrons who needed to prove they were bigger and badder than he was. Perhaps it was considered safer calling out Wild Hunt's lead singer than tangling with Felsh, Malgrove, or some of the other serious muscle that guarded the Pentacle's management. It was an unwritten law: nobody messed with Costanza's people.

Ham had always been there, dragging him away when Alan would rather have stayed to complete the education of some churlish club patron. Ham was always there, too, on the mornings after a particularly bad one, gluing his head back in place when it felt as though it was about to fall off and roll away.

Sitting up, Alan took a deep breath and decided: if anyone deserved the dubious honor of confidante and friend, Ham had won it with his own blood. And his friend was right. He did desperately need to talk to someone. Still, how was he ever going to explain that he was—or had been—Alan Kolkey, owner of Space Tech and the misplaced adulation of Earth's teeming billions, or that he was a burned-out psychokinetic telepath? Ham would either think he was being made the butt of a very bad joke, or that Alan had finally succeeded in permanently pickling his brain.

The best route, he decided, was simply to edit out all reference to his former identity and lost psionics. So he told Ham of his problems as a child prodigy, how his parents had died on a trip to visit an old friend for advice concerning his education, of the guilt he had never overcome at having been the cause of their deaths. He spoke of the empty years of isolation, growing up in the old professor's mountain retreat, lost but safe in a world of books, music, and scientific research.

Unable to face Ham, he bit his lower lip for control as he stared up at the ceiling, "The old people who raised me: their worst crime was indulging my need to hide away. By the time I finally found Dawn, I was so fucked up I couldn't even handle a relationship with one tiny girl. I screwed up so bad I drove her out into a violent rainstorm, running from the biggest explosion since Krakatoa. She's dead now too, on my account."

"Is that the 'Dawn' you're always shouting for in your sleep?" Ham pulled on a shirt then dragged a chair up close to Alan's bed. Straddling it backwards, he sat down. That was Ham. Wake him up with one of his nightmares, and he was still, not only willing, but demanding to listen.

Alan nodded, awash in the flood of remorse he had so carefully cultivated for most of his life. "I wish you'd known her, Ham. She had a smile that made spring obsolete. You'd swear she'd stolen it from the Goddess, herself. She was so full of love, so full of life! Death Himself must have been caught as off-guard as I was. I saw it happen; but something inside me still can't accept it. She's dead, Ham, and it's my fault. I murdered her, as surely as I murdered my parents. You were right about me trying to kill myself. It doesn't look as if the Gods are going to let me off so easily though. Believe me, Hitler should be alive right now and feeling like I do."

Ham was lost within the silent country of his thoughts for several agonizingly long moments. Finally, he looked up, offering token of a fleeting humorless smile. "The way I see it, suicide's sort a' like crashin' a party you ain't been invited to: It ain't cool. So forget it!" His smile solidified into iron as he gave Alan's face an emphatic slap to assure himself that he was being listened to. "Another thing: the sympathy-patience-and-maybe-he'll-snap-out-of-it-on-his-own routine didn't work. You only crawled deeper into your bottle and drifted so far out by now it'd take a space ship to haul you back in."

"Even a space ship wouldn't help. I already tried." Alan's sullen reply was far more literal than Ham could have suspected.

"Maybe so. But a little hard truth might. So, here goes. An' if you're lookin' for any more pity from me, forget it! Pity don't cost nothin', but it ain't worth nothin' neither. You can't eat it, you can't wear it, an' you sure as hell can't screw it."

"But..." Alan tried to protest.

"Shut up!" Ham snapped like a short-tempered alligator. "Sympathy don't cut it no more. Remember?. It's reality time now! So, tell me again: how'd your folks die? Just the facts, Little Brother. Just the facts!"

"They died in a crash. Car skidded on an oil slick during a bad rainstorm."

"An' I suppose you arranged for the storm an' the oil slick, then talked your folks into goin' out in it."

"But they were out there on my account."

"Were you holdin' a gun to their heads?"

"No..."

"Well, did you at least ask them, 'Please, Mommy an' Daddy, can we go for a ride in the big bad storm tonight?'"

"No, I..."

"Seems to me, then, it was their decision, not yours. An' what about Dawn? What happened to her?"

"We had an argument. I wanted her to go back home where she'd be safe from me. I'd already come too close to killing her on three separate occasions."

"How?"

"There's no way to explain without you thinking I'd lost it. So let's just say I'm a jinx. At any rate, that last time, she got furious, slipped past me, and was out the door before I could stop her. There was a terrible storm that night, like the one that took my parents, and…"

"Never mind the weather report! What happened? Just the facts, OK?"

"She was shot."

"By who?"

"A deputy, a family friend, out looking for her too. He thought she was being kidnapped. He fired—hit her—by mistake."

"Ah-hah!"

"But dammit: she wouldn't have been out there in the first place, if I hadn't…"

"You mean you ordered her out into that storm, and she went, like a good little do-bee?"

"Of course not! I…"

"Well did you at least arrange for that clown your deputy friend thought was kidnappin' her?"

Alan shook his head, unable to speak or even open his eyes.

"Then, for chrissake, man, wake up! Ain't nothin' but a perverted form of egotism takin' the rap for other dudes' bad trips. Next thing you'll be sayin' you're to blame for that 'Kali' comet, or whatever it is, up there. An' while we're on a roll here, why not the mess the whole world's in, for good measure.

"Come on, grow up, an' quit playin' all these mind-screwin' games with your own head. Believe me, no one's gonna' holler if you resign as general manager of the universe. Honest!

"An' another thing," Ham added impaling him on a long bony finger. "Seems to me your problem's not so much the isolation you been bitchin' about, as it is a matter of in-sulation. You're bleedin' for a fox who's dead. Your mind says so, but your gut won't let go. An' you won't let anyone else in to help plug up the holes. Man, you've turned down every single chick I've ever lined up for you.

"Think about it: all that talent in the chorus line goin' to waste!" Ham paused to offer a lecherous grin. "And what about some of those classy broads out in the audience, every night? Some of 'em have the hots for you too. Big time. But not a tumble from you. I gotta' confess, I was beginnin' to think maybe you were… Well, you know, one a' them."

Alan laughed bitterly. As if the Gay community didn't already have enough problems as the targets of mindless prejudice without having to take the blame for him too! "I've tried, Ham. I really have. But getting Dawn out of my system has been like trying to deflea a dog: just when you think you've finally killed the last one, he starts scratching again.

"Ever since I lost her, I've been in a kind of limbo," he continued, staring at a small crack in the ceiling and trying to lose himself inside of it. "I'm not alive; but I'm not dead either. I can't let go of the past; it won't let me live in the present, and I don't give a flying fuck about the future. It was easy falling into this hole I dug for myself, but I don't see how I'm going to be able to crawl out again. I don't really even give a shit whether or not I ever do. Oh fuck it all! Goddess, what I wouldn't give right now for a fifth of something and a few fucking heads to knock together! Goddamn, fuck it all! Screw the whole fucking world! I've had it!"

Ham leapt to his feet and threw his arms around Alan's neck, hugging him and shaking him ferociously. "Atta' boy, little Brother! Get even angrier! But let it out now! As long as you're dumping all that garbage inside your head, there's hope. It's only when you keep it buried away an' rottin', deep inside, that it can destroy you.

"Do you realize that's the first time since we met, you've actually come out with some real honest-to-Christ, good healthy cuss words? Five 'fucks' an' a 'screw.' All in one breath! I'd say that's a fuckin' good sign. Y'know, Life could be a rose garden, if only there was some way of gettin' rid of all the pricks in the world. But ain't no way that's ever gonna' happen. So stay angry, Al! It's your strongest weapon. Only keep the anger directed somewhere outside a' you, where you can recognize an' handle it.

"Damn! It's good to see you like this!" Ham celebrated, slapping him on the back. "Outside a' deckin' a few deservin' honkeys, the only times I've seen you sober an' actin' alive is when you're up on stage, makin' love to that guitar of yours. An' talkin' about makin' love, when's the last time you got it on with someone?"

"I—uh—never… Well, like I told you—I've never been comfortable with people—and we lived way out in the mountains…" Alan's face burned red-hot with humiliation as he fumbled and stumbled over his confession of virginity.

"Not even Dawn!" Ham's features registered incredulity. "Dammit! No wonder the poor kid ran outta' there screamin'.

"OK, Al, baby! I guess it's now officially un-fuckin' time." Ham collapsed back onto his chair. "Let's us say, for argument's sake—'cause of whatever it is you don't want to tell me, 'cause I might think you slipped your mainspring—that you really were the reason for Dawn an' your folks bein' dead. Now, supposin' too, while we're both playin' 'Let's Pretend', there's a heaven where folks go when they've cashed their chips in for wings an' harps. Now: how happy d' you think the three of them'd be knowin' they died for nothin', seein' you down here killin' yourself with booze, by slow degrees, but still as sure as if you put a gun to your head an' went 'bang!'

"So you gotta' pay back for what you think you done. An' pay-back's a mother!" Ham bent closer almost rubbing noses in his determination to be listened to. And heard. "But why not at least do it constructively for a change, by tryin' to be the best at whatever you know they would a' wanted you to be. Dedicate your life to that! Make it worth somethin' again! What was it your fox wanted for you to do?"

"Rule the world." Once more, Alan's apparent sarcasm was more truthful than Ham was in a position to appreciate. Dawn had never pressured him, but her deepest, unvoiced sentiments had always been with Moshey. Like the African, she had seen him as a common denominator that might some day be able to unify the nations of Earth under one centralized, peaceful, and functional, global federation. They had both been such fancifully idealistic dreamers.

"Kiddin' aside, Al. You know, you almost could," Ham grinned. "We're only the house band, but you bring in more customers than most a' the headliners. Costanza knows it. That's why he pays us so good. He don't want us tempted away by better offers.

"You know: if you got off the sauce an' let us accept some a' them super concert an' recordin' offers we been gettin' lately you could be another Presley." Ham's grin faded as he started pacing impatiently. "Al! You got the stuff it takes to be the next King: the 'Big Daddy Cool of Country Rock 'n Soul.' There's this strange, hypnotic magic between you and the audience. Your audience! I see it every night. Your music cries an' they cry with you; you laugh an' they're dancin' around the tables. I swear: if you stopped in the middle of a set an' told 'em all to go to Hell, they'd run right out an' start lookin' for the place."

"I don't want to be king of anything, dammit!" Alan snarled, recalling how it had felt to be the caged lion at the petting zoo. "So forget all the 'tempting' offers! If there's any hope for me ever getting my shit together, like you seem to think, it sure as hell won't be while I'm tearing around the country, being mobbed by deranged fans."

"OK. Agreed!" Ham raised his hand in surrender. "I sort a' like stayin' planted in one spot, myself. Still: from now on, you're gonna' start listenin' to me, hear? Any more a' your shit, an', I mean it, I'm walkin'. Startin' right now: you're off the booze, an' eatin' right for a change! You've lost so much weight the ladies in the audience who used to drool over that fantastic physique you once had are all wantin' to play nurse and mommy now.

"I swear, Al! If you got closer to Hell each time you took a drink, you'd be past it by now." Ham was hovering over him now, pleading, demanding, with eyes and hands that held Alan in their iron grip. "Like I said, you don't need the stuff. You're only usin' it—the same way you been instigatin' most a' them fights you're always gettin' me caught in the middle of—hopin' some slime bucket'll finally succeed in doin' your dirty work for you. Probably the only reason you haven't succeeded so far is 'cause there's another part a' you that wants to live, just as bad. No matter what you may think, deep down, you're a survivor, Al. How about givin' that side some help for a change. Maybe together we can get down there where you really live and give yourself a kick-start.

"You can do it Al, Baby! I know you can. So listen up good!" Ham smiled grimly, giving him another love pat on the cheek. "From now on, if you got problems, you work 'em out in Costanza's gym, pumpin' iron and punchin' out a bag instead a' rowdy customers. The Man ain't likin' how you been lookin' lately, himself, so I don't think he'll mind a bit."

"Yes sir!" Alan saluted half-seriously. He was trying to cover up a kaleidoscope of emotions, warring against each other, within him. Finally, breathing relief, he stretched himself out across his bed and surrendered to the inevitability of Ham's wisdom. Looking out at the world from the inside of a whiskey bottle had been a nightmare he would be glad to see the end of. He was sick of running away, or more accurately, drifting aimlessly, bumping against submerged rocks, and continually beaching himself on the sand. Ham had offered, no, demanded, to be his temporary rudder and sail. For the first time, Alan looked up, clearly seeing a friend: one who deserved a hell of a lot better than what he'd been getting. He closed his eyes and swore an oath to the Goddess Dawn's indwelling spirit had started him invoking as well, that this was one friend whose trust he would not betray.

"Oh, one other thing," Ham's voice intruded on his thoughts, "we gotta' see about gettin' you deflowered. It's about time, don't you think? Look, I got a friend who's a workin' girl. She owes me. An' guys with problems like yours are her specialty. She's a real lady, and an artist. She'll break you in like a yearlin' colt, an' have you feelin' fine as peach fuzz in no time.

"Something else too, while I got your attention," Ham was not going to let up, it seemed, "you are also gonna' start socializin' with people, 'specially our own guys in the band. Now I'll admit, they are a little off the wall at times," Ham raised his hands to ward off protest. But, sure as hell, no worse 'n us. An' surprise! They got problems too. Believe it or not, you ain't the only dude in the world who's hurtin'. Some folks even got real problems: like Sam, the head bartender. His wife's dyin'. Cancer, he says. An' Chen Lu, the pastry chef: he got word last week that an earthquake over in China just wiped out his entire family. Then there's our own little friend, Petie: washin' dishes down in the kitchens, hangin' around an' runnin' our errands for us whenever he's off duty. Poor little guy's so lonely, so hungry for someone, anyone, to pay him some notice!" Ham rose and headed for the door. Before closing it behind him, he turned to add a final postscript. "It wouldn't hurt, y' know, to start thinkin' a lot more about them for a change, and a whole lot less about poor, poor you."

Drained, head throbbing from too much whiskey last night, Alan nodded stiffly. Perhaps it was as well, letting Ham take charge of his life. For too long now he had stood immobile, directionless, without purpose.

"'Dear God,'" he prayed silently as he drifted back to sleep. He was remembering lines from Robert Frost that Dawn often quoted, "'If you will forgive the many little jokes I've played on you, I'll forgive the great big joke you played on me.' And please, deliver me from my greatest enemy: myself!"

•••

Desiré Storm dropped the key back into her purse, opened the door, and flicked a light switch. With a sweeping gesture of her hand, she invited Alan into her small ,tastefully furnished apartment. Still laughing, he closed the door then turned to help her off with her coat. "I was a total wreck all evening, right up until your false eyelash fell into my martini. You know, you haven't lived until you've had a sexy olive winking up at you from a cocktail glass. That's when I finally managed to loosen up and start enjoying myself.

"I can't remember the last time I laughed as hard as I did tonight," Alan added, looking down at her with gratitude and, yes, even budding fondness. "I've always been so afraid of losing control. Then suddenly you had me laughing at myself and seeing how ridiculous I really was: what a pompous, gloomy, breast-beating egotist I've been all my life."

"Congratulations! Realizing you're an asshole is half way there to not being one any more." Desiré took his coat and draped it, along with hers, over a convenient chair. Her laughter was infectious and made him forget again that she was a high-priced call girl, and that he was only her client for the evening. "When I promised Ham I'd take you on, I figured, 'Oh boy! What am I letting myself in for: another crispy critter?' But you know, you're nice, really nice! Now, I'll admit the evening did get off to a pretty shaky start. Like you said, after the eyelash incident and we were finally able to stop laughing, well it was like having dinner with an old friend. Honest: was Ham putting me on about you actually being—untried?" She was trying to be diplomatic as she made a visible effort to hide her incredulity.

"No. He wasn't joking. It's true all right." Alan was beginning to feel very, very foolish and terribly awkward again.

"Care to talk about it?" She poured generous amounts of whiskey over some ice cubes, then handed him the glass. Apparently, she had decided to adopt a matter-of-fact approach. "You're not…"

"Gay?" he laughed. "You don't know how many times that tag's been pinned on me. No, I'm not. It's not a medical problem, either. It's all in my head, Ham keeps reminding me. He says I'm suffering from a hyperactive conscience with a virus-infested program. If I try to explain any further beyond that, I'll be here all night boring you to tears. Believe me, as someone who was once very dear to me would have put it: it's a three-hanky story that belongs on the afternoon soaps."

"That's encouraging. I suppose," she frowned. "Well, enough with the preliminaries! Class is in session and it's time to get to work." She picked up a remote from the coffee table and activated the entertainment center. Soft mood music began to flow from every corner of the room. Reclaiming his untouched drink, she set it down on the table next to the remote and poured herself into his arms.

"Now relax! Don't go getting yourself all worked up trying to perform like 'Superstud' your first trip between the sheets," she crooned, wriggling seductively against him. "One thing you need to remember: making love is a lot like sleeping or acting natural: the harder you try to do it well, the worse it gets. So make believe we're kids again, playing Simon Says or Follow the Leader, and I'm it. OK?"

Alan managed an anxious smile and tried to relax, but as she unbuttoned his shirt and started drawing feather-soft circles on his chest with finger tips that teased and titillated, he suddenly froze. The old sentinels were still up. Why, when he knew his psionics were dead and there was no longer any need to fear for the safety of this woman? Had Dawn been right, after all? Had his fear of them been nothing more than an unconscious rationalization to hide behind, rather than admit he could not handle the even more potentially dangerous energies of untried and intractable emotions? Had *they* been the unseen enemy all along? He had to admit, he had never been comfortable with commitments, emotional situations of any kind. Children, though! Somehow with them, at least, and with Stan's boys especially, he had always been able to be spontaneous, cheerful: himself. Except for little Hassan, back in Tabriz: a bond of mutual need had begun forming, and had to be as quickly severed.

"What happened? Is something wrong?" Desiré looked up from her work with more than merely professional concern mirrored in her eyes.

"I was afraid, for a moment, that I might hurt..."

"You're not into S & M are you?" she frowned suspiciously.

"Hell no! Only..."

"Afraid you might be too big for little me?" Amusement replaced the frown.

"Uh... Yes. I guess," He stumbled over his words. Lying never sat well with him.

Amusement exploded into a gust of deep-throated laughter that sounded almost condescending. "When I was younger, just starting out on the streets, I had more than my share of weirdos with their whips and chains and their kinky hang-ups. I was ripped open more than once before I finally wised up. Other than that, there hasn't been a prick yet that I couldn't accommodate."

Alan smiled at the meaning she had taken. Soon enough, she was going to decide that the only thing big about him were the delusions of grandeur he was laboring under. For now, the irony helped him untie a few more knots in his brain.

Desiré was a handsome woman with long, silky black hair done up in a braided twist. She might even have gotten away with being described as 'voluptuous.' She was taller, much more bosomy than Dawn had been, and certainly dressed more tastefully, more seductively than Dawn ever had. Even under Gertha's calculating manipulations, clothing had been her special place to hide out inside of. In her own way, she had been running as hard and as desperately as he had. Small wonder they had never been able to find each other!

Alan's soul echoed, hollow as a cavern, with the vain wish that the woman in his arms, as tantalizing as she was beginning to prove herself, might have been Dawn. She was dead, he reminded himself once more with brutal candor. Growing acceptance had granted him a small pocket of comfort in the realization that a tiny part of her was still alive within him, that part of them both which had inseparably merged during their mind-fusion. Some day, perhaps, it might prove a beacon that would lead her back to him, her soul reborn into another body. Until then, he promised himself, he would wait, ever-patient, ever-searching.

For now, however, he had to go on with the business of living. He owed Ham, and he owed himself that much, at least. During these past few days of enforced sobriety, reality had started to become more real, more tolerable. Besides, Desiré's skilled caresses were beginning to awaken strange new urgencies within him. He closed his eyes, took a long, deep breath, and let go of his fear.

Under her laughing encouragements, he fumbled nervously with zipper and brassiere hooks. So clumsy! Such a total klutz! Alan could not believe these were the same hands that had once performed the innumerable, infinitely delicate operations necessary to crafting, and later, navigating a space-going vessel. Again irony pinched him with its strange twist of humor, and once more, he was able to laugh at himself.

Laughing along with him, Desiré helped, guiding his fingers, teasing, and encouraging. At last, her dress and undergarments lay in a pile at her feet.

As a boy, he had occasionally drooled over contraband magazines smuggled into the house. But that was before he decided to stop tormenting himself with temptations of pleasures he must never permit himself to indulge in. Aside from them, this was the first time he had ever seen a woman naked—'skyclad,' Dawn used to say. He preferred the euphemism, himself. It sounded so much more poetic.

Hesitantly, he reached out to touch her full breasts. He could not believe how warm, how wonderfully velvet-soft she was as she guided his awkward caresses. She laughed with throaty sensuality when a fingernail run up and down his spine sent delicious shivers on incredible journeys through his entire body.

Delighted at the discovery that he could respond so readily, he bent to kiss her with an eagerness and abandon that startled him.

"How the hell did a hunk of beefcake like you ever manage to hang on to his—cherry for so long?" Wriggling out of his embrace, she took his hand, and started pulling him toward the bedroom. "I'll never understand why some enterprising broad never managed to sneak her way past your defenses before this."

Alan would have liked to credit Ham with the preliminary ground-breaking, but somehow he was not in the mood for chit chat right now. Perhaps later he would give the bastard his due, he decided, as he followed unprotestingly. He made no protest either when she unfastened his belt and pants, hitched them down, then shoved him unceremoniously onto the bed, pulling them off, shoes and all. He had never before so fully appreciated the psychologically protective function of clothing as now, lying utterly naked before her intense scrutiny and unconcealed admiration.

"I've got to admit: you are big. But, like I said, not so big, I can't take you on." She was grinning wickedly as she climbed down beside him. As his mouth claimed hers, once more, her tongue began darting in and out, curling around his own. She pulled away, then pressed her lips to the nipples on his chest, first left then right, tickling with her tongue, nibbling ever so gently: titillating, enticing, drawing out responses he never dreamed himself capable of. The warmth, the softness of her body wrapped around him like this was a wonderful intoxication that no amount of alcohol could ever compete with. He marveled and celebrated the adventure of this new world of sensation she was opening up to him. Eagerly now, he learned the touches, the intimate caresses, the secret places to explore with his mouth and hands that inflamed his partner, making her redouble her own efforts to arouse him yet further.

When she guided him into her, a part of him grieved that this magical awakening, this moment of transcending discovery could not have been shared with Dawn. If it was this good with a near-total stranger, what would it have been like with the woman-child he had so loved, and to whom he was still soul-bound, despite the separation of death. He kissed the living woman in his arms once more, and his body sang a strange and savage new song: a song that demanded to be played out to its last, final bitter-sweet note.

Though his body sang, his soul as yet could not. He wondered if it ever would learn again, as it had once sung at Dawn's merest touch. There was a time when his spirit had flown on the wings of a great spotted eagle and looked out through the eyes of a woman. He had been tall then, as tall and mighty as the mountains he dwelled among. Irrational fear and pointless guilt had finally succeeded in stripping him of everything, leaving him without family, without love, without purpose. Condemned to a life of esper-blindness, he was immune now to all but the narrowest range of audible sound and visible light. Without the esper senses he had once so despised, and would now have given anything to once more reclaim, he was nothing but a psychic cripple.

Forcing his mind back to the present, Alan intensified his exertions, drowning himself in his new-found sensuality. He almost cried out with joy when he discovered a still-living ember of the esper faculties that once had blazed so fiercely. He fed it, fanned it, coaxed it until it flamed once more: tiny, no brighter than a candle, but a flame, nonetheless. It was sufficient, at least, to allow a faint empathic awareness that informed him each time his touch was too heavy or when he moved too fast, too forcefully, causing her pain or discomfort. It also told him when he pleased, each time a caress or a thrust in concert with her excited, brought her closer to fulfillment.

Her pleasure and desire, echoing within him, enhanced his own. Her mounting passion inflamed him yet further. Her body became a musical instrument from which the sweetest, most intoxicating harmonies of melody and color could be called forth. He played her until both their songs roared to triumphant crescendos and she lay back, beside him, limp and wrung dry.

"You know, you just went and blew it for me." Desiré lifted her head after a long while, making a feeble attempt at anger. "A working girl shouldn't let herself come when she's on the job. You start climaxing with a john, and next thing, you're emotionally involved. Then he starts thinking he's doing you a favor, allowing you to taste his magnificent prick.

"Dammit!" She sat up, suddenly furious. "You and Ham really set me up! He had to get me back for that last one I pulled on him, didn't he?"

"Set you up?" Alan lifted himself up on his elbows, puzzled.

"Oh don't give me that innocent routine! You're about as inexperienced as my old pimp, back when I was working the streets."

"Desiré, honest! We didn't set you up. I swear, this was my first time. It's only that you are one hell of a teacher." His reassuring smile and quiet sincerity finally melted her.

"Well, mister, if you're telling it straight, and you can swim like that your first time in the water, believe me, I plan on hanging around for a couple of extra laps. And maybe for a whole lot more."

"Is 'Desiré Storm' your real name?" Her blatant admiration made him uncomfortable. He needed to change the subject: a game Dawn had been equally skilled at playing.

"Hell no! That's only for the trade. To my friends, and, I hope you'll count yourself as one from now on, I'm Barbara." Her smile was wickedly suggestive as she wrapped her arms around his shoulders and started nibbling at his neck.

"Oh goodie! You mean they make a Barbie Doll us big boys can play with too?" As delicious shivers ran down his spine, he laughed and flipped her over on her stomach. slapping her smartly on her rump.

"Knock it off, buster! Tired over-worked jokes like that were part of the reason I changed my name." As she rolled back over, her frown suddenly inverted, transforming itself into a wicked grin. "Hey! In the mood for another lap or two around the pool?"

"Definitely! But feed me first, woman. I'm starving!"

"You're hungry again already? Good grief, we only ate a couple of hours ago!" She sat up impatiently. "Oh, what the hell! All right. I suppose a little more meat on those bones will mean a few less bruises on me. My God! Doesn't Ham ever feed you?" She climbed out of bed, and pretending impatience, grabbed a hand, and started pulling him up onto his feet and out toward the kitchen.

"Oh, he throws a bone or two into my cage, now and then when I've been good." Laughing as he allowed her to lead him by the hand like a spoiled child, he gave her bare fanny a playful pinch to hurry her along. His appetite had begun returning these last few days since he had stopped drinking his meals, but tonight he was insatiable.

•••

Al Falcon, Wild Hunt's lead man, was finishing his last number in the evening's final set. Peering over his guitar, he fixed his gaze on the 'sweet young thing' sitting alone at a table close to the front of the stage, slightly off to his left. For two weeks now, ever since Ham had called his attention to her, he had been noticing the tiny brunette, always at that same table. She was there nearly every night, turning her back and a deaf ear to every hopeful male who approached.

"That poor deluded kid worships the water you walk on," Ham had said, pointing her out that night. "Look! Life can go awful slow when there's no lovin' in it. And by 'lovin',' I don't mean all the bed-hoppin' you been doin' these last four months ever since Barb showed you the ropes.

"Sometimes I think we created us a damn Frankenstein. Man! Can't you ever do anything without turnin' it into a three-ring flea circus? You know, you could do a hell of a lot worse than latchin' onto that sweet little lady out there. An' not for no one-nighter either, you hear?"

Tonight, that 'sweet little lady' was wearing something frilly and green that reminded Alan of a dish of lime sherbet and vanilla ice cream. It made him wonder how *she* would taste for dessert.

Keeping tempo with the music, he danced toward the corner of the stage closest to where she sat. As he went down on one knee, aiming his guitar like a rifle, he turned on his most disarming smile and fired several of his song's most erotic stanzas directly at her. Acting on Ham's direction was getting to be a habit lately.

His moment of attention was rewarded by two sad eyes immediately lighting up like miniature suns. She was surprisingly pretty when she smiled that way, he noted. Since Barb was tied up with a paying client tonight, and since he had not as yet made other arrangements, he decided she would be a very pleasant and refreshing change.

She looked so terribly young and vulnerable though. Still, how young could she be to have made it through Costanza's scrimmage line? He was very cautious about being caught selling liquor to minors. And how innocent, coming alone to a place like this? All the same, she looked so out of place, so lonely. She would indeed be refreshingly different from the jaded fare available around here. Ever since his Barbie Doll initiated him into the sacred rites of Eros, he had become a willing convert, eager to trade the limbo of the grape for the equally transitory euphoria of sex.

The sherbet girl looked up at him with large, helpless fawn eyes that were almost the same shade of brown as her long straight hair. An expression akin to worship made her almost beautiful now. He suddenly found himself wanting to protect her, especially from bastards like himself who only wanted to borrow a warm responsive body for the night. But then again, if he didn't, someone else would grab her off and doubtless use her a whole lot worse than he would. At least he always sought to give back as much pleasure as he took for himself.

Barb had been a very good teacher and a wise, sensitive lady. She had helped rekindle a faint specter of his old empathic sensitivity that first night with her. Through it, he was discovering that the more gratification he gave, the greater was his own. With increasing ease, he knew when he gave pleasure. The more he fed his partner's fires, the more he fueled his own desire, and through a loop of empathic feedback amplified hers even further, which in turn...

When he left her tomorrow morning, this little lady would be sated, knowing for the rest of her life, that on this night, she had been loved! It would be only this one night he would give her. He had learned about women like her from unhappy experience. Spending any more time with them than that led to annoying emotional entanglements he could very easily live without. He finished his final number for the evening, took his bows, unplugged his guitar, then leaped down from the stage before the applause had time to die down.

"Buy you a drink?" He offered. His smile and body language were both programmed for seduction. He was already feeling horny and wanted to get this show on the road.

"Uh...y...yes. Thank you." She flustered and fidgeted like a nervous schoolgirl out on her first date. When she finally met his gaze, he found himself staring into eyes that overflowed with adoration and unquestioning trust, melting a little of the permafrost around his heart.

"You're new to the 'Frisco area, aren't you?" he guessed as he sat down next to her, parked his guitar in a vacant chair, then waved a waitress down. He had bedded her the night before, and from the way her own body language was shouting at him, he must have performed well beyond the call of duty.

"Vodka Collins! And could I have a lot of cherries?" the sherbet girl volunteered. She was making a brave attempt at controlling the quiver in her voice.

"A lot of cherries for the lady!" Alan repeated the rather unusual request. "And a beer for me, Mandy." He sent her off with a promise for later in his wink.

"You're right. I grew up in Colorado: a small town I'm sure you've never even heard of, called Indian Hills. It's hiding out in the mountains southwest of Denver."

"What brings you so far from home?" Alan asked, making small talk to help put her more at ease.

"My boyfriend, Rick. We eloped—if you want to call it that," she said. Her features reflected the bitterness of her disillusion. "He had a job waiting here, and we were supposed to get married. We were only here a month though when he met this other girl and took off with her.

My folks never liked him. They warned me he'd do something like that, and insisted on me waiting at least till I finished high school. But Rick's job offer wouldn't wait for another six months so we took off on our own. After he dumped me, I was too ashamed to go back. So, I found myself a job in a laundry. It was all I could get. Then I moved into a much cheaper place, one I could afford alone, and... Oh dear, I must be boring you to tears. I didn't mean to..."

"Six months short of graduating from high school! And in town for only a few months?" Catching his breath, Alan almost shouted, as he leaned back in amazement. "How old are you, girl?"

"I... I'll be eighteen in October." She looked as if she had been about to jump up and run, but instead, impaled now on the sharp point of his frown, she sat motionless, no longer fidgeting.

"Seventeen years old!" It took an exercise of will not to shout this revelation for all to hear. "Lord and Lady! How the hell did you ever get past Costanza's storm troopers?"

"Before we left Colorado, Rick had a friend of his forge me some fake i.d.'s. He took me here our first night in town. I've never heard anybody make a song come alive— or spell magic with a guitar the way you do," she suddenly gushed, spilling emotional syrup all over him. "I was telling a friend at work about you. How sensational I thought you were, and how much I wished I could hear you again. Well, it turned out she's got a daughter who dances in the line here, and has some pull with the Maitre d'. They're friends, or something. Anyway, he never questions my i.d., and if I get here early enough, he always gives me the same table. The cover charge is a killer, but worth it. Now I have something to look forward to at the end of the day."

Alan stared at her long and hard, feeling a twinge of guilt for wanting to take such unfair advantage. But only a twinge. He was still looking forward to the warm smell of her naked body, aroused and eager for him.

She blushed under the intensity of his scrutiny. Dammit, the girl was actually blushing! He leaned back and laughed, suddenly disarmed himself, and utterly delighted with her. She laughed too, self-consciously at first, but then, as she lost some of her timidity, she began loosening up and enjoying the awkward humor of the moment as much as him.

Their drinks arrived. He gave the waitress a conciliatory pat on her posterior, then sent her off with a twenty, gesturing for her to keep the change.

"By the way, do you have a name, or should I just whistle when I want to get your attention?"

"Oh! I'm sorry," she giggled, once more the embarrassed schoolgirl. "Actually, it's Frances Morino. Only everybody back home always calls me Muffin."

"'Muffin?'" Alan found himself laughing again as words like 'trite,' 'cliché,' and 'pure Colorado cornball' paraded across his mind.

"I know! It's a silly name," she giggled, "something you'd call your cat or poodle. But when I was born, the doctor told Mamma and Daddy that he thought I was cuter than a muffin, and... Well, the name just sort of stuck. I'm so used to it, if anyone called for Frances, I wouldn't know who they were talking to." She giggled self-consciously again, but weakly this time, looking a bit pale and disoriented.

Alan looked at her drink. Except for having wolfed down the cherries, she had hardly touched it, and the drink, ordered when she first came in, she had been nursing all evening, so she wasn't acting that way because she was tipsy. Now that she had his full attention, he noticed her color: it looked none too healthy either, even in this dim lighting. And her dress hung a bit too loosely about her excessively lean figure. For whatever reason, she had not been eating well, or regularly, lately.

"Hey! Drink up and let's get out of here!" he grinned, nudging her with a tap on her shoulder. "The main kitchen's closed down, and a sandwich isn't going to cut it. I know an all-night place close by that serves up a steak dinner you wouldn't believe."

"Ooooh! That sounds wonderful!" She crooned and then flustered, embarrassed again for having sounded so overly eager. "I... I'm sorry. It's only that... Well, I've been having to dip into my grocery budget to keep coming here as often as I do."

"And you'd rather be listening to my noisy throat-clearings than eat?" Alan was having a hard time chewing on this latest confession.

"Oh, but it's worth it! After spending all day at the laundry, then going home to another evening in that awful one-room apartment: it's too depressing. While I'm listening to your music, I can forget everything for a little while, at least, and pretend you're singing only to me. Anyway, I need to dump some weight."

"Sure, you need to dump some weight, girl. Like Venus de Milo needs a manicure," he laughed derisively. "On second thought, forget the drink! That steak will do you a whole lot more good." He stood up, grabbing his guitar as he impatiently shoved his chair out of the way. Taking a firm hold of her hand, he started dragging her along in his wake

"Don't you want to change out of your stage costume, first?" she asked, breathless as she struggled to keep pace with him.

"What for? As long as I don't have to worry about getting arrested for indecent exposure, who cares! Hey, Petie," he called out as they cut through the almost deserted kitchens, hailing the little dish washer who was stacking the last of the plates he had just run through. "Can you put my guitar up in my dressing room for me?"

"Sure, Al! I'm getting ready to go off shift now anyway. I can bring it upstairs right away," the plump little dark-haired man smiled obsequiously as he took the instrument, handling it with reverence. Burdened by a slight spinal deformity and partial paralysis of facial muscles that made most people uncomfortable in his presence, he was as desperately lonely and eager as always to please. Alan paused to watch as Petie hurried off, feeling a pang of conscience for the way he took such continual advantage of the little man's desperate need for acceptance.

"Every time I see you you're in black. Don't you ever wear any real colors?" the sherbet girl asked, calling his attention back to her.

"I suppose it's the color I most identify with." Amused, he smiled down at her, Petie happily forgotten once more. "I'm hardly the first though. There was St. Germaine, back in the eighteenth century. And of course Johnny Cash, the most famous 'Man in Black.'" The high priest in a coven of witches was also often referred to as The Man in Black, Alan noted silently as he once more found himself unconsciously accessing Dawn's memory patterns. "I guess I stand in pretty good company. I do have this one costume though. It's white with red trim, a lot of glitter, and a neckline that opens almost to the navel." Alan shook himself free of Dawn's ghost and managed to laugh as he recalled his one concession to Ham's complaint about the monotony of color in his stage attire. "Now come on, girl! Do we stand here in the middle of this kitchen, blocking traffic for the roaches while we discuss my wardrobe, or keep our date with that steak dinner?"

Looking like a contrite child, she offered up an embarrassed grin and then allowed him to drag her along once more.

•••

"Oh, won't you please come in—at least for a little while? I don't have very much, but I can put on a pot of coffee for us." Muffin's eyes pleaded with him as her fingers searched frantically for a key lost somewhere at the bottom of her purse.

Alan surprised himself by accepting. During dinner, paternal feelings for this innocent child had begun stabbing him with barbs of guilt for the way he was planning to use her. During the taxi ride he had firmed up his resolve to walk her safely to her door and then leave. But after seeing the neighborhood, and now this building...

Erupting in a tiny, triumphant war whoop, she materialized the key, waving it high over her head.

Well, at least for whatever was left of tonight, she would not be left unprotected, he promised himself as he scooped up the key and fitted it into the ancient lock. The building was old, smelly, and roach-infested. No wonder Muffin dreaded spending any more time here than she absolutely had to.

As she flicked on a light, he found himself staring into a one-room slice of drab, furnished in neo-yard-sale. That bed was going to be way too short and too narrow to comfortably accommodate six feet, three inches of heavy bone, and lately a lot more muscle. It had been rapidly building up again, since Ham had begun imposing his program of force-feeding and regular work-outs in Costanza's gym. This promised to be a sleepless night, curled up like an embryo, but he had made a promise to himself that he was not going to break.

While Muffin bustled about performing her coffee ritual, Alan opened the one small window the 'apartment' boasted. Even the all-pervading smell of the city had to be better than breathing in the musty decay of this crumbling ruin that ought to have been condemned decades ago. Surprisingly, the air was not too bad tonight, he noted gratefully. It was warm and there was a faint tang of salt on the occasional breeze stirring in from off the bay. It was well past three in the morning. Down on the street, several drunks were wandering aimlessly, oblivious to the taunts of a gang of youths who apparently had nothing more interesting with which to occupy their time. The more he saw of this neighborhood, the less he liked it and the idea of this small, defenseless girl living here alone and unprotected. It was a minor miracle she had not already been raped a dozen times over in the few weeks she had been living here. Alone for the first time in her life. His growing concern made him feel more protective toward her, and the more protective he felt, the hornier he grew.

"Never mind the coffee for now," he commanded softly as he walked back across the room, turned off the fire under the pot, then gathered her into his arms. Her pliable body melted obediently against his.

She made no protest when he eased her out of her dress and then gently laid her across the ancient bed. But neither was there any glow of anticipation. He found only passive acceptance. This was the expected price for dinner and the protection of his company for the night. Although lovemaking seemed to hold no promise of pleasure at all for her, there was a look in those gentle eyes of almost worshipful adoration as she quietly watched him undress. He could not help wondering what kind of insensitive clod her runaway 'lover' must have been to have left her so cold to something so wondrous, so joyous, that needed to be shared in order to be truly savored. He could only hope that moving very slowly, with generous applications of TLC, he might erase at least some of the damage that had been done to her. Taking his pleasure off her without being able to give in return would have been no better than using her body to masturbate off of. Believing that her body was nothing more than a playground for somebody else's pleasure: that had to be the scrapings from the bottom of life's barrel.

The wheel of karma must have been spinning a whole lot faster for him lately. Only a few short months ago, his Barbie Doll had helped him break free of the chains that had bound him so securely for most of his life, and already it was his turn to try and free Muffin from hers. If he could only get her to understand what he was doing and to work along with him!

He bent and kissed her, long and deep. Then, kneeling beside her on the bed, he began massaging, then caressing with feather-soft fingertips, every inch of her body. As he worked, he talked to her. Keeping his voice as soft as his touch, he told her about his music, about Ham, and even how Barb had so recently helped him. Slowly she relaxed, opened up to him. And slowly, ever so painfully slow at first, he felt her body begin to respond under his touch. Cautiously now, he began exploring the secret places that gave the most pleasure, that fanned desire to its hottest flame. Every time he struck a responsive chord in her, he felt it vibrate within himself as well.

Ever since his first time with Barb, he had been aware of the gradual resurfacing of at least one of his old esper faculties. Tonight Alan was more empathically in-tune with this small girl than anyone else since losing Dawn. Her steadily mounting ardor was beginning to turn his own desire into a rampaging inferno, almost impossible to contain. Cautiously, daring to hope, he pushed out with his mind, trying to project his exquisite agony for her to feed on, to share with him, as he now nourished himself on hers. His efforts were finally rewarded with an answering moan as she drew him down on top of her.

It had taken infinite patience, self denial that had long since gone beyond mere physical discomfort, and it had taken all the skills, but so recently acquired, to bring her close to climax. But at last her body, writhing and coiling like a hungry python, crying out for him in its now all-consuming need for release, he allowed himself to enter her. Each thrust deeper inside her brought groans of pleasure and whispered encouragements that spurred him on to greater boldness. At last: the supreme and rare delight of climaxing together!

She was still clinging to him, weeping softly as he lay back, utterly spent. But her tears were for joy. It was a joy he shared with her, silently, wordlessly, encouraging her with gentle caresses to empty herself as she lay in the crook of his arm, her head resting on his chest.

"I never dared to dream it could ever be like this. Rick always told me I was frigid and I'd never be any good."

"That bastard's the one who was frigid." Alan spat the words out like venom sucked from a snake bite. "His brain's probably never been out of cold storage since the day he was spawned."

"You shouldn't have put yourself through all that on my account."

"Believe me, Muff, you were worth every bit of it." He put on his most reassuring smile as he brushed his lips against her forehead. "I'm certain the next time won't have to take so long. Although there is a lot to be said for prolonging the enjoyment of it," he added, punctuating his after-thought with a lecherous wink.

She looked up at him, surprised that he would even consider a second time. Alan had to admit, it came as rather a bit of news to him as well.

Muff finally fell asleep, snuggled deep in his arms, still desperately clinging to him. Unable to sleep, he looked down at her. Dawn had been so much stronger, so much more self-sufficient, than this child. And yet there was some intangible, disquieting something that reminded him of the woman he had lost. He was suddenly forced to take another long hard look at himself: the restless, promiscuous, half-person he had become. At least there were no more nightly drunks, nothing more interesting with which to occupy his mind than knocking brainless heads together. Ham was still the only friend he allowed close to him. But he was making a sincere effort at establishing friendships with the other members of Wild Hunt. With some small measure of success.

Granted, sex had a lot more going for it than sitting around trying to drown himself inside a bottle, but his frantic running from female to female was still only that: running. Nothing more. He was always just as empty again the next morning as when he was coming up out of a drunk. They both numbed the pain, only in different ways. And the opiate they both provided was so limited, so temporary.

Dawn's memory was still too sacred, still too warm and alive within him to ever dare hope he could love that deeply again, but he had to try, to seek at least, and in some fashion, recapture that sense of caring, of bonding with another.

He also needed the stability of a one-woman relationship: a trusted companion as well as bed mate. The girl now asleep in his arms was hardly more than a child. How much of himself he might now or eventually be able to confide in her was still highly conjectural. The only certainty he could lay hold of at the moment was the fact that this was no place for a lone young girl to be staying.

Something heavy crashed to the floor in an adjacent apartment, precipitating a violent argument. A door slammed open and then footsteps pounded up and down the hall punctuated by obscenities. Muffin started awake, her eyes wide with terror.

"Dammit! That finally does it!" Alan's neck muscles swelled with outrage. "You're coming back home with me. Tonight! Right now! Get dressed and pack enough only for a couple of days. I have Monday off. We'll come back and get the rest of your things then."

"But…"

"No 'buts'! Move!" He climbed out of bed, gathered up her discarded clothes, and threw them at her.

"I can't! My job…"

"Fuck your job! I'm getting you out of this death trap. Now! You don't need that shit job, Muff." He softened his tone as he took time from adjusting his belt to gather her into his arms. They could spare the few moments needed to reassure her. "You can work for me. There's always a million things needing to be done that I never have time for. And if you can cook: I haven't had a decent home cooked meal in over a year!

"I am going to impose one condition" he whispered assertively as he drew back slightly to look deep into her eyes. "You're going back to school. After you've got your high school equivalency, I'm enrolling you in a good liberal arts college until you can decide on a major. I like women well rounded, upstairs as well as downstairs. He aimed a lascivious grin at the small girl that made her blush again. He had never seen anyone actually blush before. Until Muff, it had been something that only happened to the heroines in nineteenth-century pulp novels.

"I know you mean well, but colleges cost! You can bet your guitar, and all the rhinestones on that costume of yours, they're not going to let me in on my looks alone."

Good! She was showing a little spirit. He doubted he could have lasted long on a steady diet of Pollyanna and cream puffs.

"Don't worry, girl! You can check with the IRS: I'm an equal opportunity employer; I pay well; and I offer terrific fringe benefits too." His small attempt at humor was rewarded with an emotional hug and a long, wet kiss.

"I love you already, if only for proving to me that all men aren't like Rick. But, honest, you'd only be wasting your money. When I was in kindergarten I even managed to flunk sandbox. Since then my only two best subjects have been lunch and recess."

"So humor me a little. I'm one hell of a tutor, if you haven't already guessed. I guarantee: with me to cheer you on this time around, you won't flunk sandbox. Now, finish dressing and packing. And let's get the hell out of here!"

While Muff busied herself gathering up her few belongings, Alan reheated the coffee, gave her a cup, and then poured another for himself. Walking aimlessly over to the small window again, he stared out at the street below where the same drunken youths were playing chicken with the few cars and trucks still out on the pre-dawn streets. As his thoughts turned inward, he found himself scrying the spider-web pattern of cracks in the walls, trying to see the future in them.

With all this talk about school: he had just flunked Basic Lechery 101. Again! He had begun the evening looking for a simple, uncomplicated one-nighter only to end up playing Sir Galahad and rescuing yon damsel from the evil dragons of the big city. Not once, mind you, but twice in the same night. Ham was not the only one, apparently, who went about collecting strays. He laughed at himself and then winced at the thought of the teasing he was going to be subjected to when he got home.

CHAPTER XII

ALAN TOSSED about restlessly trying to court sleep but his mind was wound on an endless spool. All these months with Wild Hunt, despite half-hearted attempts at fostering friendships, except for Ham, the band members had made almost no impact on his life beyond the music they made together. Until last night they had merely been there: crutches to lean on. He was on stage with them for five, sometimes six nights a week; endless hours were spent rehearsing; occasionally they all partied together. Yet he knew little more than vital statistics about them:

There was Chey Valantin. Long, lanky and good-looking, he had an easy-going Latin charm that won him friends and more than his share of women. On those rare moments when Alan had allowed him close enough, he had felt the warmth of a smile that was totally disarming. Too disarming. It had made him feel dreadfully vulnerable. Chey played a great rhythm guitar and a red hot fiddle. More than once his fiery solos had won him standing applause.

Tall, skinny, and almost as dark-skinned as Ham, Henri Lefleur played base and more than passable banjo. He owed his nickname, 'Bongo,' to his love for banging on the bongos and singing calypso songs at parties and between sets up in their dressing rooms. Dressed usually in jeans, flamboyant western style boots, and an oversized Stetson that dwarfed him, he loved to brag, in exaggerated Haitian accents, about being the world's only true Calypso cowboy.

Then there was John Derrickson. Short, cherub-faced, his deceptively innocent eyes were such a light blue they could almost have been classified as colorless. He was better known as 'Buzzy' for always having a buzz on, no matter what time of day or night. Alcohol, pot, coke, he was perpetually airborne on something. They had been frequent drinking companions until Alan finally found his way out of the bottle last year. Even then, Buzz had never really been a friend, only a warm body to bounce empty words off of. That tired axiom about misery loving company had certainly proved itself in their case. Now they had nothing left in common except their mutual passion for music. Alan grudgingly had to concede, though, high or straight, Buzz could play the hottest drums this side of Hades. He had choreographed some of their best featured spots, had done the arrangements for many of the standards, novelty pieces, and even some of the originals Alan and Ham had written. Buzz showed promise, himself, as a composer. If only he would learn to discipline himself enough to put a saddle on that bucking talent of his!

That, in essence, was all Alan had bothered to know of them. Until last night.

Chey and Bongo had drifted into his dressing room after the last set of the evening, wanting to talk. It had taken forever for them to get beyond the neutral zone of shop talk to the real topic of concern: Petie, the band's self-appointed gopher. Alan, too, had begun noticing his increasingly frequent and progressively longer absences during the past few months, but only in proportion to the degree of inconvenience imposed having to locate someone else to run his errands—Muff usually,. But most especially when he was forced to run them himself.

Almost from the beginning Petie had developed an attachment for Alan that distinctly bordered on worship, maintaining at all times of course, the 'respectful' distance of an acolyte to his high priest. He had found some measure of camaraderie with Buzz, however, following him about more in the manner of a starving puppy.

Chey, usually spokesman for the others, had been the one to finally fire the arrow into the target. He had overheard gossip among the kitchen staff suggesting that their withdrawn little gopher was playing around with an insidious new drug that had been sweeping the city during the past two years. Because it worked on the limbic regions of the brain, it had originally been called 'paradise.' Injected subcutaneously, the drug created an experience of one orgasm after another, until it spent itself, leaving the exhausted user in a state of euphoric collapse. It was psychologically rather than physically addictive, though essentially no less deadly. Hearing of it the first time had called to Alan's mind early experiments with laboratory rats who'd had tiny electrodes implanted into the pleasure centers of their brains. Each time they touched a particular lever placed in their cages, a microscopic current would surge through the electrodes, stimulating an intense pleasure response. It had not been long at all before the rat's sole activity was pressing that lever until they eventually died from exhaustion and malnutrition.

No doubt inspired by those early experiments, paradise had essentially the same effect on its victims. They worked, stole, prostituted themselves solely for the purchase price of their next 'ecstasy.' Once addicted, users were seldom known to survive longer than a year. Their last "ecstasies" were always particularly intense, literally burning the victims up as they went out, one flashback after another, earning it the increasingly more common street name: "nova." "Going nova" referred to that inevitable final hit that triggered a chain reaction: one intense orgasm after another, until the victim eventually went into cardiac arrest. Although this was common knowledge on the streets, the demand from new users was said to be still outstripping available supply.

Alan had been tired last night and in no mood to listen to needless agonizing over imagined nothings. Petie's attention span was about as long as the gap between his two front teeth. It was nothing less than miraculous that his obsessive devotion to the band had lasted as long as it had. No doubt, Petie had simply drifted off to a new interest and new friends. Alan had pointed this out to Chey and Bongo, suggesting they talk to Buzz. He was the one most likely to know what Petie was up to these days. Ham had come in just as the other two were preparing to leave. After being given a brief synopsis he had turned and left with them, throwing an accusing glance over his shoulder as he slammed the dressing room door behind him. Making an effort to become more involved in the lives of the rest of the band had been an oft recurring theme since Ham had begun managing his life.

Was it guilt or something else about the Petie situation that was bothering him now, making sleep impossible?

Alan had finally begun drifting off, when high-pitched voices intruded themselves into consciousness. Coming from the other side of the bedroom door, they were too rapid and too muffled for his sleep-fuddled brain to sort out.

"Dammit Muff, can't you and Darcie at least take it into the kitchen?" he mumbled, too groggy to crank his vocal chords up to audible range. He turned over on his stomach and buried his head under the pillow. Well, he had only himself to blame. After all, he had encouraged Muff's friendship with Darcie. A popular dealer at the Pentacle, she was taking courses during the day at a local business college. She had hopes of some day managing the casino, perhaps eventually even becoming Costanza's second-in-command. Alan had foolishly hoped some of Darcie's assertive self-reliance and ambition might rub off on Muff.

More and more, with the agonizingly slow return of his esper faculties, Alan was being faced with the realization that he would not always be here for Muff to lean on. He was already beginning to outgrow the comfortably protective cocoon he had spun for himself. Eventually, he would have to come out of hiding and go home, to start repairing the shambles he had left behind. It was a life he knew Muff would never be able to adapt to. She was content with Al Falcon, the musician. The Lady alone knew how she would handle the revelation of his true identity, and worse yet, the fact that he was a psychokinetic telepath as well. He wondered, too, how it would sit with the rest of the world as well. Here was one Witch who would soon be done with hiding out in broom closets.

Witch? More than once Dawn had referred to him as a natural Goddess-initiated Witch. After all, she had pointed out, candles, herbs and incense were merely props, true magick was a disciplined function of the higher mind, no different from his esper faculties. And he was so much more powerful than any other witch she had ever met. Gaia most certainly had big plans for him. He had laughed then at so preposterous a notion. He was no longer laughing.

After he left, and he knew now that it was only a matter of time, Alan needed to know that Muff would be able to take care of herself, financially as well as emotionally self-reliant, like Darcie.

Darcie! What the hell was she doing here anyway at such an ungodly hour of the morning? The sun could hardly have been up for more than an hour. Two at most.

The bedroom door burst open with an insistent bang. "Al!" he heard two female voices shouting in duet. Before he could force his eyes open and try to sit up on his own, he felt two pairs of hands tugging at him, rudely ripping away the last precious remnants of sleep from his exhausted brain.

"Al! Petie's gone nova. Chey and the others are with him. They sent me to get you," Darcie persisted, still shaking him.

Muff was in her dressing gown, he noticed as he reluctantly sat up trying to rub the blur from his vision. Her hair was still a hopeless tangle from last night's bout of between-the-sheets gymnastics. God, the woman was getting good! Barb must have been giving her secret lessons. She had even begun initiating the love-making lately. Surprisingly imaginative, she was forever finding erotic new incentives to excite desire, often even, on mornings when he had dragged himself...

Petie! Gone nova? Poor innocent little Petie, who... Petie: playing around with nova? No! He could not believe it. Why hadn't he noticed, he asked himself over and over again as he jumped out of bed, shouting for Muff to do likewise as he broke speed records getting dressed.

"Where are they, Darce?" he demanded, pulling on his jacket as he followed her out the door, downstairs, and outside. They paused a moment for Muff to catch up and then climbed into the taxi Darcie had kept waiting. "Buzz called us from his place," she replied as Alan slammed the cab's back seat door behind him. "He says Petie's been asking for you especially.

"We felt there was a better chance of convincing you to come if one of us fetched you in person," she added, almost apologetically as the driver cautiously pulled out into the bumper-to-bumper madness of San Francisco's morning rush hour traffic.

Better chance of convincing him? Was that how little they thought he cared? Was he still distancing himself that much from the other band members? Dammit! They had a right to feel that way. Why hadn't he questioned when he first noticed how much weight Petie had been losing during the past few months? Those increasingly lengthy and frequent absences he had found so inconvenient: why hadn't he questioned those, as well?

"Did anyone have sense enough to call an ambulance?" Alan tried to bury his self-condemnation under an impatient display of gruff.

"Yes! And the cabbie already knows where to take us." Darcie replied from behind a wall of ice. The big-bosomed girl was plumper than Barb, and round faced, with suspicious eyes that were sharp as daggers. No casino customer ever pulled a slight-of-hand on her and got away with it. "Chey said he'd phone the cab company's dispatcher as soon as they found out which hospital Petie was being taken to. The Cabbie promised he'd keep checking in while he was waiting for me to come back down with the two of you."

"Darce! I'm sorry," Alan repented, smoothing out the harshness in his voice as he hurriedly gentled his manner. "It's my own blind stupidity, I'm upset about. I've been using that poor little man—taking him fro granted—more than anyone else. I've been so wrapped up in only myself for so long. Costanza himself could be manufacturing nova right under our noses and I wouldn't have noticed."

With a toss of her head, flaming curls caught the morning sunlight in an astonishing display of fireworks. The daggers in her eyes, aimed threateningly at him, were sheathed now. Her features softened gradually into a more understanding smile. As she gave his outstretched hand an understanding squeeze, the temperature in the cab returned to a semblance of normal.

"Where is he?" Alan demanded as he came to a skidding halt in front of Buzz.

"Treatment room A, Al. Over there!" Buzz raised a tremulous arm to point the way. "Where's Darce?"

"Back with Muff. They'll catch up in a few minutes," he called as he shot past, following the direction of the drummer's finger.

Hesitantly opening the door to the emergency treatment room, his nose was assailed with the stringent smell of antiseptics. His eyes were dazzled by the bright overhead light, and his mind was caught up in the quiet frenzy of the trauma team fighting a losing battle with death. A nurse looked up and was approaching, when she was cut off by one of the younger physicians who had been huddled with the others over the gurney in the middle of the room.

"That's all right, nurse, I'll handle it." His tone was crisp, professional, and as antiseptic as the air around him. "Are you by any chance the 'Al' that Mr. Sweet has been calling for?"

Alan nodded, ashamed once more, that he had not even known Petie's last name. That was all the little man had ever been to him: just "Petie."

"Goodness!" The young doctor's manner warmed momentarily as he somehow managed a fleeting smile. "Aren't you Al Falcon of Wild Hunt? Excellent group. Took the family to see you last week." The smile faded, and it was back to the business of medicine once more. "I don't know if your presence will help any, but it certainly can't hurt. We still haven't found any effective treatment when they go nova on us like this. All we can do is administer metabolic depressants, intravenous fluids. And prayer."

"Al! That you?" Petie looked up through red-rimmed, watering eyes as Alan bent over to nest his head in the crook of his left arm. He was nothing but bones loosely wrapped in a skin ten sizes too large for what was left of him. "I... I never knew anything that could feel so wonderful could hurt so bad at the same time... Oh God! Oh Fuck! It's happenin' again!" Alan felt the little man's body stiffen and then go into rhythmic spasms as his badly swollen and distended penis went into an abnormally large erection clearly visible through the flimsy sheet that covered him. Petie had always been so shy, so timid, so very proper. He turned Petie toward him, hovering closer to shelter the frail body from the dispassionate scrutiny of the medical staff.

"Al..." Petie whispered hoarsely as the last spasm finally spent itself, releasing him from its grip. "Al... I know I'm done for. I..."

"Petie, if there's anything I can do," Alan encouraged gently.

"Yeah!" he smiled weakly, gesturing for Alan to lean even closer. "I promise: I ain't never said nothin' to no one, but remember when you first came to the Pentacle?" he whispered. "You didn't have no beard then, or all that hair. You looked so much like that Alan something-or-other. I forget the last name. But you know: that spaceship guy who saved everyone from Kali. I was always so sure you was him. I mean, not just a look-alike. Please, Al: If you really are..."

"I am... At least I was him, Petie. You weren't imagining." Alan smiled down as he whispered so only the little man could hear. He gave the shaking hand he was holding a squeeze of assurance

"Oh gosh! Oh wow!" He looked up with an ecstatic smile that added a counterfeit glow of life to his pasty, skeletal features. The smell of death was so overpowering Alan had to hold his breath and try not to turn away. "How about that! I... Oh no, please, not again!" he added, whimpering as another cycle of fierce thrusting spasms forced an enormous, incredibly painful erection. Through his resurfacing empathic awareness, Alan could feel Petie's pain washing like an electric shock, wave after shock wave, though not at all as severely as Petie was experiencing them.

Ever since Ham and Barb had begun stirring him back to life, the walls that had entombed his esper faculties for so long had been slowly eroding. Yet they were still nowhere near what they had once been. Had they, he might have been able to do something to break this bio-chemical chain reaction. As he held the failing body close, desperately trying to will life back into it, he felt it slip away like quicksilver, forever out of his grip. The racing heart finally collapsed into arrhythmia, then stopped altogether.

Alan stepped back to let the medical team go to work, knowing as well as they how fruitless their efforts would be. Nonetheless, procedural policy still had to be followed. Paddles were being lubricated as he turned his back on the little man who had been such a silent and loyal friend. Just how loyal, he had never known until tonight.

This time he would not sink into self-recriminations and manufactured guilt, he promised himself. He was finally done with that. You can't go back and change what has already happened. The past is immutable. But the future is not. If he could learn, grow from what Petie had taught him, if others might be pulled back before they were lost down that particular pathway to Hell, at least, then perhaps he could give some meaning to the little man's living and dying. He had ignored poor Petie when he was alive and starving for attention. He would not give such short shrift to his death.

"Even the least of us have treasures to share, lessons to teach. The smallest bird may also have the sweetest song, if we only have ears to hear." The words surfaced into consciousness: something Dr. Mishra had once told Dawn. He wondered that it had been called up now, unbidden, from the buried trove of her memory engrams after so long.

Dawn: still with him, still reaching out to him from beyond the grave, in his present need.

Petie's death had pierced like a surgical incision. Without virtue of anesthetic, it was cutting into the tumorous growth of grief, grief for his parents and grief for Dawn, that had been encapsulated and walled up for so long. At the time, their loss had been too painful to permit expression, and so he had buried the hurt safely away in a dark corner of his mind. At last the floodgates were open and he found himself weeping unashamedly, unafraid: for Petie, for his mother and father, and for Dawn. It felt as if an impossible weight was being lifted from his heart.

"Clear!" one of the doctors called out as Alan retreated back into the hallway.

Tears were still pouring down his face, cleansing and healing him, as the band members converged on him. Muff's arms were suddenly around him. Darcie, huddling close, materialized a tissue, and started daubing at his face. Chey, Buzz, and Bongo, formed a tight, protective circle, reaching out to him silently with reassuring touches. Moments felt like hours before the tears were all used up and he was finally empty and whole once more.

"Is he gone, Al?" Chey asked redundantly, needing to say something to break the painful silence.

"Where's Ham?" Alan asked as he gave an affirmative nod, he was missing his friend's familiar spoor as he looked up with an affirmative nod.

"He said Petie once told him he had family in Buffalo. He's gone looking for a phone to see if he can locate any of them," Chey replied, raking fingers through his long meticulously styled hair, the way he always did when deeply troubled.

"It's finally over for the poor little guy, isn't it?" Bongo asked, stepping back to allow Alan room to move.

The exaggerated Haitian accent he usually wore so proudly was barely perceptible now.

"It's finally over, Bongo," Alan managed, barely above a whisper.

"No it's not, Dammit." Chey fired his outraged words like bullets from a rifle. "I want to know who turned Petie on to nova. He sure as hell didn't just go out on his own, one day, looking for a supplier."

"Who the fuck do you think?" Set deep, in a hard, lean face that was all sharp angles, softened only by a close-cropped, pencil-thin mustache, Bongo's coal black eyes shot accusing arrows at Buzz.

"Hey, wait a minute!" Buzz squirmed defensively, backing slowly away. "I've never touched that stuff. In fact, I warned him he was playing with a loaded grenade, the first time I heard he'd tried it." Buzz always reminded Alan of an unmade bed, a shocking contrast, standing next to Chey, but this morning, he looked like the unhappy by-product of a nuclear accident. "Maybe so. But who the fuck dragged him along to all those parties where anybody with a few dollars and an appetite can score?" Chey looked as if he was about to take a bite out of Buzzy's leg.

"Who was his supplier, Buzz?" Alan demanded softly as he pried himself from the protective embrace of the two women and began stalking the band's retreating drummer.

Only once before in his life had he been a deliberate emissary of Death, dealing it out to the mob soldiers sent out for him, some years ago, after cleaning out a crooked gambling house. It had happened on one of his early 'fundraising' expeditions to feed the Peregrine's ravenous construction costs, or so he had always rationalized in order to justify the rush: the excitement; the sense of power; the thrill of danger they afforded. At gunpoint, unable to defend himself any other way, he had struck back reflexively with his PK, causing massive capillary 'explosions' inside their brains that had killed them both instantly. He had felt no more remorse at the time than he would have for the necessary extermination of any other vermin. For nearly a week after, the experience had left him sick with nausea, self-loathing and dread that he might yet become the fulfillment of his parents' as well as his adoptive parents' greatest fears for him.

At this moment Alan would have been willing to endure the experience again and yet again for the opportunity to permanently neutralize the organization that was manufacturing and marketing the drug that had killed little Petie.

"I don't know who they are, Al. Honest. They had Petie so scared he would never tell me. But I swear, I'll keep checking around till I find out." Buzz had reason to cower. He had never before seen such fury blazing in the gaze that was now leveled at him.

Chey stepped forward to stand beside Alan, his own mood almost as lethal. "Buzz, I think I can speak for the whole band, right now. We lost a real good lead singer when Vince OD'd. I called his folks last week. They say he's still not much better than a vegetable. And talk about loaded grenades: you play with a handful every day. Well we've had it. Petie's dying was the last straw.

"So hear me, and hear me good!" Chey jabbed an outraged finger into the drummer's rib cage to underscore each word. "You're signing yourself into a rehab program. We'll stick by you every step of the way, and you'll still have a place with Wild Hunt when you get out. But only for as long as you lay off the booze and junk. You guys with me on this?" he added looking up at Alan and Bongo.

The Haitian's features were set and grim as he signed an angry thumbs up. Alan offered only grudging consent. At the moment he was more in favor of using the bastard for a floor mop. Gradually reason returned, cooling his passion and reminding him that whatever else the man was, he was still part of Wild Hunt. And they had been drinking buddies not so very long ago. A quick inventory suggested that the pluses still outweighed the minuses.

"Buzz, please don't let Petie's dying be for nothing," he pleaded as the anger drained away. Muff moved closer, giving his hand a squeeze that told him she was proud of him. Buzz always sought her out when he needed someone to confide in. She valued the confidence he placed in her and was prepared to defend him. "Do what Chey's asking. If not for Petie, then at least for yourself. Look, I kicked it, thanks to Ham, Barb, and Muff, here. Maybe I wasn't as far gone as you at the time. But you can too, if you really want to. I'll help. We all will. We're Wild Hunt, aren't we? We're a team. Hell, we're family." Alan was suddenly aware of Chey and Bongo. As he turned to look at them their eyes lit up and their faces cracked open in smiles that spilled warmth all over him.

Dithering self-consciously, he smiled back briefly. Standing a little straighter, a little prouder, he turned his attention back on the band's drummer, still frozen in place, his back against a wall. "Dammit, Buzz! You've got as much talent as any of us, if you'd only let it come out. Chey and I have both seen so much potential in the original scores you've shown us. But that's all it'll ever be: one more promise you never kept, as long as you stay hooked. For Petie, for Wild Hunt, but especially for yourself, give it a try!"

It was Buzz's turn now, as Alan stepped forward, allowing him to weep softly on his shoulder. He could feel Chey, Bongo, and the girls crowding closer to offer their support. As he looked up to exchange glances with each of them, his own tears brimming over once more, he saw the beginning of respect and affection. They had finally accepted him. He was one of them now. And he had accepted them as well. Ham would be pleased.

•••

Leaving unnoticed through the deserted kitchens, Alan took a deep cleansing breath then stepped out into the service alley behind the Pentacles. He had been incredibly restless since meeting that party of vacationing geologists and their spouses after the first show. They had dropped rather a large wad of money in the casino before coming into the dinner theater. So, when some of the women begged for an introduction, Costanza was quick to order him to join them at their table between sets. Their stories of an imminent pole shift had greatly disturbed him.

For a long time, scientists have been predicting a major pole shift within the next hundred years. But, according to recent findings the party of geologists had shared with him, for Goddess-only-knows what reason, all these Kali-spawned upheavals had drastically increased the wabble to the Earth's axis of rotation. The concensus among his learned hosts now shortened the earlier predictions to between ten and fifteen years before another disaster of such immense proportions, this time, that civilzation would be wiped off the face of the planet like playing cards in the wind.

Several members of the group had voiced regret over the loss of Space Tech's owner. A leader of such heroic proportions would be missed even more desperately during the approaching crisis, they noted. Though nothing short of divine intervention could forestall the inevitable, the hope and trust he inspired, the symbol of unity he represented, around which people might rally, pooling courage and resources would have been invaluable. Under Kolkey's leadership, *something* perhaps might have survived the coming cataclysm.

"You guys are a nauseating bunch of romantics," one of his hosts had objected: an older man who had reminded Alan, all too painfully, of his adoptive father. "Be real! Kolkey isn't dead. Don't you remember? His ship came back home on pre-programmed auto-pilot. The bum just couldn't stand the heat anymore and ran out of the kitchen. As soon as President Moshey authorizes us to go public with the information, maybe, if Kolkey's half the man we used to think he was, he'll come forward and help out again. If not, shit on him! We'll muddle through anyway." Alan had liked the man's style.

Apparently none of the vacationing party had recognized him under all the hair, beard and stage make-up. Or had they? It had taken a monumental effort of will to resist the temptation to probe their minds. Perhaps he had 'resisted temptation' because he really didn't want to release a genie that could not be rammed back into the bottle. Still, why was information, not yet available to the public, being subtly spoon-fed to someone they knew only as Al Falcon, lead man for a popular country rock band? Could Moshey have… No! The idea was absurd, bordering on paranoid.

The smell of the bay was in the cool damp air as Alan left the alley and began walking in the general direction of the docks. He needed time alone now to rethink the events of the last six months that seemed somehow to have been leading up to this latest bombshell.

Buzz had been out of rehab for weeks now, staying clean and starting to compose some of Wild Hunt's most exciting new originals. His arrangements of Ham's and Alan's compositions, as well as many of the Top Forties dance music the band played almost every night, were also inspired. They were all proud of him.

As Alan began growing closer to the band, Muff had begun drifting further and further away. Increasingly remote, at times she seemed almost fearful of him. Ever since Petie's passing, as if it had been a catalyst, the re-surfacing of his psionics had accelerated until at last they were once more as powerful as ever. It was an exercise in self-discipline not to violate the privacy of Muff's mind to learn what was bothering her.

More and more, as well lately, he had been craving solitude: working out in Costanza's gym, routinely doing his katas once more, and taking these long pre-dawn walks along the waterfront. He desperately needed these hours alone—to think, to gain the insights and master the disciplines that would make possible a healthy and stable readjustment to being a psychokenitic telepath in an esper-blind world. He had to train himself in effective sheilding and damping techniques. Living and working in the middle of this teeming city, awash in a crossfire of mental activity, such skills were more necessary now than ever if he and his hard-won sanity were to survive. They had to become automatic, second nature, like his katas.

For the thousandth time, as he walked along deserted side streets, he wrestled with the priorities of conflicting loyalties and affections. They pulled at him from two worlds: Al Falcon, the musician, or Alan Kolkey, owner of Space Tech and heir to the African's idealistic dream of a UN that would one day evolve into a stable and permanent global federation.

Noticing Buzz's growing interest in Muff, Alan had encouraged it. Someone would have to be there for her when he was gone. Was that what was bothering her? Had she been aware of him deliberately distancing himself, and pushing her at the band's drummer? Perhaps he had been a bit too obvious. Though forced to endure Ham's well-intentioned nagging about all the times lately that Buzz had been the one to escort Muff home from the club at night, he had no choice. From the very beginning, weaning her of dependency on him had been his primary goal. He had encouraged, wheedled, cajoled, even shamelessly bribed, trying to get her to continue her academic schooling. Failing that, he had tried steering her toward vocational training. All to no avail. It was not that she was slow, but aside from studying for a general equivalency diploma, there was simply no interest. The only exception had been the cooking classes she still regularly attended. She was content living in his shadow, her entire world revolving, like a satellite, around his.

A fine misty rain began mixing with the fog coming in off the water. The sound of his feet hitting pavement echoed between the jutting docks and moored freighters. Alan suddenly found himself having second thoughts as he contemplated his return home. Alone. Granted, conversations with Muff were anything but feasts of reason. Grammatically correct English was an unfamiliar dialect to her. In a contest between Stanford, Binet, and Wechsler she would have lost, and Mensa would have laughed her off the stage. But the girl possessed her own very special brand of genius. She always intuitively knew when he needed to be alone and would disappear or stand guard, jealously protecting the solitude he so often craved. When he needed to deaden the pain of the bottomless void still gnawing at his soul since losing Dawn, she would always be there, merrily chattering like a hyperactive magpie.

Muff had become a comfortable crutch. He could sleep better with her lying next to him. In his dreams, Dawn was still alive and convinced that it was he who was dead. The dreams where she had called to him, pleading for him to hear, to answer, to find her had all but ceased lately. The silver-haired warrior of his recurring dying-priestess nightmares was becoming an increasingly larger part of the landscape of his dreams. Although Dawn still reigned over his hours of sleep, the further she now drifted from him, the closer she approached the emerald-eyed demon warrior, and the larger he grew. Alan always woke from those dreams abruptly and in a cold sweat, calling Dawn's name. The agonizing emptiness that followed could more easily be endured when he was able to reach out and find Muff. She was always there for him. Perhaps it was these increasingly more frequent episodes, more than anything else, that was driving her away.

The more he thought about it the less he liked the prospect of sleeping alone once more. He relished the prospect even less of trying to find another woman as sensitive to his needs as she. Muff was about as close to loving another woman as Dawn's still-vital presence within him would ever allow.

Tomorrow, he decided, he would inundate her with roses. Winthrop Hayes, Costanza's silent partner, had a private beach home and owed him a favor. He would borrow the key, rent a car, and Monday they would spend the entire day and all night, alone, mending the huge rift he had so foolishly created between them. He had always been so certain she would feel too much out of her element living in Alan Kolkey's world. Perhaps he was selling her short. It was time to start adjusting her to the idea. It was time for 'true confessions' with Ham and the rest of the band as well.

The sky was filling up with morning and somewhere close by a roost of pigeons was warbling greetings to each other. Misty rain was rapidly being replaced by a drenching downpour when Alan paused in front of a well-lit sign that proclaimed the building behind it to be "Duke's Gym Open All Night, Every Night." Located close to a popular fight arena, it catered to professional boxers and wrestlers as well as to merchant sailors, amateurs and wanna-be's.

Alan decided a heavy workout would help dull some of the static in his mind: as good an excuse as any to get out of the rain and dry off a bit before heading home. It was his first venture outside Costanza's private gym. He had long since outgrown the puny weights the Pentacle's owner used. There was no longer any challenge left, either, in the larger set he had purchased for himself last year, after Muff had come to stay, sharing his bed and his life. Lately, it had begun taking longer and longer to work himself into the exhaustion that allowed him to sleep through the nightmares without waking everyone. He knew how much it bothered Muff when he woke suddenly, shouting Dawn's name. Perhaps using a far better equipped gym like this on a regular schedule wasn't such a bad idea. Perhaps now was also the time for searching out a good dojo, as well, for the time remaining, before he had to return home. There was no urgency about leaving immediately; the threat of the pole shift was still ten years away—give or take a year. Three or four more months was certainly not going to alter the course of history, and his esper 'muscles' still needed more refining.

The rigorous disciplining of his body was helping him to better control his returning psionics, a control that was finally allowing him to almost totally block out all unwanted background 'noise.' It was a skill he was finding especially valuable when he wanted to focus on a single predetermined target and then selectively tune for either surface scan or deep probe. Finding the idea of invading the privacy of friends and even casual acquaintances abhorrent, he had reluctantly adopted the lesser-evil policy of practicing on strangers. Only out of desperate need for the practice that afforded refinement of control, he assured himself. It was a rationalization, but helped justify somewhat using even total strangers like guinea pigs. He found no voyeuristic pleasure wandering around inside the heads of others. The very idea of parasitizing or controlling the behavior of his fellow beings had become even more frightening than it had been before. As far back as he could recall, his natural and adoptive parents had both harbored the silent fear of him growing into some sort of manipulative power-hungry despot. He had always been painfully aware of their forebodings, though unvoiced and carefully repressed. At times, they had been as much afraid of him, as for him.

The challenge of the weights was gone, but Alan still enjoyed his workouts in Costanza's gym. The trapeze swings and gymnastic equipment were sorry substitutes for the heady intoxication of free, unencumbered flight he had once enjoyed, mind-linked with Garuda. Lord and Lady! He hadn't thought about that big spotted bird in months. Missing him now and wondering if he was still alive, Alan found himself slipping into the old mind link. Suddenly he was floating on an updraft between familiar twin peaks. The sun's disk was just becoming visible over a mountain-jagged eastern horizon. Far below, a mother gopher was scrambling out of her burrow in pursuit of an adventurous pup. He stooped to his kill. The feel again of wind whistling past with increasing velocity was exhilarating. He felt the sympathetic rush of adrenaline in his distant bipedal body as the avian half of him braked, reached out with dagger-tipped talons, then, in a mad beating of flight feathers and screams from the captive delinquent, caught another updraft and regained altitude.

They were coasting toward an outcropping high on a rocky incline to consume their meal, both halves now aware of the other. An impatient voice, grating on his nerves suddenly called the Alan half back to his own body.

He found himself inside the front lobby of the gym, leaning against a counter. The attendant looked at him suspiciously as he rented a locker, sweat suit and towel then followed the man's finger to a locker room that reeked of liniment and sweating bodies. Fortunately, he was wearing his own sneakers. Working out barefoot would have been preferable to renting foot gear.

As he changed, he thought back on the comfortable rut he had dug for himself. His music was as satisfying an outlet as ever. The originals he composed for the band, in a style affectionately classified by Ham as 'Country Rock-n-Soul,' were always enthusiastically received by the crowds at the Pentacle. He had found some very special friends among the band and staff. And Muff was always there when he needed her.

It was going to be a very hard rut to leave when the time came and he ran out of excuses for delaying just a little bit longer. He slammed his locker door and walked out into the large gym. Nonetheless, he had to. It was time to stop running from old hurts, time to stop running from his destiny, from what he was.

Come on, Al, he chided himself. You know you want to go home. You miss your family, and dammit, you even miss Moshey. You're just scared shitless they won't let you back in again. Zarkov and Gertha had loved Dawn almost as much as he had. The African too. He had come visiting, brief but frequent trips during Dawn's lengthy convalescence, despite a backbreaking schedule. Alan doubted he would ever be free from the pain of her loss, but at least, thanks to Ham, he had stopped blaming himself. Hell, they had both been little better than irrational children that night! But could the old people—his parents—ever forgive him for having driven her out to her death? If they found him on their doorstep, would they let him back in? The African, too, could he ever forgive, or trust again, even with the added threat of a pole shift looming over his head?

As Alan looked around the large well-equipped gym, surprisingly busy for such an early hour, he decided the place would do. And tomorrow he promised himself, he would start looking for a good shotokan dojo. He would reap a lot more physical and spiritual benefit, under the wisdom of a skilled master, than all the weights he could lift here and at Costanza's gym. He had gone as far as he could, practicing his katas alone. He needed others to practice with, to compete against.

"Hey, ain't that the singer down at the Pentacle?" The sandpaper voice cut through Alan's thoughts like fingernails scraping across a chalkboard.

"Yeah. That's him all right. Ever since the bastard started screwin' around with my—brother's ol' lady, last year, she won't have nothin' to do with him no more." The second speaker, with an equally unpleasant voice, looked like the end product from an unfortunate mating between a toothless walrus and an orangutan, and probably weighed as much as both hypothetical parents combined. A quick scan had confirmed his suspicion that the 'brother' had been a hasty face-saving invention. Alan could well understand why the lady no longer wanted any part of him.

"Hey Killer, why don't you take him? Them musicians is all wimps. This one wouldn't even make a good sparrin' partner; but breakin' a few of his bones might help you warm up." The one with a shovel-full of sand caught in his throat was offering some very foolish advice. This musician would prove no easy victim if they persisted. Still, he sincerely hoped they wouldn't. Fighting had lost its flavor and challenge. The anger was no longer there to fuel it. The inferno that had for so long raged within him had been laid to rest. No longer was there the burning need to bash ignorant heads together. Like those here in this gym. It had taken two years, along with all of Ham's and Muff's combined patience, but Alan had finally made peace with his emotions. Enjoying, rather than fearing and suppressing them now, he had even begun finding pleasure in the small spontaneous gatherings that were always converging around the band members after hours. Right now, at this very moment, all he craved was the chance to flex his muscles and his psionics in peace. All he needed was time. Time to think. Time to pump iron until all the cobwebs were cleared from his brain and he could begin to re-sort his life and his priorities. It was a crazy way to meditate, not exactly the way it was taught in the dojos where he had trained, but it had always worked for him before.

As he walked over to a chinning bar to start warming up, he decided to ignore the two muscle-bound cretins and the small audience they were attracting. He was not scheduled to go on stage again till this evening. Until then, he was making no plans for providing free entertainment for anybody.

"I dunno, Gravel-Pit. He sure ain't built like no wimp I ever seen." At least somebody in Killer's retinue was capable of rational observation.

On stage or off and like it or not, it looked like he was about to become the main event. There were four options he saw open to him for dealing with the situation: he could walk out right now (but he had never run away from harassment before and he was not about to start now); he could try verbally defusing the situation (that might work); and no way in hell was he going to stand still and let them beat him to a pulp in the quixotic hope they would eventually grow bored and leave him alone. The only workable alternative Alan could foresee, if Killer persisted in demanding his pound of flesh, was to defeat him so thoroughly it would immediately squelch any further such notions, from him as well as from those other flunkies.

The small entourage trailing in their wake, Killer and Gravel-Pit were advancing on him now. All of them professional fighters and body-builders, he doubted they would be daunted by any display of gymnastics, but it was worth a try. If nothing else, it would loosen him up for the coming battle that was becoming an ever-increasing certainty.

He chinned himself, one-handed, several times, grabbed a firmer hold this time with both hands, then lifted his feet up and swung over the bar. Letting go with his hands next, he hooked his knees over the bar and hung upside down for several moments. He pulled up from the waist and, grabbing hold once more with his hands, hauled himself up to a sitting position. After several intricate maneuvers in rapid-fire succession, he swung up to balance atop the bar, standing straight and proud. Pausing only long enough to hurl a contemptuous smile over his shoulder at the two stalking predators behind and below him, he leaned backward, hands at his side. As he began falling, he snapped himself into a fast tuck, back-flipped to a clean landing right in front of his unappreciative audience, then immediately spun about to face them.

The black expression on Killer's walrus face was a perfect match for the murderous mood he was broadcasting. Surrendering to the inevitable, Alan decided that radical surgery was the only available therapy for ridding himself of this annoying growth.

"Big deal! Swingin' from monkey-bars is for kids an' guitar-pickin' queers." Gravel-Pit's professional appellation matched, and no doubt had been inspired by the quality of his voice. He was hardly an improvement over his walrus-orangutan friend.

Alan was amazed at how clinically he was responding. A year ago, faced with the same situation, he would have long since plowed through this garden, harvesting over-ripe egos with a vengeance. Now there was merely the expedience of dealing with the situation, rather than inviting worse by walking away and leaving these poor benighted fools with the false impression of having frightened him off. Somehow between all the music, drinking, and screwing, he had managed to do some growing up along the way.

"Bet you think them whiskers an' all that hair make you look tough, huh? OK, 'Guitar Man.' Well, let's see how much of a 'man' you really are." Built like an engine of war, Killer pasted on a contemptuous sneer as he squatted in front of a curl bar, with two-hundred pounds of weights attached, that somebody had just rolled up. He took several deep breaths, grunted, then hauled it up to chest level.

Alan read his challenger's intent and, placing his right foot back, slightly to the rear of his center of gravity, he braced himself for the assault.

Pretending to lose his balance, Killer staggered in the direction of his intended victim. 'Stumbling,' he suddenly rammed the curl bar into Alan's chest, intending to knock him to the floor, and with any luck, crack several ribs in the process.

Alan was ready. Catching the bar in an overhand grip, as far from his chest as he could, he used the momentum of the weights to execute a 270-degree clockwise pivot. Twisting his torso for proper angling, he slammed the leading end of the bar, with its attached weights, into the pit of Killer's stomach. Flying backward several feet, the wrestler landed on his back, turning several shades of red as he gasped and wheezed for breath. The weighted bar landed next to him with an ear-shattering crash-clang, scattering Killer's pack of yapping hyenas.

"I don't think those two clowns are going to question your manhood again." A grinning, dark-haired young wrestler came forward to shake Alan's hand. He was a good deal shorter, bull-necked, and built low like a tank. His features were pleasant, his manner easy. Not at all like the others. His eyes twinkled with good humor and his smile radiated sincerity. His speech was accented with a faintly detectable flavor of Canadian French: another painful reminder of Dawn. As though he needed any. Her father had been of Canadian French ancestry, also. Born and raised in central New Hampshire, however, there was more New England twang than anything else about his speech.

"Hi! Name's Rick Turelle." the wrestler added, introducing himself as he continued his vigorous hand pumping.

"Al. Al Falcon." He smiled back, returning the greeting. It was a friendly harbor in this sea of mindless hostility.

"Hey, if you can fight as good as you toss weights around, and if you ever decide to trade in your guitar for wrestling trunks, I sure as hell wouldn't mind tag-teaming with you sometime." Turelle's smile suddenly inverted itself into a frown as he looked past Alan's shoulder. "By the way, even if you were planning on saying yes, I—uhh—think it's going to be a whole lot sooner than either of us would have planned."

Alan glanced behind him, following the direction of Turelle's gaze. Somewhat recovered and on his feet once more, Killer had joined forces with Gravel-Pit. Together they were advancing on him. Two more of the walrus's cronies were also closing in behind Turelle.

"Looks like two for you and two for me. Sound fair enough?" the young wrestler grinned as he turned to face the pair stalking his rear. Alan did the same, then standing back-to-back with his new ally, waited for the foursome to make the first move.

Gravel-Pit launched himself like a kamikaze hell-bent on suicide. Once more he had foolishly underestimated his 'victim.' Alan side-stepped to the left, cross-blocking an outstretched arm that was reaching for a choke hold. As the wrestler swept past, Alan drove the point of his right fist knuckle sideways into his attacker's neck, below the ear and behind the jaw. Out cold in mid flight, he hit the floor with a loud splat.

Spinning around to face Killer, Alan could feel the man's powerful surge of emotion. Gravel-Pit had only been fighting to win brownie points with his friend and stature among his peers. Fully recovered, Killer wanted revenge, twice now having been humiliated. A simple knock-out or fall was not going to do it for him. He was on a blood scent.

Killer launched a vicious upward groin kick. Alan grabbed his ankle from a double wrist block. As he lifted the foot to chest level, beginning to trace a high arc, he saw dawning awareness of impending doom reflected in the man's features. Uncrossing his wrists as the foot traveled higher along the arc he rapidly and viciously twisted the ankle. The arc continued over his head and then downward. Screaming out his fear and surprise, Killer's body turned a cartwheel in the air. Alan felt the snapping of bones under his hand then released his hold, watching the heavy walrus body land on its side with a sickening thud.

As soon as Killer realized he was beaten, he lost the anesthesia of total concentration typical of a fighter in battle mode. He was now fully open to the agony of crushed bones and traumatized tissue. Tripping and scattering his erstwhile admirers, he was screaming and rolling along the floor as Alan turned to check on his ally. Turelle had dispatched one opponent; the other, however, had him locked up in a full nelson. So engrossed now in his enjoyment of the advantage his much greater size and weight gave him, Turelle's tormentor had not noticed as Alan casually approached from behind and tapped him on the shoulder.

Momentarily distracted, the wrestler weakened his grip long enough for Turelle to wriggle out, spin around and slam an elbow along the side of his jaw, momentarily stunning him. As Turelle grabbed him by the arms, Alan yanked at his feet, heaving the man's hulking mass into the air to dangle helplessly between them like a hammock suspended between two trees.

Grinning in surprised delight, Turelle started swinging as he sang Rock-a-bye Baby. Joining in duet, Alan increased the swing. The chorus had reached its raucous, off-key crescendo when, on Turelle's signal, they both let go, giving the man a well-earned flying lesson.

Alan suddenly found himself surrounded by congratulators. They were back-slapping so hard they almost accomplished what Killer and Gravel-Pit together had failed to.

"Mister, that was one hell of a performance. How'd you like to sign with me? Climbin' into that ring with a guitar and a song before deckin' your opponents would be a super crowd-pleaser. Shave off that jungle in front of your face, and if what's behind ain't' too ugly, we might let ya' be one a' the good guys. We'll even throw in the white hat. What d'ya' say?" A short pudgy middle-aged man was shouting up at him, somehow managing to make himself heard above the bedlam. He had an odd-looking bald spot at the top of his head and a trace of mustache across his upper lip. The fat cigar dangling from the corner of his mouth had gone out and was sprinkling ash with every word.

"Come on you assholes! Back off and give the guy room to breathe!" the strange little man bellowed once more in a voice that was bigger than he was. "Hi! Lou White. My associate here's Merlin the Magician. We handle only top wrestlers. And believe me: you have what it takes to become one of the best in our stable. Easy."

"Thanks, but stables are for horses. I have other more

pressing plans. So, if you'll excuse me…" Alan smiled with impatient amusement. "I do appreciate the offer though," he added. That was about as polite as Alan was capable of managing at the moment, as he started easing his way through the small riot of congratulators. They were still competing with each other for the chance to shake his hand. Shit! He couldn't even come to a damn all-night gym without attracting a crowd.

"Hey man, we are talkin' big bucks here. You could make it. Really make it, with a gimmick like my partner was suggesting. The chicks go crazy over sexy macho-type wrestlers." Merlin was slightly taller than his partner and a good deal leaner. He had a weasel face that Alan would not have trusted with his psionics cranked up to full throttle.

"I wish you'd consider my offer, Al." Turelle followed as Alan nodded to several more well-wishers and continued moving away from the two promoters. "We sure would make one terrific team. By the way, that was quite a stunt you pulled back there, throwing the bar back in Killer's gut like it didn't weigh nothing at all. Say, how much can you bench press?"

"I don't really know," Alan shrugged, not terribly concerned with numbers at the moment. "The largest weights I own are fifty-pounders, and I can only crowd eight of them on my bar.

"'Only,' he says!" Turelle laughed in mock disbelief. "Man, if you're pressing four, and toss two around like that, I bet you could do another hundred real easy.

"Hey! That bar on the bench over there's got five hundred on it." Turelle suddenly grabbed Alan's arm, stopping him short. "Killer's been bragging on how he'll be pressing it by next month. All he can manage right now is four-fifty. Why don't you put the screws to him one more time. Come on, give it a try!"

Alan stopped and stared, wondering. Curiosity and Turelle's challenge finally won out. Walking over, he chalked his hands, sat down on the bench then leaned back. Taking several deep breaths while he focused his mind, he lifted the bar off the rack and slowly lowered it to his chest. As he fought against this unaccustomed amount of weight, his chest and arms threatened to explode from the strain. At last, the bar began moving up. Slowly. Every inch was purchased with pain as his muscles screamed in protest. Knowing the risk he was taking, not having warmed up properly, he continued pushing the bar upward, all the way, until he locked his elbows then held it high and proud, in perfect motionless balance. He was about to return it to the rack when he heard Turelle's half-serious challenge over the whistles, applause and shouts of approval, to do it one more time.

Slowly bringing the bar back down to his chest, he called on a reservoir of strength hidden deep within him. Pretending that somehow Dawn was watching, silently cheering him on, he gritted his teeth and, with one giant final thrust, brought the weighted bar back up to full extension. Muscles trembling from an excess of exertion, he cautiously returned the weight to the rack and slowly sat up.

This time his accomplishment was rewarded with wilder cheers, louder applause, and more unnerving back-slapping that almost sent him to his knees as he struggled to stand up. When he finally managed to leave the gym, after several promises to give Turelle a call, he was followed halfway home by some faceless non-entity who wanted to train him for an equally obscure weight-lifting competition.

•••

Ham was up when he walked into their small apartment. He was sitting on the arm of an over-stuffed chair, staring out the window.

"Muff still sleeping?" He tried avoiding the other's gaze. Ham was wearing one of his it's-time-for-another-long-talk looks.

"Al!" His voice was sharp, anchoring Alan to the spot when he would rather have retreated to the safety of the bedroom he and Muff shared. "OK! What the fuck's goin' on? You've always been moody an' needin' time by yourself. Muff an' me, we understand that. We're used to it an' we can live with it. But these last weeks. Man, you have been impossible. Disappearin' for hours durin' the day when you should a' been rehearsin' with us; workin' out in Costanza's gym till you can't hardly walk much less sing. An' then ditty-boppin' off alone again after the last show, forgettin' all about me an' the guys. An' worse of all: Muff.

"I'm a big boy now." Ham leaned forward, determined this time that Alan was not going to evade the issue. "Look, I can take care a' myself, an' I got the rest a' the band, as well as other friends, t' pass time with. But now Muff, if you don't wanna lose that pretty little lady to Buzz, you'd damn well better snap out a' whatever you're caught inside of. An' fast! He's been walkin' her home all those nights, lately, while you're off in your own private world, pumpin' iron like your life depended on it.

"Come on, Al, baby! You ain't talkin' t' me again. I know somethin's eatin' away inside a' you. Now out with it!"

"You're right, Ham," Alan conceded in a voice that was barely audible, even to himself. Ham's intuition, as usual, had been razor sharp. He suddenly found himself grateful for the confrontation. He did need to talk. Ironically, his encounter with Killer, Turelle and those ridiculous promoters earlier had given him the resolve needed to do now what should have been done a long, long time ago. "There are some things I've had to deal with lately; things about myself that I've never been able to talk about before. You—wouldn't understand."

"No kiddin'. Like who you was before you landed here, maybe? Well, 'scuse me, Massah! Please! I keeps forgettin' my place. I's jes' a po' dumb nigger who don't knows no better."

Alan's head shot up. Ham always went into his Stepen-Fetchit-dumb-nigger routine whenever he felt himself being patronized. Alan too frequently fell into the egotistic trap of grossly underrating his friend's capacity for understanding and caring. Breaking his self-imposed injunction against invading the privacy of Ham's mind, he sent out a hesitant surface probe.

"How long have you known?" He was almost relieved.

"Pretty much right from the beginning. I should a' put two-an'-two together that first day, but who'd a' connected the owner a' Space Tech with some guitar-totin' hobo walkin' in off the street, drunk, dirty, an' doin' 'The Dozens.'"

"Why didn't you ever say anything?"

"Why the hell didn't you?" Ham shot back angrily as he jumped to his feet and began pacing back and forth. Then pausing and turning to face Alan, he added, more contritely, "You gotta' go back, don't you? Is that what's been buggin' you so bad?"

Alan nodded.

"Al, seems obvious you didn't like bein' the UN's glory boy. Hell! Look what it done to you. What makes you think it'll be any different now?"

"It won't. But I will. Thanks to you. Muff. The band. Barb, too. I'm a whole lot stronger now than I was back then.

"Goddess knows I don't want to leave, Ham." He looked up, pleading with his eyes for his friend's understanding. "I thought I could leave that part of me behind;

but I can't ignore it anymore: those Kali-spawned earthquakes are getting worse lately and people are dying who
might have been saved if I were out there helping."

"So, people have always been dyin'," Ham shrugged
with fatalistic cynicism. "An' they're awful stubborn, too.
They're gonna' keep right on doin' it whether or not
you're there."

"Everything dies eventually," Alan conceded with an
answering shrug. "But maybe I can buy some of them a
little more time, improve the quality of their lives. If only
just a little.

"Petie's death hammered the message home. I don't
want his dying to have been in vain. I don't want others
dying because I couldn't be bothered. I left a lot of broken
fences and a lot of hurt people behind that need mending,"
Alan said, trying to explain while he studied a coffee stain
in the carpet.

"Al, you ain't…"

"Going back out of guilt? No! Thanks mostly to you,
I'm done being a travel agent for my own guilt trips.
Remember that night you finally managed to start pounding some sense into me? You said I should be doing something constructive with my life, something that would have
made Dawn proud, rather than destroying myself the way
I was. Well, that's what I'm going back to do. I also need
to start being me. Not the owner of Space Tech, not
Moshey's generic culture-hero. And certainly not a Coun-
try-Rock-n'-Soul singer, either. But me. Will the real Alan
Kolkey please stand up!

"There's an even more important reason too for going
back. I only found out about it last night." Alan plopped
down in his favorite chair, emotionally drained, and then
proceeded to tell Ham about his meeting with the vacationing geologists back at the club.

"So when's this big blue marble of ours supposed to do the big flip-flop?" Ham asked, folding his arms across his chest and looking very pensive.

"Ten, maybe fifteen years…"

"Shit! An' what the hell you expect to do about that?" Ham sounded flabbergasted.

"Well, whatever I can…"

"So what do you plan on doin' about Muff?" Ham turned to stare out the window again. He had decided the matter was a useless pursuit. "You must a' had somethin' like this in the back of your mind way back when you first started insistin' on her goin' back to school."

"I suppose," Alan shrugged. "Deep down, ever since you dragged me out of that bottle I was trying so hard to drown myself in, I've known I'd eventually have to go back. I've always known, too, I'll never be entirely free of Dawn. Even dead, she's still too much a part of me. But, again thanks to you, I can at least live with it now.

"I really do care a great deal for Muff." Alan walked over to stand next to Ham, staring blankly at the same street below. It was already beginning to fill up with cars and people, dashing madly for jobs all over the quickening city. "Maybe it's selfish and unfair. Maybe I'm only using her like a security blanket. I don't know. All I do know is that I want to take her back with me. If she'll come, after she knows the truth. You don't think she already does, do you, Ham? I mean if you've known all along…"

"Man! You are one dude who does more talkin' in his sleep than he ever does awake." Ham laughed sarcastically. "She's gotta' know. But I think she's playin' a game called 'I Know, only I don't wanna' know I know.'"

"I wonder if that's why she's been acting so distant lately. Almost as if she were afraid of me."

"Maybe I'd be a little rattled, too, if I was a fox an' I just found out the dude I been bunkin' with used to lasso comets an' run commuter service out to the planets for a livin'." Ham turned, looking squarely into Alan's eyes. "As a matter of fact, I was, myself. For a whole week. An' I ain't no fox. It took nursin' you through a couple a' pretty bad hangovers to realize you was human, you was hurtin' awful bad, an' you could fuck up as bad as the rest of us. After that it was all clear sailin'—through hurricanes, floods, an' 'Frisco rush hours."

"Al! How'd it happen?" Ham paused to rest a compassionate hand on Alan's shoulder. "That was one hell of a fall, from where you was then, to where you was when I found you."

"I'm sorry I didn't confide in you right from the start. But honest, Ham, how could I have ever expected you to believe that burned-out mess I was back then was all that was left of the Great Alan Kolkey: Champion of Earth; Defender of the Downtrodden, and all that other garbage they were always hanging on me. Besides, I was trying my damnedest at the time to die. And something else inside me was equally determined not to let me."

Alan spent the next several hours telling Ham everything he had never been able to before. It was a gamble talking about being a psychokinetic telepath, but nothing else, so far, had frightened his friend off. He owed the man that much.

"Shit!" Ham muttered angrily when Alan had finally finished. "Took me all that time to get used to the idea of who you was, an' now I gotta' start all over again with what you are. Then again, maybe I ain't gonna be gettin' much of a chance for that. When you plannin' on leavin'?"

"At least not until you and the band can find a satisfactory replacement for me."

"Then forget it! You ain't goin' no place! 'Cause there ain't no way in Hell that'll ever happen."

"OK. So, at least until you can find someone Costanza will buy in place of me." Alan amended, warmed by the passion of Ham's declaration. The smile he gave his friend was generated, in part, out of love for the man, and partly to cover an embarrassing flush of emotion.

"Like I said before: ain't hardly no way that'll ever happen, either. You're a bigger, steadier draw than most a' his headliners. Man! Is the shit ever gonna' hit the fan when you lay the news on him. I've heard stories about what happens to people who cost him money.

"But, hey! How about showing me a few parlor tricks with them 'psionics' a' yours." Ham threw himself into the big over-stuffed chair as he hurried to change the subject. He was doing a rather fair job, himself, at hiding his own feelings behind a hastily constructed grin. "Only a couple, though. We gotta' grab some z's before tonight's show."

CHAPTER XIII

INDIAN SUMMER had brought with it a brief respite from the gathering bite of winter. There was a brisk breeze coming in off the bay that cleansed the air of pollutants and exhaust fumes, despite the heavy home-bound rush hour traffic. Alan breathed deeply, enjoying the sharp salt tang as he slowly walked the fifteen-block route to the Pentacle. Ham strolled silently along close beside him, as deep into his own thoughts as Alan was in his. Withdrawn into a fantasy of window shopping, Muff was lagging almost half a block behind. Announcing his intention, earlier, of walking to the club this evening, he had been pleasantly surprised when they both offered to accompany him.

It was going to take time, a lot of it, seasoned with plenty of diplomacy, gentle persuasions, and endless reassurances to convince Muff. When he returned, he wanted her with him. Was it fair though dragging her off where there would be constant reminders of Dawn, where the differences between the both of them would be so relentlessly visible? Could she handle the knowledge that he was a psychokinetic telepath or a life lived in the middle of the corporate/international political arena?

On the other hand, did he have the right to abandon her after having taken her this far? So many options, so much to be considered. He would have to move very, very cautiously. Muff's needs were most certainly as vital as his own and demanded equal consideration. He must not force her to follow him simply because he needed a convenient bed mate.

And what about Ham? What was best for him was equally as important. More than ever, Alan would be needing his friend's irrefutable, though sometimes hard-to-swallow wisdom as well as the companionship and moral support he had come to rely on. Yet, how could he ask Ham to go back with him, to share the loneliness and isolation living in the shadow of Alan Kolkey would most certainly bring? He would be so far out of his own element, distanced from old friends, no longer free to chart a course through life of his own choosing. He had come to depend so much on the friendship and support of these two especially. How would he ever manage to fill the void if he had to go on without them?

The late afternoon sun dipped low over the bay, turning its water to molten gold and reflecting off the windows of the buildings around them, like burnished promises for tomorrow. Alan decided to table his concerns long enough at least to enjoy the brief show nature was putting on and the warm proximity of his two dearest friends. It was not as though he were leaving tomorrow, he reminded himself. There was time yet to search for answers. There was time yet for sunsets such as this and pre-dawn walks between the worlds where Dawn might yet be found, if only in his dreams.

"Al!" Ham said, looking up from his preoccupation with counting the cracks in the pavement. "What are you going to tell the rest of the band?"

"Everything, Ham." Alan replied, breathing relief now that the decision had finally been made. "They have a right to know. The public too. When I get back—if President Moshey still wants anything to do with me, after running out on him like I did—I'll tell him everything, especially about my psionics, and let him release what he wants to about me. I'm through hiding. I'll just deal with the after-shocks, one at a time, as they come up. Not before.

Suddenly a small part of himself was soaring high above the city, circling lower and lower. Searching. It was Garuda! The great spotted eagle had found him. Or had he found Garuda earlier this morning?

The heady thrill of unencumbered flight once more! The freedom to float, to dip and soar with no walls, ceil-ings, or floors to confine! He had almost forgotten the deli-cious sensation, the intoxication of it. It was the key he had needed to open that final door to freedom after two years of self-imprisonment.

"Al! You're leaving me again. You sure you're all right?" The serrated edge of Ham's concern forced Alan reluctantly to reel consciousness back within the narrow confines of his body.

"Never better. Sorry Ham; I was traveling again." His eyes scanned the patchwork quilt of sky visible between the towering buildings that walled them in, searching for the dark spread of wings. Suddenly there they were! Directly overhead, Garuda was descending, gliding down in a tight spiral pattern. With an ear-piercing scream of triumph that could be heard over the din of rush-hour traffic, he sud-denly went into a power dive.

Alan sent out a frantic call to warn him away, but to no avail. The huge raptor was homed in on the object of a two-year search and would not be put off. Still bound by their mind-link, Alan's re-surfaced psionics must have been the beacon that had led him here.

They were at a busy intersection where a patrol officer was standing in for a malfunctioning traffic light. All around him, necks cranked skyward. Grid-locked vehicles took on the appearance of multi-headed hydras.

Keeping an anxious eye on the patrolman who was nervously fidgeting with the weapon at his belt, Alan hastily doffed his jacket and wrapped it tightly around his left forearm. The officer's fidgeting turned into action when Garuda let out a second joyful screech and two women, close by, screamed. His gun hastily unholstered, was now apprehensively being aimed skyward.

"No!" Alan shouted, diving for the officer. His PK had kicked in reflexively, knocking the weapon out of the man's hand a heartbeat ahead of the actual tackle. A moment spared to celebrate silently his once more fully functional psychokinetics, as he stood straddling his victim's prone body, and then Garuda was overhead, turning, braking the speed of his descent with a loud beating of mighty pinions. Talons reaching, grabbing hold, he came to roost on Alan's outstretched arm.

Stroking the bobbing head, and quieting the huge bird with soothing words and calming mental contact, he finally remembered, and reached down to help the angry, cursing officer find his feet.

"Please! My deepest apologies; but this eagle is an extremely valuable, highly trained animal," he lied in his most placating tone of voice.

"What the hell's the matter with you, Mister!" the patrolman shouted back, brushing the dust of the street off his uniform. "Why ain't that… that thing locked up! You got a license to own a dangerous animal like that?"

"My apologies, again, Officer. I don't know how he got free. I assure you, it won't happen again." Alan didn't need a telepathic scan to realize the man's pride had suffered a serious blow and he was not about to be put off so easily. The very thought of mind-control was as abhorrent as ever. But there was no way Alan was going to suffer the indignity and inconvenience of explaining himself to a judge. Nor was he about to invite the awkward possibility of being fingerprinted and identified, his whereabouts suddenly made public. He was not quite ready yet for that. Despite President Moshey's assurances to the contrary, he knew his prints had been lifted by numerous law enforcement agencies and put on file.

He sent out a tendril of thought that entered and insinuated its way along the maze-like convolutions of the officer's brain. His name was Humphry, Jake Humphry. Neighbors and friends on the force called him 'Hump.' A fight with his wife that morning, followed by a chewing out from his watch commander had set the tone of his day. Alan's flying tackle had put the proverbial icing on the cake. He was past the cerebral cortex now and entering the regions controlling the autonomic system. He induced just enough muscle relaxation and then withdrew back into the limbic area, stimulating release of endorphins into the surrounding brain tissue to create a mildly tranquilizing, slightly euphoric effect. He was backing into the cortical regions once more, intending to plant a few appropriate telepathic suggestions when some deeper, wiser level of himself cried out. Enough! He jerked his head up, shaking it violently, and then withdrew completely.

Planting a 'harmless, innocent little suggestion' or total mind-control: where would he draw the line? It would be too easy to rationalize, to justify each manipulation until people eventually became no more to him than puppets, finally fulfilling the worst fears of those who had birthed, loved and raised him.

The power he wielded had a capacity for infinite evil as well as limitless good. The choice was his alone to make, and one he would be forced to make, over and over again, every single day, for the rest of his life. He looked at Muff, standing close to Ham, and remembered Dawn. He remembered his parents, too, both sets. And The African, with his impossible dreams of a unified and better world. Alan smiled, suddenly realizing how easy the right choices were, after all. Temptation would always be a carrot, dangled in front of his nose. Doubtless, there would always be occasions when he weakened, or when there would be no other available alternative, but he had already been through several tours of hell. He had no intention of taking up permanent residence there. Besides, he was just beginning to like the person he was becoming. One more friendship he was not about to compromise.

The patrolman's tirade had ceased. He breathed deeply several times, re-pocketed his citation pad, and offered a confused and slightly embarrassed smile. "Sorry, Buddy. Bad day for both of us, I guess. Just don't let it happen again; hear? Get a license for that thing. And keep it caged! It's a dangerous weapon." Looking around at the crowd gathered about, he huffed self-consciously. "What's the matter? Don't any of you 'good citizens' have homes to go to? Come on; let's break it up!" Then he was off, wading through the vehicle-choked intersection to start untangling the snarl.

"Al! What the hell's goin' on? You did somethin' to that cop, didn't you?" Ham's features were a canvas for gathering storm clouds.

Not trusting himself to answer, Alan started walking, setting a pace that forced his friends to run. Muff looked too frightened and confused to speak. He knew she had seen the gun fly out of the patrolman's hand. It was really going to be fun trying to reassure her now. Garuda had forced his hand. He would have to make time for that first long talk tonight. Tell her everything and pray she understands. Would Ham even, for that matter? It was one thing showing him a few parlor tricks, early this morning, but quite another seeing serious PK in action. He did not have to look back to know Ham was having a difficult time. Alan was grateful when Muff hung back, once more out of ear shot, her back to them as she watched the patrolman's progress unraveling the Gordian knot left behind in their wake.

"What I did back there, seeing what I can really do, it's bothering you." Alan checked his speed, allowing his friend to catch up. Keeping his voice down to make certain Muff wouldn't overhear, he continued stroking Garuda's head and back, calming him sufficiently so he could be carried.

"You're fuckin' right, it's botherin' me. It bothers the goddamn shit outta' me." Ham snapped like a cornered pit bull. He paused to take several deep breaths, giving his anger time to slowly dissolve into concern. "Does that mean you always know what I'm thinkin'? Can you make Muff an' me do or think, or feel whatever you want us to?"

"I could. But I wouldn't. I have to respect the privacy of other people's minds. I couldn't stand living in a world full of puppets and wind-up 'friends.' I don't think anyone could. Why else would I have needed to ask your opinion about Muff?"

"Yeah. I guess. Only, you gotta' admit: it's scary. By the way, where'd that come from?" Ham managed a nervous smile as he gestured toward the huge eagle, now quietly perched on Alan's arm, luxuriating in the attention being lavished on him.

"Garuda? He's an old friend. We—sort of—reconnected—mind-linked early this morning. He must have 'locked on to my signal,' so to speak, and followed it all the way here." It took an effort of will to look up and meet his friend's anxious gaze.

"You, Muff, the band, even Barb, I owe all of you so much more than I could ever repay." Words began flowing, unbidden. "But you, most especially. I'd probably have been dead a long time ago if it hadn't been for you. I love you all."

For a pleasant change, it was Ham's turn to be rendered speechless, flustering and fumbling self-consciously. After a pause that lasted several lifetimes, he finally looked up, grinning. Alan began breathing once more. He hadn't lost his closest friend.

As they were passing a large cathedral, one he had passed a thousand times before on previous such walks, Alan suddenly stopped short. Inexplicably, it had taken on a totally unfamiliar flavor, capturing his rapt attention. It was not particularly old, though decades of urban smog made it appear ancient. The architecture was not pure Gothic; but inspiring, nonetheless. Its slender spires seemed to be straining to pierce a direct route to heaven by the sheer power of steel and Rocky Mountain Granite. Something within its walls was reaching out, calling insistently for him to enter.

Perhaps it was only nostalgia stirred up by the imminence of his return home. He suddenly found himself recalling childhood trips with Gertha to Sacramento and San Francisco. Visits to such sanctuaries of worship had always been on their itinerary. His mind drifted back even further to the many times he had accompanied his grandparents to Temple, before they died. Although Zarkov and Gertha had won legal custody they had not only allowed, but encouraged frequent visits. After the death of his father, though, the heart had gone out of the old people, and they gave up any further attempts at having him bar mitzvahed.

There was something else, however, drawing him even more irresistibly. A common theme, among many of his recurring dreams, was finding himself inside an immense temple. Always, garbed in ceremonial robes, he would be leading thousands of worshippers in sacred rites. He and the priestess at his side, who much too painfully resembled Dawn, were the focuses and channels of giant energies flowing through them for some divine purpose.

In another version of that same dream, he was being mobbed by those same followers, pleading for him to lead them on a holy quest to rescue that same priestess. Had those dreams been nothing more than conjurations of a troubled soul? Or were they memory fragments from an ancient incarnation, beginning to surface now, to force completion of a mission or destiny as yet unrevealed and unfulfilled. As soon as he returned home, Alan decided, he would swallow pride and seek out Dr. Mishra. Perhaps the little Hindu parapsychologist might be able to help him sort out the true meanings behind all these hauntingly realistic dreams.

Empty of Sunday or Sabbath worshippers, there was an ineffable quality of serenity within such monuments as the one now capturing his total attention. It lent credibility to belief in a Supreme Deity which he had never quite been able to capture, pumping iron or doing katas. Once more Alan felt something or someone within the great cathedral calling out to him, and oh, how he longed to answer the summons! If only Muff and Ham had not been with him! If only the rest of the band were not waiting for them! There was an early show in the main upstairs banquet room and they were already late. Even so, it took several nudges and tugs on his arm from Muff, accompanied by a stream of colorful invective from Ham, to get him moving again.

•••

"What in hell was that all about, out there tonight?" Harry Costanza's anger cut through the deafening applause as Alan came off stage after his third encore, finally managing to escape into the hallway across from the main kitchen.

"What was what all about?" he answered impatiently with another question.

"All those hymns, spirituals, and inspirational garbage you were dumping on the customers. Dammit, this isn't a fucking church!"

"What are you griping about? The audience loved it! Can't you hear them still clapping out there?" Alan had a feeling this conversation was going to end in trouble.

"Look! Adopting an eagle as mascot for a group that calls itself Wild Hunt: great!" Costanza was wound up tight, arms gesturing wildly as he continued his tirade. "Training that overgrown canary of yours to fly out there ahead of you and perch on one of the floods during your sets: terrific! And I don't know how you got him to fly down to you in the middle of one of the busiest intersections in 'Frisco, during rush hour yet, but it was inspired. Pure genius! You were recognized, of course. The Examiner and The Chronicle are both sending reporters out tomorrow to interview us. It means tons of free advertising. For that I have nothing but praise. And upstairs, earlier: all that syrupy pie-in-the-sky music? No big deal. They requested it, and they were a bunch of holy-roller teetotalers, anyway. But down here?" Chewing on his cigar, the Pentacle's owner paused once more for dramatic effect, making certain his message would sink in. "By the time you'd waded through your first set of nothing but sentimental slush, nobody was dancing. Or drinking. There wasn't a dry eye in the place and twenty of my steadiest customers took the pledge. Shit. The liveliest piece you played all night was 'Too Old to Die Young'.

"Now I'm warning you, nigger-lover," Costanza's kvetching complaints had suddenly congealed into threats. He was in deadly earnest now as he jabbed a diamond bedecked finger almost up Alan's nose. "Next time you feel the urge to play that sob-sister drivel, save it for Sunday mornings down at the mission. They'll love you. Here: next show, you sing thirsty music the customers will want to dance—and drink to! Or else I start leaning on you real hard."

"So lean all you want. I was planning to stay on only long enough, anyway, for the band to find a replacement for me. All of a sudden I don't think I even care to finish out the week." Alan had never liked being threatened. Neither had he ever liked Costanza. And right now he was not liking him a whole lot more.

"OK! So I'm sorry already. Hey, lighten up!" Looking worried, Costanza suddenly took a placating stance. "What's the matter, don't I pay you enough? Dammit! Look, you want another raise for you and your boys? You hear me complaining? You want your own private john in your dressing room? It's yours."

Alan shook his head and started walking toward the service stairs next to the kitchen. They led up to the dressing rooms on the next floor, where Alan desperately preferred being right now.

"OK, so at least tell me who pirated you away." Costanza grabbed his arm, dragging him to a halt. "How much did they offer you? At least give me a chance to better it."

"Nobody's made me any offers; and money or fringe benefits are not the problem, Costanza. I'm just fed up and I want out." He took a deep breath and tried pretending he was a statue erected to patience. It really didn't work; but it kept him from feeding Costanza's head to Garuda, still perched on the floods out in the main room.

"I wouldn't start packing my bags just yet, if I were you, Falcon." Costanza geared back to menacing once more. "I still have a couple of arguments I think will convince you to stay. In fact I know they will." The Pentacle's owner sounded supremely confident as he turned, hurled a menacing sneer over his shoulder, then stormed down the hall toward the rear of the main lobby. The mirrored play of emerald fountains was just visible from here.

Threatened again! To hell with scruples about invasion of mental privacy!

"Oh, so that's it!" Alan muttered under his breath as he sent out a silent tendril of consciousness to probe the mind of the Pentacle's owner. Small wonder Costanza was so desperate about holding onto him at any cost! Alan's immense popularity was a steady draw for large drinking and gambling crowds, perfect detergent for laundering illegal money! The rowdy fans and constant activity percolating around the entertainers also provided an excellent smoke screen for another in-house venture. Harry Costanza was also dealing! And it was his operation that owned the underground labs where nova was being manufactured. And the Pentacle also provided the perfect cover for marketing it. Petie had probably found his source right here under their very noses.

Dammit! If only he had not been so wrapped up in himself for so long! He would have known about this months ago. It made him sick to think he had unwittingly been helping that monster enslave and destroy the lives of so many, poor, innocent little Petie among them.

There had been something else, half-formulated, hatching in Costanza's mind. It was only vaguely readable behind the static of the man's intense rage. All he could glean right now were tenuous fragments concerning someone who might prove advantageous and something else about nova being a useful leash to keep the dog from straying. He would have to wait until they had both cooled down before trying to probe for clearer, more detailed information. For the moment at least all he could do was watch and wait. The time for action would come soon enough, he promised himself. Petie, and all of Costanza's other victims, would be avenged.

Slowly opening the swinging door that provided access to the dining room for the kitchen staff, and praying he would not attract too much attention from the audience, Alan sent out a silent call. Every eye in the room turned on him as Garuda came flapping noisily down to roost on an arm hastily padded with a tablecloth from a nearby laundry cart. Sensing Alan's chaotic emotions, the huge raptor continued nervously fanning the air with his wings and providing a screeching distraction for the headline act now on stage. He ducked hastily back out into the corridor separating the kitchen and the dinner theater. Stroking the downy, bobbing head, and soothing with verbal and mental assurances, he hastened for the back service stairs that lead up to the dressing rooms on the next floor.

There was a door leading to the main kitchen on the first floor landing of the stairwell. Alan peeked through the glass inset to see if any of the clean-up staff was still around to fetch him some raw meat scraps to feed Garuda. The place was spotless and abandoned, with only a security light left burning. The walk-in refrigerators would all be locked up except for the small unit in the sandwich pantry just off the casino's main bar. It was on the other side of the building, and besides, Garuda preferred his food unseasoned and uncooked. It looked as though they would both have to wait till after the last show and a long talk with Muff, Ham and the rest of the band. They had a right to know what was happening.

As he climbed the stairs, each step felt as though he were dead-lifting the 500-pound weights he had been showing off with early this morning. There were two certainties his life now revolved around: Costanza had to be brought down and the job was his responsibility, one this time, he would relish.

It would have been so simple to have just burnt the man on the spot, but then he would only have had Costanza. Someone else would have moved into the key position he presently occupied and the pulse of the organization would hardly have skipped a beat. There was another consideration as well that he must never allow himself to forget. Were he to set himself up as Costanza's sole judge, jury, and executioner, no matter how the bastard deserved what he dealt out, again: where would it all end? "Power corrupts, and absolute power corrupts absolutely." It was one of Zarkov's favorite clichés that Alan had grown up hearing endlessly repeated.

Opening the fire door on the second floor landing, he walked past the other dressing rooms to his own at the end of the narrow access hallway. It was the only one that boasted a window. It only looked out on a sunless service alley, one story below, but it was a window nonetheless. It made the small room feel a bit larger and less suffocating. Everyone gathered there for impromptu after-hours partying, whether he was there or not.

Setting his guitar down in a convenient corner, and Garuda on the back of a heavy armchair, he unbuckled the ornate silver belt that was part of his sleek black costume. He threw it on the chair next to him then sat down on the broad studio couch, where he often grabbed siestas between shows or after heavy workouts in Costanza's gym. Looking across at the eagle, now contentedly preening itself, Alan wondered if there were such things as omens. Was the giant raptor a warning that the time for shedding his comfortable cocoon was coming far sooner than he had planned?

What was going to happen with the Native American community, he worried, when it was found out he had one of their Sacred Spotted Eagles? He hoped they would not make an issue out of it as some devout Hindus had, after equating his family name with Kalki, the promised Tenth Avatar of their god Vishnu.

Alan cringed, recalling he would also have to be dealing with that mercifully small Islamic following that Iranian Defense Minister Jafar Shoja had warned him about. Determined to pronounce him to be Islam's prophesied al Mahdi, they had not been put off the scent by the fact that the other half of him was Jewish. Descent was traced through the mother, and his mother's lineage was said to trace back to the Prophet himself.

Perhaps news of these past two years, spent as a country rock musician might provide the needed hose to cool everyone's zeal once and for all. Certainly such emotional instability was not the stuff that heroes and world leaders were made from. Perhaps people would leave him alone once more. Or perhaps he would now be perceived as Public Enemy #1. Either way, returning home was going to be like wading through shark infested waters, he decided as he stretched out on the couch and closed his eyes.

He had been drifting restlessly in and out of sleep for nearly twenty minutes when a danger alarm suddenly went off in his head. It jolted him back to full consciousness in time to hear the quiet turning of a doorknob. Felsh! Alan could 'smell' the man's unsettling mental spoor. As the intruder entered the room, taking great care not to make any noise, Alan hurriedly closed his eyes, pretending sleep. Feeling another presence behind Costanza's hulking bodyguard, Alan sent out a quick mental probe to learn the reason behind this clandestine visit.

The smaller man behind Felsh was called Tooley. He was carrying a concealed hypo filled with a double dose of nova. The plan had been for Felsh to take him by surprise, then, with a knife at his throat, hold him down while Tooley pumped nova into the nearest available vein.

So, this was how that misbegotten sewer spawn planned on convincing him to stay! A few forced 'ecstasies,' Costanza must have reasoned, and Alan would be hooked, a permanent and willing slave, with him the only game in town.

Alan lay motionless, pretending sleep as Costanza's second-in-command drew near. He felt the man's right arm reach out. The hand was just inches from his throat when Alan made a cobra-quick overhand grab for the wrist of a very surprised Felsh. Maintaining his tight grip, he twisted it to lock elbow and wrist into a solid straight bar as he slid up off the couch and onto his feet. With the open palm of his left hand, Alan gave a hard, fast thrust to the elbow, shattering it. Whipping his would-be attacker around, he smashed the man's hulking mass into Tooley, knocking him to the floor and sending the hypo flying across the room.

There was not enough room in these cramped quarters to call Garuda into the air where he might have proven a deadly ally. Still, he might yet serve as a diversion at least. Before Alan could broadcast a silent command, his ally was already on the job, leaping onto Tooley's exposed back. Talons planted deep into flesh, he hung on, pummeling with powerful wings and gouging with a beak that was sharp as a steel grappling hook.

Felsh had recovered his balance. Despite his now useless right arm, he spun around with an agility that belied such bulk and launched a new assault. Alan was ready for him. He could have put the man out with a minimum expenditure of psychokinetic energy, but he was angry now and in fighting mode. He wanted to feel bone splintering under a well-planted fist.

Felsh was unaccustomed to missing such an easy target or finding himself in the suddenly reversed role of victim. In snarling defiance of Costanza's strict orders, he whipped out a gun, aiming it at Alan's midsection.

Shrieking insanely as he thrashed about trying to dislodge his winged tormentor, Tooley suddenly collided with Felsh, almost knocking him off his feet. Alan used the unplanned distraction to best advantage. A focused burst of PK ripped the gun from Felsh's grasp with such force it took his trigger finger along with it, leaving only a blood-spurting stump behind. A rapid follow-through with a fist driven like a pile-driver into the giant's chest, shattered the fragile cartilage of the sternum and sent fragments of bone into his heart. His shrieks of agony died with him as he collapsed into a gory heap.

Turning his attention now to his other would-be assailant, Alan called Garuda off. Obediently, the bird hopped onto his outstretched arm, then back onto his improvised chair-perch. Drawing a deep breath, he began surveying the carnage wrought by his pet, even without advantage of altitude and power dive. Obviously, he had as seriously underestimated the huge spotted eagle as Costanza had underestimated him.

Tooley made a feeble attempt to rise; but a fist, hard to the jaw, dispatched him into merciful slumber. The mercy had been as much for himself as for his enemy. The man's pain was so intense it was piercing through his psi-shields.

Taking a deep breath, Alan looked up to survey the war zone. In a far corner, the smashed hypo leaked a sickly green puddle into the carpeting. Behind him, Felsh lay like a discarded accordion atop a pile of wrecked furniture. At his feet sprawled the aftermath of Garuda's vicious attack. Between the strips of shredded clothing, scarlet rivulets trickled from torn flesh and collected in tiny coagulating pools on the floor. Half an ear was missing; and gouges dug deep into the man's face promised lifelong scars.

He regretted having had to kill Felsh, much as he had loathed the man. But a dead enemy cannot come back to haunt you later, when your back is turned: disciplines imposed from years of martial arts training had transformed this cold hard fact into unconscious reflex. You cannot pull punches or hesitate to ponder issues of morality when you're fighting for your life. The first commandment is survival. In combat, there is no time for thinking or feeling anything; only reacting. You become a computerized fighting machine, every attack and parry purely reflexive. Perhaps it might have been different if psychokinetic telepathy were more efficient as a weapon. It takes a lot, though, to get through the natural defenses of an esper-blind enemy psyched for battle. It requires time, concentration, energy: commodities that are in very short supply during heated battle. Other than the purely instinctive burst of raw PK needed to rip a weapon out of the hands of an attacker, a tremendous drain on his reserves, there is seldom time for thinking about it, much less for the focusing of concentration necessary to use it as a deliberate weapon. Now is all the time there is; and thinking is reduced to gut-level reacting.

Alan needed some quieter, less violent solutions, a way of delivering the Pentacle's owner up to the police, along with enough hard evidence to make the conviction stick. He wanted to make certain Costanza and his entire organization would be locked up so far back, they'd have to be fed with a slingshot. He owed at least that much to Petie's memory.

It would prove not only foolish but needlessly reckless, charging out there right now like an avenging angel. A telepathic probe warned him that Costanza's small army, maintained ostensibly for casino security, was already milling about in the stairwells, hallways and covering all the exits. Declaring open war right now might satisfy his atavistic hunger for revenge, but friends, fellow employees and patrons, caught in the crossfire, would be hurt or killed. After the smoke cleared, the needless spilling of more blood would be all that would have been accomplished. Vanishing briefly, he decided, would be far wiser. After closing time, when only Costanza and his cronies were about, he would return to settle scores.

His mind reached out, sought for Ham and Muff. They were several dressing-rooms away playing cards with the rest of the band and this month's headline act. He had to leave immediately, before Felsh's men came swarming in here, looking for their vanished commander.

Alan was certain his friends would be safe for the time being. If Costanza had designs on them it would be by way of threats to force them to reveal his whereabouts. He went to the window and opened it. Despite a thirty-foot drop to the concrete alleyway below, it appeared the most expeditious exit route.

Gathering Garuda up in both hands, he hurled him through the window, high into the air. He turned a somersault to right himself, spread his wings, then started flapping frantically for altitude. Alan smiled grimly, sensing the great bird's displeasure as he circled, looking for somewhere safe to light. His instincts were not at all nocturnal and he was broadcasting the fact on their shared wavelength.

Alan grabbed a twelve-foot length of red silk fabric belonging to one of his more exotic costumes and tied one end securely to the heavy arm chair. Wedging it into the window frame after him, he climbed out onto the ledge. He gave several hard yanks to test whether the knot would hold, then lowered himself as far as he could, dropping the remaining dozen feet to the alley below.

A steady drizzling rain was falling. It gave the cold night air a biting edge, making Alan wish he'd taken time to change or grab a coat. With a neckline plunging to his waist, leaving most of his chest bare, the satiny black costume he was still wearing afforded little warmth. He feared for his friends should Costanza decide to retaliate; but images of the cathedral he had paused in front of this afternoon suddenly overwhelmed him with an irrational need to revisit it. A need that rapidly became overpowering compulsion. He fought against it, as he had once fought for the right to die, on board the Peregrine two years ago, as he had once fought against being led to the front steps of the Pentacle. Once again he lost to that same alien will now animating his body as he rode along, a helpless passenger. Above the surrounding rooftops, he heard Garuda screeching in worried protest as he followed.

The light drizzle had become a steady downpour by the time he reached his destination. Drenched to his skin, he wondered that he no longer felt cold or even uncomfortable. The heavy rain penetrated to his very soul, cleansing and purifying, like a ritual bath in preparation for coming into a divine presence. The corrosiveness of pollutants in the urban air that painted an illusion of great antiquity over the stonework, now also lent an almost magical aura to the immense structure. Utterly lost now in the thrall of his silent summons, he no longer resisted as he approached and then paused before the massive doors of finely worked redwood. Strangely now, he found himself eagerly anticipating whatever mystical reunion waited within. His PK, though fully functional once more, was still rusty where delicacy of control was required. It took several clumsy abortive attempts before the bolts finally slipped back, permitting entry.

The cavernous interior was dimly lit, the alter illumined only by the hypnotic flickering of hundreds of small votive candles. Dawn's childhood memories of having attended High Mass in large churches, though none so grand as this, were with him. There was something else too: a memory of his own, called up from somewhere infinitely deeper that made this sanctuary all the more hauntingly familiar.

He was alone, yet surrounded by thousands of ghostly followers. He could almost feel the weight of priestly robes, reminding him of sacred vows he was still bound by. If his dreams were indeed shards of memory from some ancient incarnation, then somehow in that other lifetime, he had betrayed those vows and these followers. Worst of all, he had broken faith with higher powers working through him for preservation of both the people and the land. He was shaken by a sudden realization: the enormous energies he wielded, then as now, were not of his own creation, not his at all, but only channeled through him. They were neither curse nor gift, simply a tool, entrusted to him for the execution of some appointed mission. If so, was his planned crusade against Costanza's drug operation only a minor practice skirmish? Was this grander purpose the reason for which he had been born, the reason he wielded such power? Was this what he had wasted so much of his life, so much energy, running away from? Had that purpose already been served, at least in part, when he had prevented Kali from destroying the planet? Although he hadn't succeeded in banishing her entirely, he had at least tamed her. Or had he?

According to media reports, during the last two years of Alan's self-imposed exile, global seismic activity had certainly not diminished. If anything, although no longer so severe, earthquakes everywhere were becoming increasingly more frequent. Was this a warning there was more yet needing to be done?

In retrospect, some unseen power had apparently been orchestrating his life ever since the day he was born. Why else would he so obviously have been prevented from killing himself? Why else had he so obviously been led to Ham? Ham who had helped him to once again rediscover life and love, to learn how to celebrate the true wonder of them.

Finally done with running, Alan approached the altar rail, knelt, and bowed his head. "Not my will, but Thine," he whispered, recalling the prayer so often recited by Reverend Haley at church services or when saying Grace over Sunday dinners at Zarkov's home. Silently, he reaffirmed his ancient vows to the in-dwelling Powers once more channeling through him

He promised himself a visit to Dr. Mishra, Dawn's old mentor. Perhaps a hypnotic regression might help fill in the missing gaps between the dreams and scattered shards of memory. There were so many questions begging answers: about himself, about Dawn, and especially about this Intelligence, forever driving him on with the power of obsession.

Thoughts of Dawn welled up into consciousness once more. Salt tears burned his eyes and blurred vision. He prayed to his still-nameless Deities, if indeed that was what they were, that she would be reborn to him again some day. Till then, if only just once in a while he might be permitted to reach out and touch more of her than just the memories, precious as they were. If only there were some way he could learn how to walk between the worlds and embrace her soul, wherever it now slept, and rouse it once more into being with the kiss of life!

The paternal, almost-felt touch of a hand on his shoulder made Alan start. "The time for grieving is past, my son. Your wounds have healed and your feet have found the path that soon will lead you home to us. Your priestess is safe in the arms of a distant sister." The voice was soft as a whisper, yet deep as a subterranean cavern.

Looking up, Alan found himself staring into piercing blue eyes surrounded by a heavy beard and masses of long, black, loosely curling hair. But for the size of the burly frame, half again as tall as his own, and an aura of countless eons and ageless wisdom, he could have been staring into a mirror at his own reflection. His huge visitor was garbed like an ancient hunter in tunic and leggings of forest green with brown kid boots and leather accouterments. Over his shoulders he wore an ample cloak of deepest crimson. A large hunting horn hung from his belt, a bow and quiver of arrows were slung over his shoulder. The antlers of a great stag adorned his head, seeming almost to be part of him.

A pendant on his chest was a small golden sunburst superimposed with an equilateral cross in bold relief. Each arm of the cross ended in a spherical trefoil. At the center of the cross the interlaced lines of a tiny pentagram were etched in silver. All about him the air was heavy with the intoxicating perfume of musk and ripening grapes, of deep forest pools and cold crisp mountain trails.

Alan climbed slowly to his feet, wondering if Felsh had somehow, despite all, managed to dump some kind of drug into his system.

The apparition smiled down benignly. "That which you perceive is how your species most closely apprehends what I represent. I have been called by many names throughout the nations and ages of your people. To them I represented Death and Rebirth. I was Lord of the Hunt and Lord of the Dance, the Dance of Life and Death, the Dance of the Cosmos." As he spoke, there was all the mischief, joy, and warmth of a sunbeam in his smile. "You might better comprehend that part of me which is part of the consciousness of this world-soul you call Earth.

"Behold also your Lady! Maiden and Crone, but always Mother to all beings who live upon and take sustenance from her.

Alan's eyes traveled in the direction of the apparition's outstretched hand. On his left stood a beautiful madonna-like figure in flowing, diaphanous robes of blue and silver that billowed like mist off a moonlit lake. The horns of a crescent moon adorned the crown she wore in her silver hair. "Eons before the mortal woman who bore you into this world, I am your Mother. And you are our Chosen One.

"As your Lord said earlier, we are the Collective Consciousness of this world-soul you call Earth. We reflect the active-receptive polarity of this material plane as north and south, male and female. For thousands of years our children have clothed us in flesh, called us God and Goddess: Father and Mother. Thus do you still most comfortably perceive and comprehend us. For now at least. You will grow; you are already learning to see through the eyes of your soul. But for now...

"All who dwell upon me are my children and yet part of me: one living molecule, joining with another in ever-ascending levels of complexity, vortexes of consciousness which your finite senses perceive as planets, suns, galaxies; for this is truly a living universe: mind, pure thought made manifest." Her voice was liquid and warm, her exquisite features radiant as she opened her arms in a gesture that welcomed him back. The prodigal had returned home.

"For thousands of centuries you have worshipped us as gods." the Lord smiled benignly, coming closer without having moved. His voice too was a paradox, booming and echoing throughout the vast sanctuary, although he never spoke above an intimate whisper. "Yet we are no more or less deity than you, merely a little further along; and like you, our children, we also are still learning, growing, evolving. We are all travelers on the path to True Awakening that sentient beings throughout Creation, on all planes, are free to follow. If they choose.

"As you are the sum of all the billions of cells that comprise your body, so we are the sum of all living things on this world, seen and unseen. And we, ourselves, who two halves of a single whole, lend ourselves to a far Greater Whole: a Single Supreme Intelligence, that which you perceive as 'the Universe.' And as you channel your power from us, so we in turn channel from It."

"You were summoned here tonight so We might welcome back our beloved son from his self-imposed exile." The Lady's face radiated a pride that made Alan glow with an inner warmth, the way he had felt on his twelfth birthday, giving his first concert for his parents and grandparents. He remembered how proud of him they had all been. The Lady's voice was like his mother's caress as she continued speaking. "The lessons you had to learn were purchased with great sorrow and much suffering. But you are stronger now than ever before for having endured. And now, more than ever, We will be needing that strength. For We need our children as much as they need Us.

"The comet was our messenger, sent to rouse you from your sleep. Our children need you to lead them to awareness of who and what they truly are, before they drown in their own waste or destroy themselves in wars and pestilence. Because you are all a part of us, as you evolve so do we— who in turn are but small parts of the vast Cosmic One.

"We can channel onto your plane the power you will need for the long task ahead, but you must yet learn how to reach out for it.

"She who was once your priestess shall be again. Seek her out, my son, for she is part of the Triad you must now become—and the source of your greatest strength. Call her back to remembering.

"Know that the highest magic is love." The Lord continued, bending closer, commanding Alan's rapt attention. "Through its power you can transform an enemy into a cherished ally. Seek also the Silver Warrior. It is time for an ancient enemy to become the Third Key in the Triad. A child who will be twice sired and twice born shall bind the rune. It will be a path of great sorrow and much sacrifice, lessons to be learned in sharing and giving, should you choose it. But great also will be the reward. The choice, as it has always been, is yours alone to make. You will be loved and cherished; we will always be with you no matter what path you take."

"Remember always," the Lady said, "except in your own defense or that of others, always bide the Three-Fold Law, and remember, all who choose Our path must learn to live together in Perfect Love and Perfect Trust." Her silken voice rippled like gentle waters in a woodland stream, intoxicating Alan's mind and soul.

"I... I don't understand." Alan stammered, awash in confusion and total awe. "Why would You need me, or any others, for that matter, when the insignificant power I possess, that You say derives from You, must pale to insignificance beside Your own?"

"Because We dwell on what your mystics call the Astral or Higher Realms, We are too far removed from the Earth plane. We need willing channels working with Us to focus and direct the power which, like you, flows through—not from—Us. Therein, united, lies Our true strength, and that is why you elected to return as Our emissary, my son: to be reborn into this world of matter; to be of it so that we might work with and through you. Although you are already so close to becoming one of Us, who dwell on the Inner Planes, and therefore so much more powerful a channel for us to work through, your steel must yet endure more tempering before the blade can cut as it should. There are many more trials yet ahead before you can say your work is done."

The Lady floated close, almost enveloping him. "Once more, you must become a priest of Our children. They have been returning to Us and to the Old Ways in ever greater numbers during recent years. Once more, you must call them back to Our service.

"It will not be an easy task. Like the children they still are, feeling their newfound power as they struggle against authority, their fragile egos blind them to their true purpose. Like siblings, they fight amongst themselves, tear at each other, bicker over foolish rivalries. But like true siblings, we have faith they will come together when faced with a common danger."

Alan's face twisted into a bitter smile as he remembered Gertha and Zarkov—his parents—how much it had hurt them to watch him and Dawn tearing at each other. They had been such children themselves.

A proud twinkle in the Lady's eyes told him she had intercepted his thoughts. "Go among them, Our Chosen One. Teach them what you have learned at such cost: to work together if they would truly serve Us. If they would find themselves. We will endure the coming cataclysm, as We have many others. Your people, the civilization you have built will not, unless they put aside their petty jealousies and squabblings.

"But... How can I presume to teach? I've only just begun learning Your ways myself. Besides, I don't even know who, much less where they are," Alan protested weakly.

"You may call on all magical groups who acknowledge the Earth as their Mother and seek to protect her," the Lady replied. "But most especially, look to those who call themselves Witches: the Wise Ones, the benders and shapers of reality, for the ancient roots of their teachings are the same as yours. When the time is right, you will be lead back to them. Right now your task is to seek your priestess and birth the Triad." Alan was totally drunk now on the heady sweetness of the Lady's voice. Only Dawn had ever before had such a deliciously inebriating effect on him.

"As a reminder that We are always with you, no matter where you are, take this token of our love." The Lord held out the pendent He had been wearing and hung it about Alan's neck. It was larger and the chain slightly longer than the amulet his mother had given him just before she died. Except when its chain needed mending or replacement, he had never taken it off. "Fashion another exactly like it in the equivalent materials of your lower plane, set them atop each other, and they will merge into one. Wear them always as a token of your love for Us, and as a reminder of your ancient vows as High Priest and Magus of the Old Ways."

With a thousand more questions yet on his lips, Alan reached up to touch the softly glowing medallion on his chest. But as his fingers closed around it, he heard the huge wooden doors at the back of the church burst open.

"Find your true priestess first, my son, for without both male and female, the active as well as the receptive principle, the energy cannot flow as freely. Your power as a channel for Us is but a shadow of what it can be, what it must once more become, after you and your Priestess are at last one in the Triad." The Lord's deep, resonant baritone faded rapidly as Alan's head spun around to identify the intrusion. The Lady's voice joined with his in a barely audible "Blessed Be!"

The huge wooden doors at the front of the cathedral burst open.

"Oh thank god we found you!" Muff's shrill voice, amplified by the echo-chamber effect of the cavernous sanctuary, sheered through him like a blade, severing his tenuous hold on that other dimension. As Muff charged down the center aisle with Ham hard on her heels, feelings of anger over this shattering of the moment were mixed with relief at seeing them safely out of Costanza's reach. Alan climbed back onto his feet just barely in time to catch the girl as she flew into his arms. It took several minutes for both of them to catch their breaths and for reassurances, whispered over and over again into Muff's ear, before he could make sense of anything either of them said or thought.

"Al, Baby!" Ham finally managed between gasps for air, as he leaned against the altar rail for support. "The way them hard-nose dudes was comin' on back there, I was so sure you'd 'a bought the farm before we could get to you. What in hell'd you do to get 'em so wound up like that?"

"Costanza's dealing, Ham. And manufacturing nova too," Alan frowned over Muff's head as she continued clinging to him like a frightened child. "You thought he was going to be fuming over losing the steady revenue I was bringing in; but that wasn't the half of it. All the crowds and activity around us at the club: he's been using it like a smoke screen to launder drug money and to cover up illegal in-house activities." Alan hurriedly filled them in on his encounter with Costanza, and then later with the club owner's two stooges.

"So that's why the vultures were circling your dressin' room!" Ham nodded, anger now lighting up his eyes.

"Is that why you came looking for me?" Alan asked. "How'd you know I'd be here?"

"It was Muff. She…"

"I was on my way to your dressing room to wake you for the next show." Still shaking slightly, Muff looked up at him with her frightened fawn eyes and immediately had his undivided attention. "I overheard Costanza telling his security people you knew everything and were a lot more dangerous than he'd realized. He said something too about some little old man who'd come in earlier this evening claiming to be your father and asking to see you. He was letting him wait out the first show in his private office to surprise you. After his row with you though, he said he'd decided to hold the old man as a bargaining chip to force you to sign confessions that would guarantee your good behavior. But then he saw what you did to Felsh and Tooley. He's put out a contract on you, Al. He wants you wasted the minute you're found."

Two bombs exploded back-to-back inside Alan's head: his father here! And he was being held by Costanza! No longer of any value as a hostage, he could be killed at any moment. There was a chance the Pentacle's owner might be keeping him alive for the time being as bait to lure Alan back within range of his guns. He would have to hold on to that hope. It would buy him the time he needed.

"Oh Al!" she sniffled, hugging him even more fiercely. "I was so scared for you. As soon as I could sneak past them, I ran to get Ham and then we came looking, to warn you. The rest of the band said they'd stay and try to find out where

Costanza's holding your father. I remembered how we practically had to drag you away from here this afternoon. Something told me this was the place to start looking."

"Yeah, an' did we ever have a time of it gettin' here! It took nearly an hour just shakin' the tail Costanza put on us," Ham added with a nervous grin.

As Alan turned to pry Muff loose and start back for the Pentacle, he saw figures darkly silhouetted in the arched doorway.

"Ham! How many of Costanza's people were following you?"

"Two, I think. Why?"

"Apparently, you weren't as successful shaking them as you thought. They're back. With reinforcements." Alan could make out at least half a dozen silhouettes crowding through the open doorway.

"Oh jeeze!" Ham agonized. "Muff told me what those two dudes looked like after you got done with them. It's no wonder they called out the militia."

"Muff, get behind the altar," Alan commanded softly. "Ham and I are about to have the fight of our lives; and I don't want you hurt. Good girl!" he added with a quick kiss, as she smiled up at him, and a pat to her rump, sending her off.

Alan hunkered down behind the altar rail, motioning for Ham to follow suit, then sent out a silent summons to Garuda. The great bird had found himself a comfortable perch up in one of the bell towers and was quitting it with great reluctance. Had he been capable of such logical gymnastics, he would probably have been regretting, about now, ever having returned to his old master.

"Before this night's over I'm afraid I'm gonna' be gettin' my sinuses cleared the hard way." Ham whispered, trying to present a braver front than he was actually feeling.

"I'm grateful for the help. But your hands!" Alan added, worrying about his friend.

"Screw the hands, Dude!" Ham snarled indignantly, his eyes still riveted on Costanza's advancing soldiers. "Believe it or not, there are a few things in life more important than my music. Now granted, it's a damn short list, but you an' Muff definitely occupy the top two places."

Alan felt the warmth of love that prompted Ham's outrage. He stole the moment needed to reach out and plant a grateful hand on his friend's shoulder and to return it in a fleeting smile. By the time he turned back to face them once more, Costanza's troops were almost on top of them.

"Hey Al! Don't you think we ought'a be duckin' behind pews an' lookin' for a way outta' here? Them turkeys are all packin' guns."

"Not for long, Ham. Not for long. You're forgetting, I have an equalizer of my own." His smile froze over with ominous implications.

"The boss says he wants you wasted," the giant at the head of the human convoy boomed out, coming to a sudden halt less than a dozen feet away. The troops behind him skidded to a halt, almost crashing into each other in their nervous haste. They had all seen what Alan had done to Felsh and Tooley. Already he could feel fear eating away at them like a toxic corrosive. In the flickering, spectral light from hundreds of votive candles, Alan recognized Malgrove, the meticulously dressed Maitre d' and head of security at the club.

As he resumed his slow, confident advance, he continued speaking slowly, savoring the echo-chamber effect and the fear he imagined it was inspiring in the hearts of his intended victims. "I think Costanza would appreciate a few words with the three of you first, though. I'm sure he'd like to find out how much you and the rest of your band actually know about the operation. Maybe he might even enjoy wasting you himself, afterward. So, if you clowns would like to live a couple extra hours, I suggest coming along quietly, real quietly!"

At the Pentacle it was common knowledge that ten years ago wrestling fans had known him as 'Hatfield McCoy, The Smokey Mountain Mangler.' He had come by the title with little or no help from promoters, eventually getting himself barred from professional wrestling after permanently crippling more than one opponent in the ring. It was not common knowledge, however, that his legal name was Rotoni, Anthony Rotoni, and that he'd had many serious brushes with the law during his rather illustrious career.

"Hey, Sam! Figures you'd be here too. Boy is there ever gonna' be hell to pay when they open the coffin and find you gone," Ham called out. His bravado was directed at the tall cadaverous caricature on Rotoni's right. He had just stepped forward and, using the muzzle of his thirty-eight, was gesturing in the direction he wanted them to move. Ham was maintaining a cool exterior, but silently he was broadcasting a frantic plea. *Quick, Al, do something, anything, before we're all killed!*

Alan's eyes became narrow slits of concentration. He tightened focus then released a 'blast' of PK. It ripped Sam's weapon out of his grasp and sent it flying into the pews behind him. The forty-five that Rotoni materialized to take its place followed the same trajectory.

"Hidden magnets? Whatever. Good trick anyway, guit-picker; but it isn't going to save you. You're nothing but old women masquerading as men. You don't have a prayer," Rotoni laughed, anticipating an easy kill. He had changed his mind, deciding that finishing them off now might be the better part of wisdom.

"Oh, but that was just for openers. Wait'll you see us duelin' with our knittin' needles," Ham sneered, beginning to feel braver.

"Oh, wise guy, huh?" Sam sneered back.

"Say! Now that was an original line," Ham laughed tauntingly. "How come you ain't tried 'Twenty-three ski-doo!' yet, or 'So's your old man!'?" Sensing, from past shared combat experience, that Alan could use some additional time in which to launch his next volley, Ham was buying him the precious seconds he needed.

Outside, Garuda circled, patiently waiting. *Now!!* Alan 'shouted' his mental command. Guided by a fragile tendril of projected consciousness, the spotted eagle dove at one of the stained-glass windows. Fearing it might prove too solid, injuring his winged friend, Alan tightened control and increased power. He managed, if only slightly, to weaken the molecular bond within the window glass, barely a split second before Garuda entered with a crash that haloed him in thousands of multi-colored starbursts. Swooping down in the midst of Rotoni's troops, he was a screeching, flapping, biting, clawing, feathered demon, heralded by an iridescent sea of falling shards. The distraction was all Alan could have hoped for. Like Felsh and Tooley earlier, they had been taken completely off guard. Their six stalkers suddenly found themselves the prey, as they backed off, trying to protect their eyes and shooting wildly into the air.

Alan fought desperately against the wave of weakness and vertigo that always accompanied sudden, excessively heavy drains on his PK reserves. The moment, Garuda's gift of surprise, must not be lost. Swallowing hard against a second wave of nausea, he found a hidden reservoir of strength to tap into. Limbs trembling, he clamped down hard with his teeth, then aimed his PK at the four remaining weapons. One after the other, he hurled them as far out of reach as possible before a stray bullet could hit Garuda or one of his friends.

"Man! Now that was really one far-out trick." Ham shouted, as they both dove at their disarmed attackers.

Alan connected with a fist rammed hard into the face of the cadaverous Sam, smashing bone and flesh, and permanently rearranging his features. Anything had to be an improvement, he rationalized in a feeble attempt to justify this overwhelming lust for mayhem that was now consuming him. He thought he had rid himself of all the buried anger; but learning that his father was a hostage, and now this unprovoked attack! In a temple of worship, of all places, all the more sanctified by the visit only moments ago of the Great Mother and her Consort. So much for the lecture on 'perfect love and perfect trust.' They wanted a fight; he would be delighted to oblige. But somewhere else. If he could lead his pursuers outside through the rear vestry and lure them away from Ham and Muff...

Too late! Danger right behind! Alan looked over his shoulder in time to aim a back kick at one of Costanza's soldiers, descending on him with knife held high and poised to strike. The edge of his foot connected like a battering ram, just under the man's rib cage. As his assailant went flying backward, his body describing a beautiful arc over several pews, Alan was dimly aware of internal organs rupturing. Tongue protruding, he was already turning blue as he hit the floor. He twitched several times then lay still.

A hasty check on Ham found his friend in dire need of aid. He was being held from behind while someone else was using him for a punching bag. Alan leapt back over the altar rail and launched himself at the man pinning Ham's arms back in a full nelson. As he rammed the extended fingers of his right hand upward into his victim's left armpit the arm involuntarily jerked backward, going limp and paralyzed. Then he grabbed the man's wrist, palm up in his left hand and yanked it across his own chest in an arm bar. Forcing his victim's body backward, Alan delivered a vicious hand ax to the exposed throat. Wind pipe shattered, neck broken, another of Costanza's hirelings went down.

His arms free, Ham was acquitting himself quite admirably, Alan noted with grim satisfaction. He had just delivered a vicious kick to the groin of the hired goon who was pounding at him. As his man doubled over in pain, Ham grabbed his head in both hands, holding it steady for a knee kick to the face, knocking him out. With a smashed nose, his eyes would be swollen shut by the time he came to. He no longer posed any future threat.

"Thanks bro… I… Watch out!" he yelled, pushing Alan aside and ducking under a wild swing with a heavy, carved wood chair, appropriated from the chancel behind them.

Cursing himself for losing concentration, Alan delivered a roundhouse kick to this latest challenger's stomach, doubling him over and sending him flying very obligingly into Ham's ready fist.

Rotoni alone remained, the last tree to be felled. Smug self-satisfaction had transformed itself into fear. Eyes wide with surprise and new respect for the man he was now coming up against, he licked his lips and tried to stand tall. "Well, well! 'Tinkerbell's' grown fangs. How about that!" His lips pulled back into an ugly parody of a smile calculated to conceal the fear as he hunkered down and began circling slowly and cautiously.

"Hey Al! Why do I get this funny feeling you'd like to hog 'Cuddles' here all to yourself?" Ham laughed, as he stepped back to make room.

"I haven't a clue," Alan smiled back fiercely, recalling all the veiled insults, the sarcasms and subtle indignities.

Knowing how much being the house band at the Pentacle meant to Ham and the other members of Wild Hunt, for two years he had forced himself to quietly endure them. But no more now. He was going to enjoy this opportunity to finally balance the ledger, prolonging the pleasure as much as possible. No PK this time, either. Just muscle pitted against muscle, making it worth all he had endured, for the sake of the band, at the hands of this sub-moron who suffered from major delusions of adequacy. The asshole didn't know what power really was. Alan was going to relish educating him, and...

"Damn!" He cursed out loud, remembering Zarkov. His father needed him a great deal more than the child, still dwelling within, needed to 'get even.' While he was playing around, collecting his debt of revenge, Costanza might be deciding it was time to dispatch the old man. No! He would have to finish Rotoni off as expeditiously as possible, then waste no more time getting back to the Pentacle.

Allowing his enemy to posture and feint for a moment, he gracefully accepted the invitation of a coaxing hand gesture, and walked, with seeming nonchalance, within reach of Rotoni's powerfully muscled arms.

Overconfident, allowing himself the premature luxury of self-congratulation, Alan had momentarily forgotten that his present adversary had been a professional wrestler with more than a little training in the martial arts himself. Without telegraphing his move and before Alan could block, Rotoni fired off a powerful solar plexus punch. Instinctively tightened abdominal muscles were all that saved him from major injury. Fighting to remain afloat through wave after wave of nausea, he just barely managed to counter Rotoni's left-handed follow-through punch. Suddenly finding himself on the defensive, he was forced into blocking and feinting, to avoid the speed and power of Rotoni's attacks. The nausea finally under control, able at last to clear away the last cobweb from his brain, Alan was able to retrieve his lost focus. Feigning exhaustion, and continuing his defensive posture, he waited until Rotoni, emboldened, tried once more for a punch to Alan's mid-section. This time he was ready with a block and a quick follow-through punch of his own that sent Rotoni staggering several inches backward.

Smiling as though he'd only been kissed, Rotoni was hurting as Alan pressed his advantage. He struck with all the force he could muster, driving the heel of his right hand upwards into his enemy's undefended jaw. Grabbing the jaw with one hand, he reached over behind his enemy's head with the other. Then twisting Rotoni's head, he slammed it down hard against the carpeted floor. A communicator spilled out from one of Rotoni's pockets and came to rest at Alan's feet. A red indicator light signaled that the device was locked in for monitoring.

"Come on you two! Let's get the hell out of here! Snow White's heard everything and probably has his whole organization out trolling for us and his missing dwarfs right now," Alan called out He was more anxious than ever to be out of here and heading back to the Pentacle to find his father.

"Al! Behind you! Look out!" Ham's shouted warning came hard on the heels of his own internal alarm.

"Oh shit! Here we go again!" he said. Adding a string of invective, Alan turned to face down this latest obstacle. The cadaverous Sam was back on his feet. His face had been reduced to a mangled ruin by Garuda's overzealous attack. Somehow still able to see, he was aiming a gun he had managed to retrieve from the maze of untenanted pews. Without wasting time to ponder ethics, Alan loosed a withering blast of PK that paralyzed the man, freezing his brain and toppling him like a chunk of ice breaking off from a glacier.

Alan had launched Garuda back out into the night, and was half-way through the door himself before realizing he was alone. With a sinking premonition, he turned back to retrieve his two shell-shocked friends.

As he herded them outside, Muff was looking up at him in frightened awe. The gentle man she had known for almost a year had suddenly grown fangs and fur. When he reached out in a hesitant gesture of assurance, she cringed like a cornered rabbit. Pointing their faces in the direction of the club, Alan started them moving. Like an obedient zombie, holding fast to Muff's hand, Ham started walking in wide-eyed silence.

"Damn!" He had always known people would react this way, if—no, when—they found out, as they soon enough would. No more running or hiding; he had promised himself. But still: Ham and Muff! That was a little more pain than he could manage right now. If only it could have been Dawn here beside him—instead of Muff! She would have teased him unmercifully about using wind tunnels for blowing out matches; but she never would have shrunk from him. Hardly noticing that the rain had stopped and that a bright full moon now lit the sky, he bit down hard in a desperate effort not to let his feelings surface. Quickening his pace, he pulled far ahead of his trailing friends.

"Hey, Al! Loosen up, will ya'!" Ham called out, pulling Muff after him, like a rag doll, as he ran to catch up "Give us a break, huh? We need some time to digest that last mouthful."

"Great! Only take a look at Muff, there! For nearly a year we've eaten, played, worked, slept, and, dammit, made love together. Now, all at once, I try to touch her and…"

"Dammit Al, slow down! This ain't the Olympics," Ham shouted, forcing Alan to acknowledge him and slacken his pace. "That's better. Don't you go slidin' back into the poor-little-ol'-me's again!" he frowned, stabbing a finger into Alan's back. "Muff's never been good at handlin' surprises, but tomorrow she'll be right as rain again. And you know we're brothers. So shut up!

"Hey! I didn't say you should slow down that much! Costanza's holdin' some dude says he's your ol' man. Now let's go kick us some ass. Big time!"

"Ham!" Alan stopped abruptly, precipitating a near collision. They were still several blocks from their destination. "It's going to get pretty rough in there. I'd breathe a whole lot easier if you'd make sure Muff gets home safely." He saw the troubled expression on his friend's face, felt the conflict between concern for Muff's safety and his need to stand with a brother in his hour of danger. He was afraid too, that if he left, this might be the last time they would ever see each other alive.

"No, Al!" Muff looked up, tugging on Alan's sleeve for attention. "No matter how powerful that mind magic of yours makes you, you're still going to need Ham's help in there. I won't let you send him off to baby-sit me. I'm not ashamed to admit I'm scared, but I can still handle myself. Besides, who knows what kind of surprise Costanza might have waiting back at the apartment.

"Right now, I'd feel a whole lot safer walking into the Pentacle behind the two of you than anywhere else. I promise: I'll stay as far out of sight and out of the way as possible; I won't panic and I won't get in the way. And if they start shooting, I'll duck real fast. Please?"

It was the first time Muff had spoken since the fight with Costanza's men. Now it looked as though the problem would be shutting her up again if he didn't concede. Applauding her new-found courage with a smile, he reached out hesitantly to caress the down on her cheek. She didn't pull away this time. Outwardly, at least.

"All right, Ham. Let's get the bastard!" Alan's grim smile was cast in concrete as he probed ahead along the route back to the Pentacle. "We're going to have to sacrifice speed for caution. Costanza's called out the militia. They're scouting for us in pairs and threes. The man may be a lot of things but stupid isn't one of them. He knows now, I'm dangerous and crazy enough to come back, wanting to even the score. By now, too, he probably suspects I know about his hostage; so he'll be waiting for us."

CHAPTER XIV

A LAN WAS CHAFING from the tedium. They were forced to move slowly, hugging the shadows of buildings as he cautiously probed ahead. There had been endless detours, melting into store fronts, ducking behind dumpsters in alleys as they fought to elude Costanza's soldiers. Only moments ago, when retreat had been impossible and discovery imminent, Alan had reluctantly been forced to "neutralize" a lone spotter. When the man failed to report in at his appointed time Costanza's people would be doubly alert. Alan would have loved a dramatic entrance, bursting in through the Pentacle's huge gilt doors and charging through the lobby crowds up the winding ornate staircase to the club owner's private office. Discretion ruled, however, forcing him to agree with Ham's choice of the kitchen's service entrance instead.

"That's odd. It's hardly past one an' no one's hangin' round the front entrance. The parkin' garage 'cross the street's empty too," Ham frowned, looking back suspiciously as they threaded a cautious path through the shadows and down the Pentacle's deserted service alley. "The place is locked up tighter 'n Buzzy's drums," he added, peering in through a nearby window then jiggling the double doors of the service entrance a second time. "Al! What the hell you doin' now?"

Alan shook himself out of intense concentration and opened his eyes. "I'm arranging for speedy transportation out of here when we're done." He closed his eyes once more to help facilitate concentration. It had been such a long time. For all he knew they had long ago dismantled the Peregrine or redesigned her com system. At last! Linkup! Once again, he felt the old thrill as she powered up in answer to his distant summons. It was like slipping his hand into a comfortable, well-worn glove. Through data feedback, he "felt" the hanger doors grind open, protesting no doubt from long disuse. Before withdrawing, he programmed her to home in on the city's coordinates then hover out of sight, above the low-hanging cloud cover, until he was ready to call her down.

"What the fuck we gonna' need transportation for, out'a someplace we can't get into in the first place. And what kind'a transportation, might I ask?" Ham's features darkened further with suspicion. The surprises were still coming faster than he was capable of comfortably assimilating.

"First of all: where does it say 'psychokinetic telepath can't break in'? And you already know damn well what kind of transportation." Alan was beginning to enjoy Ham's consternation.

"Thanks. I was afraid you'd say that."

Alan closed his eyes once more, this time to send out a probing tendril of thought, searching for the club's elaborate alarm network. He found one of the sensor wires, then followed it back, past each alarm circuit, to the central computer. That part had not been particularly difficult; but exploring an unfamiliar system at such a distance, overriding, then selectively shutting down only the kitchen's alarm sensors, was a delicate task requiring intense concentration.

He had spent the last few hours battling with psionic weapons for the lives of himself and his two friends. Then just now re-activating the Peregrine: it had proven a far greater drain than at first anticipated.

The world around him was slipping out of focus as his right hand instinctively sought the pendant that had been given to him by the antlered "deity" of his vision. It was still there. As real and solid to the touch as his mother's. Wrapping his fingers around it, once more obeying a silent summons, he felt himself sinking into the earth. He was merging with it, feeding from it like an infant suckling at its Mother's breast.

He had never considered it as an energy source to draw from for refueling his body's depleted power reserves. Had he once again connected with his mysterious Lord and Lady or had he only been acting on metaphysical information unconsciously retrieved from Dawn's stored memory engrams? He allowed himself the luxury of a moment's further retrospect. Either way, the basic concept wasn't that different from a favorite martial arts centering exercise used for focusing on the ki, your inner power, and recharging your energy reserves by aligning your center of gravity with the earth beneath your feet.

Alan had to shake his head several times before his eyes would open. His back was against a grimy brick wall with Ham and Muff in front, bracing him up.

"Thank God! I was just gettin' ready to go for an ambulance. What happened?" Ham was as pale as it was possible for him to look.

"Sorry I had to scare you like that. Those last two stunts were too much of a drain. Apparently my body decided to shut down for an emergency recharge," he apologized, brushing an arm across his forehead to wipe away perspiration that was beginning to trickle into his eyes. "I'm all right now," he added. Gently shrugging off any further attempts at help, he went back to work. By the time the last of the bolts on the Kitchen door had slipped back, his head had begun throbbing again.

A rapid scan before entering confirmed what they had suspected. Costanza had closed early and sent everyone except his security staff home. Activity was still coming from the dressing room area. Guards were covering the lobby, all the exits, and patrolling the halls. The greatest concentration of mental activity, however, was centered in the area of Costanza's second floor office suite.

Zarkov! His father was still alive. His familiar psychic spoor placed him somewhere close to where the Pentacle's owner was gathering his generals. With all the surrounding mental static, Alan was unable to get more than a general fix on his location. Relief at finding him unharmed was quickly metamorphosed into outrage and then fear, fear they might yet decide to shoot the old man before they had time to reach him. Running back and forth along the broad spectrum of conflicting and distracting emotions was not going to save the rancher's daughter, Alan reminded himself. He drew a deep breath, then schooled his focus on the more immediate problem of a single presence very close by, somewhere in the kitchen area. He hurriedly briefed Ham and Muff on the results of his scan.

"Looks like our former employer got the callin' card we left back at church, where we was all 'prayin'," Ham whispered nervously as he poked his head through the kitchen doors. "You're right. There's the creep over there," he added, barely audible as he withdrew, carefully closing the door behind him. "It's Twadowsky from the Casino. He's got his hands around one 'a Chen Lu's cakes. The way he's goin' at it a herd of elephants could stampede past an' he'd never know the difference. Oh. Uhh... Sorry about checkin' fer myself, Al. Old habits die hard. Growin' up in the neighborhood you learn early: no matter how much you trust the brothers, have a good look for yourself before divin' in."

The casino's floor man had to be taken out as fast and silently as possible. Alan didn't want the others on patrol alerted so soon to their presence. Twadowsky, standing off to the right near the walk-ins, was hacking off another wedge of cake with a large chef's knife when Alan eased himself silently into the kitchen from the service hallway. He smiled at the grim irony of using such a vicious looking weapon for cutting cake. Rather apropos, he found himself thinking, as the man and the situation suggested their own solution to the problem of silent neutralizing. Shaping his PK into the semblance of a hand, Alan projected it outward, grabbing the fist holding the knife. He pulled back and out, then cutting edge leading, initiated a powerful inward thrust that pierced through the man's neck, severing the trachea and both carotid arteries. Incapable of making more than a few gurgling sounds, Twadowsky's features twisted into a mask of horrified surprise before he sank to the floor, drowning in his own blood.

Fighting off a wave of nausea as a powerful flood of the dying man's emotions broke through his shields and swept over him, Alan scanned the hallway outside the kitchen and the service stairs leading up to the second floor, then waved an all-clear. Positioning himself as best he could to shield Muff from the bloody tabloid of death, Ham grabbed the girl's hand and bolted for the door leading to the stair well.

Still leading the way, Alan hugged the shadows of the dimly lit second floor hallway. Ahead of them, blocking the way to Costanza and his father, stood a guard carrying a large semi-automatic. For the moment, his back was toward them as he leaned over the balcony rail for a brief exchange with another soldier directly below in the lobby.

Alan signed for silence as he quietly approached the hall guard from behind. Reaching around with his right hand to cup his enemy's jaw, he slammed upward, effectively silencing any warning. Simultaneously, he clamped his left hand around the back of the guard's skull. With a quick left snap, up and back, he silently broke the man's neck. He made a grab for his victim's weapon just in time to keep it from clanking to the floor. As he started hauling the body back out of sight from the lobby below, he looked up to see Ham holding a door open and motioning impatiently for him to deposit his cargo inside the unlit interior.

The way was clear now, but Alan hesitated, torn between concern for Muff's safety and his need to rescue the man who had been both father and friend for most of his life. Just ahead, the door to Costanza's gym was ajar. A quick scan of the unlit interior assured him it was empty. He signed for Muff to enter and lock herself in. She obeyed, but reluctantly.

Alan paused to scan the large office. Costanza was barricaded between the far wall and the dubious safety of his huge desk. Positioned around him were a dozen of his lieutenants. Five or six of the local ranking drug lords were present as well, accompanied by their own bodyguards and aides. He was certain none of Costanza's people would dare open fire in such tight quarters; but Costanza himself was a calculated risk. He could hear the Pentacle's owner shouting accusations of incompetence at his entire staff. With mirthless satisfaction Alan noted the fear hidden behind the man's convincing display of outrage.

"Cover my back! I'm going for Costanza first," he whispered, handing the semi-automatic to Ham, who received it none too willingly. Taking a deep breath to focus himself, he kicked the door open, knocking somebody down who'd been stationed on the other side. Hoping the element of surprise would be sufficient to make it all the way through the gauntlet, he launched himself into the room. As he was shoving aside one of the local drug lords who was blocking his way, he saw Costanza reach into his desk drawer, scrambling frantically for a gun. Making a quick course adjustment for an attack, now from Costanza's vulnerable left side, Alan slammed a fist into an unguarded gut knocking another obstruction out of his path. On his feet now and still fumbling for a proper grip on his weapon, Costanza had to aim now from an awkward position, giving Alan the needed time for a head-first flying tackle. Unable to check his momentum, he reached out with his left hand, grabbing Costanza in a chin lock, as he sailed past. His head impacted with sickening force against the wall.

For a moment he was back in the cathedral with multi-colored shards of glass falling all around him. And then he was on the floor. Costanza on top of him, was dazed, confused and still caught in the chin lock. A million miles away, someone was yelling for "that fuckin' desk" to be shoved aside. Costanza was pulled free and then bodies began piling on top of him, holding him down and smothering him with the sheer weight of their numbers. Fists swung wildly occasionally connected sometimes with him, sometimes with each other. Alan was too far away to really care.

Consciousness was slipping from his grasp. Part of him remained behind, buried under a mountain of pummeling flesh, while yet another part broke free, swimming, buoyant on a sea of diffuse, unfocused energy that seemed to be emanating from far below, within the bowels of the planet. The battle erupting all around him was being played out in slow motion, like icebergs drifting along on a quiet ocean. Time slowly returned to its normal pace.

Several feet away, Alan "saw" Ham holding the semi-automatic by the barrel and swinging it like a club. He had become a raging forest fire, fighting against impossible odds to reach the side of his fallen friend. Just as suddenly, Muff had appeared. Transformed now into a she-demon, she was using a small weight bar, scavenged from the gym next door, with devastating effect. Already two participants in the pile-up, pinning Alan's untenanted body to the floor, were lying off to one side in discarded heaps. It would only be a matter of moments before Costanza's people would waken from this latest surprise attack, regroup, and swat these two into permanent oblivion, as though they had been nothing more than bothersome mosquitoes.

Alan was frantic. Ham, Muff, his father, they needed him. He mustn't fail. Not again! Not as he had failed himself and others who had depended on him so many times before! Suddenly he was back within the confines of his body, fighting against the weight of smothering bodies, to fill his starving lungs with precious air. A fist pounding against his chest was driving the hard metal of both pendants into the soft flesh of his chest, forcing painful awareness of them into consciousness. He fought vainly to tap his body's depleted energy reserves for one final burst of PK.

The Lady's soft voice suddenly insinuated itself into awareness, "There is no need to deplete yourself, My Chosen One. Draw from My body! All that you need is yours. You have only to reach out to me."

Gratefully, like a starving man, he sent a part of himself deep into the Earth, like the roots of a tree, drawing up the gift of her precious life force. He needed only to focus, to open himself more fully now to its flow as it strengthened, restored him. The new power began flowing through him in seemingly inexhaustible supply. Resolve hardened into the anchor he needed to pull himself back to full consciousness once more.

He was amazed at the ease with which he was now able to free himself, like a dog shaking water from its fur, until he looked up and found himself surrounded by the entire band. Ham and Muff had been joined by Chey, Bongo, and Buzz, all grinning fiercely, as they hovered over him. Unconscious at their feet were most of the soldiers who'd had him pinned. Chey and Bongo both held out a hand, helping him back onto his feet.

Costanza's mob had regrouped and was rushing them once more. Reacting automatically, Alan loosed a blast of PK. It was like a nova exploding within him that hurled everyone in the room to the floor. Their casualties forgotten, those few of Costanza's forces who were still able to, scrambled back onto their feet and out the door.

"How can any dude possibly have more fun than this, unless maybe he's lucky enough t' have four impacted wisdom teeth an' a dozen kidney stones all singin' the same tune." Struggling to get his shaking legs back under him, Ham was trying once again to camouflage astonishment at this latest demonstration of raw power that had taken even Alan by surprise.

"Oh man! What the hell was that?" Chey sat up, shaking his head. He was debating silently about the wisdom of trying to stand up too soon.

Buzz lay speechless and unmoving. Propped up on trembling elbows, his eyes were tracing the pattern in the rug.

"Al! We're family. We'll back you all the way. But I think it's time for some answers." Bongo's voice had lost its playful Haitian cowboy patois. Deadly serious now, he was the least shaken of the group. "I suspected who you really were the first day you joined up with us, but Chey kept telling me I was crazy. And how could I argue with him? I mean, really, why would Alan Kolkey, with all his money and power, be knocking around with a country rock band no one ever heard of before?

"I guess that's none of our business, man; so I won't ask. But, dammit, what the hell are you?"

"I'm not sure anymore myself, Bongo." Alan confessed, shaking his head in total bewilderment. Until now, knocking guns out of people's hands, one at a time, and unlocking bolted doors had been the most his PK was capable of.

Muff didn't shrink from him when he reached out to pull her back up, but she was saucer-eyed and shaking. She had no clever repartee or feigned indignation to duck behind like Ham, who was busy dusting himself off and muttering under his breath. Bongo was helping Chey shake sense back into Buzz as they hauled him back onto his feet.

Alan suddenly felt his father's familiar psychic imprint clearly this time. He was very close, confined inside a dark, cramped space somewhere behind that far wall over...

"All right, Falcon! You had your fun; but playtime's over now. Either you and your pals come along quietly, or the pretty lady, here, cashes her chips in." It was Rotoni, his lips curled back in a triumphant sneer. Bursting through the office door, he had grabbed Muff in a hammerlock and was holding a knife to her throat. His eyes were red hot faggots, burning holes in his skull. Framed in blood streaming down his face from a deep scalp wound, they gave him a ghoulish appearance.

"Like I said the day we met, Al: Darwin was right. There's your proof." Ham's initial fear for Muff had almost instantly turned to anger, with its own brand of courage. He began circling like a hunting cat, trying to divide Rotoni's attention between the two of them. "Man, you don't learn too quick, do you? Messin' with m'man over there's a short cut to the bone yard."

Damn! Alan cursed himself for such disastrous carelessness. Why hadn't he taken the time to put Rotoni permanently out of action, as he had most of the others? Recalling the lessons of the last two years, he hurriedly redirected anger where it belonged: toward the enemy now menacing Muff. His outrage suddenly blazed white hot and molten. He collected his fury, rolled it into a ball and hurled it. Rotoni froze. For a moment his features twisted themselves into a grotesque mask of pain; and then his entire head exploded into flames.

If possible, Alan's astonishment was even greater than that of his audience as he hurriedly pulled Muff from the now lifeless embrace of her erstwhile captor. He nudged her gently toward Ham, then made a quick grab for the body before it fell to the floor. Again! Until now, directing such concentrated fury only resulted in death through neural overload or destruction of cerebral blood vessels.

With its skull charred now to an unrecognizable cinder he hauled the corpse up to chest level. Three more of Rotoni's soldiers stood paralyzed in the doorway, looking like bowling pins waiting to be knocked down. Obligingly, he aimed and hurled, scoring a clean strike as "ball" and "pins" went down together. A frantic scramble to untangle themselves turned into a mad rout across the mezzanine and down the spiraled stairs to the main lobby.

"That ought to keep the bastards quiet for a while." Ham said, flashing a hesitant, very nervous grin as he allowed Muff to crowd deeper into the shelter of his arms.

"For a while," Alan agreed. "But only for a while. It won't take long at all to psyche themselves for another attack. Next time it'll be with guns drawn and spitting lead." Gesturing needlessly for silence, he resumed his search. His hands became antennas, sounding the walls as he paced once more around the office perimeter. He stopped in front of a walk-in closet where Costanza kept supplies and a small safe. Behind it, he felt a camouflaged panel, beyond it, a concealed chamber. And his father!

With no patience remaining to search for concealed buttons, he rolled the heavy safe aside and smashed his own way through.

In the dim light filtering from the room behind him, he saw a toilet and sink in the far left corner, partially obscured by a folding screen. To his immediate left was a counter holding a hot plate, a small portable refrigerator, and above it shelves, stockpiled with tins and boxes of preserved food. On his immediate right were more shelves containing books, a radio, a phone and a TV. Directly across from him, a door, bolted and padlocked from the inside, led to a hidden exit below, at the back of the building. No doubt, the room was used primarily as a safe place for associates of Costanza who were refugees from the law and rival organizations.

As Alan's eyes rapidly accustomed themselves to the darkened chamber he located the light switch and flicked it on. Looking toward a far right corner where he had only been able to distinguish the outlines of a bed, he found the old man who had raised and loved him for so many years—gagged and tied spread-eagle to the antique metal frame! With a cry of outrage, he leapt to his side. Reaching for a convenient kitchen knife on the nearby table, Alan cut through his bonds, then eased the gag from his mouth. He helped the beloved old man sit up, then began very gently kneading circulation and life back into his aging limbs.

Ham moved closer as Muff knelt beside the bed to help. "Name's Ham. Ham Davis, Sir," he said after an uncomfortably long silence. "This here's Muff—I mean Frances

Moreno. Those other clowns over there are Chey Valantin, Henri Lefleur, better known as Bongo, and John Derrickson, also better known as Buzz," he added, gesturing toward the tunnel of light pouring through the chamber's entrance where the other band members huddled in confusion.

"I'm sorry," Alan dithered self-consciously. Awkward embarrassment suddenly transformed itself into pride as he added, "Everybody, this is Dr. Heinrich Zarkov. My father!"

The old man's eyes glowed moistly at the sound of the word, "father." He suddenly threw his arms around Alan's neck and wept unashamedly. "I never doubted for a moment you'd come, Son." He finally managed a feeble smile after several minutes' struggle to recapture his lost dignity.

"We'd better get out of here while we still have a chance. Can you walk, Sir?" Alan asked when he was finally able to trust himself to speak.

"Of course I can! I'm only sore and stiff from being tied to that bed for so long. Not crippled. Now help me up!" The old man's familiar, gentle blustering was a wonderful, welcome sound.

Alan smiled, trying to camouflage a saline trickle down one cheek as he offered a supporting arm. He led the way over the battlefield casualties littering the office. At the door leading out onto the mezzanine, he paused to listen.

"Hear anything?" Ham inched forward, poking a cautious head out to scan the hallway for himself.

"Yes. Downstairs," Alan whispered. "Costanza's been passing hash around and by now has them all psyched into thinking they're pretty damn near invincible. Any minute now there's going to be a charge up 'San Juan Staircase' with guns drawn and blazing."

"What's our chance of making it out through the kitchens?" Chey asked, crowding close to take an anxious look.

"They've already got it blocked off," Alan replied after a quick psi probe in the opposite direction as well. "The casino exit below us, even tighter."

"How about the fire escapes?" Bongo suggested. "There's one in this wing, right at the end of the hallway over there. And another one in the main banquet hall above the dinner theater."

"Too late, again." Alan shrugged after scanning these as well. "They've already got men outside covering them. On those narrow stairs, we'd be ducks in a shooting gallery. There's only so many guns I can take out at one time. Even one-at-a-time would be a challenge if the gunmen are hidden. Costanza also thought to post a heavy guard at the exit from the concealed room where my father was being kept prisoner. So don't bother mentioning that either," Alan added in frustration.

"So what do we do, make a run for it, hoping at least a few of us will make it, or wait for them to come after us?" Buzzy's angry words were more challenge than question.

"If we're takin' a vote, put me down for the blaze-a'-glory bit," Ham added, smiling grimly. "I don't much relish waitin' for the grim reaper to come lookin' fer me. I always figgered, when my time came, I'd want to be meetin' him at the door with a drink in my hand."

"We're not voting," Alan announced grimly, ending all discussion. "There's one escape route they haven't blocked off yet; because they don't know it exists.

"Ham, you and the others, I want you to take Muff and my father on ahead with you. The service stairs we came up earlier open onto the roof. Wait for me there."

"Well, if we're about to die, I suppose we may as well be doin' it with nice clean air from off the bay in our lungs," Buzz commented angrily. He was doing his best to mask a fear that was turning his insides into jello.

"An where the fuck are you gonna' be, while the rest of us are haulin' ass up there, Al?" Ham snapped. He knew what Alan was planning.

"I have to, Ham." He pleaded with his eyes for understanding. "I need to be at the rear to draw their fire in case they try to rush us before we can make it to the roof. And nobody's going up there to die, Buzz," he added for the benefit of the others. "I arranged for transportation earlier, and loading dock's up topside."

"Oh, shit! I should have known," Chey laughed nervously, as he turned to face Bongo and Buzz. "Men, brace yourselves! We are in for the ride of our lives. Next stop: Mars."

"So! Is it safe yet to make our run for it?" Ham asked, peering up and down the mezzanine once more.

Alan raised his hand in a holding gesture, and turned to check once more on the motionless bodies strewn about the floor like discarded garments. Satisfied that none was in any condition to pose any immediate threat, he was about to turn back, when his attention was snagged on the wall plaque behind Costanza's desk. It was a copper disc, graven with a black pentagram, the club's logo. Deliberately hung that way, in an inverted position, representing the Satanic principle, disturbed him. Despite the urgency of their situation, Alan surrendered to an overwhelming impulse, walked over, pulled it off the wall, turned it right-side-up, then replaced it. Relieved somehow, he was once more free to turn his attention back to the crisis at hand.

"Now?" Ham asked with anxious sarcasm. "Or would you like for us to wait till you've dusted and vacuumed, too?"

"Now!" Alan snapped back after another quick psi scan. "But keep low. And as far back as possible against the wall when you're crossing the mezzanine. Some of those bastards gathering down in the front lobby are marksmen."

"I hear what you're singin' to me, Brother." Ham flashed a nervous smile, grabbed Muff's hand, and hunkering low, launched himself down the hall. Zarkov and the rest of the band members followed close behind.

"Faster, Ham! They're starting up the stairs." Alan crowded closer, urging them to greater speed.

They were almost across the stretch of mezzanine that opened onto the lobby below when the vanguard of their pursuers reached the top of the stairs. Before Alan had time to turn and face them, he heard a loud report and felt the near miss of a bullet as it whizzed past. Muff suddenly stopped running, crying out as she crumpled to the floor, and lay still.

Recalling another bullet that had ripped away all he had once held dear, he whirled about to face his enemy. Rage became a living demon. Enveloping him, it swirled like a scarlet mist before his eyes, ripping a cry from his throat that echoed like Thor's own thunderbolt. Bearing down on his tormentors like a maddened bull, another blast of PK sent weapons flying, and men scattering in blind panic back down to the lobby. Alan grabbed the nearest of the few still on their feet and still foolhardy enough to stand their ground. Lifting him sideways, Alan hurled the man after his retreating comrades with all the force he could conjure. Grabbing every body, conscious or unconscious, that he could lay hold of, he hurled them down the stairs and over the bannister rails.

Those able to disentangle themselves from the growing pile-up at the bottom of the ornate staircase stampeded through the main entrance and out into the night.

The last of this second assault wave, now utterly demoralized, had vanished. With unspent rage still in need of venting, Alan was about to launch himself on a hunting expedition, when the desperate urgency in Ham's voice, called him back to sanity.

"She's bleeding very heavily, Son. Get back up here and do whatever you can. Quickly!" His father was kneeling on the floor beside Muff when Alan arrived. He had rolled his jacket into a makeshift pillow and was tucking it under her head in a pathetically futile gesture.

Alan knelt beside the old man, closed his eyes and took several deep breaths to center himself. Focusing his inner vision deep within the girl's violated flesh, he located the bullet. It was lodged in the wall of the right pulmonary vein, close, too close, to her heart. It had not managed to rip entirely through, damaging the heart itself, as in Dawn's case; but still, the similarity was too painfully close. If he wasn't able to do something, and right away, Muff would also be just as dead before an ambulance could get here. For the moment at least, any attempt at pulling it out would be like removing a badly fitting cork from a bottle whose contents were under pressure. The steady trickling away of Muff's life blood would become a gushing torrent; unless... Recalling the horrifying pyrotechnic display his PK had created earlier, he wondered if he could generate it again, but this time under controlled conditions. If he only he could manage to funnel his PK into a living laser! If he could convert those giant energies, now flowing through him, into controlled heat, at a very tight point of focus, and then manipulate that focal point with the delicate precision of a surgeon's scalpel... Damn! If only there were time to practice, and on something else other than Muff!

With a silent prayer to his newly-discovered patrons, very cautiously, very slowly, Alan eased the bullet away. Holding back the flow of blood, he located the severed ends of the right pulmonary vein and carefully eased them together. Visualizing himself as a living laser projector, he began welding. He could almost smell the searing of flesh as he focused and powered up. Drawing a tiny white-hot point along the tear line, he cauterized the vein back to a semblance, at least, of its original integrity. There was a bit of leakage as he allowed the blood to flow once more, but normal clotting action would soon seal those small remaining perforations. Finally, ever so cautiously, he eased the bullet out through its original point of entry.

With audible relief, and a silent bouquet of gratitude to the Lady, Alan looked up and found himself staring into Buzzy's worried face. He had been hovering as close as Ham's and Zarkov's restraining hold on his arms would permit. Chey and Bongo were also leaning close, their faces once more frozen in expressions of awe.

"She gonna' be all right, Al?" Buzzy's voice broke between a croak and a whisper when he finally rediscovered it.

Alan managed an affirmative nod, adding. "Please! Someone call…"

"Way ahead of you, Al." Chey managed an anxious smile. "I ran back to Costanza's office to call the police and an ambulance the second Muff went down."

"Thanks, Chey." Climbing to his feet, Alan turned to face his friends. "Look, I don't want my father mixed up in this. Would all of you stay with Muff till the ambulance gets here? Tell the police I'll be back in the morning to answer their questions. After Petie and now Muff, assure them: I want Costanza and his entire organization more than they do.

"More important though: listen carefully! I don't think Muff's in any danger of going into shock, but still, if she regains consciousness before the ambulance arrives, get some fluids into her; but please, nothing with any alcohol content!"

Alan directed the remainder of his instructions at Chey as well as Ham. Next to his closest friend, he was the band member least likely to garble the message. "Tell the paramedics, when they get here, that the bullet damaged the right pulmonary vein. The repairs I was able to make are only temporary, at best; so tell them to move her very gently and to keep her sedated if she wakes up. When you get to the hospital, tell the doctors where the damaged vein is. They'll have to go in right away to mop up all the pooled blood in her thoracic cavity—her chest—and to effect more permanent repairs. If they try to waste time arguing, tell them Alan Kolkey said so. I don't think you'll have too much trouble convincing them. By now the Peregrine is hovering only a few hundred feet above this building, in plain view of the entire city."

Satisfied Muff was no longer in immediate danger, Alan disconnected the last psi-link with the girl. Suddenly something distastefully familiar insinuated itself back into awareness. Shifting focus once more, he sent out a probing thread of consciousness. Finding nothing but themselves on the second floor, he 'traveled' down to the main level. Nothing there, either. A search outside found Costanza's people still prowling about. They were waiting to take pot shots, from the safety of concealment, at anyone leaving the building. It was none of them his radar was flashing alarms on. The basement was the only place he hadn't yet checked. Wait! There! In the wine cellar! Costanza, himself: the author of all this suffering and death.

"Buzz, give this to the police. They'll be needing it." Alan handed him the bullet he had just removed from the body of the girl at his feet. "And take care of Muff for me."

"You won't have to ask twice… uh… A… Al…" He answered, suddenly uncomfortable with the familiar contraction of Alan's name. He was visibly overjoyed however at the prospect of having Muff placed in his charge.

There was nothing Alan could do at the moment to mend the rift he had foolishly created in his fragile relationship with Muff. Forcing back the stab of regret he now felt, he turned his back on the band's drummer, and focused his attention on more immediate concerns. "Ham, take my father up to the roof and wait with him till I catch up. I just discovered a few loose ends that need tying up."

"Sure, Al. C'mon, Doc!" Ham had to tug on the old man's sleeve to get him moving.

He needed a running leap to hurdle the log-jam of bodies at the base of the great curving staircase. Turning right and reversing direction, Alan raced past stilled fountains and the silent sentinels of the Tarot's major deck, watching from the mirrored walls. He paused for a moment at the cash office underneath the rear overhang of the mezzanine that circled the Pentacle's main lobby like a crown. Satisfied his prey was still hiding somewhere in the basement, he turned toward the left wing. Running past bookkeeping and clerical, past the kitchen manager's office, past the employees' lounge, and kitchen supplies, he stopped finally at the service stairs between the freight elevator and kitchen. Costanza's "smell" was growing stronger.

In the wine cellar at the bottom of the stairs, Alan could feel him even more strongly. He had been here only moments ago. Following the psychic spoor, he walked past the maintenance shop and rows of dust-covered storage bins. The trail ended at a heavy wooden door. It was bolted from the inside. Costanza's "scent" leaked through strongest here. Even with the boost from the powerful adrenaline high he was on right now, Alan doubted he could have broken through. The attempt, however, might have placated, somewhat, his need to be pounding his own brand of justice into Costanza's sneering face. It took a giant effort of will, but he managed at last to quiet his mind sufficiently to engage his PK. Moments masqueraded as hours; but patience was finally rewarded with the feel of leaden bolts beginning to slip back.

No wonder so much effort had been needed to move them! They were enormous! The interior surface of the door, designed apparently to hold off a small army, had also been bullet-proofed. Wetting his lips in anticipation, he reached for the latch and pulled. The door opened on rusty hinges that creaked like the gates of a haunted castle in a low-budget horror film. There was at least one small corner of his mind still capable of appreciating the irony of rusting hinges, dark musty cellars. And a secret laboratory! In place of the stereotypical Hollywood film variety, however, this small chemical factory manufactured a different sort of monster: nova, Costanza's hottest, most lethal commodity.

There was his prey, sitting behind an ancient, battered, reagent-stained desk in a far corner. He was aiming a thirty-eight, trying unsuccessfully to steady it in both hands. The air down here was cool, yet his forehead was beaded in sweat.

"You're wasting your time, Costanza. Haven't you been listening to any of the stories your people have been telling about me, or the witness of your own eyes?" Alan's voice coiled like a bullwhip snaking along the ground, ready to be drawn up for the next strike.

"I didn't see anything. Those clowns up there are nothing but a bunch of ignorant, superstitious assholes." Costanza's attempt at camouflaging panic with contempt was so blatantly transparent, even a psi-blind child would have seen through his bluff.

"Then why are you hiding down here? And why are your hands shaking like that?" Alan injected all the venom he could conjure into his words and all the menace possible into his slow, serpentine advance.

"You're a dead man, Falcon, or whatever the hell your real name is. At this range I can't miss. The bullet will blow a hole in your chest I could stick my fist through."

Alan kept smiling and walking, enjoying Costanza's feeble effort to mask rapidly escalating panic behind this smoke screen of bluster. The man was already so close to paralysis, it was almost a waste of energy freezing the cortical region that controlled his voluntary muscles.

He grabbed his victim's weapon and hurled it across the room where it smashed into a shelf-full of glassware. Leaning over the desk, he planted his face scant inches from Costanza's. "Don't worry, scum. You haven't bought it. Yet. Before I'm done though, you'll be doing more singing to the police than I did my entire two years here." With each word the whip hissed and cracked, striking closer and closer.

"Wha'... What are you going to do?" Costanza choked on a terror that made his eyes bulge and constricted his throat till he could barely breathe or speak intelligibly.

"Nowhere near what you really deserve, you slime-spawned parasite. Have you ever taken a good look at them, your victims, after six or seven months on the poison you peddle? I have. They're nothing but walking skeletons, living for nothing else but their next "ecstasy.' They're only detouring through 'paradise' on their way to Hell, and Hell is the only real estate you deal in. That stuff makes heroin, and all the other junk your organization peddles, look like candy by comparison."

Remembering defenseless little Petie and Costanza's plans for enslaving him as well, Alan plunged into his captive's brain with a force far in excess of need, caring little how much pain he was causing. The man's anguished screams finally broke past the anesthetic barrier of adrenaline surging through Alan's veins. Costanza's agony, now echoing inside his own brain, made him pull back just short of killing. There were too many others involved in this drug cartel, and Costanza knew the location of each rat hole. If he died now, they would be free to set up shop somewhere else and continue their bloody business of destroying lives.

There were ways, however, to "program" a mind like a computer, feeding the right "software" directly into the correct cortical memory centers on a telepathically subliminal level. Conscious mind and logical process were defenseless here. Lifting inhibitions where they blocked access to previously classified information was simple enough. Planting his own "program" and pulling out any stops that would otherwise have protected Costanza from spilling everything to the police gave Alan not the slightest pang of guilt. As far as he was concerned, the moment the Pentacle's owner first started dealing, he surrendered all rights to privacy or autonomy of action. Those who enslave must themselves inevitably know slavery. That was the law of karma; and tonight he was its enforcer.

Grateful at last to be done with his loathsome task, Alan wasted no time withdrawing from Costanza's mind. No matter how many showers he took, it would be weeks before the man's stench would cease to permeate his every thought and nightmare.

One last chore remained: making certain this lab, at least, would never again be used for the manufacture or processing of nova. At the far side of the room was a second door, as heavily armored as the first. Beyond it lay an underground tunnel that connected with another adjoining building, an old warehouse, also owned by Costanza & Associates. With methodical deliberation, he walked over and slipped the inside bolts into place so no one could gain entry from that direction.

Turning his attention back to the lab, he became an engine of destruction, toppling shelves, smashing delicate electronic equipment, hurling larger pieces across the room. It was a catharsis that left him emotionally drained but satisfied when he finally stopped. Not even counter tops remained in usable condition. The reagent-stained desk behind which Costanza still sat in zombie-like death trance had also been reduced to a splintered ruin.

Alan smiled with grim humor. No need for binding him, or even locking the door as he left. It would be weeks, months perhaps, before the bastard would be capable once more of any independent thought or action.

Alan ran out onto the second floor mezzanine where Buzz, Chey, and Bongo were huddled around Muff. She was still lying on the floor, but covered now with a blanket someone had scavenged from somewhere. Outside, he could hear the sirens of arriving police and ambulances.

"Tell them they'll find Costanza down in the base-ment, Buzz," he said as he knelt to check on the small girl.

"Is he...?" Bongo stammered.

"No. But I'll bet he wishes he were. They're going to find him extremely cooperative!" he answered with grim satisfaction.

Muff had regained consciousness, and was watching silently while he reassured himself that the cauterized ends of the damaged artery were still holding together. "I have to get my father out of here. He's too old and he's already been through too much tonight. Neither of us are ready to deal with the police, at least not right now. But I promise: I'll be back for you." He gave her hand a gentle squeeze.

"No, Al! I'd die for you. You know that. I almost did. Only I don't think I can live with you any more, knowing who—what you are, what you're going back to: I just couldn't handle it. Oh, I do love you. And in your own way, I know you love me, Al; but you're not in love with me. It's someone named Dawn you're really *in* love with; and she's dead. How do I fight a ghost who haunts your dreams every night?" She paused to offer him a sad, apologetic smile. "I've thought a whole lot about it since I finally quit trying to fool myself. For a while I was sure I'd be happy just being able to be with you wherever you went. But after tonight, after seeing what you can do…" Her voice was barely audible as she made a feeble attempt at sitting up.

Gently easing her back down, Alan touched a finger to her lips, silencing her protests. Now was no time for arguing pros and cons. She was too weak. Dammit, where were those medics?

Oh shit! Those were shots being exchanged outside. Costanza's soldiers were still out there and, apparently still high on Costanza's hash, were determined to fight to the last man. No telling how long his makeshift patch job would hold. And who the hell was he kidding? Even if Chey and Ham managed to deliver his message ungarbled, who would take them seriously, even with the evidence of the Peregrine in the Sky over the city. They would still be taken for nothing more than a couple of tripped out musicians. And what if Costanza's goon squad decided to retreat back into the Pentacle for a final stand? This was no time for running out on friends, on family.

"There's a shoot-out going on down there," he announced, looking around as he stood up. Now that resolve had been firmly hammered into place he felt calmer, despite continued concern for his father.

Chey was crouched low, peering down between the mezzanine balusters, his gaze anxiously riveted on the main entrance. Bongo, shielded behind a large potted palm, was watching the stairs, Costanza's office, and the hallway beyond. Buzzy, hugging the floor, was using his body to shield Muff against any possible attack from the other hallway. They were all armed with weapons that had been hastily scavenged from the human debris littering the great staircase.

"Muff needs to get to a hospital. Now! I'm going to have to go out there and see if I can break the log jam," Alan announced. He suddenly found himself overwhelmed by two apprehensive but eager volunteers. Buzz continued hovering close to Muff. She was still his sole concern.

"Thanks Chey, Bongo. But right now stealth is my strongest ally," Alan smiled, basking in the rekindled warmth of their concern for him. "Besides, in case I don't make it back, or Costanza's soldiers try to retake the place, I need you here for Muff and my father. Which reminds me: would one of you go up and get those two back down off the roof? Takeoff's been indefinitely postponed."

Muff was too weak from blood loss to argue. But her fear for his safety was palpable, deepening the sunken shadows around her eyes. A hurried handshake from Buzz was followed by emotional embraces from Chey and Bongo.

Alan ran for the service stairs, the "worlds only calypso cowboy" close behind. As he bolted down to the first floor landing, Bongo headed for the roof, his long legs easily taking two steps at a time.

Entering the dimly lit kitchen, he hunkered down below the level of the counter-tops. One of Costanza's people might be peering through the single window that faced out on the alley. The smell of death hung heavy in the air around him as he edged past Twadowsky's body. It was lying in a large pool of coagulated, slowly drying blood, the carving knife still clutched in his lifeless hand.

Alan was suddenly not at all proud of what he'd allowed Costanza to goad him into becoming. Yes, he'd killed before; but that was years age. The confrontations had been deliberately engineered, but only as sparring matches, opportunities for testing his martial and psi skills under real battle conditions. It had been Ego, with a capital E, and yes a lot of anger too, in need of venting. But the killing had only been accidental: frying a brain with more PK than intended, or an instinctive survival response when confronted by weapons, drawn and firing. Twadowsky could as easily have been temporarily decommissioned. Alan caught himself. He must not fall back into the old patterns of wallowing in guilt and self-condemnation, especially now, when the lives of people he loved were at stake.

Shaking himself back to reality, he crouched even lower, then very cautiously, very slowly opened the door, just a crack. The alley was in almost total darkness. Stray bullets must have taken out the lights. He would have to probe the night with other senses.

A faint rustle of movement came from the direction of the large dumpster. It was followed by a flood of conflicting emotion that almost gave him vertigo: hate, anger, defiance, despair, unreasoning fear of capture and imprisonment. Better to die than spend the rest of your life in a cage.

"I don't know about you, Charlie, but I'm takin' as many of them fuckin' cops with me as I can." The whispered words were barely audible over the acoustic distortions of surrounding walls and damp night air.

"No! We can hide, Ray. I know all Costanza's private squirrel holes. If we can manage to get back inside, they'll never find us."

A moment was budgeted to take stock before taking action. Alan was still in costume. As usual, he was all in black except for some glitter on the collar, which he hastily tucked out of sight. It was scratchy and itched. His mane of black hair and beard were ample enough to conceal most of the light skin of his face, neck and shoulders. The night was his ally. Stealth was his weapon. What a shame he hadn't majored in Ninjitsu. He would have aced Invisibility and perhaps gone on to become a famous assassin. Oh well, he shrugged with dark humor. On with the hunt!

A shake of his head sent even more long black curls cascading over his face like a mask. Concealing the light-reflecting flesh-tones of his hands behind his back, he began inching out the door. He wished he had thought to bring gloves from his dressing room. Pressed against the wall of the building, he slowly inched his way in the direction of the dumpster. Good! Only two minds. He would be able to handle the second before the first hit the ground. But no more killing! Only a little closer now. A visual lock would make it easier to separate the two minds from each other for better focus. There was no actual connection between his psi faculties and his biological senses. It was purely psychological; but it helped, nonetheless, especially where he was so close to the end of his reserves. Anger or crisis, no doubt, could still access raw power; but exhaustion was making a deliberate, fine-tuning of his PK increasingly difficult.

There was enough residual light to barely separate two figures as he cautiously peered behind the dumpster. It would have been so much simpler to deep-fry both brains and be done with it; but no! It was bad enough in the heat of battle, but setting himself up as a mobile kangaroo court, deciding, on the spot, who will live or die, based on whim, anger or simple expediency, again, where would it all end?

Alan eased himself into Charlie's brain. He focused on the multiple regions concerned with the complex functions of consciousness and triggered a cascade of neural misfirings. It would be hours before the man would be able to once more coordinate enough voluntary muscle action to function beyond the level of a six-month-old infant. As Charlie slid to the ground, babbling incoherently, his weapon slipped from nerveless hands, hitting the concrete pavement of the alley with a metallic thunk. Before Ray had time to react, the same therapy was applied to him, with equal effectiveness. Another weapon out of commission.

Crouching low and hugging the shadow of the building, Alan became a shadow himself as he started moving toward the street. Ahead, hiding just inside the fire exit: another one! With no time and no taste right now for originality, he administered a third dose of the already proven remedy. Another recruit for the diaper brigade!

At the junction where the Alley spilled out onto the street, Alan hesitated, clinging to the last remnant of shadow. From here on, his task would become infinitely more complicated by the swirling vortex of confusion surrounding the building that until tonight had housed the fashionably exclusive Suit of Pentacles. Police and ambulance vehicle lights melded with searchlights, probing the fast retreating darkness. Voices, tense and shrill, were shouting orders back and forth. Demands for surrender blared from portable loudspeakers. As shots were exchanged from places of concealment, their ear-shattering reports rent gaping holes in the tattered fabric of the night. Trying to focus in the midst of all this bedlam was going to tax him to the limit.

Flurries of movement, the glint of light reflecting off metal, followed by gun powder flashes pinpointed the locations of three no four more of Costanza's troops. One was concealed in a doorway. Three others, close together, were hunkered down behind parked cars across the street. One by one, he brought them down.

"I got you now, you fuckin' bastard!" The voice, hoarse with exhaustion and desperation sounded familiar.

Shaken out of intense concentration, Alan did a rapid about-face to find himself staring down the barrel of a thirty-eight. He was standing out in the middle of the sidewalk, almost directly under a street light where he must have unconsciously drifted. Four targets taken down in rapid-fire succession without time to 'recharge' had proven the proverbial straw. Disoriented, and shaking with fatigue, he could only watch helplessly. That cliché about your life flashing before you was just so much romantic bullshit. All he was feeling was emptiness and futility at the imminence of death. Had it all been for nothing? He could not yet have taken down enough soldiers to have ended the battle. By the time help got through, Muff would probably already be dead. And what of the others, should Costanza's men decide to make a final stand inside the Pentacle?

Looking past the unwavering weapon to the hatred in those familiar bloodshot eyes, Alan recognized the hard, bone-angled features of Kopek, one of Felsh's security people. They'd traded blows on more than one occasion during his early months with the band. He had been drinking too hard and fighting even harder then with anyone willing to oblige him.

Head pounding, every muscle in his body slowly melting into jello, Alan let himself down on one knee. Perhaps, by seeming to break, he might be able to buy enough time to rally what remained, if any, of his strength. Cradling his head in his hands, he encouraged Kopek's silent gloating.

The gun remained pointed dead-center at his heart. The hammer clicked back. Kopek was milking the moment for all he could.

From deep within, Alan felt himself being pulled up out of his pit of exhaustion. Again, that feeling of maternal reassurance he had experienced back at the cathedral. Had it been hours or generations ago?

The sensation vanished almost as quickly as it had come. He felt suddenly revived and unaccountably stronger, though not by much. But at least his muscles had stopped shaking and his mind had relocated its center of gravity.

"Bye-bye, Bastard! Payback's a mother, ain't it," Kopek sneered as he slowly began squeezing the trigger.

Raw survival instinct kicked into auto. Alan's mind shot out a feeble burst of PK, deflecting Kopek's aim away from him, but not quite far enough. As he launched himself at his attacker's midsection, the gun went off. He felt searing pain track across his left temple. From somewhere close, he heard the sharp crack of a rifle. Kopek's body suddenly jerked out of reach. At the apex of his trajectory he hit only empty air, and darkness.

It was war and he was waging an uphill battle, fighting his way back to consciousness through the thunder inside his head. When he was finally able to open his eyes, he found himself lying on a stretcher with a pressure bandage on his head. Hovering above him, a paramedic was monitoring life-signs and talking to someone at the other end of a mobile phone. He was surrounded, half-blinded by the strobing lights of police vehicles and ambulances. Uniformed officers were everywhere shouting orders back and forth to each other and to groups of morbidly curious bystanders.

Muff! His father! What was happening? Shoving the protesting paramedic aside, Alan sat up and looked around. Several medics were wheeling a stretcher out through the Pentacle's massive gilt doors. Fighting back alternating waves of vertigo and nausea, Alan struggled to his feet. Reeling drunkenly, he pushed his way through a sea of hands. He managed an intercept as the stretcher was about to be hoisted into an ambulance. It was Muff! She was still alive and still conscious, though just barely. Thank the Goddess! She had lost a great deal of blood.

Turning to face the annoyed paramedic closest to him, he was about to speak when his hands were grabbed, yanked behind him, and then cuffed. An officer suddenly materialized and began reading Alan his rights.

He shook his head, trying to rid himself of the cobwebs and immediately regretted it. Biting down hard on the pain, he closed his eyes and took several slow, deep breaths, trying to focus the spinning kaleidoscope of pain and conflicting emotions within himself. The pounding in his head was still there, but he finally managed to push it far enough into the background so he could function almost rationally once more.

"Officer, please. I need to speak to these medics. It's urgent." Alan had to shout to make himself heard over the bedlam. "Ms. Moreno, here, was shot. The bullet punctured the right pulmonary vein. I did a temporary patch job but it won't hold for very much longer. ER needs to know. They've got to get her into surgery as soon as she gets there.

"From what I've heard, you sing a pretty mean song, break a lot of hearts, and play a guitar that can melt steel. Since when do these qualify for an MD after your name?" Captain Finley was average in height, but under a deceptively soft layer of fat he was big boned and heavily muscled. He was middle-aged with cold iron in his eyes. During his many years with the SFPD he had seen much and heard all the excuses. "Lets cut the crap; what's your real name, mister; and what's your connection with all this?"

"My real name's—Alan Kolkey; and you'll find my connection down in the Pentacle's cellars." Shit was about to start hitting that overworked fan in bucketloads. Deciding he had better get ready for it, he sent out a PK command to the Peregrine. Another small finger of tightly focused PK probed the lock on his handcuffs.

"Right! And my name's Tinkerbell." Finley wasn't buying.

"As I said before, check the cellars. I left an early Christmas present for you down there." Alan's patience was close to its limits. "Since you're having trouble believing I'm who I say I am, take a look. My calling card just arrived," he added, gesturing toward the region of sky immediately over Finley's head as he handed the police captain his cuffs.

Finley looked up, stammering in disbelief. Alan had brought the Peregrine down below the cloud cover where he had "parked" her earlier. She was hovering now just above the surrounding rooftops. Her familiar contours, silhouetted against diffuse city lights reflecting off the higher clouds, left no more questions in the police captain's mind as to his "prisoner's" identity.

"Now, Captain Finley," Alan announced over his shoulder, as he climbed into the ambulance behind the medics, "if you'll permit me to accompany Ms. Moreno to the hospital, where I fear I'll be needing a bit of patch work, myself. You have my assurance: as soon as she's out of danger, I'll answer all your questions and cooperate in any way possible. In the meantime, I'd appreciate it greatly if you'd personally see to the safety and comfort of my friends and my father, Dr. Heinrich Zarkov."

EPILOGUE

T HE EASTERN horizon was glowing with the soft pastels
of early morning as Alan exited precinct headquarters
with Zarkov, Ham, Chey and Bongo. On the sound advice
of Captain Finley they left by way of the basement garage,
where police vehicles were housed and maintained, to
avoid having to wade through reporters and cameras. It
hadn't taken long for word to leak out, then spread like a
forest afire during a severe drought. Buzz had elected to
stay with Muff at the hospital and keep an eye on her.
Zarkov was almost too exhausted to walk as they crowded
into the waiting cab and headed for Golden Gate Park. It
was the closest open area where the Peregrine could safely
land. The old man, propped against Alan's left arm, nodded off almost immediately. For the rest of them the brief
journey was passed in strained silence. By unvoiced con-
sensus, everyone was putting off the ordeal of promises,
hurried last messages, and final farewells until the last possible moment. More fortunate than the others, Alan was
able to fill the void with necessary busy work. First, he
shifted focus to his giant ship, "parked" once more several
thousand feet above the city. Her computers recognized his
command and switched to auto. She would be waiting and
ready for final set-down when they arrived.

Another shift linked him to Garuda, circling high over the city. He was not a nocturnal animal, but had been obliged to stay alert, and hungry, all night tracking the erratic movements of his human half. He was screeching annoyance as he descended and began circling the cab. The huge bird was not going to be a willing passenger, Alan feared.

The sun's disk, clearing the eastern horizon, was broken into golden fragments, gleaming through tiny breaks in the autumn foliage, as the cab pulled away. It would return in an hour to pick up the three remaining band members. Gazing skyward the small group watched, still silent as the Peregrine came into sight, then slowly began filling up the sky. Bringing her in safely for a tight landing in this clearing occupied all of Alan's concentration. Finally she was down, her starboard passenger lock open, and boarding ramp extended.

This was it. No more dragging out the inevitable. So many conflicting emotions! He looked forward to seeing Gertha. His mother. President Moshey too, though he dreaded going back again to being perceived as the last living hope of the planet. The agony of facing Dawn's family and friends also lay ahead of him. He owed them that much. Perhaps seeing her parents again, the place where she had been born and raised, meeting the people she had loved might breate new lefe into the treasured memories.

The Alan Kolkey who existed before her had been born out of the inferno that had taken his parents. Dawn's death had been the catalyst for a rebirth. The man he was today, who could love and allow others close enough to love him in return, had been reborn during that second holocaust that had torn her away from him as well. But not forever, and not totally. Yes, her body was dead, lost somewhere out among the stars. Yet she lived on, as the Lord and Lady of his vision had assured him. Her memories, her love, her essence, bonded to him during that fateful mind fusion, so long ago, had merged with his, becoming the Alan Kolkey who stood here now.

He turned to look back at what he was leaving behind. A world filled with Muff, Barb, Darcie; and music. Music shared with Ham and the rest of the band. Little Petie too. Especially little Petie! They had all taught him so much and given him the courage to love. Living among them he had carved out a comfortable niche for himself. Muff would never be Dawn, nor could she ever have replaced her. Yet he had loved the tiny brunette. It had been a warm, patient, comfortable, often paternal love. And she had been so good in bed! Damn, he was going to miss that!

"I... I guess this is it. *Yo tambien te quero, me hermano.*" Chey's voice was barely audible and cracked several times along the way. As he came closer, he had difficulty meeting Alan's gaze. Then suddenly his arms were around Alan's neck with a strength that belied his size. Then just as suddenly he backed away.

For once, Bongo was speechless as he followed Chey's example with his own self-conscious embrace. "We fight good together, hey?" he grinned, after a painfully long pause. He had finally relocated his missing vocal chords. "We play some damn good music together, too. *N'est pas?*"

Alan forced out an awkward smile. It would have to do. Words had become elusive for him as well.

"Dammit, man! Do you have to leave? Wild Hunt ain't never gonna' be hot, like it was, with you gone," Chey protested. His macho invulnerability was teetering on a precarious edge.

"You'll never know how much I want to stay here, Chey." It was a desperate struggle to find words. "But it's broken and there's no way we're ever going to put it back together again the way it was before last night. Besides, I had a life, such as it was, BWH: Before Wild Hunt, that I made a pretty big mess of. There's some serious fence-mending and shit-shoveling I have to take care of."

"Ham...?" How was he ever going to say good-bye. He couldn't imagine life without Ham there to pound sense back into his stubborn head whenever he started slipping off the deep end. Who else knew him so well? Who else was left with whom he could so totally and comfortably be himself? Goddess! As much as he wanted to, did he have any more right dragging the poor man off out of his home element than he would have, Muff? Dawn! Muff! Now Ham as well?

The sound of cars and vans screeching to a halt brought Alan back to cold reality. Voices started shouting orders as cameras and equipment began unloading.

"Sure didn't take them bloodhounds long to get back on the scent," Chey swore under his breath. "Hey, her-mano! Better get while gettin's still good."

"Man, you can't buy publicity like this," Bongo complained. "What a waste."

"Maybe not, old friend," Alan smiled, somehow managing to see some irony in the whole thing. "Wild Hunt won't be hurting for bookings for a long time, even with a new lead man. That's a fact.

"This isn't good-bye forever, friends. I'll be back. As often as you can stand me: when I need a reality check, when I need someone to tell me I'm full of shit," he paused to smile sadly in Ham's direction, "but most especially when I just need to be with my friends." He threw a pleading glance at Ham as he sent out a silent call to Garuda.

"Oh Hell!" Ham suddenly burst into laughter. "I've always made it a policy to stick with dudes who have a future and foxes with a past. Why quit now!" Tossing keys in Chey's direction, he put an arm around the old professor who was still yawning and sleep fuddled, and started herding him up the hatch ramp. "Can you guys try to rescue Al's guitar collection from his dressing room? And take care of the apartment for Muff? We'll be back for our stuff as soon as possible. Hey, Al! You waitin' to serve tea to them reporters?"

Relief, liberally mixed with joy, washed through Alan's veins as he hurriedly wrapped the worn jacket Bongo handed him around his outstretched arm for Garuda to land on. He almost regretted throwing Chey and Bongo to the wolves. Almost. Those two clowns could be counted on to mine the situation for all they could get out of it. Right now, he had to get this tub off the ground and his father safely home. Maybe his mother would make them some of those incredibly fluffy pancakes of hers for breakfast.

As the hatch slid closed, Alan realized it was closing on a part of his life he would never be able to return to. Friendships, if they managed to continue on, would never again be the same or quite so close. He had lost Dawn and now he was losing Muff. That hurt worst of all.

Dawn! He had felt the bullet rip through her heart. She couldn't possibly still be alive in the literal sense. Yet, last night at the Cathedral, he had been counseled to seek her out… Once more, he had to touch the pendant the Horned One had given him to convince himself they had not been merely figments of a tortured mind. Perhaps Dawn wasn't totally lost to him after all. She still existed somewhere out there on another higher plane. And he was a Witch, a Priest of the Old Ones. A walker between the worlds.

The End — For Now

About the Author

Diane DesRochers (Groton, Mass.) holds a Master's Degree in Psychological Counseling. She is a Witch and high priestess of the coven AppleMoon and recognized clergy in the Commonwealth of Massachusetts. She serves as New England Regional Director of the Witches Anti-Discrimination Lobby. Leading pagan publications around the world have published poetry and articles by Diane. This is her first novel.

To Write to the Author

If you wish to contact the author or would like more information about this book, please write to the author in care of Llewellyn Worldwide and we will forward your request. Both the author and publisher appreciate hearing from you and learning of your enjoyment of this book and how it has helped you. Llewellyn Worldwide cannot guarantee that every letter written to the author can be answered, but all will be forwarded. Please write to:

Diane DesRochers
c/o Llewellyn Worldwide
P.O. Box 64383-K224, St. Paul, MN 55164-0383, U.S.A.
Please enclose a self-addressed, stamped envelope for reply,
or $1.00 to cover costs.
If outside U.S.A., enclose international postal reply coupon.

On the following pages you will find listed, with their current prices, some of the books now available on related subjects. Your book dealer stocks most of these and will stock new titles in the Llewellyn series as they become available. We urge your patronage.

TO GET A FREE CATALOG

To obtain our full catalog, you are invited to write (see address below) for our bi-monthly news magazine/catalog, *Llewellyn's New Worlds of Mind and Spirit*. A sample copy is free, and it will continue coming to you at no cost as long as you are an active mail customer. Or you may subscribe for just $10 in the United States and Canada ($20 overseas, first class mail). Many bookstores also have *New Worlds* available to their customers. Ask for it.

TO ORDER BOOKS AND TAPES

If your book store does not carry the titles described on the following pages, you may order them directly from Llewellyn by sending the full price in U.S. funds, plus postage and handling (see below).

Credit card orders: VISA, MasterCard, American Express are accepted. Call us toll-free within the United States and Canada at 1-800-THE-MOON.

Postage and Handling: Include $4 postage and handling for orders $15 and under; $5 for orders *over* $15. There are no postage and handling charges for orders over $100. Postage and handling rates are subject to change. We ship UPS whenever possible within the continental United States; delivery is guaranteed. Please provide your street address as UPS does not deliver to P.O. boxes. Orders shipped to Alaska, Hawaii, Canada, Mexico and Puerto Rico will be sent via first class mail. Allow 4-6 weeks for delivery. **International orders:** Airmail – add retail price of each book and $5 for each non-book item (audiotapes, etc.); Surface mail – add $1 per item.

Minnesota residents add 7% sales tax.

Llewellyn Worldwide
P.O. Box 64383-791, St. Paul, MN 55164-0383, U.S.A.

For customer service, call (612) 291-1970.

Prices subject to change

THE RAG BONE MAN
A Chilling Mystery of Self-Discovery
Charlotte Lawrence

This occult fiction, mystery and fantasy is a tale of the subtle ways psychic phenomena can intrude into anyone's life—and influence the even the most rational of people!

The Rag Bone Man mixes together a melange of magickal ingredients—from amulets, crystals, the tarot, past lives and elemental beings to near death experiences, shapeshifting and modern magickal ritual—to create a simmering blend of occult mystery and suspense.

Rian McGuire is a seemingly ordinary young woman who owns a New Age book and herb shop in a small Maryland town. When a disturbing man leaves a mysterious old book in Rian's shop and begins to invade her dreams, she is launched into a bizarre, often terrifying journey into the arcane. Why is this book worth committing murder to recover? As Rian's family and friends gather psychic forces to penetrate the mysteries that surround her, Rian finally learns the Rag Bone Man's true identity—but will she be able to harness the undreamt-of power of her own magickal birthright before the final terrifying confrontation?

ISBN: 1-56718-412-X, mass market, 336 pp. $4.99